PAULA GOSLING was born in Detroit and moved perma-
nently to England in 1964. She worked as a copywriter
and a freelance copy consultant before becoming a full-
time writer in 1979. Since then she has published four-
teen novels, has won both the John Creasey and Gold
Dagger Awards from the Crime Writers' Association, and
has served as the Association's Chairman. When she isn't
committing murders by typewriter, cooking or reading,
she can be found in her sewing studio, creating abstract
embroideries and patchwork quilts. She has a wonderful
husband, two beautiful daughters, one lovely cat, and a pet
overdraft which she is grooming for Gold in the Banking
Olympics.

UNDERNEATH EVERY STONE

PAULA GOSLING

WARNER BOOKS

A *Warner* Book

First published in Great Britain in 2000
by Little, Brown and Company

This edition published by Warner Books in 2001

Copyright © Paula Gosling 2000

The moral right of the author has been asserted.

A CIP catalogue record for this book
is available from the British Library.

ISBN 0 7515 2534 0

Typeset by Palimpsest Book Production Limited,
Polmont, Stirlingshire
Printed and bound in Great Britain by
Mackays of Chatham plc, Chatham, Kent

Warner Books
A Division of
Little, Brown and Company (UK)
Brettenham House
Lancaster Place
London WC2E 7EN

*This one is for my wonderful husband, John,
without whom I couldn't.*

Underneath every stone there lies hidden a
a scorpion, dear friend.
Take care or he will sting you. All
concealment is treachery.

Ancient Athenian drinking song

IT WAS VERY EARLY ON a crisp October morning in Blackwater Bay. The sky was blue, the air was clear and there was a dead man in Cotter's Cut.

Moony Packard lay under the scarlet leaves of a poison sumac, the back of his head crushed and bloodied. Nearby, his mail-bag lay on a dirty curd of week-old snow that had been preserved from the daily thaws by the shadow of a sycamore. He lay there for an hour and forty-three minutes, undiscovered.

Then Albert Wimshaw, whose eyesight was poor at the best of times, turned into Cotter's Cut on his way into town to pick up a morning paper. He tripped over the outstretched foot of Moony Packard and fell heavily, hitting his head on a large rock that lay beside the path.

A short while after that, Stephenson J. Gardiner the Third came through Cotter's Cut accompanied by his dog, Ferdinand. Spotting the two outstretched men, to say nothing of the blood, Mr Gardiner suffered a mild heart attack and collapsed onto the path. Pinned down by his leash, which was still convulsively clutched in Mr Gardiner's hand, Ferdinand began to bark.

Eleven minutes later Davy Lewin, on his way to school, came upon the three supine men and the frantic dog. He ran down the path to the home of the Widow Parker and banged on the door. When the Widow Parker appeared, her white hair in rollers and wearing her second-best peach-coloured housecoat, Davy told her to dial 911. Suspicious of pranks (she'd been fooled before), the good

1

Widow Parker asked why. Davy told her what he'd found. She promptly fainted, leaving Davy to phone the Sheriff.

That's the way it goes in Blackwater Bay.

Just one damn thing after another.

ONE

BY NINE FIFTEEN COTTER'S CUT was swarming with representatives of the law. Sheriff Matt Gabriel was there, along with his Chief Deputy, George Putnam, plus the few other deputies who worked for him year-round. Had it been summer he would have had many men (and a few women) to deploy, for they hired extras to handle traffic and other misdemeanours during the summer season – mostly college students who appreciated the money and the brief taste of power.

Matt glared at the crime scene. Just when he thought it was safe, he was back in hot water. He crossed his arms over his chest and growled to himself. George, on the other hand, was full of enthusiasm.

'First of all, do we think the same person who killed Moony Packard also hit Albert Wimshaw over the head?' George asked in a solemn voice, glancing over at the new recruit who was listening intently to all that was going on and taking copious notes. The new recruit was young, female, shapely and far too smart to fall for George's poses. But George was ever the optimist.

'I mean,' George continued, 'did Wimshaw witness the murder and try to do something about it?'

'I don't think so, George,' Matt said. 'I heard Albert tell the paramedic that he tripped over something. I guess that would have been Moony's foot – seeing as how it was sticking out over the path. And seeing as how there is blood on that big rock there. And seeing as how Moony looks to have been dead for quite a while – his blood has

3

clotted while Albert's is still fresh – although we'll have to wait on the doctor for actual time of death.'

'Right,' said George, nodding and writing furiously in his notebook.

The new recruit, Susie Brock, raised her hand as if still in school. 'Sheriff?'

'Yes, Susie?'

'This is definitely murder?'

'Oh, I think so. It's pretty hard to bash in the *back* of your head all by yourself,' Matt said solemnly and smiled at Susie. 'Did you think it was suicide?'

'Oh, no – but he could have fallen on that rock earlier and hurt himself, got up and then collapsed,' Susie said. 'Earlier this morning there could have been an icy patch there under the bush. He could have slipped on it and gone over backwards because of the weight of his mail sack. There could be his blood under Mr Wimshaw's on that rock.'

'Good for you, Susie,' Matt said. 'George, arrest that rock.' Susie grinned appreciatively.

'You mean take it in for questioning?' George said, getting into the spirit of the thing.

'I mean make sure it gets to the forensic lab along with everything else we find,' Matt said in a more business-like tone. He glanced around at the crushed grass and other signs of the two men who had fallen on either side of Moony's body, plus the paramedics who had attended them, and sighed heavily. 'It's a shame we've had so much interference with the murder scene.'

'Wimshaw couldn't help tripping, he's as blind as a bat. And Mr Gardiner is a *very* sensitive guy,' George said, with a bit of a sneer. 'What do I put the rock in? We haven't got any evidence bags big enough . . .'

'Wrap it in newspaper and put it in the trunk of your car,' Matt said patiently. 'Did you get to bed late last night, George?'

'No later than usual,' George said defensively.

'Ah,' said Matt, guessing George had been drowning his

4

sorrows again over the loss of his previous girlfriend and the continued resistance of Susie Brock to his charms.

Susie was twenty-two, just out of college and eager to learn law enforcement, much to the dismay of her parents. Susie was a modern woman. The fact that she was very, very pretty was a source of constant annoyance to her because she wanted to be taken seriously. She cut her auburn hair short. She never wore make-up. She affected a very severe appearance in uniform. None of this made any difference to George Putnam. In fact, if anything, it just made things worse.

Susie Brock was a Real Challenge.

'Better get on with the pictures, George,' Matt said. 'And get the tape up.'

'Right,' George said, putting away his notebook. He turned to Susie. 'Brock, get the tape out of the car.'

One of the other deputies came forward. 'Sheriff, I just heard that Moony Packard had an argument with Frog Bartlett last night in the Golden Perch. Frog said he would kill Moony Packard next time he saw him. And now Moony's dead.'

'Aha!' said George.

Matt sighed again. He had just got through with another murder investigation that had left him exhausted and a little fed up with the job of sheriff. He was beginning to wonder if he should give it up and retire. The election was coming up soon. He had two opponents, Jack Armstrong and Tyrone Molt. For a moment he thought, the hell with it, let one of them take over. Then he took a deep breath and told himself to stop being so negative and to get on with the job.

'We'd better get hold of Frog,' George was saying to Susie.

'What?' Matt was startled out of his reverie. 'Oh, yes. George, you get Frog – Susie and I will go talk to Frank Packard.'

'Who's Frank Packard?' Susie asked.

George gave a short laugh. 'You'll see.'

'I want action, dammit!' shouted Frank Packard. He was a tall, wiry man with astonished grey hair – it stuck up straight from his scalp as if trying to get away from him. The hair in his ears seemed similarly inclined. 'Moony was my brother and I want justice for him.'

Packard was a local eccentric, a paranoid firebrand, seeing threats around every corner, certain of conspiracies, fearful of aliens, suspicious of kindly gestures or interest. He was supposed to be on medication, but rarely took it. He seemed, perversely, to enjoy living on the edge of his nerves and everyone else's. He'd been getting worse lately. The news of his brother's murder had rocked him at first, but now he had rallied.

'I assure you that we are—'

'I don't want assurances, I want someone in jail!' Frank shouted. He seemed to be addressing some invisible gathering.

'Did you have anyone specific in mind?' Matt asked with interest.

'Yes. No. I don't know. That's your job, isn't it?'

'I am always grateful for information,' Matt said evenly. 'Sit down, Mr Packard. Relax. Perhaps you can be of help.'

Frank sat. The living-room of the house he had shared with his brother was sparsely furnished but very clean. Packard himself was dressed in what could have passed for Army fatigues and, while his voice was shaking with emotion, his bearing was rigid and rather intimidating. He was accustomed to being the centre of attention, much to the chagrin and annoyance of most of Blackwater's citizens who encountered him picketing various businesses, making speeches in the park, daubing signs on convenient walls, writing wild letters to the editor of the *Blackwater Bay Chronicle* and in general making a noisy nuisance of himself.

'There was a lot of people jealous of Moony,' Frank began. 'Because he had that important job and all.'

'He delivered the mail,' Susie said in an amused tone.

'You think the mail isn't important?' Frank bellowed.

She quailed. 'Of course it is, but—'

'He knew about everybody,' Frank said.

'Yes, but—' Matt began. His mouth felt dry, and he wished he could interrupt and ask for a drink of water.

'And there were people who were against him,' Frank went on, leaning forward. 'Government people who had it in for him because he knew too much. Wouldn't surprise me one little bit if the CIA or the FBI had him bumped off by some contract killer. He wrote to them, you know, he wrote to them and told them what he thought of them. I bet that made them mad. Moony had a lot to say about what this so-called government is doing to this country. He was disgusted by it, same as me.'

'I really don't think that—'

'He wasn't afraid to speak his mind and neither am I,' Frank announced, straightening up again. 'I know Moony wasn't liked, but that wasn't his fault. Some people can't take the truth, you know. Some people just can't handle criticism.'

'It isn't that—'

'Take that Armstrong guy that built that god-awful mall, for instance. Moony didn't like him one little bit. And that other one who wants your job – Molt? Damned used-car salesman, crooked as a dog's hind leg. He punched Moony once, in the bar. Knocked out a tooth.' He eyed Matt malevolently. 'Moony didn't much like you either.'

'So I gather,' Matt said. 'How did he feel about Frog Bartlett?'

'Funny you should mention Frog Bartlett,' Frank said in an almost normal tone, which for him was comparable to a whisper. 'They never did get along, not even from kids.'

'Oh?'

'You think Frog Bartlett killed my brother?'

'At the moment, I have no—'

'Could be, could be,' Frank said, sitting back a little. 'Moony kind of did like to tease old Frog.' He squeezed his eyes shut – it might have been a smile although the rest of his face gave no indication of it. 'Moony could be like that. Have to admit it. Maybe not smart, but he got the devil in him sometimes. Not that he would allow it was the devil – more like some avenging angel. Moony was a righteous man. A God-fearing man. He knew the difference between good and evil. He kept track of it all too.'

'I'd be very interested to see his room,' Matt said.

'Well, now, I'll just bet you would!' Frank said, his voice suddenly loud again. 'You got no right to go poking around in Moony's stuff.'

'As it happens, I do. It often helps to know about the victim in these cases,' Matt tried to explain. 'There might be something there that—'

'I'll be the judge of that,' Frank said. 'He left everything to me and with me it will stay.'

'I could get a court order,' Matt said reflectively.

Frank stood up. 'Oh, yeah? Well, you just go ahead and do that. Why would you want to see Moony's stuff? What are you looking for? Maybe *you* killed him, hey?' Frank was getting over-excited again. There were little deposits of spittle in the corners of his mouth. 'There would be the perfect crime – the Sheriff did it. And who investigates? The Sheriff. I don't trust you.'

'Look, Mr Packard—' Matt stood up too.

Frank backed up towards the door. 'Don't you go threatening me. I can go to the Mayor, you know. To the Governor. I can get you fired – don't you think I can't.'

'Mr Packard.' Susie Brock's voice was sharp and almost as loud as Packard's. 'Sheriff Gabriel has his duty to do. The victim almost always can supply us with some clues to his or her killer.'

He whirled on her. 'You're probably in it with him. Maybe you're his paramour, maybe you did it together to keep Moony from telling everyone about your disgusting ways. Moony was against things like that. We both

8

are. You might have stopped Moony but you won't stop me!'

'I don't want to stop you, Mr Packard. I want to help you to find your brother's killer,' Susie said in a no-nonsense tone. 'Don't you want that too?'

'I can do my own detecting,' Packard muttered, apparently rather mollified by Susie's standing up to him.

'But we're professionals,' Susie said. 'Won't you at least let us see his room? It might help a lot. We should all work together.'

Packard eyed her and then Matt with suspicion, but gradually his enmity boiled away and his quasi-military bearing slumped a little. 'All right,' he said. 'But you're not taking anything away but what I say so.'

'That's fine,' Matt said. He and Susie followed the man down the hall. As they passed one open door Matt glanced in and saw a bedroom that was even more spare than the sitting-room, with an Army cot tautly made up, a footlocker, a small side table and a straight chair. There were military posters on the walls and, over the bed, a shelf of what looked like books on survivalism and military history. It seemed to be a cross between a barracks and a monk's cell. That must be Frank's room, he thought.

The late Moony's room was quite the opposite.

For a start, it was much larger. Two walls were entirely covered by huge aquariums, and between the tanks was a bookcase stuffed with volumes on the breeding and care of tropical fish. The aquariums were lit and the fish within the clear water were spectacular.

'Moony liked fish,' Packard said rather unnecessarily.

Here there was a double bed, made up with quilts and comforters. A large, overstuffed easy chair was set so that the occupant could watch both aquariums in comfort. A small bookcase sat beside it. Matt glanced over the titles – mostly murder mysteries and what looked like a long run of *Ellery Queen Mystery Magazine*. Beside the easy chair was a swing-across table and beneath it a stack of legal pads. For keeping all those 'records', presumably.

'I'd like to look through your brother's papers,' Matt said.

'Why?' Packard's voice was belligerent, but more subdued now as he looked around at the room that had belonged to his dead brother. Anger had been replaced with something like regret – or so it seemed.

'Oh – in case he left any indication of who might have had something against him, recent appointments with people, that sort of thing,' Susie said casually.

Packard shifted from one foot to the other. 'He never wrote down anything like *that*,' he said sullenly. 'Never made appointments or anything like that, except maybe with the dentist. He just did the bills and all. Me, I'm more of an action person.' He straightened his spine and squared his shoulders.

'Even so—' Matt said.

'Go ahead, then, I don't care,' Packard snarled. He stood by the door watching them as they went through the few papers on the small desk that stood under the single window overlooking the rear garden. There was nothing that could be of help. No diary, no appointment calendar and, oddly, no letters of any kind aside from bills marked 'Paid'.

'Did your brother keep papers anywhere other than this desk?' Matt asked, turning to Packard. 'Things like insurance policies, bank accounts, maybe a will or other family papers?'

Something flickered in the man's eyes. 'I don't know anything about that. We got no kin at all. Just the two of us. You don't think he'd leave me without a home now, do you?'

Matt thought he was holding something back, but decided to let it go for the moment. He would check with the bank – Moony might have had a safe deposit box.

'How did you get along with your brother, Mr Packard?' Matt asked.

Anger reappeared and coloured Frank's cheek-bones bright red. 'What the hell do you mean by that? We got

10

on fine. Only two years between us, me the older. We got on fine.'

'Do you work, Mr Packard?' Susie asked.

'Sometimes. I do painting and decorating.'

'But your brother was the main wage earner between you?'

'You could say that.'

'And what will you do, now that he's gone?'

'The best I can, young woman. The best I can.' He glared at her.

'Thank you,' Susie said. 'We'd like to see the rest of the house, please.'

'How come?'

'It gives us an idea of what your brother was like,' Susie explained as they went from room to room. The house was neat and clean, but all the furniture was old-fashioned and worn.

'How long have you and your brother lived here, Mr Packard?' Susie asked, as she opened a cupboard in the kitchen and peered in.

'All our lives,' Packard said, still glowering. 'And there's nothing in there but soup cans and cereals.'

'Who did most of the cooking?'

'Moony,' was the sullen answer. 'You through yet?'

'I guess so,' Matt said, after a brief glance at the basement from the stairway above it. Just the furnace and some kind of work-bench back in the shadows next to a washing machine. Despite living there all their lives, the house reflected very little in the way of personalities, aside from the two contrasting bedrooms. Probably it hadn't changed since their parents furnished it.

Packard followed them back into the sitting-room. 'I appreciate you coming to tell me yourself,' he muttered rather awkwardly. 'About Moony, I mean.' Then he took a deep breath and addressed that invisible audience once again. 'I want whoever did this to be caught and punished,' he announced. 'This kind of thing is what is ruining our country. Murderers everywhere, nobody respecting the law of the land, people taking advantage, people lowering their standards. I want action on this, Sheriff! I want results!'

'We'll do our best,' Matt promised, thinking as he did so that Packard sounded as if he were issuing orders. He didn't need to be told to do his duty, nor did he take kindly to people like Frank Packard bellowing at him. Apparently the man hardly knew how to speak any other way, except under duress. 'And if you come across any other papers and so on, please let us know. Did your brother have a lawyer?'

'I don't know.' For a moment Frank looked perplexed, then his chin came up. 'I'll have a look around,' he finally said. It was clearly as much co-operation as they were likely to get.

In the car, Matt leaned back with a sigh and drank deeply from a bottle of mineral water he kept there. Thirst was always a problem lately. 'There must be papers somewhere. He was sure nervous.'

'Let's go back and really search the house,' Susie suggested, puzzled by Matt's lack of enthusiasm.

Matt shook his head. 'By the time we get a search warrant he'll have dealt with it. We can look around a victim's home and possessions, but we have to have probable cause for a full in-depth search, unfortunately. He might *give* us cause, if we watch for it. A couple of the posters on his bedroom wall were of private militia groups. I wonder if he's into that kind of thing.'

'I didn't like him much,' Susie said. 'He was kind of scary, the way he kept shouting, and his eyes . . .' She shivered.

'Interesting,' Matt said.

'What is?' Susie wanted to know.

'How two brothers could be so different. Moony Packard was unctious, opinionated and holier-than-thou, but he spent a lot of time in the Golden Perch and was very gregarious. His brother Frank, on the other hand, is a loner who hates authority and never has a good word to say about anyone.' Matt cleared his throat as he put his key into the ignition. 'You have to wonder,' he said slowly, as the engine caught.

'Wonder what?' Susie asked dutifully.

'What actually went on in that house when they were alone.'

TWO

FROG BARTLETT WAS ONE OF the ugliest men in Blackwater Bay County.

He sat in Matt's office, hunched and glowering, resembling his nickname in everything but colour. Frog was thickset, with a big head that seemed to rest right on his shoulders, a wide mouth, a flat nose and beady little eyes.

'I'm glad Moony's dead,' he said to Matt. 'He was a preaching, sneaking son of a bitch and deserved killing. God knows I *felt* like killing him from time to time, like everyone else, but I just hadn't never got around to it. Now somebody's done it for me.'

'You admit you had a fight with Packard last night in the Golden Perch?' Matt asked, finishing his second cup of coffee.

'About twenty people can tell you we had a fight,' Frog said. 'Sure I admit it. Proud of it. Wish I'd punched him out, but they drug me off. Spoil-sports.'

'What did you have against Packard?' Matt asked.

'Hah! What didn't I have against him?' Frog wanted to know. 'He was sly. He made fun of people behind their backs. Gossip? He could gossip you into the ground and then yell down the hole after you. I think he used to read people's mail too, by God. Not just postcards neither. People complained but there was no way of proving it. He was clever. Damn know-it-all. Wonder he lived so long.'

'Anything else?'

'You got to have more?'

14

'I've got to find a reason why he was killed.'

'Why? He's dead. Let it go. Be glad.' Frog smiled. It was an expression that sat oddly on his squat face and Matt felt a little unnerved by it. 'How long you going to keep me here, anyways?'

'Till I find out all I want to know,' Matt said wearily. 'I'm not keeping you here, but it would look better if you stayed and answered my questions.'

'Look better to who?'

'To me. Maybe, eventually, to a judge.'

'You going to pin this thing on me?'

'Not if you're innocent.'

'Hah!' Frog was unconvinced. 'So if I haul ass out of here, that makes me guilty, is that it?'

'No. But it makes me more interested,' Matt said.

'In what?'

'In what you think you have to hide by avoiding my questions.'

'Full circle,' Frog said triumphantly. 'You have George drag me in because I had a fight with the deceased, you ask me questions to see if I'm a killer, I say I'm not, you say okay, but you don't really believe me. Then, when I get tired of your questions, which any sane man would, you say that's okay too, you don't have to ask 'em no more because if I leave I'm guilty. And you done all that sitting down too.'

Matt had to laugh. 'What I believe or don't believe isn't the point, Frog. It's what I can *prove* that counts. Where were you at five this morning?'

'In bed, asleep. Is that when Packard got it?'

'You were in bed alone, I take it?'

Frog went white, then bright red. 'Now that's a damn fool question.'

'No – if you'd had a companion it would have given you an alibi.'

'If I'd a known I would need an alibi I should have hired some girl to sleep with me, is that it? Damn – sure missed out there, didn't I? Never had a respectable reason to go whoring before.'

'What time did you get up?'

'Seven. I always get up at seven. What time did you get up?'

'About seven.'

'There you go. Moony, now, Moony got up about four he used to brag. Liked to get to sorting the mail for his route early. Did you know that?'

'Yes, I did.' Duff Bradley had gone over to the Post Office to see what he could find out about Moony Packard's usual routine and if there had been any variation that morning. There hadn't – apparently Moony had behaved normally before going out on his round.

'Guess just about everybody did, he used to go on about it often enough. You'd think he'd invented the dawn or something. Like nothing started around here until *he* flipped the switch. Conceited bastard.'

Matt looked down at the notepad on his desk. 'Would you have any objection to our looking around your place, Frog?'

'What for?'

'General enquiries. I could get a search warrant, but it would look better for you if you made no objection.'

Frog waved a hand. 'I got no objection, long as you don't mess my stuff up. I keep a neat house, like it to stay that way.'

'Fine,' Matt said. 'Thank you.'

'That it?' Frog started to stand up.

'I'd still like to know what you argued with Moony about last night,' Matt said.

Frog sat down again. 'Dumb,' he said. 'It was just dumb, is all. The guy pissed me off, everything he did pissed me off. Last night he made some remark about the election, said . . .' Frog suddenly looked embarrassed.

'Said what?'

'Said Armstrong was a lousy candidate. Said Molt only was interested in selling cars. Said he wasn't going to vote for you neither.'

'Well, he didn't have to,' Matt conceded.

'It wasn't *what* he said, it was the way he said it,' Frog

went on. 'You got to understand, everything Packard said had at least two meanings, maybe more. He said *he'd* make a better sheriff than you ever were. Sorry, but that's what he said.'

'We still have free speech in this country,' Matt pointed out.

'Some people take advantage,' Frog growled. 'You caught plenty of bad guys in your time.'

'With luck and a following wind,' Matt admitted. 'Had some help, of course.'

'That's what else he said. That you always needed help, that you couldn't do anything on your own.'

'We all need help, Frog.' Matt was just about managing to keep his temper. Good thing *he* hadn't been in the Golden Perch last night, he might have killed Moony Packard himself.

'Well, anyways, I had a few beers and he got me going,' Frog said. 'Ever since we was kids, he liked to get me going. Then he'd start to laugh . . . I don't mind people not liking me, but laughing . . . he had this way . . .'

'I understand,' Matt said. And he did, because he himself had seen Packard in action on other occasions. If Frog had had an argument with Packard last night, then it had merely been Frog's turn. Packard had been a man of loud opinions, fond of starting arguments, of baiting people.

How angry had Frog been last night? How drunk? Enough of both to kill? It seemed unlikely and yet possible. Frog was an odd man. He'd begun a career in the Army but had been invalided out. Now he lived on his own in the house he'd grown up in, spent his life in his garden or fishing. For a man with such an easy life, Frog Bartlett was amazingly crabby, Matt thought. Maybe he was bored. Animals can turn nasty when they're bored – and then Matt wondered why he classed Frog with the animals. It was the look in the eyes, he decided. Frog's eyes were all black, hard to read, suspicious in their setting of frowning lines, like animals Matt had seen in zoos. His hair – what there was of it – hung raggedly over his forehead and he peered through it, head down.

He didn't want to think Frog was guilty.

But he had no reason not to think so.

Not yet.

There was a tap at Matt's door, and George Putnam opened it slightly and looked through the gap. 'FBI's here, Matt. Brokaw again.'

'Thanks, George. Give me a few minutes.'

'My, my,' Frog said, when George had withdrawn. 'The FBI, hey? How come?'

'Moony Packard was a mail carrier. Killing a mail carrier in the course of his rounds is a Federal offence,' Matt said with considerable lack of enthusiasm.

'Jesus,' Frog said. 'I didn't know that.'

'No. The killer probably didn't either.'

'Then you believe me?'

'Not necessarily, Frog – I just said you and the killer were in the same boat – not knowing the FBI might be taking over.'

'Does that mean you won't be doing the case?'

Matt stood up and shrugged. 'I don't know. Maybe. Maybe not.' He sighed. 'We'll drive you back home in a few minutes – you can wait over there. Tilly will give you some coffee and a doughnut.'

'Free?'

'Absolutely.'

'Almost worth getting arrested,' Frog muttered.

Agent Brokaw had been in the office before, when a man who had been enrolled in the Witness Protection Scheme and placed in Blackwater Bay had gone missing. He was a handsome African-American, an Alan Ladd look-alike in ebony. He greeted Matt in a friendly manner, which made Matt wary. Smiles on an FBI agent often meant trouble.

'Sheriff,' Brokaw said, shaking his hand. 'How are you?'

'Fine, thanks. And you?'

'Oh, fair to middling. You've got a dead mail carrier on your patch.'

'Yes. Moony Packard.'

'Wish you could have left the crime scene intact for me,' Brokaw said with another kind of smile.

'If I'd known you were coming . . .'

'You'd have baked a cake, sure. But you have pictures?'

'Of course. George, get the Polaroids of the Packard crime scene for Agent Brokaw.' George produced them instantly. He had been waiting. 'Have a look for yourself,' Matt said, handing them over.

There was a long silence while Brokaw slowly and carefully went through the stack of photographs and drawings made at the scene. Matt and George waited, saying nothing. Brokaw was a man who knew how to dress and was as self-contained as a cat. It was a pleasure to watch him. Every time he lingered over a particular picture or note, Matt and George would exchange a glance.

'Nice work,' Brokaw finally said, closing the folder.

'Thank you.'

'The mail-bag.'

'Yes?'

'It doesn't appear to have been opened.'

'No. We looked into it – nothing seemed to have been disturbed. The mail was sorted into packets with rubber bands around them – that was apparently Moony's habit, according to the people at the mail depot. And everything was stacked in the bag according to streets and so on, still in proper order. We just handed the bag back and they got someone else to deliver it.'

'Interfering with the US Mail is a Federal offence, you know.'

'I knew that. Once we had satisfied ourselves that nothing had been disturbed, we handed it straight back.'

'Uh-huh.'

'I know killing a mail carrier is a Federal offence,' Matt said. 'So we've been expecting you.'

'That's nice to know. *Un*fortunately, in this case, we have no jurisdiction,' Brokaw went on in a pseudo-sad voice.

Matt was surprised. 'Why not?'

'Because your victim was not employed by the Federal government, but by a sub-contractor who handles all the mail in this county. If the mail had been tampered with it would have been a different story. As it is, we don't come into it. We'd like to – but we can't. Unless, of course, you *ask* us to come in.'

'Not . . . at this moment,' Matt said.

'Uh-huh.' Brokaw leaned back. His suit adjusted to his changes in position like a second skin, the soft material obviously very expensive, as was the tailoring. Matt thought, not for the first time, that the FBI dressed its people very well.

'I like to solve my own problems,' Matt explained, although he knew no explanation was necessary. The remark made by Moony Packard the night before his death – that Matt always needed help to solve his cases – still rankled.

'I can understand that,' Brokaw said. 'But don't forget we have national resources, information . . .'

'I don't think this is a national case,' Matt said. 'I think it's what we might call a little local difficulty.'

'And you don't want us horning in,' Brokaw concluded.

'Not really, no,' Matt admitted. 'But if the offer stands—'

'Oh, it does, it does,' Brokaw said. 'We're always happy to help local law enforcement officers, when required.'

'More than happy,' George put in.

Brokaw looked directly at him for the first time. 'Deputy Putnam, isn't it?'

'Yes.' George was suddenly aware he should have kept his mouth shut.

'The idea that the FBI is fond of "taking over" is a false one,' Brokaw said very quietly. 'We have plenty to do on our own without taking on other folks' problems. Funny how people get the idea that we are Big Brother watching them. We aren't.' Brokaw smiled that smile again. 'Unless they get in our way, of course.'

'I don't think George meant that,' Matt said. 'I think he meant that you are there to serve and happy to do it, isn't that right?'

'Oh, that's right enough,' Brokaw agreed, standing up. 'We are happy to serve.' He extended his hand to Matt. 'Nice seeing you again, Sheriff Gabriel.'

Matt and George watched Brokaw move down the office and out through the door, closing it quietly behind him.

'So damn smooth,' George said irritably.

'Highly educated, highly trained, highly paid,' Matt said. 'We'd be smooth, too, under those circumstances.'

'I like the highly paid part,' George said rather pointedly. He'd been angling for a rise for months, now.

'So would we all,' Matt agreed. He stood up. 'Frog had no objections to our looking over his place. I think we should get right on it.'

Dispatching Duff Bradley and Susie Brock to the house, Matt and George started with the garage – for no particular reason other than they had parked in the drive and it was closest. It was a fortunate choice. Frog had a large two-car garage, half of which was filled with his old van. The other half had been turned into a very comprehensive workshop. On one end of the bench sat a water pump, presumably out of his garden pond, partially disassembled. On the other was a rocking chair that was obviously being stripped down. The walls above the long work-bench were covered by pegboard, on which hung all Frog's tools, each one carefully outlined in marker pen to show where they went. One outline was empty, but it didn't take them long to find the missing item.

A large monkey wrench, with blood and hair on the working end, lay in plain sight on an old barrel. The wrench had Frog Bartlett's initials on it.

Frog was astonished. 'How did that happen?' he growled.

'At a guess, I would say when it came into contact with Moony Packard's skull,' George said in a nasty voice.

'Well, I didn't contact it,' Frog stated. 'Last time I seen

that wrench it was hanging up with all the rest of my things. Right there—'

'Well, it's not there now,' George observed.

'Wouldn't I have washed it and put it away if I'd a used it to kill somebody?' Frog demanded, his normally croaky voice going a bit high with tension. 'Would I have left it lying there like that?'

'I don't know,' Matt answered. 'Maybe you couldn't bring yourself to touch it again.'

'I never touched it in the first place,' Frog said.

'We'll see.' George bagged the wrench in plastic. 'Your fingerprints may be on it.'

'Well, of course my fingerprints will be on it,' Frog said. 'It's my wrench, dammit.'

'I noticed you don't keep your garage locked,' Matt commented.

'No need. Folks don't bother with me, much,' Frog said. Matt knew that was true, because Frog's temper was legendary. 'And I don't have much worth stealing, either. Nothing that can't be replaced real easy. I like it that way.' Frog's voice was rather belligerent. 'No need to worry like that. No need to think about anything like that. See?'

'So someone could have come in and taken the wrench, used it to kill Moony Packard and then thoughtfully replaced it,' Matt observed.

'Sure, sure, that must be it!' Frog said, relieved. 'Sure, that must be the answer.'

'Who would want to do that?' Matt asked.

'I don't know,' Frog said.

'No,' Matt agreed. 'Neither do I. Seems a very complicated thing to do, doesn't it? So much easier to buy a wrench or something like it for cash from one of the big stores. So much easier just to throw it in the bay when you'd finished killing Moony. Or even into the quicksand in the Mush. So who would go to all the trouble of coming over here and taking your wrench, use it to kill someone and then replace it?'

'I don't *know*,' Frog said again. 'It wasn't me, though.

I would have done what you said. I would have bought a new one. I would have thrown it away. I sure wouldn't have brought it back here and left it like that . . . Nobody would.'

'People do funny things when they've killed,' George mused. 'Maybe you just wanted to threaten Packard. Maybe your temper got out of hand. Maybe when you'd killed him you were so horrified that you just weren't thinking straight.'

'I always think straight,' Frog protested, beginning to perspire. 'Besides, that doesn't have to be Moony's blood. Maybe I used it to kill a rat.'

Matt looked at him. 'Did you?'

'Did I what?'

'Use it to kill a rat,' Matt answered patiently.

'Yes. No. I don't know,' Frog said, twisting his hands together and rubbing his knuckles. 'Maybe.'

'Well, that's easy to find out,' George said. 'The forensic lab will tell us all that.'

'They can do that?' Frog asked.

'Oh, yes – the forensic lab can tell us whose blood this is, right down to his chromosomes,' George said pointedly. 'Don't you worry about that.'

But Frog looked very worried indeed.

'Move it a little to the left,' Daria shouted, gesturing.

Larry Lovich obliged, shifting the poster more towards the centre of his window. 'There?' he mouthed through the glass.

Daria made a circle with thumb and forefinger, then came back inside the café, shivering with the cold, as Larry applied tape to the corners of the poster showing Matt looking fierce and powerful, a true guardian of peace and safety.

'I hope it doesn't get spoiled with condensation,' Larry mused, stepping back. 'We get a lot of condensation. It's the coffee machines that do it.'

'Never mind,' Daria said. 'These are left over from last

time. We plan to print some new ones, if I can just get Matt to sit for an up-to-date photograph.' Daria Grey ran the local art gallery and was engaged to Matt Gabriel. She lived with an elderly aunt on Paradise Island, a cosy enclave of cottages overlooking the bay that was a little society all its own.

They moved to the back of the café, past the tables with upended chairs, past the display case of cakes and pastries, past the still-hissing coffee machines and the small sink with the tap that wouldn't stop dripping.

'Just Desserts' was exactly what its name implied – a coffee shop that served tea, coffee and desserts. But what desserts! Luscious gateaux, rich cakes, crumbly cookies and succulent brownies – all home-made and all delicious. The owners of Just Desserts were Larry Lovich and Freddy Tollett, a gay couple who also lived on Paradise Island. They had thought long and hard about what kind of establishment to open – what would be the most pleasant to run, the most profitable, the most attractive – and had settled on good coffee combined with irresistible calorie-laden confections. A lot of these were made for them by Nell Norton, a widowed neighbour on Paradise Island and a compulsive baker. She had won many awards at county fairs for her baked goods and the café gave her an outlet for her most creative talents. She shared a cottage with Margaret Toby, also a widow, whose speciality was making quilts. And not just any quilts, but quilts of such spectacular design and workmanship that they hung next door, in Daria's art gallery, where they sold for very high prices.

These two good ladies were among the group gathered at the back of Just Desserts, all with a common aim – To Get Matt Gabriel Re-elected.

'Molt's no threat. It's Jack Armstrong that's the problem,' Freddy said.

'He plays dirty,' Lem Turkle nodded. Lem was one of the respectable Turkles, an old Blackwater Bay family whose members had a wide range of distribution and morality.

24

'I could tell you things about that mall you wouldn't want to know.' Lem was a builder whose contacts with Jack Armstrong had been frequent and bitter. They had vied on many a contract, and Lem knew to his cost what crossing Armstrong could mean in terms of quick beatings in dark parking lots, equipment sabotaged and materials stolen on jobs he had won over their bids. Not all Turkles were to be trusted, but Lem was the best of the lot. He also ran the local taxi service. 'You hear all sorts of things, driving a taxi,' Lem was known to boast. And it was true that Lem knew a lot of things about a lot of people, most of them scurrilous, some of them lies, but all of them fascinating. Especially to Lem.

'What kind of things?' Nell asked.

'Oh, substandard stuff being used, corners being cut – the roof is going to start going in a few years, you'll see. There was talk about kickbacks, too. And some kind of fancy dancing with the workman's comp. The steel joists were minimum size – and he used cheap timber, too. Somebody might be under that roof when it goes.'

'You hope,' said Larry, knowing Lem's propensity for enjoying disasters that happened to others.

'The big problem – the only real problem – is this new murder,' Margaret Toby said gloomily. 'It's come at such a bad time. If Matt could solve it quick then there would be no question about his getting re-elected. It would be a shoo-in. A landslide.'

'He's got trouble, right here in Blackwater Bay,' Freddy Tollett said. 'Armstrong is already hollering for "results".'

'He's doing more than he appears to be doing,' Daria said, then looked as if she regretted saying that much, for all the others turned to stare at her. She shrugged. 'Like the swan – quiet on top of the water but paddling for dear life underneath.'

'Well, in terms of the election, he's sitting on his hands,' Nell Norton snapped, complicating the metaphor. 'It's not just that he has to do something, he has to be *seen* to do something. He has to arrest someone.'

25

'Who?'

She raised her hands and shrugged. 'I don't know. Someone. Anyone. Give the papers someone to talk about, to think about. Anything to get the pressure off him and what he *isn't* doing.'

Daria smiled and looked around. 'Any volunteers?'

'He can arrest me if he likes,' Mrs Toby said staunchly.

'Margaret, Moony Packard was murdered, not appliquéd,' Nell Norton said.

'What about me?' Freddy Tollett's voice was less than steady. 'People would be willing to believe the worst about me. You could count on that.'

'Not funny,' Larry said to his friend. 'Not remotely funny.'

Daria shook her head. 'It's not as easy as that.' She sighed. 'Matt is tired. I'm worried, frankly. I can hardly get him to talk about the election.'

'Well, somebody has to get him onto it, or he'll lose, that's for damn sure,' Lem said flatly.

'I heard they have a suspect already for Moony's murder.'

'Frog Bartlett,' Freddy said.

Lem nodded. 'Moony liked to get people riled up, taking a righteous stand just to make someone angry. Frog used to fall for it all the time. Although he wasn't alone. Moony was tolerated, because he used to buy drinks for everyone, but he wasn't really liked. And some folks hated his guts because of his holier-than-thou attitude. Me included.'

'Did you kill Moony?' Larry asked, not really meaning it.

Lem got red in the face. 'No, dammit, I did not!' he said loudly.

'Only kidding.' Larry raised his hand in supplication.

'Not funny,' Lem muttered, subsiding. 'Point is, there's a lot of people might have been pushed too far by Moony Packard. Not just Frog. Frog's the last person I would pick for it.'

'There's some who would disagree,' Nell Norton said.

'Frog's got a short temper and he doesn't suffer fools gladly.'

Freddy sighed. 'You grow up looking like Frog Bartlett and you might well be short-tempered. Kids taunt him all the time, did you know that? Grown-ups shun him or are rude to him because they think he's thick-skinned, but he isn't.'

'How do you know that?' Larry asked.

Freddy picked up a paper napkin and folded it carefully into smaller and smaller squares. 'Ever looked into his eyes?' he said quietly. 'They're full of pain. He can't help looking like some kind of small-town Quasimodo.'

'He's not that ugly.' Daria frowned. An artist with a growing national reputation, she had often felt the urge to paint Frog Bartlett, his face and form were a challenge. And she knew what Freddy meant about the pain in his eyes. It *was* an ugly face, but a face full of character too.

'No, well – people can be stupid sometimes,' Freddy said. Larry reached over and laid his hand over his partner's.

'We're getting off the point,' Mrs Toby said. 'We've got to get Matt re-elected, so stop with the amateur psychology and start thinking about what we can do to put Matt on the map. Who's going to be the first one to try on one of these patchwork VOTE FOR MATT hats I've made up?'

THREE

MATT WAS CORNERED.

He sat in his office with his arms folded across his chest and glared at them. 'I don't want my picture taken,' he grumbled. 'I hate having my picture taken. I haven't got *time* to have my picture taken – I have a murder to investigate. There are things—'

'Well, you have to have a new picture,' Daria said firmly. He was slumped in his chair like a naughty little boy – or rather, a naughty six-foot-three boy – with his lower lip protruding sulkily. 'The one you used on your last election posters made you look like a "Dangerous – Most Wanted" candidate.'

'I got re-elected, didn't I?'

'Only because people knew you.'

'Well, then—'

'You didn't have much opposition then,' Tilly Moss pointed out. She was busy writing lists. Tilly ran the sheriff's office and lists were her speciality. 'It was only Tyrone Molt doing his usual bid for free advertising and nobody ever takes him seriously. But now you've got Jack Armstrong . . .'

'The All-American Boy,' muttered Matt.

'. . . against you and he could cause trouble,' Tilly went on, ignoring him. 'He finished building that new mall in record time and everybody thinks it's great, new jobs, new shopping facilities, all that.'

'Nothing to do with policing a county,' Matt said. 'He's the kind who smiles and then rides roughshod over everything in his path. I wouldn't trust him as far as I could throw him.'

'Since when did people vote on the basis of suitability for a job?' Daria asked. She pushed Max, the large orange station cat, over a little and sat beside him on the edge of the desk. Max yawned. 'It's all a popularity thing now, I'm sorry to say.'

'That's a very cynical attitude,' Matt said, giving Max a brief scratch and reaching for his coffee mug.

'Well, maybe I've become a cynical person,' Daria retorted. 'It seems to me it's the person with the best television ads who wins the votes these days.'

'I'm *not* doing a television ad,' Matt said rather too loudly. 'I'm not going around kissing babies, I'm not laying a wreath on the Veterans' Memorial, I'm not doing a tap-dance in the Town Hall, I'm not—'

'You are,' Daria said.

'You are,' Tilly said.

'You are,' George Putnam said. 'That is, not the tap-dance. Unless you *really* want to get votes, of course.'

'Mm,' Matt muttered. He had to admit things had changed. Since that last election, a series of fairly spectacular murders had brought Blackwater Bay to the attention of the state capitol. The big city media, having 'discovered' Blackwater Bay as an idyll threatened and a haven for eccentrics, were reluctant to let its good stories go unreported. As each successive case had brought more and more attention their way, the Powers That Be had deemed it necessary to update and modernize things. Money had poured in from the capitol and, reluctantly, from the city council as well.

The Sheriff's Department had spent the past year surrounded by builders, chaos and noise. Now Blackwater Bay had a spanking new complex that housed offices, jail, a special secure records and evidence room, garaging for their fleet of squad cars and jeeps, and a proper apartment for Matt 'above the shop'.

Meanwhile, Election Day was coming closer and closer. 'There's Moony Packard's murder to deal with. I need to concentrate on that, dammit.'

'Oh, that's going to be easy,' George said confidently.

29

'We're just waiting for confirmation from the forensic lab. Should be able to put Frog away any day now. And just before the election, too. Couldn't be better.'

'Big deal.' Matt glowered. He was still not happy about the evidence against Frog Bartlett. Something was wrong there. It had been too pat, too easy. As a consequence he'd played the investigation by the book so far. They'd questioned everyone who worked with Moony and all the people who had been at the Golden Perch with him the night before his death. They'd talked to everyone who could possibly have a connection with Moony, but they'd all been surprisingly uncooperative. Word of finding the bloody monkey wrench in Frog's garage had got out – like George Putnam, many people had already decided Frog was guilty. Others, Matt among them, weren't so sure. But pressure was being brought to bear on Matt to make a quick arrest. He hated being forced into doing something against his better judgement.

'It's a perfect time to step up your election campaign,' Tilly said triumphantly. 'Show Jack Armstrong that you are still the right man for the job.'

'He hasn't got a chance against Matt,' Daria stated loyally. 'What's his platform?'

George looked uncomfortable. 'He was in the Golden Perch last night, buying drinks for people. He's saying Matt only got the job because he was his father's son.'

'That's a god-damned lie!' Tilly was outraged.

'I didn't say he was right,' George said. 'I just said that was what he's going around saying.'

'Nobody's listening to him, surely?' Daria asked.

George shrugged and glanced at Matt. 'Some people might. He can be real charming, you know. Especially to the ladies, but the men like him too. Some people are impressed by a glad-hander and overlook things like sharp business practice.'

'All you have to do is arrest someone. Be a sheriff and you'll *stay* a sheriff,' Tilly finished. 'Isn't that right, Daria?'

'Well . . . I suppose in a manner of speaking . . .' Daria was reluctant to endorse this plan of action, especially if it involved Matt getting beaten up or shot at. 'Wouldn't it be easier just to make a few speeches?'

'Armstrong is talking to the Rotary on Friday,' George put in. 'You should call Don Overton and demand equal time.'

'And say what?' Matt wanted to know.

'Good policing is good for business – they'll like that,' Daria said promptly. 'And then there's the PTA, and the Junior Achievement, and the Algonawana Lodge, and I'm sure we can get you an interview with John Parsons on WMBCTV, and on the radio, and set up a debate at the Town Hall, and—'

'I'm no good at public speaking,' Matt protested.

'Rubbish,' Daria said, picking up and unbending a defenceless paper-clip. 'You taught college students a boring subject—'

Matt stared at her. 'I beg your pardon?'

'Well, not boring to you, but heavy going for a freshman footballer,' Daria amended quickly, dropping the ruined clip into the waste basket. 'And you kept their attention, didn't you?'

'More or less,' Matt conceded. 'But talking about Descartes is a little different from boasting about yourself. I feel uncomfortable doing that.'

'Oh, you don't have to do *that*,' Daria said impatiently. 'You just have to talk about what your job entails, show that it takes a certain kind of person to do it, that *experience* means everything, that—'

'And that building a damn mall is no recommendation,' Tilly put in. 'Just because Jack Armstrong was a big football star in high school here, and handsome, and has a lot of money to throw around . . .'

'Whereas I am old and ugly and poor?' Matt asked, raising an eyebrow.

'I didn't mean that,' Tilly said, flushing bright pink. 'I meant—'

31

'I know what you meant.' Matt smiled wryly. 'Let's see, now – what are my qualifications for office here? I used to teach a boring subject in college, I am no longer young and handsome . . .'

'You're just being awkward,' Tilly snapped.

'And I'm awkward,' Matt added.

'You're not all *that* bad-looking,' George said assessingly. 'Kind of reliable and craggy. And you still have all your hair. Armstrong is beginning to go a little thin on the top.' George was very proud of his own hair: thick, blond and kept in trim by a very nice redhead down at the Topknotch Unisex hairdressing establishment. He glanced over to see if Susie Brock was listening, but she was doing some filing and had her back to him.

'Would you care to count my teeth?' Matt asked him. 'Just in case the subject comes up?'

'It might get the dental vote,' George said brightly.

Matt groaned. 'I *hate* this.'

'We gathered that, dear,' said Daria, less and less amused by his intransigence.

'How about a wedding?' Tilly suggested suddenly. 'If you two were to tie the knot some time in the next few weeks it would get all kinds of publicity.'

'That's a rotten reason for getting married,' Matt said reprovingly. Daria said nothing, but gave Tilly a meaningful glance. Tilly didn't press the point.

'And you have to have a slogan,' Daria stated.

'A slogan?'

'Yes – like "Win with Wilkie" or something.'

'Who's Wilkie?' George asked.

'I've got it,' Tilly announced. 'How about – "If you support Gabriel, blow your horn"?'

'Oh, my God.' Matt buried his head in his hands.

The phone rang and Tilly answered it. She listened, nodded, asked for them to fax it through right away and put the phone down. She went into Matt's office and beckoned for him to join her.

'Well, you've got your proof,' she said, when he'd closed

the door behind him. 'That was the guy from the State forensic lab. That's Moony's blood on the wrench all right. They matched it right down to the DNA, so there. They're faxing the report over now. You've got what you need, Matt. You can arrest Frog Bartlett.'

FOUR

'LUTHER BURBANK BARTLETT—' THE JUDGE intoned. A ripple of giggles and snorts ran through the spectators.

The judge continued, 'You stand accused of the wilful murder of one James Montgomery Ward Packard—' A few more giggles.

'How do you plead?'

'My client pleads Not Guilty,' said the lawyer who had been appointed by the Public Defender's office to represent Frog at this preliminary hearing. He spoke in a hurried voice, shuffling through some papers before him, his mind on another case.

'God-damned right!' shouted Frog, pounding the table in front of him with a large gnarled fist. 'Not god-damned guilty!'

The judge's gavel snapped down smartly and he glared at the dishevelled figure who glared back at him, eye for eye and sneer for sneer.

'The prisoner will be held in custody pending trial.' The judge reached for his calendar and flipped through the pages. 'One month from today be convenient for you, counsellor?' He glanced down at the lawyer. 'Counsellor?' he said again, more loudly.

'He's talking to you, meat-head,' Frog snarled, jabbing the lawyer in the ribs with his elbow.

'Ouch! Oh – yes, Your Honour. One week from today,' the lawyer mumbled as he struggled to replace the papers in his already full briefcase.

'One *month*, he said,' Frog growled, raising his elbow again.

'Uh – yes, fine, request bail,' the lawyer said automatically, dodging to one side and glancing at the clock on the wall to his left.

'Bail set at—' The judge paused. Frog growled. The judge's eyes narrowed. 'Bail set at five hundred thousand dollars.'

There was a shocked silence.

'What the hell for?' Frog shouted.

Even the lawyer was startled out of his distraction. 'That does seem rather excessive, Your Honour. The defendant—'

'I am familiar with the defendant. Bail set at five hundred thousand dollars,' the judge repeated and banged down his gavel with satisfaction. 'Court adjourned.' He stood, gave Frog one final glare and marched into his chambers.

Frog turned to his lawyer. 'He gonna be the judge at the trial?'

'Probably.' The lawyer was gathering up his things.

'Can't you get me another judge?'

The lawyer looked at his watch. 'Why?'

Frog mumbled something as Deputy George Putnam took hold of his arm. He was led away, still muttering to himself. The lawyer turned to the crowd who were now filing out of the court. 'What did he say?'

A man in a plaid mackinaw obliged. 'Frog said he should have shot the judge when he had the chance.' He looked the lawyer over from head to toe, taking in the city suit and shoes. 'You're not from around here, are you?'

'No,' the lawyer admitted.

The man in the mackinaw nodded. 'Figures. Nobody from around here would stand by Frog Bartlett.' He leaned forward and spoke confidentially. 'Afraid of gettin' bit.' Guffawing, he moved away.

The lawyer sighed and closed his briefcase. After another glance at the clock on the wall he hurried out.

The double doors swung shut behind him. Silence descended. Then a chair scraped back. In the rear corner of the court room Sarah Marsh stood up, struggled into her coat, stuffed a fistful of sodden tissues into her handbag and sidled down the row of chairs to the door.

There was a very determined look on her face.

Dominic Pritchard looked with some consternation at the woman seated on the other side of his desk. It was relatively early in the morning for the young lawyer and he'd hardly had a chance to digest his breakfast. His second cup of office coffee was still to come. 'But I understand Mr Bartlett *has* representation,' he said.

'Just some court-appointed idiot who doesn't come from around here and can't tell his ear from his elbow,' Sarah Marsh said with disgust. 'You could get him out of the way in no time.'

'Look, Miss Marsh, I'm very much a junior member of this firm,' Dominic began. 'You'd be better off talking to Mr Putnam or Mr Taubman—'

'You'd charge less,' she interrupted.

'Yes,' he agreed. 'And with good reason. I'm inexperienced. I've never handled a major crime defence. I've barely done any trial work at all.'

'You handled my boundary dispute with that Armstrong fellow just fine,' she said, leaning back with every evidence of satisfaction.

'That was absolutely straightforward,' he protested. 'The law was perfectly plain and everything was documented.'

'I think you can do it,' she insisted. 'You're young and have lots of energy. It will take energy to find out the truth. Matt Gabriel should never have arrested Frog, never in a million years.'

'Well, I don't know.' Dominic was doubtful. 'From what I understand, he didn't have much choice. Mr Bartlett and Mr Packard were enemies from way back. They'd had a loud argument the night before in the Golden Perch that nearly came to blows.'

'Doesn't mean a thing,' Sarah said abruptly. 'Always have been like that, the two of them, right from schooldays.'

'And the weapon was found in Frog's garage—'

'The *alleged* weapon.'

'With his fingerprints on it. And the blood matched Packard's.'

'Somebody put it there,' Sarah said stubbornly. 'I'm sure I heard something in the yard that night. I live right next door. I heard somebody opening Frog's garage door – it squeaks. And he never locks it.'

'I'm sure they'd be glad to have you as a defence witness, Miss Marsh,' Dominic ventured. 'But a squeak doesn't have a name on it. It doesn't tell us *who* opened the garage door, does it? It could have been Frog himself.'

'Sleeps like the dead, Frog does,' Sarah said flatly. 'Because of the drugs.'

'Drugs?' Dominic was startled.

'Frog's not a well man,' Sarah explained. 'He's got something wrong with his spine, something with a long name. It's why he walks bent forward and twisty the way he does. Why he's always so damn cranky. It's the pain. He's in bad pain all the time. Has been for some years, now.'

'I see,' Dominic said, leaning back. 'This thing that's wrong with his spine – would it prevent him from hitting someone over the head?'

She glared at him. 'No,' she admitted. 'It would probably hurt his back and shoulder, but he could do it. He works in his garden all the time, no matter that the doctor told him not to do it. Must hurt a lot, but he lives for that garden. His pride and joy.'

'I see. So he's not actually disabled.'

'Not so he'd ever admit, no.'

'A squeaking door isn't a defence, Miss Marsh.'

'But it's all circumstantial,' Sarah protested. 'The argument and the wrench and all the rest of it. It's not as if anybody *saw* it happen – except whoever actually did it, that is.'

Dominic nodded. 'I happen to know that Sheriff Gabriel was not all that happy about arresting Frog, but the evidence – even though it's circumstantial – *is* pretty strong.'

'But he never confessed,' Sarah said. 'He would have confessed if he'd done it.'

Dominic looked at her sympathetically. She was a tall woman in her late fifties, or early sixties perhaps, unmarried, not beautiful, overweight and burdened with a lack of style that would have been laughable if it hadn't been so pathetic. She wore a red coat that was too tight over a flowered dress that was too loose and hung below the hem of the coat in scallops. Sensible shoes graced her long flat feet. Her hair was a mousy brown streaked with dull grey and she wore it in a very unflattering style, scraped back into an old-fashioned bun. Her face was plain, but her features were even, her eyes were a warm shade of honey brown and she had a beautiful smile when she permitted herself to show it.

'You seem to know Frog Bartlett rather well,' Dominic stated.

'I ought to. I've lived next door to him all my life and his. We grew up together, more or less. Well – side by side, anyway. Our parents were friends when they were alive,' she said.

'You're his friend, then?' he asked.

She shook her head. 'He hates the sight of me,' she replied. 'Always has. Teased me a good deal when we were young.' She almost smiled. 'But he's not a bad man, Mr Pritchard. He's a good man. People know that, they like him despite his short temper. He's just rather – prickly.'

It was his turn to smile. From what he knew of Frog Bartlett, which admittedly wasn't much beyond gossip and what he had occasionally observed at the Golden Perch, prickly was a vast understatement. Yet he also knew Bartlett had many loyal friends. The dominant feeling in the town was that the Sheriff was wrong to arrest Frog – but there was nothing anybody could do about it at the moment because no alternative suspects had been turned up, no matter how hard the Sheriff had tried to find one. It seemed a foregone conclusion that Frog would be convicted. Sarah Marsh apparently thought otherwise.

'It's the pain,' she went on. 'And–' Now she did smile. 'And he takes a perverse pleasure in being "an ornery cuss", like his father before him. Oh, he's a good friend to have, he'll stick with you through thick and thin, but he can't handle sympathy. He teased me all right, but he got teased himself even more, because . . . well, you've seen him. He's odd-looking. And children can be cruel, you know.' She sighed. 'Some grown-ups too, come to that.'

'I really don't think I'm the person to help you,' Dominic said wistfully. It wasn't often a murder defence dropped into a young lawyer's lap. 'I could talk to Mr Putnam for you—'

'No, I want you,' she said stubbornly. 'Are you refusing to take the case?'

'I'm not refusing, exactly—' he began.

She sat back. 'Well, then.'

'It's simply that I think you'd be wasting your money. The prosecution—'

'Scared?' she asked suddenly.

'Well . . . yes,' he admitted. 'It's a big responsibility and every man is entitled to the best defence he can get.'

'He's not getting it now,' she said pointedly. 'The yahoo they sent him doesn't give a damn and watches the clock all the time. You would *care*.'

'Well, of course I would care, but—'

'You talk to Mr Putnam, then. You ask him if he thinks you can do it.' She stood up. 'It's not the money. I have enough money for Mr Putnam to defend him, I just think you would do a better job. I have an instinct about things like that.'

'Many people think they have an instinct about—'

'Well, I do. I taught for many years and I know young people. It's my money, after all. I can spend it the way I like. I received an inheritance from an aunt that will be plenty and it's just sitting there, now. The only thing is – the *only* thing is – he mustn't know it's me.'

'I beg your pardon?'

'He mustn't know it's me paying for his defence,' Sarah Marsh said. 'Ever.'

'But why?'

'One, he wouldn't accept it. Two, if he was desperate enough to accept it, he'd hate me even more for being beholden to me. And three – I just don't want him to know. Anybody to know. Is that clear?'

'Not really,' Dominic said, standing also. 'But if that's the way you want it I have no objection.'

Her face lit up. 'Then you'll do it?'

'I'll talk to Mr Putnam about it,' Dominic answered cautiously. 'I'll see what he says.'

'Fair enough,' Sarah allowed. 'I'll call you tomorrow and see what you've decided.'

'No, I'll call you,' Dominic said. 'Either way, I'll call you.'

'Do *you* think you could handle a first-degree murder defence?' Carl Putnam asked his young associate, when they were sharing an in-office lunch-hour. He was a handsome man, with greying blond hair and the build of a lifelong tennis player.

'I don't know.' Dominic was always painfully honest with himself and others. 'As far as I know at the moment, the evidence *is* circumstantial. Of course, Matt may have something he's keeping quiet, something the prosecution felt able to build a case on. I wouldn't know unless I took it on – then they'd have to tell me. She seems absolutely certain that Bartlett is innocent.'

'Sarah Marsh is not a frisky woman,' Carl observed, starting to peel an apple with his penknife. 'Nor is she a profligate one. If she's willing to put up money for Frog's defence, she must have good sound reasons.'

'In which case you'd think she'd want the best,' Dominic said. 'She'd want you.'

Carl smiled. 'But she wants you.'

'So she says. I can't understand it.'

'Oh, I can,' Carl mused. 'I bring a lot of baggage with

40

me into the court room. Country club, yacht club, all that crap. I think it's not really a matter of wanting you as much as Frog not being likely to accept me. Sorry if that dents your ego.'

'Not really,' Dominic admitted. 'Is he any more likely to accept me?'

Carl shrugged, dropping the long strip of apple peel on the newspaper he'd spread out as a table-cloth. '"D" for Dominic.' He pointed with his knife to the peel. 'Seems like a sign.'

'Could be "D" for "dope",' Dominic observed wryly. 'Or Dumbo.' He was sensitive about his ears, which were not large, but to him seemed enormous, especially when he'd just had a fresh haircut.

'You hang out at the Golden Perch, don't you?' Carl asked.

Dominic grinned. 'Only when Emily lets me off the leash,' he said. Emily Gibbons, a young reporter on the local newspaper, was his Significant Other, as she liked to put it. 'Maybe once a week. And some lunch-times. They do a good steak sandwich.'

'I remember.' Carl nodded. 'That's the trouble with "moving up" in society – the food just gets worse and worse. Nouvelle cuisine everywhere, which means I never get enough of anything I like and too much of things I hate, like broccoli. Maybe I'll drop in at the Perch for a steak sandwich tomorrow.' He closed his eyes suddenly. 'No, I can't – I'm meeting Jack Armstrong at the yacht club about the summer race schedule. Maybe the day after.' From his wistful tone it didn't seem all that likely. As he himself said, Carl Putnam was 'up' in society. He had money, a big house, a beautiful young second wife and a thriving small-town law practice. He was not ambitious, however, having resigned as District Attorney as it took up too much of his playtime. He was good-looking, athletic and popular. Dominic would have hated him if he hadn't also been a fair and decent man. He also happened to be the father of Deputy George Putnam – a source of occasional friction between Dominic and George, who tended to be a little jealous of his father's protégé.

'Well, Dom,' Carl said. 'As far as I'm concerned, you can take the case. Things aren't too busy here at the moment, so you've got the time. And the experience will be good for you. If you have any problems, feel free to come to me.'

'Okay.' Dom started to fold up the detritus of their meal. He felt sudden excitement, as well as a faltering kind of elevator drop in the pit of his stomach. 'The thing is – will Frog Bartlett *want* me to defend him?'

'There's only one way to find out.' Carl grinned sympathetically. 'And don't be put off by his manner – he's like that with everyone.'

'I feel well warned,' Dominic said. 'But how bad can he be?'

'Fuck off!' Frog Bartlett croaked. His voice was deep and came from far down in his throat. 'I don't want to talk to anyone.' He regarded with great suspicion the young attorney who had been brought to his cell. 'Especially some damn kid.'

That Dominic was young was true, and that he was boyishly handsome was true, although a broken nose (the souvenir of a college football match) gave character to his face. His thick hair often tumbled over his forehead when he was absorbed by something and his heavy-lidded eyes gave the impression of sleepiness. This was deceptive. Very deceptive.

Dominic held his ground. 'My name is Dominic Pritchard and I'm an attorney with Crabtree and Putnam. I'm offering to represent you in court, Mr Bartlett. At no cost to yourself.'

Frog looked at him and scowled. The effect was terrifying. 'Nothing is for free,' he said.

'Then this is an exception that proves the rule, because someone has offered to pay your costs.'

'Who?'

'I have been asked to keep your sponsor anonymous.

The person in question is simply interested in your having the best possible representation. The person feels that the attorney assigned to you by the Public Defender, while no doubt very able, is not in a position to give your case the time and attention it deserves. I am. This particular person is convinced of your innocence.'

'Hah! Must be the only one around here who is.'

'On the contrary, I understand many people in town are on your side.'

'I never asked them,' Frog growled.

'No, you didn't. But I guess people like you despite your bad temper.'

'Nothing to like,' Frog muttered. 'Nothing to dislike.'

'That gives you every chance of getting a fair trial, then,' Dominic said. He was leaning back against the bars of Frog Bartlett's cell. It was not a comfortable position, either physically or emotionally.

'This person who's paying – do I know him?'

'I'm not at liberty to say,' Dominic responded carefully. He realized he'd have to watch his Ps and pronouns in this and any subsequent conversations with Frog, who would naturally be curious about such a generous mystery person.

'Somebody local?' Frog persisted.

'That would be telling.'

'What do I have to do in return?' Frog asked suspiciously. 'They want me to sign over my house or something? I've said it before and I'll keep sayin' it, I won't god-damn sell!'

'There are no strings attached,' Dominic said. 'The party concerned was very clear about that. No obligation of any kind.'

'I bet it's the guys down at the Perch,' Frog muttered, half to himself. 'I bet they got together. They didn't like Moony any more'n I did.'

'I didn't know Packard, but I must have seen him at the Perch,' Dominic said. 'What did he look like?'

'He wasn't no oil painting,' Frog answered. 'Almost as

43

ugly as me. About my height, skinny, kind of curly reddish hair going thin on top, long pointy nose, mouth like a mailbox, which is suitable, because he was a mailman. You must have seen him around. He was always around someplace, pretending to be important,' Frog went on. 'Always acted like he was the backbone of the Postal Service – that's how he spoke of it. "The Postal Service", with trumpets if he could've had some. It was either that or his damn tropical fish.'

'Oh – *him*.' Dominic nodded in sudden recognition. 'He spent about an hour, once, telling me about guppies.'

'That's him all right. Only man I ever knew who could make breeding tropical fish sound dirty.'

'You say he wasn't popular.'

'He was popular all right, but nobody *liked* him. See, he wasn't tight with his money, bought beers all round, so everybody put up with him. Boughten friendship, that's what he had. But he was so full of himself he never noticed. Thought he was "a beloved town character". Damn fool. Not a bit of character to him is what I always say. Said.'

'Did you kill Packard?' Dominic asked bluntly. He knew it was a question that defence lawyers often avoided asking, alleging that it was irrelevant to the proper presentation of a case, but he wanted to know. He was new to this and he needed convincing.

'I god-damn did not!' Frog shouted. Then, in a quieter voice, he added, 'I'd say that anyway, wouldn't I?'

'Not necessarily.' Dominic levered himself away from the bars and rubbed his shoulder. 'Do you mind if I sit down?'

'Help yourself.' Frog shrugged, moving down to the far end of the bunk. He took up a considerable proportion of it and Dominic settled himself gingerly on the edge.

'Mr Bartlett, I won't be able to find out what the prosecution actually has in evidence against you until I am officially appointed as your attorney.'

'How long you been out of law school?' Frog demanded.

'Three years,' Dominic said. 'I work for Carl Putnam.'

'That fancy-ass.' Frog snorted. 'Wouldn't catch *him* down here among the dead-beats.'

'He said you'd feel that way, but he's a good trial lawyer. He'd be willing to represent you himself if you'd prefer.'

'I don't prefer.'

'He's an excellent attorney—'

'Aren't you?'

'I don't know yet. Mr Putnam says he has every confidence in me and that he feels I would do a good job for you. I suppose that might tell you something. Frankly, I haven't had very much trial experience.'

'How much?'

'Well, a few accident cases, one or two misdemeanours, some property work—'

'But no murders?'

'Ah . . . no.'

'The office boy, in other words?'

'Not quite. I was top of my class in law school.'

'School,' Frog said in a disparaging tone. 'Not the same thing.'

'We did trial work – quite a lot of it. In practice.'

'Wow, I'm impressed.'

'It's still a matter of law, Mr Bartlett. I know the law.'

'Backwards?'

'I beg your pardon?'

'People usually say they know stuff backwards,' Frog said, with a glint of amusement in the black eyes.

'Oh.' Dominic, playing along, seriously considered this. 'I can't see that it would be much use,' he said finally.

'Me, neither,' Frog agreed. He looked away and stared at the window high in the wall above them. 'I hate being in here,' he muttered.

'I'm sure you do. I was amazed to hear how high the bail was set,' Dominic said.

Frog shrugged and winced. 'Pickett has it in for me,' he mumbled. 'If he's the judge at the trial, we're finished before we start. I shot his dog.'

'You what?' Dominic was horrified.

'Only with rock salt,' Frog added. 'Damn mutt kept digging up my backyard. Gave it to him one day, right in the ass. Never come back again, that was for damn sure. Only protecting my property. But Pickett, he didn't see it that way. Tried to get me arrested for cruelty to animals. Matt wouldn't play, that time. This time it's different. This time Matt's playing along all right.'

'What do you mean by that?'

'You'll see,' Frog said darkly.

'Then do you want me to represent you?' Dominic asked.

'For free – take.' Frog shrugged. 'That's what my grandad always said and so I'm saying it to you. Somebody wants to waste their money on me, fine. Not that I think you'll do any better than that bozo the Public Defender sent up. Nobody will. They've got me nailed and nailed good, you'll see. But I've got nothing against you. You might as well practise on me as anyone else.'

'Fine.' Dominic was not sure whether to be pleased at the challenge of a first degree murder case or daunted by his new client's lack of enthusiasm. 'I'll go and make the necessary arrangements.'

'You do that,' Frog muttered. 'Go play your little games. Won't make a damn bit of difference, you'll see.'

'It's my understanding that the evidence against my client is purely circumstantial,' Dominic said formally.

Sheriff Matt Gabriel looked at him with amusement. They were good friends, having once lived in the same boarding-house. 'Your understanding?'

Dominic grinned and relaxed. 'All right. I'm trying to be dignified. What have you got against him, Matt?'

'Not a lot, but enough,' Matt admitted. 'I have to tell you that I wasn't all that happy arresting Frog, but there are other interests in this.'

'Political?'

Matt sighed. 'I'm afraid so. Plus Packard was killed in uniform, apparently on his mail round, which got the FBI nosing around until they figured it wasn't really their concern. He liked to start work early, apparently, and always showed up at about five o'clock in the morning to sort and arrange his delivery. His mail-bag was still shut, but if the killer took something and refastened it, we'd have no way of knowing. It wasn't sealed or anything, but because it wasn't obviously tampered with the Fibbies backed off. Frog has to be grateful for that. I guess I do too.'

'I see. And what evidence do you have against Frog for this?'

Matt counted off on his fingers. 'We have the argument that he had with Packard the night before. We have the weapon which was found in his garage with blood on it that matched Packard's blood type.'

'And what type is that?'

'A-positive.'

'One of the most common types,' Dominic said disparagingly. 'My client may have the same type.'

'Oh, he does, he does.' Matt nodded.

'Well, then—'

'But the DNA matched Packard's,' Matt concluded.

'Ah.' Dominic was silent for a moment. 'Is that all?'

'We have motive, we have means and we have opportunity,' Matt said.

'What opportunity?'

'Your client has no corroborated alibi – claims to have slept late that morning. Alone, of course.'

'So?'

'We have a witness who says otherwise,' Matt told him. 'We have a witness who puts Frog Bartlett in his van on the road at just after six thirty that morning. Driving at speed.'

'How good a witness?'

'Another mailman,' Matt said. 'Homer Brophy, on his way to work. Knows Frog, knows his van. And he apparently has no axe to grind. I'm sorry, Dom – it may be circumstantial, but it's pretty strong. In the end, I had to charge him.'

'Because you had no one else?'

47

'There's that, too. No one else with a motive, much less a weapon. It was Frog's wrench, Dom. His name was scratched on the handle. You could read it quite clearly, through the blood.'

'You mean the killer didn't wash the blood off the weapon?'

'Obviously not.'

'That seems a little odd, doesn't it?'

'Yes, it does. I've been worried by that too. But the facts remain. Maybe he was in a state of shock and meant to wash it off later on, perhaps he was so horrified by what he'd done he couldn't bring himself to look at it or touch it again.'

'Then why bring it back home with him? Why not just throw it into the lake someplace?'

Matt shrugged. 'Who knows?'

'He says he didn't do it.'

Matt just looked at him.

'I'm going to defend him, Matt. I'm going to look into this.'

'Good,' Matt said. 'Anything I can do to help, you just let me know. I feel really bad about having to charge him, but my hands were tied. I couldn't pretend the evidence wasn't there. And I couldn't stall them any longer.'

'Who's "they"?'

'Let's just say people I can't argue with. I'm only a county sheriff, Dom. In one way I have a lot of power. But, in the end, I have to do what I'm told. And I was told to arrest Frog Bartlett.'

'Told by whom?'

'The District Attorney, who else? He feels the case is solid.'

'He's wrong,' Dominic said firmly. He wished he believed it.

'Maybe. But that's not my only problem.'

Dominic looked at him. They were friends and he knew immediately what Matt was referring to. 'The election,' he said, not without sympathy.

48

Matt nodded. 'People were beginning to wonder why I wasn't arresting somebody.'

'You mean Armstrong was,' Dom said. 'I heard him talking around town.'

'Yeah. The DA and I are in the same party, Armstrong is in opposition. Of course he made as much of it as he could.'

'Is that why the DA forced you to arrest?'

'I think so,' Matt admitted. 'I don't *like* to think so because nothing was actually said, but . . . it was clear.' He banged his fist on the desk. 'I hate this election crap. Hate it!'

'Let's have some lunch,' Dominic suggested. 'It sounds to me like your blood sugar is low.'

Matt gave him an odd look, then shrugged. 'Are you staking me to a steak?' he asked as he stood up.

'No,' Dominic said firmly. 'You're in such a rotten mood you might arrest me for attempting to bribe an officer of the law.'

FIVE

THE GOLDEN PERCH WAS FULL of noise and the smell of steak and onions. A lot of men seemed to have had their fill of pre-winter tasks and were looking to relax, full of virtue at having hammered in a few nails and given deep thought to clearing out the gutters, possibly tomorrow. Or soon.

There had been a general turning of backs when the three men walked in. The Sheriff's arrest of Frog Bartlett was definitely not popular here. Matt ignored it and went to his usual table.

'What do you know about Jack Armstrong?' George asked Dominic, when they had made major inroads on their steaks and fries.

'George,' Matt warned. 'Leave it alone.'

'No, I want to know,' George said stubbornly. 'We have to know what you're up against.'

Dominic shrugged. 'I don't know much. Your dad handles all his legal stuff. I've seen him in the office, but I've never talked to him or anything. He's kind of impressive, I suppose. Powerful presence – you know when he's in the room. He's smart, I know that.'

'Rats,' George muttered.

'I'm smart too, George,' Matt said mildly. 'Remember?'

'Yes, sure . . . but that isn't what you meant, is it, Dom?'

Dominic shook his head. 'He's smart like a shark is smart. Knows what he wants, goes after it, won't be stopped. He got that mall built over some tough opposition.'

'Anything dirty?' George asked. 'Anything we could use?'

Dominic chuckled. 'Ask your dad. Nobody else in the office sees anything of Armstrong's business. I'm not saying your dad would condone anything illegal—'

'Of course not,' George said stoutly.

'But then Armstrong might not tell him everything,' Dominic finished. 'He's got a reputation for playing his cards very close to the chest—'

'Ah,' George said.

'I don't *know* anything,' Dominic reiterated.

'Of course not.' George's expression was solemn.

'But I could ask around,' Dominic offered. 'Look around. I know there have been plenty of rumours about his methods. Strong-arm stuff, intimidation, harassment and things like that. Everybody knows it goes on . . .'

'But there's never any proof and nobody will complain,' George said. 'We know.'

'You have enough to do.' Matt reached for his third glass of water. 'We don't need—'

'We damn well do,' George contradicted. 'You're going to pussyfoot your way right out of a job, Matt. This is politics. We need ammunition.'

'I'd sure hate to have to work with Armstrong as sheriff,' Dominic stated. 'He's too single-minded – all ego and no flexibility. You're a good sheriff because you see all sides of a situation, Matt.'

'And get hung up between them,' Matt said morosely, pushing his plate away. 'I'm *too* fair – I let things ride because I think a lot of problems will work themselves out naturally.'

'And they do,' George agreed.

'Sometimes. But maybe single-minded would be better from a law enforcement point of view. Maybe if I were more single-minded I would have found out who killed Moony Packard by now.'

'He's depressed,' George said to Dominic. 'He doesn't know what he's saying.'

'I'm right here, George,' Matt said. 'I'm not a deaf invalid, you know.'

'I'll ask around,' Dominic offered, looking at his watch and starting to get up. 'I'll see what I can find out.'

'Good,' George said. 'We have to smash this guy.'

Dominic grinned down at him. 'Nobody could say you weren't single-minded, George.'

'Damn right,' George agreed. His attention was then distracted as Susie Brock came in. She was with one of the new deputies George didn't know very well yet. This deputy, one Bob Flatly, was not married. George scowled. His lunch began to churn in his stomach. Thoughts of the election fled.

'I want more posters up,' Jack Armstrong told his campaign manager. 'Get all the good places covered before Gabriel gets off his butt – if he's ever going to get off his butt. Complacent bastard.'

'He's very well liked in the town,' Irwin 'Win' Otis observed, making a note on his spiral reporter's pad. 'I still don't know why you're running against him and not the Mayor.'

'That's because you're a stranger here,' snapped Armstrong. 'Have you ever *seen* Merrill Attwater?'

'Oh, come on. He's big and muscular, I admit, but that's hardly . . .'

'Merrill *looms*,' Jack said impatiently. 'He has them all eating out of his hand because they're afraid he'll eat them if they don't. He's not a bad man – he just doesn't know his own strength. Anyway, he hasn't got enough of what I want.'

'Which is?' Win asked.

'Power,' Armstrong said with a certain degree of relish. He was a big, handsome man who had retained the musculature of his college football days. 'Do you know, all the time I was putting up the mall, all the time I was putting up the estate, Matt Gabriel was around helping the building inspectors "enforce" the codes? Wherever I turned, there he was, pointing things out, telling me about "arrestable offences" and all that crap. He can do that. He can do a lot of things, but he doesn't take advantage of it. Man has no vision. He's a small-town sheriff with a small-town mind.'

'You were born here too,' Win pointed out. 'You are a local boy.'

'Yeah, sure.' Armstrong grinned. 'But a local boy made good. And that's the difference. I didn't come back until I'd made a couple of million and knew my way around people and corners. Gabriel just came back with his tail between his legs when his father died. Big difference. He's reached the limit of his ambitions – I'm just starting.'

Otis, with the image of the tortoise and the hare firmly in the back of his mind, just smiled. He liked an optimistic candidate, it was a real advantage in the race. But unlike Armstrong, he did not discount Matt Gabriel's position in the town. The present incumbent of the office of sheriff was liked and respected. If he was not flashy or on the take, that was the measure of the man. Otis had no doubt that if Armstrong became sheriff, things would be done very differently than they were at present. He was under no illusion that they would be better – probably the opposite. But that wasn't his worry. His job was to get Jack Armstrong elected, that was what he had been hired to do and that was what he would do. Lean and wary, veteran of many political campaigns, he knew his stuff and charged accordingly. But Armstrong could afford it.

He just wished he knew his candidate a little better than he did at the moment. He wished he could believe in him. It made things so much easier if your heart was in it. 'More posters,' he said. 'Anything else?'

'Yes. When am I going to go head to head with Gabriel?'

Otis checked his schedule. 'Thursday night. At the local high school. A debate on law and order.'

'Perfect.' Armstrong looked pleased and turned to go out of the room.

'I have one of the researchers on it right now,' Otis said. 'There will be plenty of ammunition for you when you need it.'

'I'm not worried,' Armstrong called from his executive

wash-room, gazing at himself in the mirror over the basin. 'It's just one of the steps along the way.'

'Oh? And where is it you're going?' Otis asked.

There was a chuckle from the wash-room and the sound of running water. 'Oh, I want to build up my grass-roots appeal first. A few years as sheriff will give me a nice "law and order" base on which to build.'

'Build what?'

'A career, my friend, a career in politics. Power at the top end where big things are done. I have the vision for it. So many people don't. But I have humility too. I know you have to have a solid and deep foundation to put up a tall building. I am in that business, after all, right?'

'So you only want to be sheriff for one term?' Otis was surprised – he hadn't heard this before.

'One, maybe two. That will be enough. Of course, I will need to do things right, get some publicity, get known beyond Blackwater Bay. The big-city papers love this place, you see. Gabriel spends all his time trying to play it down. I won't make that mistake, believe me. When things happen in Blackwater Bay, the big papers take notice. If they're kept informed, that is. And I intend making certain that they are.'

'I see.' This put a slightly different complexion on things. Otis wished fervently that Armstrong had mentioned it before. 'Is this plan something new? When you hired me there was no talk of anything beyond the sheriff's job.'

Armstrong appeared in the wash-room doorway. 'I've been talking to some people from the capitol,' he said. 'They made me realize that I was setting my sights too low. They know quality when they see it.' He came across to Otis and put a hand on his shoulder. 'I sound like the worst kind of egotist, don't I? Don't mean to be.' He squeezed Otis's shoulder and moved back behind his desk. 'But I know my worth. People take to me. They like the image. It gives them confidence, excitement, enthusiasm. Gabriel is just *there*, like a tree or a rock. No sexiness, no charge, no pizzazz.'

'I would have thought that being as solid as a rock was a good recommendation for the job of sheriff,' Otis observed wryly.

'As solid and as thick. Take this murder of the mail man,' Armstrong said. 'It's obvious to me that he has the right man in jail. I've heard a lot of people say the same thing. But does he talk to the press about the hunt for the killer, the capture? Does he take any credit for himself, any glory? No – he shuts the door on it and he shuts his mouth. Pathetic. He could have used it as a real asset in his so-called campaign, but no . . . he just sits there.'

'I haven't been paying much attention to the murder,' Otis admitted. 'Was it difficult to find the killer?'

'Not really, apparently it was easy, they found the weapon in his garage with his fingerprints on it. But Gabriel could have made it *look* tough. All the better when he finally got around to arresting this man Bartlett. Even if it was routine – does he get any mileage out of how careful he was, how painstaking? No, not even that. I'm telling you, this man knows *nothing* about politics whatsoever. He's just a hick guy in a hick job in a hick town.'

'But he's not stupid. I understand he used to be a philosophy professor,' Otis commented.

Armstrong clapped his hands and held them out. 'There you go – see what I mean? Head in the clouds, no idea of what the real world is like. Took the job for an easy life and that's what he's got. Well, that's not what I want. I want more and I mean to have it. But the first step is winning this election, so get out there, man, and make sure I do. That's what I'm paying you for, right? That's why I gave you the job!'

'Oh, right, right,' agreed Win Otis, standing up. 'More posters. I'll get right on it.'

'This isn't going to work,' Matt said.

'Shut up and keep still,' growled Harry Foskett as he adjusted his focus. 'Look noble.'

'I feel like a damn fool,' Matt growled back.

'And you look like one,' Harry told him. 'Lift up your chin and look over at that cactus in the corner.'

Matt did and started to laugh. 'Did you send away for that from Playboy Enterprises?' he asked. The cactus was a very defensive phallic symbol. 'Or is it a warning to women not to come too close?'

'Very funny,' Harry said.

Harry's studio was in the basement of his house on Clifford Street. Once you got used to having to walk past his wife's washing machine and his kids' bicycles, it was quite a professional set-up. Draperies backed a raised podium where he did portraiture and various props were ranged around the walls for his more artistic efforts, particularly fashion shots for local boutiques and hairdressers. One wall featured some of the impressionistic studies he had been doing for the past couple of years, many of which had been sold through the art gallery run by Matt's fiancée, Daria Grey. While this aspect of his profession gave Harry encouragement and nourished his creativity, he had never lost sight of the fact that baby pictures, wedding and graduation photos formed the backbone of his income. Harry was a practical man. He lifted his head from the viewfinder and glared at Matt. 'You still look like an idiot.'

'I can't help it.' Matt shifted uncomfortably on the tall stool. 'I always photograph badly. You're on a loser here, Harry.'

'I refuse to accept that,' Harry said stubbornly. 'Try thinking about the dignity of your profession, upholding right and order, protecting the innocent.'

'Nobody's perfectly innocent, Harry,' Matt said wearily. 'And nobody's perfectly guilty, either. There are always circumstances. It makes my life very difficult.'

'You think too much.'

'You just *told* me to think.'

'Okay, my mistake. Stop thinking.' There was a pause. 'Now you look like you've had a pre-frontal lobotomy.'

'I told you.'

Harry sighed and straightened up, flicking off the lights that were focused on his subject. 'Let's take a break.'

Matt stood up and stretched. 'Sorry, Harry.'

'It's only because I want you to look good,' Harry explained. 'To look right for the job.'

'I really don't think all this is necessary,' Matt said, as Harry poured out coffee for them both. 'People know me, they know the kind of job I do, they can make up their minds on my record.'

'Balls. People expect a bit of hoopla. They would think you didn't care if you didn't put up some posters and kiss a few babies.'

'I'm not kissing any babies,' Matt said.

'Figuratively speaking,' Harry told him.

'I'm not kissing any asses either,' Matt went on.

'All right, all right, I get the idea, you are true-blue incorruptible and want to stand on your record. Fine. But you have to make an effort, Matt.'

'I have to spend some money, you mean. Which I would, if I had any to spare.'

'Well, that, too. But I told you I'm not charging you for these shots; they're my contribution to your campaign.'

'I appreciate that, Harry. I really do. It's just that I hate taking the time to do all this kind of thing when I should just be getting on with the job.'

'Well, unfortunately for you we live in a democracy,' Harry said wryly. 'People don't get jobs for life here, they have to stand up and get elected now and again, just to keep their hand in. It's only every four years, after all. You're too idealistic. Everything is politics and image these days. And that can be pretty powerful stuff, believe me. I know what a picture can do.'

Matt looked at him over the rim of his coffee cup. 'What do you know that I don't?' he asked suspiciously.

'Well, have you heard about Frank Packard?' Harry enquired.

'That he's going around spouting off about who killed

his brother? At the moment his favourite candidate seems to be me. I heard all about it. People are used to Frank raving about stuff – nobody ever believes him,' Matt said confidently.

Harry looked uncomfortable. 'Maybe Frank isn't your biggest worry. Jack Armstrong has impressed a lot of folks. They think he's the kind of guy who gets things done.'

'Yeah – at any cost,' Matt said.

Harry nodded. 'I know, he's a pushy bastard, but that could come across as efficiency.'

'Unless you happen to have been in his way.'

'Maybe.'

'My problem is I can't see *why* he wants to be sheriff,' Matt said.

'You've got a lot of power in this county, Matt. Just because you don't go exploiting it doesn't mean it couldn't be put to use, one way or another.'

'Meaning?'

'Oh, I don't know. If he decided to be on the take . . .'

Matt smiled wryly. 'There aren't that many opportunities to be on the take in Blackwater.' He knew of one, of course. Armstrong himself had offered him money to back off on enforcing the allegations of building code infringement. If he had charged him at the time with attempting to bribe an officer of the law, maybe . . . It hadn't been that overt. Armstrong had picked his time and place very carefully, had spoken very circumspectly – but the offer had been clear. That meant there would only be his word against Armstrong's. Matt's response then had been a warning. Bringing it up now would simply look like electioneering. Nobody would believe him.

'Okay, I could be wrong,' Harry conceded. 'He might want to do good for all concerned. Maybe he just likes the image of sheriff, gives him a bit of swagger.'

'My God,' Matt said. 'Do I swagger?'

'Hell, no. But you could if you wanted to, I suppose. Goes with the badge, doesn't it?'

'My dad never swaggered that I remember. He never

gave me swaggering lessons, either.' Matt smiled to himself, remembering his father.

'Mostly I think it's because of the Town Council,' Harry said.

'What about them?'

'You've got a vote there, haven't you?'

'Yes.'

'And for the past million years or so, they have always voted pretty well split down the middle on most things, just for the hell of it.'

Matt grinned. 'True. They switch from time to time – when it really counts.'

'Yeah – well, zoning is something they split even and pretty consistently on. You got Berringer, Soames, Brackett and Glaister for keeping things as they are, and you got Field, Tonnitti, Murphy and Merrill Attwater for gung-ho development. Sometimes they go one way, sometimes another, but mostly they split just that way, right?'

'Right.' Matt was beginning to see where Harry was going with this.

'Now all of those guys are pretty secure on the Council. I don't think Armstrong could shift any of them they've been there so long, but you . . .'

'But I am vulnerable.'

'You're *more* vulnerable because he can whip people up about law and order, but he can't whip people up about Soames, Brackett, Field, Tonnitti, Murphy . . .'

'I see.' Matt saw only too clearly.

'What's more, if he gets his projects through it means lots of jobs become available. If he were sheriff he could hold the deciding vote, dangling those jobs as carrots,' Harry ended.

It was true, Matt thought. He should have seen it from the beginning. He hadn't even thought about the Town Council because he couldn't always attend the meetings. His mistake. 'Well, fine, Harry. And thanks for the warning.'

Harry wasn't finished. 'He's also good-looking and . . .'

'Now, just a minute,' Matt said.

'And is willing to spend a lot of money on television ads and stuff like that,' Harry added quickly. 'He's after the female vote.'

'I haven't seen any TV ads,' Matt said, scowling.

'You will. He paid a friend of mine at the Hatchville TV station to shoot them for him on video and I hear they're pretty impressive. Lots of kids and dogs and Mom and apple pie. Preserving the peace in our corner of America, that sort of thing.'

'Oh, for crying out loud.' Matt was disgusted. 'Do you really think voters around here are going to fall for that?'

'They might. Not everybody in Blackwater went to college, you know, not by a long shot. And even smart people can be lazy thinkers. TV is a very powerful medium. Pictures speak to everyone, Matt. I ought to know.'

'Yes, well – I sure as hell can't afford TV ads,' Matt grumbled. Was he really going to lose his job to some rich pretty guy with delusions of grandeur? He remembered Jack from high school – vain, full of himself, a glad-hander. His fellow students *seemed* to like him. Yet Jack hadn't been elected class president. Matt had. That had been an upset, totally unexpected. A secret vote, of course, perhaps reflecting the student body's real feelings. Could he expect to win on a secret vote again?

'Don't people think I'm doing a good job?' he asked Harry rather plaintively.

Harry looked away. 'Some people think you put Frog inside too quick,' he said quietly. 'There's been talk around town . . . maybe Armstrong started it, maybe not . . . but they're saying it was politics put him in jail, not proof.'

'They're right,' Matt admitted. 'And I'm not proud of it. Oh, there's evidence enough. Too much, if you ask me. Don't think I haven't been worried about it. I have been. I still am.'

'Well, then—' Harry began.

Matt put down his coffee cup and reached for his hat.

'Hey, wait a minute – we've got to get this picture,' Harry protested.

'But I want to—'

'Siddown,' Harry snapped.

Reluctantly, Matt did as he was told.

Harry took a series of shots, then straightened up and looked at Matt over the top of the camera. 'That's great,' he said. 'That grim, determined expression is just what I've been after all along.'

SIX

IT WAS 'I LOVE JACK Armstrong Day' at the brand-new Blackwater Mall. At least as far as Armstrong himself was concerned.

He was spending the afternoon glad-handing his public as they shopped in the new mall he had built so efficiently. As Mrs Peach, who ran one of the most famous guest-houses in town, edged by, he saw her and caught her by the hand. 'Mrs Peach, how nice to see you. Out shopping for treats for your boarders, are you? Have you seen the sausages in the delicatessen – ah, you have. Oh, really, you make your own? Well, I'm delighted to hear that, family recipes should be preserved. You have a nice day now.'

Mrs Peach walked away, wishing she had told Jack Armstrong where to get off, but she was Southern-born and Southern ladies did not display bad temper in public. She didn't know which she disliked more – the man or the mall. She had always loved her walks along Main Street, going from shop to shop for this special thing and that. Walking through the mall wasn't the same at all. But . . . and this was a big but to a woman with a reputation for fine cooking to keep up . . . there was a delicatessen in the mall that carried the most amazing things, ingredients she'd often had to send away for in previous years. She needed those things to keep her guests happy. But she had to grit her teeth to go there to get them.

She wasn't sure whether it was the bright lights or the constant background music, but she went in, got what she wanted and got out as quickly as she could. She couldn't understand the people who spent whole afternoons in the place. Especially the teenagers, who seemed to have adopted it as Fun Central, probably because of the four coffee shops, one on each side of the open-plan structure that surrounded what was – she admitted it – a very pretty little garden.

On her way out she passed her friends Mrs Toby and Mrs Norton, who lived on Paradise Island. 'Watch out for low-flying politicians,' Mrs Peach warned in an ominous tone.

'Not that Tyrone Molt again, is it?' Margaret Toby asked, craning past Mrs Peach's shoulder to get a look. 'I can't stand that sleazy snake. He asks for your vote and then tries to sell you a car. Man's a menace.'

'No, it's Jack Armstrong,' Mrs Peach said huffily. 'Smiling all over the place.'

'Well, he's not as bad as Molt,' Mrs Norton said. 'He built this place, after all. Very useful.'

Mrs Peach regarded her friend with displeasure. 'You think so?'

'I admit it's a little garish,' Nell Norton conceded. 'But having the supermarket here as well as—'

'Mr Naseem's little market is fine for me,' Mrs Peach said stoutly.

'Then why are you here?' Mrs Toby asked, eyeing her plastic shopping bag which, admittedly, was bulging.

'I only come to the delicatessen,' Mrs Peach said virtuously.

'What – you don't even look into the fabric store?' Mrs Toby asked, amazed. Mrs Peach was a member of the Blackwater Bay Magpies, a very popular quilting circle. 'It has a fabulous range of calicos just in. And some metallics . . .'

'I might have glanced in, going by,' allowed Mrs Peach, flushing a little.

'And what about Luxurious Ladies?' Mrs Norton wanted to know, referring to a shop that featured clothing for ladies above a certain girth. 'They have some nice things in there.' Both ladies showed their enthusiasm for cooking and baking in their waistlines.

'I *did* find a very nice shirtwaist in there,' Mrs Peach admitted slowly.

'So you think the mall has some advantages?' Mrs Toby asked.

'Oh, I suppose so,' Mrs Peach admitted irritably. 'But it isn't the Taj Mahal, is it, although Jack Armstrong apparently thinks it is. Anyway, I'd never vote for anyone but Matt and neither would you, so all Jack Armstrong's smiling isn't going to get to us, is it?'

'Of course not,' said Mrs Toby firmly.

'No way, José,' said Mrs Norton just as firmly.

'It's his wife I feel sorry for,' Mrs Peach mused. 'She's up in that Mountview Clinic again, I hear.'

'Heart,' Mrs Toby said.

'Nerves,' Mrs Norton said.

'Drink,' Mrs Peach said. They had all spoken at once and looked at one another with raised eyebrows.

'Well, it's something that keeps her going back there,' Mrs Peach stated, after a minute. 'Don't suppose she gets much sympathy from *him.*' She jerked her head back towards the crowd that had gathered around Jack Armstrong.

'No time,' Mrs Toby said.

'Too busy,' Mrs Norton said.

'Too selfish,' Mrs Peach said.

The three ladies looked on as the crowd around Armstrong built up. Suddenly there seemed to be an argument. Someone was shouting.

'You killed him! You had him killed! You're all alike, all you bastards!' The cause of the ruckus was Frank Packard, as usual, this time being wrestled out of the crowd around Armstrong by two very muscular-looking young men. 'Don't think I don't know about you. Maybe you and the Sheriff are in it together . . . everybody has something to hide,' Packard continued to shout as he was dragged away. 'I'll tell the Governor on you!' came his parting shot as he and Armstrong's 'attendants' disappeared towards the parking lot.

The three ladies looked at one another and sighed heavily.

'Yesterday he was saying it was Granger Gibbons who had killed Moony,' Mrs Toby said. 'Tomorrow it will probably be Reverend Allwood.'

'Or maybe you or me.' Mrs Norton snorted. 'The man's a menace. He never takes his pills, you know. It would be a lot quieter around here if someone had killed him and left Moony alone.'

Mrs Peach was shocked. 'You don't mean that, Nell Norton.'

Nell shook her head. 'No, of course I don't. But the Packard boys have always been trouble in this town, we all know that. Frank because he's crazy and Moony because he was a sanctimonious blowhard. There have been times when I wanted to kill both of them myself and that's the truth. Perhaps I just have an evil nature.'

'Well,' conceded Mrs Peach. 'I doubt that, but I guess I know what you mean. Nobody is exactly *sorry* Moony is gone, which is a sad thing to have to say. I will admit he was a very good mailman. The one they replaced him with isn't nearly so efficient. Unfriendly, too. Never stops for a chat.'

Mrs Toby and Mrs Norton nodded solemnly. Something *had* been lost when Moony died and that was the latest news. He had been a particularly fecund source of gossip and anybody knows that gossip is important in a small town. How else would you know what was going on? And what to do about it? You could find yourself being perfectly friendly to somebody who should have known better and you wouldn't know it until too late, and then what would everyone say?

The three ladies parted with mutual assurances and wishes for a good day. As they walked on, Mrs Toby and Mrs Norton were silent for a moment.

Then Mrs Toby spoke: 'You don't suppose Frank Packard is right, do you?'

'About what?'

'I don't know. He seems to blame everyone. Almost as if he were covering up . . .' She stopped. 'What if Frank killed his brother? What if that's why he's going around accusing everyone else – to take attention from himself?'

'That's an interesting thought. We should tell Matt about that.'

'I expect he's already looked into it,' Mrs Toby said complacently. She had faith in Matt. 'Do you think Armstrong has a chance of winning?'

'I hope not,' Mrs Norton responded, as they passed Jack Armstrong's campaign display laid out at an intersection of the corridors of the mall. He seemed to have fully recovered his equilibrium after the altercation with Frank Packard. Certainly his two 'attendants' had returned without Frank and all seemed peaceful once again. Armstrong was talking to several quite pretty girls, all of whom had adoring looks on their faces. The two women exchanged a worried glance.

'The youth vote,' Mrs Toby said.

'The dumb vote,' Mrs Norton said. 'No respect for tradition.'

'There are a lot more of them since that first subdivision of Armstrong's sold out,' Mrs Toby added. 'Lots of new young families out there. Two votes for every house at least.'

'But it would never be enough to beat Matt . . .'

They looked at each other. 'Would it?'

There had been a bookshop on the corner of Main and Trumbull for over fifty years, but it had become Bookery Nook only thirty years before, when Helen Smith took it over from old Mr Beevor, who had decided he'd had enough of northern winters and moved to Florida. Now, three decades later, twice married and dogged by ill health which she faced with humorous defiance, Helen (now Pollock) had to admit that she couldn't face customers on a day-to-day basis, so came in only from time to time. Cancer was one thing – she'd dealt with cancer, she'd known where she was with cancer. Customers were another thing altogether, totally unpredictable.

'I'm sorry, Mr Hutchings, I don't know anything about your special order,' she told the irritated man standing before her. 'Let me check the book.'

Mr Hutchings was not to be placated. 'If I'd gone to that big new Borders bookshop in Hatchville I'd have had it by now,' he snapped.

'I doubt it,' Helen said calmly. 'They use the same suppliers we do, Mr Hutchings. I'll call you the minute the book comes in, I promise. We do have some other new books in the horticultural section, however, that you might like. Have you seen them? There's a particularly lovely one called *Tropico* that just came in on Monday.'

'Oh?' Mr Hutchings perked up. 'Who did that one?'

'Omri Peterson – she's supposed to be an excellent—'

But Mr Hutchings was off on his quest, tossing gruff thanks over his shoulder as he headed towards the horticulture section at the rear of the shop.

'Bet the manager of Borders didn't know about that one,' Lisa Cummings said to Helen, when Mr Hutchings had returned and paid for his copy of *Tropico*, going out a happier man.

'No.' Helen nodded. 'It's from a small press that hasn't been in existence for very long. But I took some copies because I know we have several horticultural vultures in town. It was worth the risk.'

Lisa sighed. 'That's the advantage of a small bookshop,' she said loyally. 'We know our customers.'

'We hope we do,' Helen told her. 'I wish I had the energy to come in more. I feel as if I'm losing touch with everything – orders, stock, sales – the whole shebang.'

'Nonsense,' Lisa contradicted. 'You still know more about the business than the rest of us put together.'

'I wish that were true,' Helen said with a sigh. 'For example, there are boxes of books in the back from a continental supplier I don't remember ever dealing with.'

'That's a special order,' Lisa said quickly.

'Oh. Well, there are about fifteen new periodicals I've never heard of on the news-stand. We've had four authors visit whose books I've never read, and both Doubleday and Warner's have changed their reps around *again*. I don't seem to be in touch with things any more. I must make more of an effort to keep up.'

'Why?' Lisa asked in a practical manner. 'You have Muriel to run the office, you have me and Dean and Jane and Scotty to sell. The bookshop is doing very well. Why don't you relax more, do a few of the things you've always wanted to do? You've earned the right to retire, especially with your health problems.'

'My dear, the only way to deal with my health problems is to ignore them.' Helen's eyes were bright. 'Keeping busy is the answer to pain, believe me. I intend to come in more, not less, in future.' Lisa looked rather alarmed at this and started to speak, but they were interrupted.

Dominic Pritchard had come over to the desk with a list in his hand. 'Good-morning, Mrs Pollock,' he said politely. 'I wonder if you could help me.'

'Only if you call me Helen,' she told him. 'I've spoken to you about that before, you know. Handsome young men calling me by my first name makes me feel young again. You should consider it a duty, a kindness to the elderly.'

He laughed. 'Okay, Helen – I have a challenge for you.' He handed her a list. 'Can you get these for me?'

'My goodness,' Helen said, reading down the list. 'Are you setting up on your own?'

'Hardly. But I need these particular books to help me in my new case. I'm defending Mr Bartlett.'

'Defending Frog Bartlett?' Helen was amazed. 'But I thought he was pleading guilty.'

Dominic frowned. 'Who told you that?'

'I don't know.' Helen looked confused. 'It seems to be the general consensus. Something about letting his lawyer go?'

'Oh. It's more a case of taking on a new lawyer – me. A

very new lawyer,' he added, half to himself. 'I think he's innocent and I'm defending him.'

'Frog Bartlett innocent?' Lisa said, coming over. 'I don't believe it.'

'No?' Dominic asked. 'Why?'

'He and Moony Packard hated one another,' Lisa answered. 'Everybody knows that.'

'Well, I hope "everybody" isn't on the jury,' Dominic said crossly. 'I may have to ask for a change of venue.'

'So Frog is denying it, is he?' Helen enquired.

'Absolutely,' Dominic told her. 'He says he was asleep in bed at the time.'

'Well, he would say that, wouldn't he?' Lisa's tone was disbelieving.

Dominic frowned. 'I don't understand why some people are so ready to believe the worst about him,' he said plaintively.

'Have you met your client?' Lisa asked.

'Yes, of course I have.'

'And you found him full of old-world charm, I suppose?'

Dominic had to smile. 'Not exactly. But a short temper isn't exactly—'

'Who else would have killed Moony if not him?' Lisa interrupted. 'Mr Packard was one of the nicest men around Blackwater.'

'A little egotistical, perhaps,' Helen said thoughtfully.

'He was a pillar of the community,' Lisa snapped. 'He went to *our* church.'

'Well, that excuses everything, does it?' Helen asked.

'What do you mean?' Lisa's tone was defensive.

'My dear girl, there have been axe murderers who were church-goers,' Helen said gently. 'And Mr Packard was not exactly shy about giving his opinions to people whether they wanted to hear them or not.'

'He spent a lot of time at the Golden Perch,' Dominic pointed out. 'He certainly wasn't teetotal.'

'No,' Lisa agreed. 'But he was a *good* man. That's why his

getting murdered was so awful. And Frog Bartlett did it. Everybody knows he's been threatening to kill Mr Packard and anyone else who crossed him for years.'

'Ah,' Dominic said. ' "Everybody" again.'

Helen looked at him. 'That's what bothers you, isn't it?'

'Exactly what bothers me,' Dominic agreed. 'I hate foregone conclusions. Especially where justice is concerned.'

'Good for you,' Helen applauded.

'It would save the county a lot of money if he would just plead guilty,' Lisa said briskly. 'But then, I suppose you wouldn't get *your* fee, would you? Or are you defending him for free?'

'Lisa,' Helen snapped. 'That's quite enough.'

'Well,' Lisa said sulkily. 'Everybody knows lawyers are just in it for the money.'

' "Everybody" certainly gets around,' Helen commented. 'And "everybody" seems to have some unpleasant opinions.'

'You meet him everywhere,' Dominic agreed.

Lisa glared at them both and walked away to attend to another customer.

'I'm sorry, Dominic,' Helen said.

'Oh, we're used to it.' Dominic sighed. 'It started with Shakespeare – "first we kill all the lawyers" – and it's gone steadily downhill ever since. On the one hand people ask you what you do and when you say "lawyer" they immediately do one of two things – ask for free advice or introduce you to their unmarried daughter. But on the other hand, if you ask them what they *think* of lawyers, their general estimation is somewhere between jackal and politician.'

'Not a very wide gap,' Helen said wryly.

'No.' Dominic grinned. 'But there again you get the dichotomy. "Call your Congressman" when you want something done, but "dirty politicians" in general.'

'Same with the police,' interjected Matt Gabriel, who had been standing behind him for a few minutes. 'They hate us until something in their life goes wrong.'

'Now booksellers don't get that,' Helen mused. 'I suppose we're lucky. Or totally without character. Good-morning, Matt, what can we do for you?'

'I wondered if my order was in,' Matt said. 'David Canter's book on offender profiling.'

'Yes, here it is.' Helen produced it from a shelf behind the counter. 'We had to order it from England.'

'Thanks very much.' Matt glanced at Dominic. 'How's it going with Bartlett?'

'I'm working on it,' Dominic said rather grimly.

'It will take you until the trial to read all these books you've ordered,' Helen put in. 'That's assuming we can get them in time.'

'Books?' Matt asked.

'Looking for loopholes.' Dominic smiled. 'Always looking for loopholes. Thanks, Helen – if you could get them quickly it would be a big help.'

'I'll do my best,' Helen promised and watched him walk out. 'He's a nice young man,' she said to Matt. 'I like him a lot.'

'So do I,' Matt agreed. 'I just hope he doesn't break his heart trying to defend Frog Bartlett.'

'Is the case against him so solid?' Helen asked.

'It's not bad,' Matt replied. 'But Dom's problem will be getting a clean jury. He has a lot of friends, but there are also a lot of people like your girl there who *want* Frog to be guilty.'

'Why?'

'Because he's ugly and short-tempered, and has no family,' Matt said sadly. 'And because if he didn't do it, they'd have to consider the possibility that somebody they knew did. Maybe a friend, or an acquaintance – maybe somebody in their own family, or church. Maybe the man next door. And that scares them. They want their murderers to fit the part. And Frog Bartlett fits all too well.'

SEVEN

DOMINIC PRITCHARD WAS GIVING A strong performance of outrage at the offices of the *Blackwater Bay Chronicle*. His audience was his own fiancée, Emily Gibbons, daughter of the paper's owner and its star (only) reporter. She was, as usual, viewing his overtures with suspicion.

'The least you could do is run a small feature article on it,' Dominic said. 'You have the fact that he's changed his lawyer and I could make a statement. I want to get it into circulation that there is reasonable doubt about Frog's guilt. Just reasonable doubt, that's all I'm after at the moment. All I'm asking for is fair play. Put the whole story in as my opinion – do an interview if you like. Otherwise—'

'Otherwise what?' Emily asked.

'Otherwise I am prepared to go to the papers down in Grantham with the whole story of a local paper turning people against an innocent man,' Dominic said flatly. 'I know a couple of reporters on the *Free Press*, as a matter of fact. You know how they love stories about crazy Black-water Bay.'

'You'd go to *them*?' Emily asked, aghast. 'Against *us*?'

'Only if I have to,' Dominic replied. 'I need all the ammunition I can get. I'd prefer to get it here.'

'All right, all right.' Emily surrendered, reaching for her notebook. 'I'll put something in the next edition. But this is blackmail.'

'No, it isn't. It's balanced reporting and I'm glad to see you doing it. For me.'

'Oh, no, you don't,' Emily said, still undecided whether to be cross with him or not, threatening her like that. After all, they were engaged. He shouldn't be so hard on her. 'I'm doing it for Frog and justice. But it's not going to do Matt Gabriel any good in the elections. It will look like he's made a mistake.'

'Matt Gabriel can look after himself,' Dominic said. 'And speaking of the elections . . .'

'Hah! Don't get me started on the elections.'

'Actually, that's just what I *would* like you to get started on,' Dominic said.

'What do you mean?'

'Jack Armstrong.'

'What about him?'

'Would you like him to be sheriff?'

Emily sighed. 'Absolutely not. Matt is a good sheriff – or at least he always has been, up to now.'

'Is the *Chronicle* backing him?'

'We aren't backing anyone, we're impartial.'

'Oh, come on . . .'

'No, seriously . . . Dad says we're going to remain neutral on all the issues and all the candidates.'

'Admirable,' Dominic said. 'And implausible.'

'Well, we'll *try*,' Emily amended.

'George Putnam asked me to see if I could find out anything about Jack Armstrong,' Dominic said. 'I've been asking around, but I haven't come up with anything usable yet.'

'Usable?'

'You know what I mean. I want to see Matt re-elected as much as you do. But I also want to see Frog get a fair trial.'

'Matt will be re-elected all right,' Emily stated.

'Well, I'm not so sure.' Dominic looked worried. 'Armstrong is a strong man and he's been working hard at this thing.'

Actually, Emily had been glad of Armstrong's decision simply because it allowed them to fill columns of print with

73

election news and conjecture. This hadn't been so easy when the results were a foregone conclusion. 'His agent keeps coming in here with press releases.'

'I know,' Dominic said slowly. 'When Matt didn't make an immediate arrest it was an opportunity for Armstrong to imply Matt was incompetent. Then Matt arrested Frog, which took the wind out of Armstrong's sails for a minute. Now he's saying Matt acted too quickly. Guy plays both sides of the street at once – a born politician, I'll give him that. Matt just can't win for losing. Or at least, that's what Armstrong is saying.'

'Maybe we ought to look at it all again,' Matt said slowly. 'Maybe we were too hasty.'

'You were as careful as you could be,' Tilly protested and counted off on her fingers. 'You had every possible alternative suspect interviewed. You went over the crime scene twice with a fine-tooth comb. But you can't argue with the forensic evidence. Frog's monkey wrench, with his fingerprints on it, along with blood matching Moony Packard's blood group and DNA index.'

'Yes – it's all there. That's what bothers me,' Matt said.

'You mean, why didn't he wash it, get rid of it?' George Putnam asked.

'Yes.'

'Because he thought nobody would look?' George suggested. 'Because he thought he had plenty of time to do it?'

'Post traumatic stress syndrome,' Susie Brock ventured. 'Or irresistible impulse – he didn't know what he was doing, and so repressed the murder and forgot about the wrench being there at all.'

'Hm,' said Matt, unconvinced. 'Or he didn't *know* it was there. The rest of the garage was as neat as a pin, every tool cleaned and oiled, and hung up in its proper spot. Only the wrench was out of place, sitting in plain view.'

'Frog said he hadn't been in the garage for days, due to the fact that he was doing some interior decorating and had everything he needed on hand indoors,' George recalled. 'We saw the ladders and paint cans in there.'

'I think we ought to look at it all again,' Matt repeated. 'The DA stampeded me, dammit.'

'He's a pistol, all right,' Tilly agreed. 'Says he's a new broom. Claims Carl Putnam let everything get slack.'

'Political talk.' George was irritated by this slur on his father. 'He was only appointed as interim DA and now he wants to get elected so he's secure. Something you ought to consider, Matt. A lot of people believe Frog did it. You open things up again, they're apt to think you're unreliable or something and vote for Armstrong.'

'I'd rather they thought I was taking a responsible attitude,' Matt said. 'Innocent until *proven* guilty, remember?'

'You're beating a dead horse,' George told him.

'No, I'm not. I was never happy about arresting Frog and when Judge Pickett set that ridiculous bail keeping him in jail, I felt even worse,' Matt said.

'It's a pretty comfortable jail,' Susie pointed out. 'The fact that he's had to stay here because County was full has made it much easier on him. He's got a decent bed, his own TV, good meals plus all the doughnuts and coffee he wants – and you even let him have a rocking-chair.'

'He needed it to ease his bad back,' Tilly snapped. 'Anyway, it only sounds good to you because you're out here,' she went on. 'He's stuck back there with no company except for the occasional drunk we bring in—'

'I'd go back and play cards with him but he's such a damn grouch,' George said. 'The only reason Pinckney plays gin with him at night is because he's half deaf and can't hear Frog cussing him out.'

'He's worried about his garden.' Tilly glanced at the clock. 'It's time for his pills.' She opened a drawer in her desk and took out a box with several bottles in it. She consulted a small card and shook out the appropriate dosage, recapped the bottles, returned the box to the drawer and stood up. 'Feel like a nurse, doing this.' She went over to a table that stood by the wall and poured out some coffee, added milk and sugar, and put a couple of doughnuts on a plate, carried them through the door in the rear wall that admitted her to the jail portion of the office building.

'See what I mean?' George protested. 'Waited on hand and foot. She goes to the library for him too.'

'He's our responsibility,' Matt said.

'He could have gone to the County jail. They could have found room somehow,' George pointed out.

Matt just looked at him. Their cells were new and clean. As for the County jail . . .

'Well,' George said. 'He did kill someone, after all.'

'I wonder,' Matt muttered. 'I really do.'

Sarah Marsh was on her knees in front of Frog's house when Dominic walked up behind her. His shadow falling across the flowerbed made her jump and she glanced up at him. 'Oh, hello.'

'What are you doing over here?' he asked.

She sank back onto her heels and wiped a dirty wrist across her forehead, leaving a small smear over one eyebrow. 'Winter's coming,' she said. 'There's a lot to do in a garden before winter, believe me.'

'I do,' Dominic assured her. 'But this isn't even your garden.'

'No – it's Frog's,' she agreed. 'But it will go to wrack and ruin while he's stuck in there. At least I can keep it tidy for him until he comes back so he'll have something to look at come spring. It would just about kill him if he found it all a mess.'

'He's asked me to get him some clean clothes,' Dominic said. 'And to check that everything in the house is all right.'

'It's fine. I have a key in case of emergency, and I've been keeping the place dusted and so on – in case he suddenly finds a way to make that bail. There's only the house for security, you see – not worth enough.'

It was a small old house, rather isolated in the middle of the large garden that surrounded it on all four sides. It badly needed painting and two of the upstairs windows were boarded over on the inside.

Sarah sighed. 'The grass will need its last cut soon. I'll get one of the neighbourhood boys to do it. At least it will be respectable.'

'Does he know you're taking care of all this?' Dominic enquired.

'He'd never ask,' she said resignedly. 'Let him think the fairies did it.'

Dominic chuckled. 'I wish you'd let me tell him how generous you're being.'

'No.' She was firm. 'I meant what I said. He'd hate being beholden, especially to a woman. Particularly to me. Always called me a fool for retiring early to look after my parents, said I should have had a life of my own. But I loved them and it was no sacrifice, believe me.'

He looked down at her. A woman with so much to give and no one to give it to, now that her parents were gone. So she had taken on Frog Bartlett at arm's length. It seemed unlikely that she might entertain romantic feelings towards the ugly, ill-tempered man, yet he thought that might be the case, whether she realized it or not. He knew now that she was younger than he had first assumed. Certainly she was doing all she could for Frog, whether Frog wanted it or not. He thought she was probably right about Bartlett resenting it, adding foolish pride to the list of his client's less attractive traits.

'I hope he has the opportunity to see what you're doing for him,' he said. 'Do you want to come in with me? I'm not sure what to take.'

She heaved herself to her feet and wiped her hands on the canvas apron which she'd wrapped around and over the mustard-coloured sweater and brown slacks she wore. Mustard was not a flattering colour for her, making her normally drab complexion look even more washed out than usual. 'Might as well. You could bring his dirty clothes back with you another time and I'll see to them.'

'He told me to take them to the laundry,' Dominic said as they went up the front steps.

'He can't afford laundry bills. Why don't they give him some kind of prison clothes, anyway?'

'Don't have any that will fit him, apparently,' Dom replied. 'In any case Matt thinks people are more comfortable in their own clothes. Says uniforms take away their personality. I said wasn't that the point of them and he said "Not in my jail".'

'Matt's a good man,' Sarah said, as Dominic opened the front door of Frog's house.

'He's a worried man, I'm glad to say,' Dominic told her as they went in. 'I'd like to think I've caused him to take a second look at everything, although to be honest I think he was already worried about the case. The DA rushed him and he doesn't like being rushed.' He paused. 'Good heavens,' he said.

The dilapidated exterior of Frog Bartlett's house was no indication of what lay within. A hallway with a gleaming wood floor bisected the house from front to back. The parlour on the left was Edwardian in feel, with tall bookcases and comfortable chairs sitting upon old oriental rugs. The dining-room, across the hall, was an almost perfect Shaker room, with a large plain table and the dining chairs hung on wooden pegs around the perimeter. The kitchen was modern with a country feel, and the rear sitting-room was relaxed early American, with homespun upholstery and pine-clad walls.

'I thought he had no money to speak of,' Dominic said.

'He doesn't,' Sarah confirmed. 'Just the house plus what his family left, which wasn't all that much, and a disability pension from the Army. But Frog likes auctions and he's very patient about getting what he wants. All this is his own hard slog. He always says there's nobody to please but himself and all the time in the world to do it. Of course he spends most of the days on the garden, but the rest of the time he works on the house.'

There was evidence that Frog had been repainting the dining-room when Matt Gabriel had come to arrest him, because there were still drop-cloths on the floor and a roller gone hard in a tray beside the paint cans. The chairs from one wall were placed carefully aside and the wall itself was half covered with a fresh coat of white.

'Why hasn't he painted the outside?' Dominic asked.

'What, and have the tax assessor put up the rate?' Sarah laughed. 'Not Frog.'

They went upstairs. The front bedroom was obviously Frog's own and it was the only room in the house that was carpeted, in a mossy green that matched the quilts on the bed. There were three, each folded back neatly. The whole house was extremely tidy.

'You've cleaned it well,' Dominic commented.

'Hah – I didn't have to do a thing except dust,' Sarah said. 'Frog keeps everything spic and span. His Army training, I reckon.'

'There's one thing that puzzles me, though. Since he keeps everything so perfect – why does he leave those two windows boarded up instead of replacing the glass? Glass isn't that expensive.'

'I don't know,' Sarah admitted. 'I suppose it's some kind of storage room.'

'On the basis that I should know all I can about my client,' Dominic said solemnly, 'I think we should take a look.'

'Well—'

'And the fact that I'm incurably nosy,' he added with a grin. They went to the door of the boarded-up room and opened it.

It was Sarah's turn to be amazed. 'Good heavens,' she said, when Dominic had found the light switch. 'Although I should have guessed – I've seen him out in the garden with a camera often enough. I just assumed he took his film to the drugstore like everyone else.'

The room had been converted to a professional-looking dark-room, with all kinds of equipment, none of which seemed particularly new but all of which was beautifully maintained – if a little dusty at the moment.

'So Mr Bartlett has another hobby,' Dominic said, pleasantly surprised. He went over to look at a row of photographic prints which were hanging up to dry. 'And he's good too. I wonder if Matt saw all this.' The prints were of the garden, close-ups of tiny details, such as a dew-spangled spider's web, a tangle of branches with a tiny bird within, a mossy mound of pebbles and so on. There were two sets of prints, one black and white and the other colour, the former emphasizing composition, the latter hue and tone. 'Very good, in fact.'

Sarah had been examining some cabinets with wide drawers and he heard her gasp. Oh, God, he thought, not something nasty. Not nudes or pornography.

But, while Sarah was blushing, it had nothing to do with sex. She had opened a drawer and found a section marked 'Sarah'. In it were literally hundreds of pictures of her, from childhood to the present day. Studies of her obviously taken at a distance, although there were some early close-ups. 'I remember him always fooling with a camera when we were at school, but I never thought much about it. We all had cameras in those days, took pictures of each other and so on. But these are—'

They were lovely. Somehow Bartlett had managed to turn Sarah's plain features into something special and in several of the prints she looked almost beautiful. In fact, beauty was the overriding theme of all his work, Dominic decided. The ugly man had spent his life in search of it, in recognition of it, in recording it. And he'd found it everywhere.

'This is me last year,' Sarah breathed. 'Out in the garden with my straw hat on, picking berries. Getting old, now.' But her voice didn't hold sadness as much as wonder, for Frog's picture showed her ageing gracefully, her face caught in a moment of pleasure at discovering a particularly plump bit of fruit, probably. 'I don't understand.' She sounded helpless. 'I never saw him take this.'

Dominic looked around and discovered what he had expected – a telephoto lens. 'Judging from the angle, he probably took it from an upstairs window. He wouldn't have wanted to embarrass you, maybe.'

'Here's pictures of a lot of folk,' she said, hurriedly replacing her 'file' and pulling out another. 'Why, here's even pictures of Moony Packard.'

It was a file marked 'Mail men' and showed Packard, as well as others, delivering mail in all weathers – leaning against wind and rain, up to the thighs in snow, in summer shirt-sleeves talking to people on their rounds.

'But these aren't all from inside the house,' Dominic said after a few minutes. 'Many have been taken in town. Didn't everybody notice Mr Bartlett taking photos? I mean, there are literally thousands of pictures here.'

Sarah had been thinking. 'His van.'

'What?'

'Frog drives an old van. I bet he would sit inside and take pictures when people didn't know it. Peeping Tom, that's what he is. A Peeping Tom.' She began to look quite indignant, Dominic thought, to cover her confusion at having been such an important photographic subject for the man she thought disliked her – for her file of pictures was enormous compared with the others. Only the one marked 'Roses' was thicker.

'Not in the usual sense,' Dominic said quickly. 'I mean, there's nothing unpleasant about his work. Far from it. Look at these shots of children – nothing nasty there. Just wonderful pictures of innocents – and not so innocents – at play.' This last comment came from his discovery of a startling series of prints depicting a fight between two lads of about nine or ten, full of disturbingly real fury. The file of children's photos wasn't particularly extensive, but very effective. Bartlett seemed to have photographed everything that caught his eye – he had a whole record of the town and its people. Wonderful work, all kept hidden from the world he had observed. 'He could have made a living from photography,' Dominic finally said, closing the last drawer. As he did so, he caught sight of something on the wall. Not a picture – but a certificate. An award from a national magazine. In fact, there were several awards there.

'Looks like he might have collected a few cheques along the way.' Dominic showed Sarah the certificates. 'Maybe that explains how he financed his equipment. Even second-hand, this set-up would have cost him thousands over the years.'

'As I told you, he was patient,' Sarah said quietly. She had been going through the 'Roses' file and Dominic came to look over her shoulder. Lush, evocative prints were in this collection, showing the blooms in full glory, richly coloured, softly focused. There was none of Mapple-thorpe's sexuality in this flower photography – Bartlett's viewpoint was a little old-fashioned and very romantic. Beauty was indeed his goal.

This was not the work of a man who could kill as Moony Packard had been killed – brutally, savagely and with forethought. Whoever had ambushed Moony Packard in Cotter's Cut had done so with the monkey wrench concealed about his person and with only one aim in view: destruction.

Destruction and putting the blame elsewhere, for the wrench had been stolen in advance and with purpose.

He had to believe that.

Someone had not only hated Moony Packard – they had hated Frog Bartlett as well.

Why?

EIGHT

JUST DESSERTS WAS THRONGED WITH the wives of the men who thought they were simply shopping. Plate after plate of delicacies were being consumed, along with the latest in gossip. The ladies were very happy amid the coffee and calories, and their voices were as of cooing doves, chittering sparrows and the occasional gull.

Mrs Toby and Mrs Norton were in their usual Wednesday place in the back corner, where they could watch everyone and catch up on town events and news.

'Did you see the *Chronicle* this morning?' asked Larry Lovich as he put down their order of bear claws and double *lattes*.

'Haven't looked through it yet. Why?' asked Margaret Toby.

'Big editorial on Frog Bartlett maybe being innocent,' Larry said. 'What do you think of that?'

'Do they actually say he's innocent?' Nell Norton asked, plucking the newspaper out of her shopping bag and opening it.

'Not in so many words,' Larry conceded. 'But they quote Dom Pritchard as saying he is. And being angry that so many people have made up their minds ahead of time. Says it's not fair.'

'Well, it isn't,' Nell agreed, locating the page and starting to read. 'They'll have a hard time getting an impartial jury.'

'Just because a man is ugly . . .' Margaret Toby began.

'I know,' Larry said. 'People just assume, don't they?'

'Well, he *is* kind of crabby,' Nell Norton put in. 'Doesn't seem to like people very much, so you can't blame them for not liking him back, I suppose.'

'Even so, he has a right to a fair trial,' Larry stated firmly. There was a 'ping' from the counter and he looked over to see his partner, Freddy Tollett, glaring at him. 'Sorry – duty calls.' Larry went quickly to pick up another order. Freddy scowled at him, Larry winked and Freddy grinned. Larry carried the order to a far table with a smile on his face.

'Well, she's certainly made some good points here,' Nell Norton admitted.

'Let me see,' Margaret Toby said, reaching for the paper. She quickly read the article, then put the paper down. 'This doesn't make Matt look too clever,' she said slowly. 'She talks about a rush to judgement.'

'It says the DA rushed, not Matt.' Nell read fast. 'Matt didn't want to arrest Frog so quick, remember? But the evidence . . .'

'Scientific tosh,' Margaret snapped. 'DNA and all that palaver. Don't believe a word of it. Just magic, that's all, magic tricks to fool people.'

'I think there's a bit more to it than that,' Nell said drily.

'Even so.' Margaret's voice was low. 'It's not going to make Matt look so good – and that's pretty important right now. Do you think Armstrong had a hand in this?'

'I doubt it. Dominic Pritchard and Emily Gibbons are engaged, remember?'

'Oh, of course,' Margaret acknowledged. 'Of course. But still, I think it's time we took a more active hand in this election business.'

'What do you mean?' Nell's tone was cautious – Margaret had a way of going off the deep end sometimes. As precise as she was in her quilting, so dear Margaret was scattered in her thinking. Brain went too fast, sometimes, Nell thought. Lost traction.

'I mean Mr Armstrong has things going his way just a bit too much at the moment,' Margaret said firmly.

'Matt needs back-up.' She gulped at her coffee and took a huge bite of her bear claw. 'Come on,' she mumbled rather indistinctly. 'Let's get down to the gallery and talk to Daria.'

Daria was seated behind her desk at the back of the premises. Around her on walls and stands were her own paintings, works by other artists, some of Mrs Toby's art quilts and a series of photographs by Harry Foskett of winter bayside scenery. The gallery was a thriving business because of Daria Grey's own fame as an artist of national stature. A beautiful, highly strung girl, she had returned to her home in Blackwater Bay after a very bad and destructive marriage, finding peace here and the gradual return of her ability to paint.

'We saw the editorial in the paper.' Nell Norton came straight to the point. 'It makes Matt look a bit bad, don't you think?'

'No worse than he looks to himself. The trouble is, he has no alternative suspect,' Daria said. 'Mind you, according to Frank Packard it could have been the CIA, the other mail man who took over Moony's route, Jack Armstrong, Matt himself, the mayor and about a dozen others. Frog is only one of a long list of people who murdered Moony, according to Frank. What he isn't clear about, apparently, is whether it was just one of them or the whole caboodle working together to spite him. Matt is doggedly following up all his allegations, but so far – nothing.'

'Hmph,' Nell Norton said. 'Hardly surprising. Frank Packard is a horse's ass. Always suspecting someone, forever going around blaming other people for the fact that he's too ornery and too stupid to get a job himself.'

'He's not stupid,' Mrs Toby protested. 'Frank was a bright boy – too bright, in fact. That's the trouble with him – his brain is too big for his boots. He suspects everyone is against him, because he reads all these terrible magazines. Helen Pollock told me he's always buying weird books and ordering more, about conspiracies and survivalism and stuff like that. She thinks he might belong to one of those crazy militia-type groups too.'

'Then why is Matt listening to him?' Nell asked.

Daria sighed and aimlessly shuffled some papers around the top of her desk. 'Because he believes it's his duty. And because he thinks if he keeps busy doing things like that, we can't force him to make speeches and public appearances.'

'Oh, tosh and nonsense,' Mrs Toby said briskly. 'Matt loves that job and wants to keep it. He can live with responsibility. He's just shy, that's all. He hates all the election hullabaloo and I don't blame him. It's undignified. But it's necessary and so he has to face up to it.'

'Well, he's having to appear tonight on the same platform as Tyrone Molt and Jack Armstrong.' Daria's voice was grim. 'We got him to agree to that, at least. It's a debate, up at the High School.'

'My, my,' Nell mused. 'That should be interesting.'

'We'll make sure everybody is there to cheer him on,' Mrs Toby said firmly. 'We'll get out and kick some asses.'

'Margaret!' Nell was surprised. 'You're getting low-down and dirty!'

'Right on,' Mrs Toby agreed and smacked her right first into her left palm. 'We're not here to have fun, you know.'

'Did you hear – Frank Packard got beat up by some of Armstrong's boys,' George reported later that afternoon. 'Seems he made a fuss at Armstrong's campaign display in the mall, and they "escorted him" away. Not very gently, apparently.'

'Does he want to bring charges?' Matt asked, interested.

'He says no,' George answered. 'I caught up with him in the ER because someone saw it and called it in.'

'Who?'

'Anonymous,' George said in disgust. 'You remember him.'

'Oh, yeah. Good old reliable Anonymous.'

'Anyways, it was kind of odd. Frank said leave it alone, that he was making a fuss and maybe he deserved it.'

'That doesn't sound like the Frank Packard I know.' Matt frowned.

'I know,' George said. 'I really tried to get him to bring charges – I mean, think how it would be tonight if you could bring it up during the debate, how Armstrong's buddies beat up an innocent bystander just because he argued with him. But Frank wouldn't play ball. He was acting real weird. Which I suppose is pretty normal for Frank, come to think of it.'

'You can't force people to bring charges,' Tilly pointed out.

'I know that, I know that. It's just that . . . hell, it would have been so good to be able to say it.' George sank down in his chair. 'It would have paved the way for bringing up other stuff – you know, about the mall and so on.'

'That's dirty politics, George,' Matt protested. 'I can't prove anything, because nobody will make a complaint.'

'Well, yeah,' George agreed. 'That's the whole point. We know Armstrong pressured people to sell their land for ridiculous prices. We know he had some of his workers strong-armed and one beat up real bad when they started talking about how he was cutting corners on the mall.'

'But nobody would testify.' Matt's voice sounded weary. 'And we couldn't get evidence. He outsmarted us every time.'

'The bastard,' George said. 'Think what kind of sheriff he'd be. Jesus, and I'd have to work with him. He knows I don't like him.' George sat up suddenly. 'He could fire me!'

'So could I, George.' Matt smiled.

'Yeah – but you wouldn't,' George said complacently. Then he frowned slightly. 'Would you?'

'Now who could I get to replace you, George?' Matt asked. 'You're unique.'

'Yeah?' George took it as a compliment, of course. 'Well,

there you go, then. But he won't think so. He'll make a mess of this place, Matt. You've really got to stop him.'

Matt gazed at George for a full minute without speaking. Then he looked up at the clock and over at the coffee machine. 'I hadn't thought of it in quite that way,' he said, half to himself.

'Why not?' George wanted to know. 'The rest of us have.' He leaned forward. 'Matt, he'd be a gold-plated disaster. We know he's slippery, we know he works just over the edge . . . what kind of law enforcement officer would that make him?' He leaned back again. 'A dirty one, that's what. You can't avoid it, Matt. It's not a matter of politics. It's a matter of defending the town against him. You can't count on everybody thinking you're great. You've got to get them to see he's no good. You got to protect *me*, Matt! And Tilly – you think he'd keep Tilly on? She knows too much – she'd be the first one out.'

'Thanks, George.' Tilly had been listening to this with interest. 'But I guess you're right.' She watched Matt digesting this. It was a tack they hadn't tried before. Maybe it would work. Maybe if they got him *real* mad at Armstrong he'd do something about it.

'Some people grow into a position,' Matt pointed out. 'He's a hard worker, nobody denies that. Maybe—'

'Bullshit,' George almost shouted in exasperation. 'Anyway, why should we have to put up with some guy who's learning the job when we have someone who already knows it? Somebody straight, I might add. Not somebody as crooked as a corkscrew.'

'There's no proof of that, George,' Matt protested mildly.

'I don't need proof, dammit. I *know*. You know. Frank Packard knows, too. And so does Mr Anonymous, among others.'

'We all know, Matt,' Tilly said. 'We all know he would rape this office for what he could get out of it. Power is what he's after. And he'll abuse it. Are you prepared to stand back and let him do it? If you get defeated in this election, how will you feel, seeing him dirty your badge?'

There was another pause. Matt glanced from one to the other. 'Nice end play.' He smiled. 'I'm impressed.'

'Did it work?' Tilly wanted to know.

'Maybe,' Matt said. 'Maybe.'

Although the night was cold, the inside of the Heckman Memorial High School auditorium was tropical. Digger Wells, the custodian, had turned up the heating system with a little too much enthusiasm and a capacity crowd didn't help. There were colds and flu germs incubating all over the auditorium as people shed their coats and scarves and good sense. For the 'debate' had turned nasty.

It had started easily enough with Mr Berringer, the Town Clerk, introducing the three candidates and allowing them each three minutes for making their cases.

Tyrone Molt was first and he made out a case for electing him because he promised to service all the official cars free of charge. He knew the town 'like the back of his hand'. He was a widower and could give all his attention to the job at hand. And he was brave, trustworthy and true. Because it was early in the evening, nobody snickered and everyone applauded politely.

Then Matt stood up. He spoke quietly. 'You all know me and you know how I've served this town for the past nine years. More important, I know you. I, too, was born and brought up in Blackwater Bay. Although I was away teaching for a short while, I came back when my father died and filled in until I could be elected at the proper time. I grew up with the law as part of my life. I know it and I love it. You trusted me then and you can trust me now. I didn't have to learn "the ways of the world" because my world is right here and it's not the same as anywhere else. Nor are the people the same as anywhere else – and haven't the big-city newspapers loved it?' (This brought the first laugh of the evening.)

'What is important in enforcing the law in a town like

Blackwater is not just getting things done – but in getting them done in a way that is right and just for the town. It's knowing when to bend, when to step back, when to allow people some freedom and when to curtail it. If I wanted to, I could tie this town up in knots by strictly enforcing the rules – because, as many of you know, our rules are a little eccentric.' (Another, smaller laugh from the audience.) 'But I don't want to do that. I don't want to rule with an iron fist.' (He glanced at Armstrong, who examined his nails as if wondering whether to exchange them for another set.) 'I don't want to exert all the power this office holds at every opportunity because that is not appropriate. What *is* appropriate is maintaining a kindly, fair-minded, even-handed approach to the law. It's letting folks live their lives as they wish to, but it also means not leaving them in danger, fear, or need. I can be tough if I have to be, you've seen me take necessary steps, but that's not as important to me as being fair. That's what justice is all about. What is—'

'How about justice for Frog Bartlett?' somebody shouted. 'Are you sure you've got the right man?'

'Of course he has,' somebody else shouted back. 'Frog's so ugly he probably scared Moony Packard to death.'

'That's not fair,' came another voice.

'Sure is,' yelled someone else. 'Frog ever have a kind word for you?'

'Did Moony?' another somebody asked. 'Talk about Mr Know-it-All—'

'Now wait a minute.' Matt raised his hands.

Jack Armstrong stood up beside him. 'I think every citizen has a right to question elected officials on their care and attention to duty,' he said.

'It's not your turn yet,' Mr Berringer whispered loudly.

'If I am elected I promise to be answerable to all citizens and not to leap to conclusions in any investigation.' Armstrong smiled smugly at Matt.

'Who leaped to conclusions?' Matt asked him. 'My job is to gather evidence. It's up to the court to—'

Armstrong ignored him and grinned at the audience. 'There are some folks whose *only* exercise is leaping to conclusions. People who believe in sitting back and doing nothing about anything in the hope that it all will go away are cowards. I won't be that kind of sheriff. If a man's guilty, I'll make sure he goes to prison.'

Tilly Moss suddenly stood up. 'No – you leap over the rules instead,' she shouted at Armstrong.

Mrs Toby got to her feet in another part of the audience. 'Yes, what about that? What about what you did to Frank Packard, here, you and your bully boys?'

'I have no idea what you're talking about,' Armstrong said disdainfully.

'Shut up, you old bat,' came a voice from the back. Matt looked and saw it was one of Armstrong's employees.

'I will not shut up,' said Mrs Toby. 'Matt Gabriel is the best sheriff this county has ever had. Except maybe for his father.'

'Yes, well, if his father hadn't been sheriff, he'd never have got the job,' Armstrong snapped in a low voice.

'I heard that,' George Putnam said. He was sitting in the front row next to Susie Brock and leaped to his feet, shaking his fist at Armstrong. 'You take that back, you bastard.'

'Please,' said Mr Berringer weakly, as more and more shouts erupted from the increasingly restless audience. Some wanted Matt to let Frog out of jail. Others wanted Armstrong to explain about the new housing development at the edge of town. How was he going to build that if he was busy being sheriff and vice versa? There were insults exchanged, names called, chairs pounded and arms waved. 'Please, ladies and gentlemen . . .'

'What about the mall?' someone shouted. 'Who got that built in record time?'

Mrs Peach stood up. 'And why is it already falling apart in record time?' she wanted to know.

'Yes – who's to blame for that and a lot of other things I could mention?' bellowed Frank Packard, getting to his feet with difficulty but glaring from beneath his bandages at both Armstrong and Matt. 'Like people getting beat up? And other people getting killed? And . . .'

Tyrone Molt stood up, pushing Mr Berringer back into the chair from which he was struggling to rise. 'I heard a bunch of the shops in that precious mall of yours had to be totally rewired before they could open up,' he said. 'What do you say about that, Armstrong?'

'I say you are an uninformed idiot,' Armstrong blurted out before he could stop himself. 'You know nothing about how to build anything.' He turned to Matt. 'Including a safe town. People getting murdered all over the place and you just sit on your ass or spend your time courting a rich woman who won't say yes.' He smirked. 'Could it be she knows something we don't?'

That, for Matt, was the last straw. He grabbed Armstrong by the lapels and shook him. Armstrong began to turn blue. 'Leave my fiancée out of it, you son of a bitch,' Matt said.

Daria stood up. 'Matt, please . . .'

He didn't hear her. After a moment she rushed down the aisle and out of the auditorium. Tilly Moss hurried after her.

Armstrong twisted from Matt's grasp and struggled for breath. He turned to the audience who had gone quiet at seeing Matt Gabriel's rarely displayed anger. 'You see?' he managed to gasp. 'Unstable behaviour. Is that what you want from a sheriff in your town? He's obviously lost his balance—'

'Now wait a minute,' Tyrone Molt said. 'You saying Matt is crazy?'

Armstrong glanced at Molt and sneered. 'Takes one to know one.' In the audience, Win Otis covered his face with his hands and groaned.

'You're the one who's crazy!' Tyrone shouted. 'You think you can get your way by pushing people around! Well, we're too smart for you!'

'I doubt that,' Armstrong commented.

'Please, gentlemen . . .' Mr Berringer said, wringing his hands and coming forward. 'Let's keep this orderly.'

'Tell *him* that.' Molt gestured towards Armstrong. Everyone knew Tyrone Molt was in the race for the publicity, he made no secret of it. He liked to strut around the town talking to people, handing out business cards for his car dealership, getting the most out of the free advertising inherent in running for office, however unsuccessfully. But although he was suspect as a salesman, he was a fair man. He saw no reason for Armstrong to out-and-out insult an opponent.

'Mr Armstrong, please . . .' Berringer pleaded.

'He grabbed me first,' Armstrong protested, gesturing towards Matt. 'He's the one who got violent, just because I pointed out that his so-called fiancée refuses to actually marry him because—'

At that point Matt swung and connected. Armstrong went down hard. There were shouts from the back of the audience and several large men began to charge the stage. That they didn't reach it as quickly as they intended was because others were there before them. George and fellow deputies Duff Bradley and Charley Hart jumped up onto the stage, but by then Armstrong had got to his feet and was trying to punch Matt. Tyrone Molt stepped forward. Mr Berringer got caught between them and was squeaking piteously, waving his arms.

More people poured onto the platform and several fist fights broke out between Armstrong's supporters and Matt's. Nobody seemed to be supporting Molt, who was growing more and more excited by the minute. The area in front of the stage and the stage itself was a mass of struggling, shouting people.

Molt, stimulated by the noise and excitement, lifted a chair and held it up, apparently intending to bring it down on Armstrong's head, but someone lurched into him and it flew out of Molt's hands, skidded across the podium and hit Mr Berringer, the Town Clerk. He went down with a shriek and what later proved to be a broken leg.

'Now, wait a minute, Molt!' Matt shouted.

'I wasn't aiming at him!' Molt shouted back over the crowd, which continued to surge over the stage like a throbbing tide, now forward, now back, as one group and then the other gained the upper hand. The noise was incredible, the heat unbearable and control seemed impossible.

Matt, in desperation, drew his revolver and shot into the air in order to get everyone's attention. There was an ominous cracking and a section of the ceiling crumbled to dust over the mêlée.

But it worked. Everyone stopped where they were and stared at him.

'There! See?' Armstrong was so delighted he was practically jumping up and down. 'He's trigger-happy. He's unstable. He's dangerous!' He climbed down from the dais. 'I'm getting out of here before he starts shooting at me!'

'Don't tempt me, Armstrong!' Matt shouted and started after him. Half-way down the aisle, he turned back to the platform, where everyone was still frozen in various postures of shock. 'I would like to point out that Mr Armstrong's company put up the ceiling that has just collapsed on you, ladies and gentlemen. Think about it.'

He made for the exit, but turned again at the door. 'George – call an ambulance for Mr Berringer.' He looked around, wild-eyed and shaking. 'And – clean this place up!' Then he went out after Armstrong.

NINE

'WHAT HAPPENED AFTER I LEFT?' Tilly asked eagerly. She had followed Daria out before the real excitement began.

George leaned back in his chair. 'Matt kind of lost it.' He shook his head and grinned. 'Have you seen the Grantham papers this morning? Somebody tipped them off that there would be fireworks there last night and I'm pretty sure it was Armstrong or that campaign manager of his.'

'I wouldn't put it past either one,' Tilly agreed.

George leaned back in his chair and smiled at his memories of the previous evening. 'I think it was when Matt shot off his pistol to restore order and part of the ceiling fell in that the reporters from Grantham really got excited. And when he pointed out that it was Armstrong's company that had put in the new ceiling that fell down, they were grinning from ear to ear. Several people had to go to the hospital with cuts and bruises, and Mr Berringer has a broken leg. He's not happy.'

'Would you be?' Tilly asked. 'He only just got over being knocked down by that runaway tractor at the County Fair.'

'He doesn't have a lot of luck, does he?' George mused.

'Neither does Matt, lately,' Tilly said. 'Daria was real upset, I took her home with me. She hated seeing him up there being jeered at, losing his temper. You know how sensitive she is. If you ask me, half the people in that audience were *paid* to make trouble.'

'That's what we think too,' George agreed. He sat forward

in his chair and drew his notebook over towards him. 'That's how I'm going to write it up, anyway.' He looked at the clock. 'Has Matt come down yet?'

'No,' Tilly replied. 'Should I call him?'

'No – let him sleep. We can handle things,' George said confidently.

He should have known better.

Susie Brock called in about ten minutes later.

She was out on patrol with Duff Bradley, much to George's annoyance. Duff was married, but that didn't make a lot of difference as far as George was concerned. He wanted Susie where he could keep an eye on her, but she stubbornly refused to stay in the office and Matt acceded to her demands for patrol duty, saying she needed the experience. George thought she should go with *him* on patrol, but Matt was on to him and didn't let that happen, even though George insisted that he could teach Susie a hell of a lot. Matt had said he probably could, but he didn't think it would be much about law inforcement. George had sulked for two days after that one.

Tilly turned to George with a pale face. 'They've just found a body out near the edge of town.' Her voice was unnaturally loud. 'Susie's pretty sure it's Jack Armstrong. He's been shot, she said.'

There was a shocked silence.

Through the open door to the cells in the back came a gravelly voice. 'Well, you sure as hell can't blame *this* one on me,' shouted Frog Bartlett.

Tilly rang Matt's apartment over the office and, when she got no reply, went upstairs, coming down a moment later with a shocked look on her face. 'He's not there. And his bed hasn't been slept in either.'

She and George stared at one another.

'Where the hell could he be?' George asked.

A faint wind rustled through the small hummocks of field-grass around them, stirring up some dust and bits of litter. They stood in a semicircle, staring down at the ground. The sun was warm on their shoulders – it was a beautiful morning. For some.

'It's his gun.' George looked at the carved ivory grip of the .38 revolver that lay a little distance from the body. 'That's Matt's gun. It was his father's.'

'Oh,' Susie said in a small voice. 'And the handcuffs?'

'Standard issue. Could be his. Could be anybody's.'

Jack Armstrong lay on the ground before them, curled into a semi-foetal position, with his hands cuffed behind him and a bullet hole in the middle of his forehead.

'It looks like an execution,' Susie whispered.

It did, at that.

Duff Bradley came back with the forensic kit. 'You want me to make a start, George? I called the coroner and he's sending someone over. And I called Doc Willis too. Mrs Willis said he was on a house call but she would call him on his beeper, so he shouldn't be long.'

Susie looked puzzled. 'We have to get him declared officially dead before the guys from the medical examiner's office can take him away,' George explained in a stunned, abstract voice.

'Oh, of course – I forgot.' Susie seemed very nervous and kept glancing at George out of the corner of her eye.

'What's wrong?' George asked.

'Oh, nothing . . . It's just . . .' Susie paused, reddening.

'You're wondering if Matt did it,' George stated.

'I'm sorry, it's just that the gun . . . and the handcuffs . . . and last night . . . he was so angry . . .'

'Now, look.' George cleared his throat. 'That's ridiculous and you know it. Matt wouldn't do anything like this in a million years.' He shifted uncomfortably. 'I know it's his gun and all, but there could be an explanation for that. Maybe somebody took it last night in the fight . . .'

Susie shook her head. 'I saw him leaving after Armstrong. He was wearing his gun as usual. I know, because it occurred to me that maybe . . .'

'Maybe he would use it? You don't know him at all,' George said in disgust.

'Why here?' Duff wanted to know, looking around. It was mostly open ground, with markers on small sticks in regular patterns, stretching into the distance. A pair of earth movers stood to one side, bright yellow in the sunshine. Meadow-grass had grown up around their wheels. Armstrong's body was lying behind a small, rather dirty trailer marked 'Office' on the door.

'This is the site of his new development,' George said, momentarily distracted from the traitorous thoughts he and Susie had been having. 'Or it was, anyway. I heard things have been held up.'

'Why is that?'

'Some folks have refused to sell their land, by all accounts,' George replied. 'We had complaints about harassment from some of them, but nobody would actually lay a charge.'

'Typical,' Duff commented, staring down glumly at the body and then glancing towards the road.

The man who earlier had run out into the road waving his arms to stop the patrol car was now sitting on its back seat, his head in his hands. George glanced over at him too, following Duff's gaze. It was Armstrong's campaign manager. 'Mr Otis regrets,' he said quietly.

'I asked him if he wanted me to call anyone, but he just shook his head,' Susie said. 'I think he's in shock.'

'Probably,' George agreed. 'The medics will give him something when they get here.' He sighed. 'What about Armstrong's wife?' he asked.

They looked at one another. 'I think she's in the hospital,' Susie answered.

'In the clinic, you mean,' George stated. 'She's in Mountview. Susie, radio Tilly to ring them and tell them what's happened, have them make sure nobody lets her find out before we get there.'

'It's very quiet here,' Duff observed. 'Where is everybody?'

'The project's been red-flagged,' George explained. 'Armstrong had to lay off his men until he could get the go-ahead on the new layout from the Town Council. To get around those folks who won't sell their land he's had to have all new plans drawn up, new arrangements for laying water, sewage pipes, electricity and roads ... all that kind of stuff. It's costing him a fortune, I hear.' He cleared his throat. 'I mean, it was,' he added. 'Don't know what will happen now.'

'There's going to be hell to pay over this.' Duff looked down at the body and the all too familiar gun.

'I know,' George agreed.

'Especially after last night,' Duff continued. He seemed quite calm, but George saw he was shaking. George, too, was shaking, not knowing quite what to do next.

Across the open field an ambulance lurched towards them, bumping over the ridges of the cleared areas, crunching through the grass of the still wild sections. Behind it came Dr Willis's car. When he had pulled up, the old man climbed out rather awkwardly and came over to them, scowling. 'You pick the damnedest times and places to find bodies,' he grumbled to George. 'Who is it this time?'

'See for yourself.' George turned away.

'Holy sutures,' Willis said. 'Armstrong. Shot in the damned head.'

'Observant of you.' George was watching Susie talking to Tilly on the radio.

'Guess this settles the election problem,' Willis said practically. He kneeled down with difficulty on his arthritic knees and laid his hand on Armstrong's throat. 'Dead all right.' He prodded the corpse, tried to lift an arm, sighed. 'Just starting to stiffen up. You can take him away when the Sheriff's men are through,' he said to the ambulance men. He reached for George's hand and pulled himself to his feet with a grunt of pain. 'All yours.'

Just then Susie came running back. 'Tilly says Charley Hart just called in. They've found Matt. He's in his car, parked in front of Armstrong's house.'

'Dead?' Duff was appalled.

'No.'

99

'Drunk?' asked George.

'No. He just won't wake up. They don't know what's wrong with him.'

Doc Willis sighed. 'I do. Come on.'

'I diagnosed him about a month ago,' Doc Willis said to George, looking down at Matt as he lay in the hospital bed. 'Diabetes. His father had it, so I wasn't surprised. I suggested treating it by diet, but that wasn't working, so yesterday I prescribed some pills to control his blood sugar. And what did you do?' he asked, glaring at Matt.

Matt flushed, but was so pale it didn't make him look much healthier. 'I took both pills at once and then forgot to eat dinner,' he mumbled.

'You did worse than that. You had to get into a rage and jump and shout and get excited. *That* is what did it to you in the end. That kind of thing absolutely burns up blood sugar and by not eating you had no reserves.' Doc Willis sighed. 'For a smart man you sure are dumb. I *told* you the point was to keep your blood sugar *even*, avoid highs and lows. Well, you've had your first hypo and it damn well could have killed you. We've filled you up with glucose, which has cleared your head, but as far as I can see that's only temporary if you're going to behave like an idiot. Maybe now you'll listen to me.'

'It wouldn't have killed me,' Matt protested.

'Suppose you had been out in the country someplace where nobody found you,' Doc Willis countered, his white hair all awry as he kept running his hands through what was left of it. 'You could have died of hypothermia, being unconscious like that. As it was . . .'

'As it was, you were found in front of Jack Armstrong's house,' George said. 'What the hell were you doing there?'

'I haven't the faintest damned idea.' Matt looked at him bleakly. 'I don't remember much of anything after leaving the meeting and getting into my car.'

'Nothing?' asked George.

'Nothing.'

'Oh, dear.' Doc Willis looked at George. 'You've got a problem, George, haven't you?'

'What problem?' Matt wanted to know. 'What's wrong, George?'

'Well . . .' George began.

'He's afraid you killed Jack Armstrong,' Doc Willis said irrepressibly. 'Wouldn't blame you if you had, but it's a hell of a way to run an election.' He was watching the monitors they had attached to Matt as he spoke.

Matt stared at George. 'Jack Armstrong is dead?' He started to get out of the bed, but Doc Willis pushed him back.

'Twenty-four hours I want you here,' he said. 'Maybe longer. And no arguments.'

Matt kept staring at George, waiting for an answer. George muttered something.

'Speak up, George,' Matt snapped.

George cleared his throat and fingered his tie absently. 'We found him out at the site of his new development. Handcuffed. Shot in the head.'

'With your gun,' Doc Willis added gleefully. 'Ain't that something?'

'My gun?' Matt asked.

'Your gun was found at the scene,' George said rather formally. 'We don't have ballistics results yet. Or finger-prints. Not that the grip would take any, being carved like it is.'

'My gun?' Matt repeated, stunned.

Doc Willis patted his shoulder in an avuncular manner. 'You take it easy now. Nobody takes this seriously.'

Matt's eyes met George's. 'George?'

'Well, of course I . . . I mean, it's ridiculous to even think about it. But . . .'

'But there it is. Or was.' Matt held up one finger after another. 'My gun. No alibi due to my own stupidity. A very public and physical argument with the victim only hours before. A victim who was opposing me for election

101

and who had implied he knew things about me that would defeat me at the polls.'

'Well.' George cleared his throat. 'Yes.'

Matt sighed and lay back with his eyes closed. 'Hubris,' he said.

'Why didn't you tell us about the diabetes?' George demanded. 'You should have told us, Matt. People should know so they can help you . . . I mean suppose this hypo thing had happened in town? Doc here says you'd look and act drunk, maybe collapse. That doesn't look so good in a sheriff, you know? We should have been told.'

'Absolutely,' Doc Willis agreed. 'I told him to tell you.'

'I meant to, but there never seemed to be an opportunity, what with the election and the Shadowman thing, and then Moony's murder.'

'Damn poor excuse,' Doc Willis said. 'You were ashamed, admit it. You were afraid they would think you were weak.'

'Not at all,' Matt protested, but he looked away.

Doc Willis sighed. 'Diabetes is *not* an illness, it is a condition,' he stated. 'As long as you watch your diet and take your medication at the proper intervals and remember to eat regularly, you should be just fine.' He turned to George. 'We sometimes see these episodes in the early months after diagnosis because people aren't used to looking after their condition properly, but eventually it becomes second nature. Mind you, I had an idea it might be more difficult with Matt because of his irregular eating habits.' He glared at Matt. 'And his penchant for doughnuts.'

'Can't you remember *anything*?' George asked plaintively.

'Sorry, George. I remember feeling peculiar and wondering if I should drive, and thinking maybe I should eat something . . .' Matt frowned. 'I remember talking to someone while I was standing by my car.'

'Who?' George leaned forward eagerly.

'No idea.'

'Man? Woman?'

'A man, I think.' Matt's forehead grew more corrugated as he tried to concentrate. Then his face relaxed. 'No idea past that. Could have been anyone.'

'Maybe someone who saw you were sick,' George said. 'Someone who wanted to help you?'

Matt shook his head. 'I wasn't sick . . . I was just . . .' He shrugged. 'It's gone.'

'Jesus, Matt, you've got to give me more than that to work with!' George protested. 'Come on, think.'

'I suggest you let it go, George,' Doc Willis said, as a nurse came in with a blood tray. 'We have to start testing his blood now. And he should rest.'

'I feel fine,' Matt said firmly.

'I'm sure you do. Lie down and shut up,' Doc said with equal firmness.

'Listen, Matt . . .' George began.

'I know, George, I know,' Matt said wearily. 'You have to consider me a suspect.'

Doc Willis stared at George. 'Now, George, you can't be serious.'

'Oh, he's serious, all right.' Matt winced as the nurse punctured his arm with a syringe and began to draw blood. 'If the ballistics come through as a match, he'll be even more serious.' Matt looked at his deputy, who was scuffing the floor with one foot and trying to pretend this wasn't happening. 'You're in charge, George. Apparently I'm not going anyplace at the moment.'

'Oh, gee, Matt . . .'

'Do it,' Matt said. 'Just do it.'

TEN

THE PRIVILEGE OF BEING ILL gracefully can be very, very expensive. For those who use Mountview Clinic, it is a price worth paying. Mountview is located just over the Black River and, naturally, on top of a hill. The original building, nearly two hundred years old, is of pinkish brick and, although extensions have been added, they are in keeping, so the whole is attractive and inviting. The medical care is excellent, the general standard as high as any five-star hotel. It is patronized by the wealthy, the famous and, occasionally, the very ill.

Head Nurse Kay Pink directed George and Susie to Mrs Armstrong's room. 'She's still pretty sick from the infection she had,' she told them as they walked down the hall. 'We thought we were going to lose her at one point, but she rallied.' Kay didn't sound too enthusiastic about that. 'She's . . . not an easy woman.'

'Oh,' said George, who was already nervous enough to admit himself to the loony bin. If one more thing went wrong he would. He glanced at Susie, who seemed calm enough. Well, she might be, but she didn't have the responsibilities he had now. Or the worries, he thought. He wished his stomach would settle down.

Kay knocked on the door and went in ahead of them. 'Mrs Armstrong? Here is someone to see you.'

Mrs Irene Armstrong was a beautiful but thin, bird-like woman. Her thick black hair was in strong contrast to her paper-white skin and lay around her face like snakes on the pillow. Her eyes were a peculiar bleached blue that was so pale as to make her seem almost blind. But she saw very well, and fixed George and Susie with a baleful glare as she put down her magazine.

'How are you today, Mrs Armstrong?' George began brightly.

'I'm in here because I'm a sick woman. How else would I be except poorly?' she snapped. 'Who are you? What do you want?'

George cleared his throat. 'I'm afraid I have some very bad news for you, Mrs Armstrong.' And he told her.

Kay said later that they must have heard the scream down in the town. It was an eerie, wounded-animal noise that sent the staff and what patients there were in the clinic into momentary cardiac arrest. And after that, things got worse.

She began to throw things.

George, ducking a water glass which shattered on the wall behind him, tried sweet reason. 'Please, Mrs Armstrong, you're only upsetting yourself.'

Another shot, more accurate this time, left him with a bruise on the shoulder and flower water dribbling down his uniform shirt as chrysanthemums cascaded around his shoes and the vase bounced and then broke into two pieces on the carpet.

'Mrs Armstrong! Stop it!' Susie shouted, going towards the bed.

Pushing her aside, Kay Pink produced a hypodermic syringe, which she'd had concealed in her pocket. 'Hold her down,' she directed Susie. Between them they got Mrs Armstrong immobile and sedated, but still glaring with wild eyes at George, whom she seemed to blame entirely for everything.

'Get out, get out, get out!' she shrieked and began to cry.

'That's better,' Kay said, seeming to see in this collapse some sign of encouragement. 'She'll sleep in a minute.'

'You were prepared for that, weren't you?' asked George, pulling a stray flower stem from behind his ear.

105

'I was,' Kay agreed. 'I had already talked it over with one of the doctors. She tends to become . . . excitable . . . if she doesn't like the way things are going.'

'Well, I don't like the way things are going,' George grumbled. 'Have you got one of those shots for me?'

'Come on, George,' Susie said. 'We have work to do.'

'I'll need to talk to her,' George persisted as they went out of the door.

'Tomorrow,' Kay suggested. 'Come back tomorrow, George.' She looked at him curiously. 'Where's Matt, anyway? He usually likes to do this kind of thing himself.'

They explained about the diabetes, but said nothing about the gun or the blank in Matt's memory. Kay nodded. 'He was lucky someone found him. I expect it's just a matter of getting him stabilized, that's all. Won't take long.'

'I hope not,' George muttered. 'I only have one other clean uniform shirt. And a sheriff has to look his best at all times.'

Kay and Susie exchanged a glance as George walked ahead of them down the corridor. 'Sheriff?' Kay whispered.

'Temporarily,' Susie answered.

'Oh, my God,' Kay said. 'Not again.' She patted Susie on the arm, but did not explain.

When they got back to the office Win Otis was still there, talking to Tilly. He seemed to have recovered some of his equilibrium, and was sitting back in the chair with a cup of coffee in one hand and a doughnut in the other.

'Mr Otis.' George' voice was stern. 'Are you ready to give us a statement now?'

'Yes, I guess so,' Otis said, finishing off his doughnut and dusting the powdered sugar off his hands. He licked the residue away and rubbed his fingers together as if to test for any remaining stickiness. Otis glanced at George warily. 'Did you see Mrs Armstrong?'

'Yes. She was . . . upset. Naturally.' George poured himself some coffee but forced himself away from the doughnuts. He felt he needed something more substantial and wanted to get this over with as quickly as possible. Time was going by and the Golden Perch would stop serving lunch soon.

'You surprise me,' Otis said.

'Oh?'

'Well, she never gave much evidence of caring about her husband. It was a real drawback for us – candidates need to be seen to be supported by their wives.'

'Mrs Armstrong isn't well.'

Otis snorted. 'So she claimed. She just wasn't interested in putting herself out, that's all. Jack himself said the heart business was an excuse – but he didn't seem to mind.'

'Maybe he felt she wouldn't be much of a help,' Tilly suggested.

Otis nodded. 'I can see that she might have turned into a liability if she felt like it. And I gather she often felt like it. It was amazing to me he . . .' He drew in a deep breath and shrugged. 'None of my business, I suppose.'

'Do you think she had reason to want Mr Armstrong dead?' George asked bluntly.

Otis was stunned. 'Good Lord, no. He was her golden goose. I never got the impression she didn't care for him. Just didn't care much what he did. I suppose she'll get it all now. That should keep her happy.'

'You don't like Mrs Armstrong?' Susie asked.

Otis shrugged again. 'Not my place to like or dislike her. As I said, wives can be a real asset to a campaign, but she refused. I've never come across that before. Usually the wives are as gung-ho as the candidates.' He smiled wryly. 'Sometimes even more so. They like the idea of being a political wife. But not her. She treated it all as if it were an annoyance and something of a joke, frankly. I didn't understand her at all. And I was glad when she checked into that damned clinic – which I understand she did regularly – it kept her out of the way.'

'What were you afraid of?' George asked.

Otis counted off on his fingers. 'Her temper, her drinking, her simple cussedness. She hated living here, she had no time for northern people, said they had no manners, she hated the weather here, the shopping, the food, in fact just about everything except Jack's money. That she liked. I think she resented his spending so much on the campaign. I understand she wanted him to build some kind of "Southern-style" addition onto their house instead.'

'All right.' George didn't quite know what to do with this information. 'Let's get on with this. What time did you arrive at the site this morning?' he asked, sitting down next to Otis and turning on the tape-recorder, indicating that he had done so.

Otis didn't seem to mind. 'I got there about ten ... around ten.'

'And why did you go there?'

'Why, to meet Jack,' Otis said in some surprise. 'I'd had a call to meet him there.'

'Was the call from Mr Armstrong himself?'

'Yes ... that is, it was a message from Jack relayed through my beeper.'

'So you can't be certain it was from Mr Armstrong.'

'If you mean did I hear his voice, no, I didn't. But I assume somebody did and then paged me from head-quarters.' He glanced from George to Susie to Tilly. 'Campaign headquarters, that is. We're over on Main and Walnut ...'

'Yes, I know.' George nodded. 'So someone there took the call?'

'I suppose so. I can find out for you.'

'We'll look into that,' George said easily, making a note. He was getting into this now. 'So you arrived. What then?'

'Well, I tried the door, but it was locked, so I knew Jack wasn't inside, so I walked round, thinking he was out back. And ... he was.' Otis swallowed, as if a bit of doughnut was still stuck in his throat. 'I could see right away that he was dead. I mean . . . well, anybody could see that.'

'You didn't try to check if there was a pulse, anything like that?'

Otis shook his head rather violently. 'I didn't touch him. I . . . couldn't. All that blood . . .'

'What did you do then?'

'Well, I started back to my car to call . . . and then I saw the patrol car coming along, so I flagged it down. It was really lucky they were going by just then, wasn't it?'

'Yes,' George agreed, glancing at Susie, who looked away. 'It was.'

George frowned – it was more than lucky, it was damned odd. Susie and Duff had no reason to be out that far from the middle of town. He opened his mouth to speak, but a glance from Tilly stopped him. He'd clear that up later, he promised himself.

'And you know the rest,' Otis finished.

'Do you have any idea why Mr Armstrong would want to see you out there at the site?' George asked.

Otis shook his head. 'No. None at all. I can't see what it would have to do with the election and that's all I'm paid for, to get him elected.' He paused. 'All I *was* paid for,' he amended. 'I've never lost a candidate before,' he added rather sadly. 'I don't know quite what the position is now. I suppose the party members will . . . it's too late to register another candidate . . .' He looked at George in some surprise. 'Looks like your boss wins after all.'

'Not really a win, is it?' George said quietly.

An odd expression crossed Otis's face. 'No, I don't suppose it is.' He smiled a little smile. 'Not yet, anyway. Jack's name will have already been printed on the ballot. You'd be surprised how many people are dumb enough to vote for a dead man. One won, once – can't remember where now. They just vote for the party, never look at the names.' He shook his head at the thought.

'Do you know of anyone who might have wanted Mr Armstrong dead?' George asked.

'Your boss,' Otis said pointedly. 'And after last night, any number of people. The way they were shouting at him and so on – it was scary.'

'But most of that was just heat of the moment,' George said hurriedly. 'I meant *serious* enemies – people from his past, that kind of thing.'

Otis shook his head. 'I didn't know him all that well. I was just a hired gun, remember. I do this for a living, it was not a soul-mate kind of thing. I do remember asking him if there was anything in his past I should be worried about, or prepared for if it came out, and he said there wasn't as far as he knew. I had to leave it there. They're not always honest with me and they should be because ... well ... things come out, as Mr Clinton discovered. But Jack insisted everything was okay, so I accepted it. I really had no alternative. He hired me to do a job and I've been doing it. End of story.'

'Did you get on well with Mr Armstrong?'

'I didn't kill him, if that's what you're asking,' Otis sounded defensive. 'I didn't know him well enough to want to kill him. He was my current golden goose.'

'You say you make your living as a campaign manager?'

'That's right,' Otis said with what seemed like pride. 'I am a professional researcher and speech writer as well. I've got a good record at it too. We were going to beat the hell out of your boss.'

'Were you?' George appeared mildly interested.

'Oh, yes.' Otis seemed very sure.

'Not any more,' George put in, before he could stop himself.

'No, not any more.' Again, that odd expression on Otis's face. 'You guys play hardball up here.'

'What do you mean by that, Mr Otis?' George asked.

'Oh, nothing,' Otis answered. 'It just seems kind of lucky for you that Jack is dead.'

George looked furious and started to stand up, then got himself under control. He spoke through gritted teeth.

'You really think the position of sheriff of one of the smallest counties in a mid-western state is worth killing for, Mr Otis?'

'You'd be surprised what people kill for,' Otis said. 'What they care about, put their money on, put their lives on for that matter. Jack wanted to be sheriff.'

'Why?' George asked.

'As a stepping stone,' Otis replied. 'He wanted to move up in politics and he seemed to think sheriff was a good place to start. High profile, made him look strong on law and order, that kind of thing.'

George was startled. 'I never thought of it that way.'

'Well, perhaps that's the difference,' Otis commented. 'You're a lawman, Jack was a politician. He knew you got covered by the city papers pretty often—'

'More often than we want,' Tilly said wryly.

'Whatever.' Otis waved a hand negligently. 'He felt he could make a mark, then move on. Matt would have got his job back next time, probably.'

'So that's what it was.'

'What what was?'

'His reason for running.'

'As far as I know.' Otis's face was neutral.

'And nothing to do with the kind of power he might have on the Town Council, maybe to get his housing project passed, or anything like that?' George asked.

Otis looked from one to the other. 'I have no idea what you mean.'

George turned off the recorder. 'We'll have that transcribed and you can sign it, Mr Otis, then that will be it for a while. The inquest will be in a couple of days and you'll need to stay around to testify at that because you were the first on the scene.'

'You mean, don't leave town because you suspect me?' Otis asked rather archly.

'I mean don't leave town as we may need to verify things with you or ask you about things concerning Mr Armstrong,' George responded. 'That's all.'

Otis stood up. 'I suppose I'd better go and give my condolences to the grieving widow,' he said reluctantly.

'I'd give it a day or two,' George suggested.

'Yes,' Susie agreed. 'Or at least until they remove all the small objects from her bedside.'

ELEVEN

'NO, MATT . . . IT CAN'T BE.' Daria looked at him in dismay.

'I'm afraid it's the only way it can be,' Matt told her. 'If I stay on the case, people might think I'm covering my own crime. So George has to take over.'

Daria hated seeing him in a hospital bed like this. Too much like finding him there because he'd been shot or beaten up. Diabetes was nothing compared with that, but he looked vulnerable and weary just the same. 'So you can't have anything to do with the case? Nothing at all?'

'Not directly, no. I can't interview people, gather evidence, any of the usual things. I have to sit at home and wait for George to come up with the answer.'

'Oh, my God,' groaned Daria, walking round in circles between the bed and the window. Her heels clicked an agitated staccato on the linoleum.

'I can always talk to George on the telephone, I suppose,' Matt mused.

'Well, that's it!' Daria said, coming back towards him. 'You can direct things over the—'

'I don't think George will like that.' Matt was rather amused at her ire.

'Matt! You're not taking this seriously.'

'Oh, I am, I am. Believe me, I am. But if George is in charge of the case, he has to be *seen* to be in charge and he has to *feel* he's in charge. It will be good experience for him.'

'But it will look so bad . . .' wailed Daria.

113

'Not at all. I asked Tilly to stop by the *Chronicle* office and give the story to Emily Gibbons. I am withdrawing from the case because I am ill and because I am under the same kind of suspicion as any other citizen in town. I feel it is the honest thing to do, etc. etc. Emily is a decent girl, she'll write it up sympathetically. Tilly thinks people will be impressed by my honesty and sense of fair play.' His mouth twitched.

'Hell's bells!' Daria shouted, which startled him. He'd never heard her raise her voice before. 'You're out of your mind!'

'No, I am innocent, that's all. It's a matter of clarifying the situation before people begin whispering and conjecturing, which will hurt my reputation even more, believe me. Can't you see that?'

She stared at him. 'I suppose . . . when you put it that way . . .'

'Exactly. George will do all right.' He crossed his fingers under the sheets. 'Somebody stole my gun while I was unconscious, that's all.'

'And that could have been anybody.'

'Yes, except that this particular "anybody" deliberately used it to kill Armstrong, presumably with the full intention of making me look guilty. The same way somebody stole Frog Bartlett's wrench to kill Moony and make Frog look guilty. There's a pattern there, Daria. I'll mention that when I make my statement.'

'You have to make a statement?'

'Well, of course. I'm a suspect – remember?'

'Oh, my God,' Daria said. 'I can't believe this is happening.'

Matt reached out and put his arms round her. 'Think of all the extra time we'll have together.'

'The hell with that,' Daria mumbled into his pyjama pocket. 'If you can't do anything about this case, then I will.'

He pushed her back and held her by the shoulders. 'And what do you mean by that?'

She sniffed and wiped her eyes with the back of her hand. 'I don't know – yet.' Her eyes brightened. 'I know – I'll get George to swear me in as a deputy.'

'Daria . . .'

'Or something,' she said miserably, coming back into his arms. 'Somebody has to do *some*thing, Matt. It's ridiculous. You're innocent, dammit.'

'Well, then, we haven't anything to worry about, have we?' Matt tried to speak confidently. But it was a poor effort. Even he didn't believe him.

'This is ridiculous,' Tilly hissed out of the corner of her mouth as she and Susie stood by the coffee maker, filling the filter for a fresh brew. 'George can't handle this.'

'Well, maybe he can,' Susie whispered back, glancing over her shoulder. 'Maybe he's just never had a chance before.'

'Oh, he's had chances before,' Tilly said in a strangled voice. 'One time Matt went to a conference in Chicago for sheriffs from all over the country and George arrested half the town for everything from double parking to walking on the grass in Heckman Memorial Park. By the time Matt got back the circuit judge was mad as hell, having to deal with all the little misdemeanours, and George was still strutting around like a randy rooster in a henhouse, eyeing everybody in town in case they sneezed out of turn. Took weeks to clear up.'

'Oh. But he might take this more seriously. I mean, he was reluctant to do it.'

'He was only caught off-balance,' Tilly said uncompromisingly. 'The minute it began to sink in, did you see his face change? I wouldn't be surprised if he threw Matt in jail as soon as he gets out of the hospital.'

'Oh, come on,' Susie protested.

'Well,' Tilly conceded. 'Maybe he's not dumb enough for that, but . . .'

'I'm sure George will be fine,' Susie stated with more conviction than was required.

Tilly eyed her. 'Just because he's pretty . . .' she began.

Susie drew herself up. 'I hope you don't think I'm that foolish.'

'No,' Tilly said. 'I don't think you are. Nobody does. Listen – we're going to have to help George.'

'Help him? How?'

'Well, sort of guide him along without him noticing, if you get my meaning.'

Susie stared at her. 'I beg your pardon?'

Tilly lowered her voice even further, causing Susie to come closer. 'I can watch out for him here, but you'll have to sort of pull him up if he gets loose outside anywheres and turn him in the right directions if he starts going off half-cocked, which is more than likely. It won't be easy. George kind of resents that you have a college degree and all.'

'Well, that's too bad, but I can't get rid of it now,' Susie said. 'I am what I am.'

'Mm. On the other hand, I think he's kind of sweet on you, too, which could help.'

'Well . . . I guess I can handle George.' Susie wore a very small smile.

Tilly turned to look straight at her. 'Done a bit of baby-sitting in your time, have you?'

Susie's smile widened. 'Lots. And I have two little brothers too.'

'That's what I like.' Tilly turned back to the coffee maker. 'Qualifications.'

'You're making that up,' Mrs Toby said to Daria that evening. It was the bi-weekly gathering of the Blackwater Bay Magpies and they were in Mrs Toby's kitchen, getting the refreshments ready.

'I wish I were.' Daria sighed. 'Matt has to turn the case over to George Putnam because Matt could be considered as a suspect. It was his gun – the ballistics came through already – although it had been stolen from him some time during the previous night.'

'That's what he *says*,' said Mrs Norton, laying cookies out on platters.

Daria whirled on her. 'That's what happened! That's what *must* have happened!'

'Now, now.' Mrs Norton's voice was calm. 'I didn't mean I didn't believe it – of course I do – but others might not. You have to be prepared for that. Not everybody in this town thinks Matt Gabriel is the end-all and be-all that we do.'

'Well, he is.' Daria wiped a tear from her cheek. 'He's a good, honest man and this is just terrible for him.'

'Of course he was *framed*,' said Mrs Toby. 'That's perfectly clear.'

'Well, of course,' agreed Mrs Norton, reaching for another tin box of cookies. She had an admirable collection of these old tin biscuit boxes from England, which kept her baked goods crisp or soft, depending on which she wanted. Her niece in London sent a new one over every Christmas and they made a colourful display in the kitchen.

'I wish there was something I could do.' Daria poured fresh water into the coffee maker and put another kettle on the stove for making tea. 'I left Matt just lying there in that hospital bed, watching television. I went in to feed Max just before I came here and I swear that cat was depressed too.'

'Max is a very unusual cat,' Mrs Toby said crisply, setting out cups and saucers on the trays. 'Matt might have done better to turn the case over to *him* instead of George.'

Daria managed a laugh, but not a very long one.

'*We*'ll just have to take over,' Nell Norton stated, snapping the last empty tin shut. 'George will never manage on his own.'

'What do you mean, "take over"?' Daria asked. 'I said to Matt that I should become a deputy, but he just got cross.'

'Well, Matt doesn't have to know, does he?' Nell brushed crumbs off the counter into her hand and dropped them into the waste disposal. 'There's you and Margaret and me,

117

and we could rope in . . . let's see . . . Larry and Freddy . . . Snakehips Turkle knows a lot of really disreputable people . . . and maybe we could get in touch with Kate and Jack . . . oh, I know lots of people who would help.'

'To do what?' Daria asked in a bewildered voice.

'Why, solve the Armstrong case before it does any real harm to Matt's chances for re-election, of course,' Nell said briskly. 'George is a nice enough boy, but he's never exactly shone with a bright light, if you know what I mean. He's eager all right, heaven knows, but he needs reining in and without Matt to keep him in line . . . well . . . it could be nasty. He might be forced to arrest Matt because he can't find the real killer.'

'What about Dominic Pritchard? And Emily Gibbons?' Margaret Toby suggested. 'They could be very useful.'

Daria sighed and shook her head. 'Emily would help if she could, I expect, but poor Dominic is caught up with trying to defend Frog Bartlett, remember? I understand from Matt that's not going too well either.'

Nell snagged a snickerdoodle off one of the platters and munched it while she thought. 'Well, why don't we take on *both* cases?'

The other ladies looked at her and one another.

'We're not exactly professionals,' Mrs Toby said tentatively.

'We're not exactly stupid either,' snapped Nell. 'If we can ask questions about one, we can ask questions about the other.'

'I suppose next you'll be wanting us to wear special suits with capes,' Mrs Toby said waspishly.

'That was unworthy of you, Margaret.' Nell sounded reproachful.

'Or slouch hats and raincoats.' Mrs Toby was on a roll.

'That's enough, Margaret.' Nell's tone was firm.

'I thought it was funny,' Mrs Toby said in a hurt voice. 'Everybody's so serious, all of a sudden.'

'It's a serious situation,' Daria said. 'Believe me, if you'd seen Matt this afternoon—'

'That's settled, then.' Nell Norton was brisk. She picked up a tray of cookies and headed towards the sitting-room. 'We'll start recruiting people tomorrow. And Tilly can liaise with George.'

'Poor Tilly,' commented Margaret.

TWELVE

'YOU HAVE TO ADMIT IT'S a possibility,' Dominic was saying to George Putnam at that very minute.

'I don't have to admit anything,' George said stubbornly. His tour of duty had ended at six, but he was so increasingly enamoured of the prospect of being in charge that he'd stayed on, casting an authoritative eye over the night staff as they came on duty. He made sure they knew the position all right. 'Moony Packard was killed weeks ago and he probably didn't even know Jack Armstrong personally. They didn't exactly move in the same circles, you know.'

'I realize that,' Dominic said in exasperation. 'But there could be some connection we don't know about.'

'How can we investigate what we don't know?' George asked, thinking to stun Dominic with this irrefutable logic.

'Isn't that what investigating is all about – finding out what you don't know?' countered Dominic.

'Not exactly,' George said. 'There's a routine, there's regular lines of enquiry, basic stuff that you have to get out of the way . . .'

'Like what?'

'Like . . . background of the victim, like who benefits from the death, like who saw him last, like . . . all kinds of stuff. I got enough to do without trying to tie together two things out of left field that don't go together.'

'Then let me do it,' Dominic said eagerly.

'Do what?'

'Tie them together – if I can.'

George considered. 'How would you go about doing that?' he wanted to know, thinking he had Dominic cornered now. What did a kid lawyer know about investigation?

'Well, first of all, by talking to my client.'

'Your client?'

'Frog Bartlett.'

'Oh, hell, I forgot to get his damn dinner.' George got up. 'Here, Buncie – go over to the Golden Perch and get Frog's dinner, would you? Tell Harlow it goes on the county bill, like always.'

'Aw, George, I was just about—'

'It's got to be done, Buncie,' George said a little louder.

'Okay, okay. Do they know what to give him?'

'Yeah, Tilly took his order over this afternoon.'

Grumbling, Buncie went out, and his patrol partner sank back down on a chair and began reading the *Chronicle.* Main Street to Wilber to Greeley to US29 would have to get along without them for a while longer.

'I want to see Frog,' Dominic said, as George sat back down.

'*Before* he's had his dinner?' George asked comically, as if Dominic were offering to go into a lion's den.

'Oh, for crying out loud.' Dominic lost his patience with George at last.

'All right, all right.' George, tired of baiting him, got up again and went along to the rear of the building to let Dominic into Frog's presence. 'You want to get out in a hurry, just holler. I'm going for my dinner now. Somebody out there will come and let you out.'

'I was really worried,' Dominic said wryly.

Through the bars, Frog seemed about as dangerous as a sick puppy. He was slumped on his bunk, glancing through a gardening magazine. He looked up as Dominic was let into his cell. 'You got good news or bad news?' he wanted to know.

121

'I have no news,' Dominic admitted. 'Which I suppose counts as good news.'

'To some,' Frog allowed, putting aside his magazine. 'Sit.' Dominic sat.

'Well?' Frog asked.

'Jack Armstrong is dead,' Dominic began.

'I know. That was good news. I heard it already.'

'Why do you say it was good news?'

'Because he was a double-dealing, no-good, fat-headed twister,' Frog said. 'If he'da been elected sheriff I woulda hung myself right off, except that would have given him what he wanted, maybe, so I guess I wouldn't have at that.'

'I don't understand.'

'I heard you talking to George out there,' Frog said. 'You want to know if there was a connection between me and Jack Armstrong? You bet your ass there was. He's been after me to sell my house to him for the past year, done all he could to make life hard for me: threats, trouble, hassle, everything short of throwing me out with his own hands and I'm not sure he wasn't thinking on how to do that.' Frog grinned. The sight was a little unnerving, but Dominic bore it with equanimity. 'But I wouldn't give in to the bastard son of a bitch,' Frog continued. 'He used to get madder'n a wet hen. Even sent a couple of his little sweethearts to break me up a little. Bad idea. I broke them up a little instead.' Another grin. 'Poor babies.'

'I see. So you had a kind of feud with Armstrong?'

'I guess you could call it that. I sure as hell wasn't going to sell to him.'

'Why did he want your house?'

'Mine and a couple others in the street. We're right at the end and it woulda made his life a hell of a lot easier if we was to give in and sell up to him. It woulda saved him about a mile of rerouting drains and water and electricity lines and all the rest of it, plus giving his development a second access to town. Which would turn our street into a freeway, by the way, so me and some others said no. A few beyond us had already said yes, mind you, making him the proud owner of several properties he had no damn use for because we were still in the way. Hence . . .' Frog took a moment to savour this gracious language. 'Hence he was a mite frazzled.'

'I see. Did he hassle you enough to make you want to kill him?'

'Hell, no. Besides, I got an alibi, right? Best kind. In jail. No problem.'

'Did Armstrong have any connection with Moony Packard?' Dominic asked.

Frog looked puzzled. 'Not that I know of.' He brightened. 'Maybe he delivered his mail?'

'Maybe,' Dominic acknowledged. 'I can check that, I suppose, but it doesn't seem a very good reason for killing him.'

'Killing who?' Frog looked even more puzzled. 'Armstrong or Moony?'

Dominic shrugged. 'What I was thinking was, maybe the same person who killed Packard killed Armstrong. If so, obviously it wasn't you.'

'Because of my cast-iron gold-plated alibi,' Frog agreed. 'But who would it be?'

'That's what I'm trying to figure out. I have to find a connection.'

'Oh.' Frog took a deep breath, then sighed it out. 'Can't see it, myself. I mean . . . what would Moony want with a cuss like Armstrong? They didn't belong to the same golf club or anything like that, Rotary or Kiwanis or the Algonawana Lodge or whatever. I don't think so, anyway. Do you?'

'No – but that's something else I can check. Armstrong didn't spend much time in the Golden Perch, did he?'

'No way. Not his kind of people,' Frog said. 'Nobody there he could take advantage of or make use of, see? And he didn't strike me like a beer drinker, much.'

'No, I suppose not.' Dominic stood up. 'Well, I'm going to work on this for a while. If you think of anything let me know right away.'

123

'What kind of thing?' Frog wanted to know.

Dominic shrugged. 'If I knew, I'd know where to start.'

Frog picked up the gardening magazine again. 'You were right.'

'About what?'

'No news.'

The news about Matt Gabriel's suspension travelled fast and by morning the whole town seemed to know about it.

At the bookshop, Helen Pollock was as shocked as anyone. 'As if people would think he did anything wrong.' She addressed Lisa Cummings. 'Matt Gabriel is the most honest man in town.'

'Power corrupts,' Lisa said in a flat voice. The fact that Matt Gabriel had pulled her up for speeding several times, finally replacing the warnings with a summons, had soured her somewhat on the subject of law and order.

'Well, it's never corrupted Matt.' Helen turned away from Lisa. 'I'm going to sort things out in the stock-room.'

'Oh, I can do that,' Lisa said brightly. 'You stay here and serve the customers.'

'No, thanks. I'll do it myself – I told you, I want to know what's going on in my shop.' Helen smiled. 'You attend to the customers – you've got some waiting now.'

Lisa turned to see two people standing by the register with books in their hands. 'Oh – sorry.' She walked over to serve them. With a sigh, Helen went back towards the stock-room, stopping by the office to see if there was anything special Muriel wanted her to do.

'No, thanks – I'm just about caught up with things for once,' Muriel said, leaning back and reaching for her omnipresent coffee mug, which was steaming gently on a table beside her. 'What do you want to do about Mr Armstrong's special order?'

'What special order was that?'

'I'm not sure – Lisa handled it. It's only down as "Special

Order" on the computer, which is a bit odd. His wife is in the clinic, isn't she? She wouldn't want them delivered there.'

'No,' Helen agreed. 'In fact, I don't suppose she wants them at all, whatever they are. Politics, probably.'

'Well, should I send them back to the supplier?'

'I don't know,' Helen said vaguely. She ran her hands through her hair in exasperation. 'Lisa will not pay attention to our rules – she orders willy-nilly, has some sort of code of her own as far as I can tell . . . it's very upsetting. If she weren't so very good with the customers . . .'

'I know. They all like her. And she is very knowledgeable about books and authors, she keeps up with the reviews and all.'

'Yes – but does she ever read the books themselves?' Helen asked, raising an eyebrow. 'I really doubt it. She has the new attitude: books are like potatoes, you sell them the same way. Which isn't true at all. Not for me, anyhow. But then, maybe I'm old-fashioned.'

'And thank heaven for it.' Muriel put down her now empty coffee mug. 'A good bookshop needs a good owner at the heart of it.'

'Hm – which is fine, as long as one of those big chains doesn't decide to stake out a branch in Blackwater Bay,' Helen said. 'I couldn't begin to compete with their volume discounts.'

'I wonder,' Muriel mused. 'There's a lot of loyalty in this town. I noticed the other day that now the first rush of excitement is over, there aren't so many people at the new mall as there were in the beginning. They're coming back to the old shops again.'

'We had a close call, there,' Helen said. 'One of the chains wanted one of the larger units. Fortunately they came too late. But if the shop that took it fails, they might be first in with an offer. And then what would we do?'

'What we've always done, offer a personal service. By the way, those books Dominic Pritchard ordered can be here by Friday – I had a word with the wholesaler and they're putting through a special order.'

'Oh, that's wonderful.' Helen was pleased.

'Well, I know the manager pretty well,' Muriel said modestly. 'I told him it was a matter of life and death – which, in a way, it is. Or would be, if the state still had the death sentence. Apparently he'd heard about the case and he's big on justice for the little people.'

'You *do* know him well.'

Muriel flushed slightly. 'We used to date in high school,' she confided. 'It's not *what* you know, but . . .'

'Amen.' Helen smiled. She turned to go to the stockroom. 'I'll check out that Armstrong shipment. If it's something we might be able to sell, I'll put them out. Otherwise they might as well go back where they came from. I assume they were on "sale or return", as usual?'

'I imagine so.' Muriel got up. 'Do you want some coffee while you're working? It gets pretty dusty out there.'

'Maybe later.' Helen went through the door at the back of the shop into the crowded area where they kept newly arrived stock.

Space is always at a premium in any shop and in a bookshop the problem is as bad as in a grocery. Books have to be ordered in multiples, and then there are the point-of-sale stands and placards, returns boxed and waiting to be shipped back, and all the other impedimenta of a flourishing establishment. Bookery Nook was the only bookshop in Blackwater Bay and, what with being a 'tourist' town in a sense of being seasonally active in the summer but incredibly inactive in the winter, there were many readers. The library did good business too, but Blackwater Bay folks seemed to like to buy books – mostly paperback, it's true – and keep them on their shelves for visitors to take to the beach in the summer. There was a seasonal pattern to the buying – more serious tomes in winter, when one could curl up and concentrate, followed by a boom in silly 'airport'-type novels in the summer, when the heat made it difficult to keep your mind on anything except what to put on the barbecue or pack for the picnic. Gardening books came in for a rush in spring, do-it-yourself manuals in the autumn. And so on. Lately there had been a greatly increased interest in craft books of all kinds, particularly needlework, pottery and woodwork. Helen loved it all and wished she had time to read every book she had for sale. Alas, it was like the cobbler's children – she was often the last to read the current best-seller.

She sighed and looked around the cluttered space, the boxes stacked high on either side of the narrow aisle. Where was that box she had noticed the other day, the one Lisa had said was for Jack Armstrong? After some shuffling and sliding, she found it tucked into a back corner and lifted it out into the light. The supplier was Dutch – not a familiar name. They got many beautiful art and gardening books from Holland, but this was a new company as far as she was concerned.

Using a short, sharp knife kept for the purpose, she slit the tape holding the top flaps shut and reached into the box to draw out the top item.

After a long, long moment, she carefully put it back and reached for another. And another. Then, just as carefully, she took a roll of tape from a nearby shelf and resealed the box. Reaching up, she pulled the chain for the light, bringing the room into complete darkness. Turning, she went along the narrow aisle by touch and back into the sudden brightness of the shop, blinking rapidly. She didn't look into the office, but headed straight for the sales counter.

'Lisa,' she said quietly. 'I want to talk to you.'

THIRTEEN

SARAH MARSH TOOK A PAN of muffins out of the oven and closed the door with her knee, wincing as she did when a creak of arthritis reminded her that her joints weren't what they used to be. She made muffins frequently, also cakes and cookies, for she hated to have an empty cupboard when people came round. People came round fairly often, for Miss Marsh had been a popular English teacher at Heckman High School before her retirement.

Despite her frumpy appearance, or perhaps because of it, her students had invariably felt strong affection for the woman who guided them through Homer and Dickens and Shakespeare and, sometimes, Faulkner, depending on what she thought a class could take in its stride. Not many ran to Faulkner, it's true, but she made sure that she exposed them to much that was good in twentieth-century literature as well as the classics. She'd had a knack for making the most difficult text accessible and alive – a rare ability even more rarely seen today – and for finding the central nerve and hidden depths in lighter offerings. When a student was particularly promising and bright, she augmented the syllabus with P.G. Wodehouse and some of the better crime novels as a reward.

The fact that she had retired early had been a great disappointment to many of her students, who had looked forward to her teaching their children in turn. But several kept in touch and often came to see Miss Marsh for advice on how to handle their teenagers. Nobody was ever turned away from Sarah Marsh's door.

So Dominic Pritchard was greeted with a smile and the smell of fresh-baked cranberry muffins, and found himself relaxing in Miss Marsh's friendly kitchen, as had many before him.

'Just in time for elevenses,' Sarah said briskly. 'My mother was an Englishwoman, and I always have elevenses and four o'clock tea. Except I prefer coffee. Is coffee all right for you?'

'Yes, please.' Dominic put his briefcase under the table and loosened his tie slightly. 'Cream, no sugar.'

'Glad to see you're not into this skimmed-milk business,' she said over her shoulder as she took cream from the refrigerator. 'Altogether too much fuss about it, if you ask me. And it tastes like chalk water too.'

'I boarded for a while with Mrs Peach,' Dominic said and that was sufficient explanation.

'My goodness, then I'll have to look to my laurels. That woman is a magician in the kitchen.'

'Took me months to get my waistline back to normal.' Dominic chuckled. 'But it was worth it.'

When they were settled with steaming mugs of coffee and a plate of the fresh muffins between them on the big oak table, Sarah sat back and looked at him. 'What have you got to tell me, then?' she asked.

'You know about Jack Armstrong's death.'

'Oh, yes.' Her eyes widened. 'Now you're not going to tell me they're blaming that on Frog?'

'No, of course not. But it occurred to me that there might be a connection. That the same person might have killed both Moony Packard and Jack Armstrong. For some reason, the same person might have wanted the two of them dead. Maybe they both knew something or someone . . .'

'Good heavens, that's quite a leap.'

'Well, two murders fairly close together and both apparently without motive—'

'Surely there were plenty of motives where Armstrong was concerned?'

'Yes, but nothing very specific. People either seemed to like him or hate him, with very little in between.'

'He wasn't a nice man.'

'No, I know that.'

'He was a politician.'

'Well, he was starting to be.'

'Only officially. He was *always* manipulative, even as a boy. I had him in one of my last classes before I retired. Full of charm, full of guile, full of . . . whatever you think politicians are full of.' She smiled. 'He liked to get his own way, managed it most of the time. Except when it came to getting elected president of the senior class. Matt Gabriel beat him out there.'

'Really?' Dominic looked speculative. Was this another reason for Armstrong's deciding to run against Matt? Another election, another challenge? This time round, Armstrong had *really* lost. But Matt had lost too – unless George was able to find out who killed Armstrong – because he was under suspicion.

Sarah reached for a muffin and broke it open. Steam rose slightly from the two tender halves. 'Yes. Young Jack thought he had it "in the bag", but it was not to be. Everyone he'd thought he had under his thumb proved to be more slippery than he had realized. He hated Matt after that, made no secret of it either.'

'Did he ever do anything to him? I mean – were there fights? That sort of thing?'

'Oh, no . . . that wasn't Jack's way. He just made life difficult for Matt in every way he could . . . little things . . . little lies, little slurs, little conspiracies, that sort of thing. And always behind Matt's back. By the end he'd taken most of the pleasure of being president away from Matt and that seemed to satisfy him. Then he went away to college and didn't come back afterwards. Not until recently, that is – when he had lots of money and could make an entrance, as it were.' She shook her head. 'He was a great disappointment to me, but some people are just mean-natured, no matter how much they smile in

130

public. Most people couldn't see past those tiger smiles, but I could. Some others could too. I don't *think* he would have beaten Matt for the sheriff's job, but he would have made it a close-run thing.' She sipped coffee. 'Frankly, I'm glad he's dead. He certainly would have turned very nasty if he'd won and worse if he'd lost.'

Dominic was learning more and more about Jack Armstrong, but it seemed to spread the net of suspicion further, rather than pulling in any suspects. 'He returned to Blackwater Bay before I came here,' he said. 'What was the general reaction to him?'

'Well, he came bearing gifts, didn't he? What do you think? He bought land nobody thought was worth anything and built a small housing development and then that new mall in record time. He gave money to the town, made money for the town. People were impressed. He had about five years, in all, for building up his position. He was about to reap the results.'

'By becoming sheriff?'

'By putting himself into a position of power,' Sarah said rather sardonically. 'And, for his own satisfaction, by beating Matt. That was a side issue, but I'm sure it afforded him pleasure just to think about it.'

She *really* hadn't liked Jack Armstrong, Dominic thought, looking at her set face. Could *she* be a suspect? The idea was preposterous, yet the scene of the crime wasn't so very far from her house. She could have walked to the site of the proposed development in less than ten minutes. And back, without anyone noticing particularly. It was, after all, her own neighbourhood.

'Did Armstrong try to buy your house?' Dominic asked.

She smiled. 'Yes, of course he did. And Frog's. And Mrs Johnson's, Mr Webster's, Mrs Spolini's and lots of others in the street. Frog and I wouldn't sell, although Armstrong had been certain we would. So certain he bought several others before getting around to us. He offered us a lot of money – more than the places were worth. But the land was what he was after. The houses would have been bulldozed in a moment.' She got up to refresh their coffee. 'I was born in this house, Frog was born in his. They aren't much, but they are definitely ours and we were not about to sacrifice them so that Mr Armstrong could have convenient access for his little ticky-tacky housing development. Why should we?'

'Does it seem very far-fetched to you that the same person might have killed Moony Packard and Armstrong?' Dominic asked.

'A bit,' she admitted, sitting back down and passing him the cream, along with nudging the plate of muffins towards him in silent encouragement. 'I can't see that there would be any connection between the two deaths – except in time.'

'Well, there is something else,' Dominic said. 'In both cases, the murder was arranged so as to make it look as if someone else had done it. Somebody took Frog's wrench to brain Moony Packard and somebody stole Matt's gun to kill Jack Armstrong. I think they would call it the same *modus operandi* in a sense, although the actual murders were different. So it *might* be the same person.'

Sarah considered this. 'Maybe. Maybe. You have to look at who benefits, don't you? Nobody really benefited from Moony's death – except maybe his brother Frank – but Frank was better off with Moony alive, as he was the only one bringing in a steady income. He didn't get robbed and nothing was taken from his mail sack.'

'But it was premeditated, because somebody stole Frog's wrench to do it. We can't say it was a random killing now, can we?'

'I don't suppose we can. A lot of people benefited from Armstrong's death – his wife because of the money, Matt because of the election and anybody else he might have crossed because of lots of reasons we don't even know about. I know he pressured a number of people to sell their land for that mall, and for that development out there.' She gestured towards the end of the road. 'Now the land the mall is on or near is worth a lot more than it ever was, far more than he paid for it, that's certain. Same with the land for that housing development. Two good farms went under for that and now where are they? One family is living in a little house in Lemonville, the other I don't know where they are. But both men lost their reason for living, I do know that, and all because Armstrong pressured them through their wives to sell up. Sweet talk sounds good to a hard-worked farm wife, believe me. Both women put living in a new house with all modern conveniences and little to do but watch TV all day against the drudgery of farm life. It wasn't much of a contest. *They* pushed the sale through. But it was Armstrong's doing.'

'Who were they?' Dominic asked, taking out his electronic notepad.

'The family in Lemonville are called Ashworth and the other family were named Platt. I don't know where they are now. It broke my heart to see those farms go under – it was beautiful land and now it's just dust and nothing.' She looked angry. 'What do you suppose will happen to the development?'

'I have no idea. I believe Mrs Armstrong inherits pretty much everything – she'll have to decide.'

'Then nothing,' Sarah said firmly. 'It will just go to weeds.'

'She might sell it to another developer,' Dom suggested. 'It might be put to some good use.'

She sighed. 'I suppose so. It couldn't be worse than what he planned.'

'By refusing to sell you had apparently forced Armstrong to redesign the development – you and Frog. Set him back months and it was going to cost him a lot of money.'

'He made that very clear,' Sarah said. 'He sent some very unpleasant people round to emphasize what we were costing him. Tried to scare us, said they would build on the land they had in this block already, some kind of juvenile facility or mental home or whatever – saying they'd pretty well destroy our peace of mind somehow or other. Or maybe put up a mini-mall where teenagers

133

would hang out, a pool hall, that kind of thing. In the end he had to let it go, but I could tell it rankled with him. He practically snarled at us in the street.' She smiled. 'We had him blocked and wouldn't move. I think it's called dumb insolence in the Army. Frog loved it. I have to admit I did too. Not very admirable, is it?'

'Depends on your point of view.' Dominic grinned. 'Personally, I'd also have enjoyed it.'

'We aren't very nice people, are we?' Sarah said. 'Have another muffin.'

'Okay, Tyrone, I want you to think back,' George said. (George was in charge. George was being forceful, thrusting and professional. According to George, that is.)

According to Tyrone Molt he was being a pain in the ass.

'I thought back.' Tyrone cast a glance around his used car lot in the hope of spotting a vict— that is to say, a prospective client. Tyrone never thought of them as victims. At least, not out loud. 'All's I remember is a lot of shouting and shoving, and then old Berringer getting his leg broke. He's suing me, you know. Not my fault he was standing there. I never saw him. Can't blame me.'

'You did lose your temper, Tyrone, you can't deny that,' George said.

'I'm *not* denying it.' Tyrone was defensive. 'I'm just saying I don't remember anything about Matt's gun being took. I didn't take it, I know that damn well. I got a gun of my own,' he added and, when George opened his mouth, 'yes, I got a licence for it too, all legal. Got to protect my business, got to have something by me when I take the day's money to the bank, don't I? I *need* my gun.' When George opened his mouth again, Tyrone went on firmly, 'What I *don't* need is anybody's else's gun.' George managed a slight croak preparatory to speech, but Tyrone rolled on: 'I sure don't need Matt's gun. Hardly a gun at all, that old .38 of his father's, although I guess now we know that it works all right. I

134

got me a Glock. Even shoots underwater, did you know that?'

'No, I . . . yes, I . . .' George managed. 'Listen, Tyrone . . .'

'I'm listening,' Tyrone said, turning to look up and down the road in case a dearly beloved customer might be bringing something in for repair, like a Rolls-Royce or a Mercedes. Hard to get parts for those foreign cars, had to charge extra and all that. The road was empty. 'Not that I go underwater that much,' Tyrone added reflectively.

'Stop that!' George shouted.

Molt turned to stare at him. 'Stop what?' He was truly mystified.

'Pay attention,' George commanded. 'I want you to tell me *exactly* what happened last night at that damn rally.'

'Well, jeez, George, you were there yourself. You saw.'

'I was busy handling the crowd, I didn't see what was going on on the stage,' George thundered. 'How many people were up there? Who were they? What did they do, *exactly*?' A few small beads of perspiration had appeared on George's upper lip.

'Matt grabbed old Armstrong by the lapels,' Molt began, eyeing George warily. 'Then Berringer tried to get him to leave go and somebody else jumped up . . . I think it was Harry Foskett with his camera . . .' He chuckled to himself. 'That Harry, always ready for a shot for the paper.' George growled and Tyrone cleared his throat. 'Then a couple of Armstrong's goons got up there and one of them pushed me out of the way, and I got mad because he stepped on my foot – I got corns something terrible on my right foot – so I shoved back and then he shoved me again, and then Isaiah Naseem tried to get everybody to calm down—'

'Did Isaiah get up on the stage?' George interrupted.

'No, no, he just kind of danced around the edge. He's a pacifist, you know. Something to do with his religion. Of course, if you ask me, these foreign religions . . .' Catching a glint in George's eye as he was about to hold forth on the influence of religion on modern-day life, Tyrone rushed on: 'Um – then there was a bunch of people pushing me back; let's see, there was Lem Turkle, Frank Packard, Bob Matthew and maybe Jim, too, and Glen Hardwicke – he was there flashing his badge. I think Milly Hackabush started shrieking about then and there was a couple of others I don't know who they were, from out of town maybe, and Duff Bradley pitched in, and then one of the Rumplemeyer boys – I think it was Weasel – started swinging and caught me one on the shoulder so that was when I picked up the chair and threw it . . . thinking to cause a distraction, you understand . . . and unfortunately it hit Berringer in the knee and he went down, and then everybody crowded around him because my Lord that man can scream and cuss, and it all sort of gets mixed up after that. I felt real bad about Berringer, I got nothing against him, other than that he's an idiot, of course, but Matt was telling everybody to back off and he kneeled down beside Berringer . . .' Molt paused. 'Maybe that was when it happened,' he said reflectively.

'What, what?' asked George, who had been writing names frantically in his notebook. 'What happened?'

'Well, Matt was on his knees, like I said, and his gun, it was stuck right up in its holster, you know, the way it would do, and then everybody was fussing over Berringer so maybe that was when somebody took Matt's gun. Because he was worried about Berringer, preoccupied you might say, and I was sort of . . . well, there was nothing I could do, so I sort of . . . tried to help get the rest of the people out of the door,' he concluded self-righteously. 'To avert panic,' he added importantly.

'You mean you ran off,' George said unsympathetically.

'I never did. I hung around for a while,' Molt protested. 'Listen, I got a customer over there looking at a '96 Chevy I been trying to get rid of. That's all I remember, George, honest.'

'Maybe you took the gun yourself – that's why you left in such a hurry,' George said with a masterful glower. 'Maybe you followed Matt out of the hall, saw he was not feeling well and took his gun from him then.'

Molt took deep offence. 'I did *not*! Why would I do that?'

'Maybe you thought Armstrong was too dangerous an opponent in the election. Maybe you thought it might be a good way of getting rid of both of them, kill one, pin it on the other.'

'Hah!' Molt said. 'They didn't worry me none.'

'Maybe he knew something he was going to tell about you that you didn't want him to tell,' George suggested, fixing Molt with what he hoped was a beady eye. It was a blue eye, certainly, but its beadiness was questionable, although George was trying hard.

'Everybody knows me.' Tyrone looked furtive now. 'I got nothing to hide.'

'Are you sure about that?'

Molt glanced around to see if anyone was nearby. 'What have you heard?' he asked in a low voice.

'Oh . . . I hear stuff all the time,' George said smugly. He had him on the run now all right, all right.

'That stuff about Dolly Boot and me is a god-damn lie,' Molt mumbled. 'Anybody knows me knows that.'

'Uh-huh,' said George, looking wise.

'And that bookie Haven, it's his word against mine,' Molt went on. 'There's nothing writ down whatsoever.'

'Right.' George nodded.

'As for the Rumplemeyer girl . . .'

'Which one?' George asked quickly. He knew two or three of the Rumplemeyer girls quite well. One very well.

Molt drew back and smiled a crocodile smile. 'You don't know, do you?'

'Know what?' George blurted out before he could stop himself.

Molt tapped the side of his nose. 'Ah ha,' he said, and walked away towards the man and woman who were circling the Chevy.

'Oh, shit,' George muttered and shut his notebook.

FOURTEEN

HELEN POLLOCK CAME INTO THE sheriff's office looking very distracted.

Susie Brock was behind the counter and she sensed right away that there was something wrong. 'Are you all right, Mrs Pollock?' she asked anxiously, knowing the woman's history of ill health.

'Oh, I'm fine, dear, just fine,' Helen assured her. 'Is Matt about anywhere?'

'He's still in the hospital,' Susie said.

'Oh, yes, I heard about that. And about him not working on the Armstrong case. Seems so silly, all that. As if he would kill anyone.'

'Is it something I can help with?' Susie asked.

'Well – I'd really rather talk to Matt.'

Susie didn't want to push. Sometimes people came in just wanting to chat because they were lonely, although she didn't think Mrs Pollock was one of those. There was definitely something on her mind and when she was ready she'd no doubt come out with it. Occasionally people had to come back twice or three times before they got up courage to talk about something that embarrassed or upset them. Not wanting to appear foolish was a very human trait. 'I understand. You've known him a long time.'

'Oh, I've nothing against you, dear . . .' Helen flushed.

'I know you don't.' Susie smiled. 'I'll tell Matt you came in and want to see him. I expect he'll come over to the bookshop as soon as he's up and about.'

138

'Oh. Good. That would be best, after all,' Helen said, brightening a little. 'There's something he should *see*.'

'I'll tell him,' Susie promised. 'The minute I spot him.'

'It won't work unless we *all* do it.' Mrs Toby looked around at the people gathered in her living-room.

'Yes, that's what usually goes wrong in the books,' Mrs Norton put in. 'You see, one person, the amateur detective, goes around asking questions, and people get suspicious and he ends up getting beat up in an alley.'

'Oh, swell,' said Larry Lovich. 'That's a nice prospect.'

'Hush, let them finish.' Freddy Tollett pushed his partner's arm impatiently.

'Stop that,' Larry snapped.

'Well, then, listen,' Freddy snapped back. They were not in a good mood, having had a spat about clotted cream after dinner. Larry thought they should introduce it at Just Desserts in a real English afternoon tea service and Freddy felt American desserts were good enough for him, thank you, and they should be good enough for their customers too. This was the first time they had spoken to one another since arriving.

'I don't know what the hell I'm even doing here,' complained Snakehips (Sam) Turkle.

'You're our low-life expert,' Mrs Toby said.

'Well, gee, thanks.' Snakehips grinned, rather gratified at the title. 'Nice to know I'm good for something.'

'What does that make me?' Emily Gibbons asked. 'High-life expert? In which case you've got the wrong girl. I'm shy, I lead a cloistered life, you know.' She grinned at them.

'No, I want you to be our co-ordinator because your office is right in the middle of town,' Mrs Toby said.

'Oh.' Emily was slightly deflated.

'Maybe I'd just better start at the beginning,' Mrs Toby continued.

'Good idea.' Daria Grey raised an eyebrow, quelling further remarks from those gathered.

'As you know, Matt Gabriel has been suspended from

duty and is still in the hospital,' Mrs Toby said. 'Which leaves George Putnam in charge.' A few groans were heard. 'Now George is a good man,' Mrs Toby went on firmly. 'But he's young and inexperienced.'

'And an idiot,' somebody said.

'No, not really. Not if you explain things carefully enough,' Mrs Norton contradicted. 'The trouble is getting him to listen.'

'May I continue?' Mrs Toby asked in a rather icy tone.

'Continue,' Mrs Norton said grandly.

'Thank you. Matt needs help. He needs *our* help. I talked to Tilly Moss about this and she agrees. She'd be here herself but her mother is poorly. Now, as Nell said, in the books one amateur sleuth goes around asking questions and that raises suspicion. But if we *all* go around asking questions, sort of casually, you know, well then it might not raise any kind of suspicion at all, because nobody will make any connection. We'll each ask different questions of different people at different times. See?'

'What kind of questions?' Larry wanted to know.

'Well, we have to break it down. The idea is to cover all the areas of the investigations to see if we can come up with any information that will help George. Tilly can then sort of . . . insert it . . . into his mind for us. She's used to George and she knows how he thinks.'

'Nice choice of words, "thinks".' Snakehips giggled. 'I don't know why Matt keeps him on.'

'George is *reliable*,' Mrs Toby said in the deputy's defence. 'He's loyal and he's strong.'

'He's not all that reliable,' Freddy put in. 'He goes off half-cocked at the least thing.'

'Yes, well . . . be that as it may. I am suggesting that we augment George's investigations, give him more eyes and ears than he has already, sort of unofficially help him out. We don't want this thing to hang over Matt's head any longer than it has to, do we?'

They all agreed that they didn't.

'You may have to spread the net wider than you think,'

Emily said slowly. When they all turned to look at her she blushed a bit. 'It's just that ... well ... you all know Dominic Pritchard.' Everyone nodded. 'He's defending Frog Bartlett and he believes there is a connection between the two murders. He thinks maybe they were committed by the same person.'

'Good Lord,' Mrs Norton said. 'What an idea!'

'Well, he has some good reasons for thinking that.' Emily proceeded to list them: the lack of apparent motive, the closeness in time and the fact that in each case an attempt was made to blame someone specific for the killing. 'And so I feel we ought to broaden our investigations to cover both murders.'

'Does that mean you think my plan is workable?' Mrs Toby asked, beaming at her.

'Oh, sure. As long as we don't trip over each other while we're being nosy,' Emily replied. 'In the city they have hundreds of police officers working on a murder. Here there's only George and a few deputies, and they have other things to do as well, like traffic and so on. We *can* be useful – even if George wouldn't admit it. But if he finds out ...'

'He mustn't find out,' Mrs Norton warned. 'That's why there's safety in numbers. For instance, Snakehips, you hang around the pool hall anyway ... so getting people talking about the murders shouldn't be any problem for you.'

'Hell, no,' Snakehips agreed. 'We already been gassin' about it.'

'Good.' Mrs Toby turned to Larry and Freddy. 'And people are gossiping in Just Desserts, aren't they?'

'Constantly,' Larry confirmed.

'Well, then, you only have to keep your ears open and add a little question now and again to find out all kinds of things.'

'I suppose so,' Freddy agreed. 'Although you're really asking us to eavesdrop.'

'Rubbish,' said Mrs Norton. 'Anyway, you do that already

and you usually join in folks' conversations too. We're not suggesting you act any differently than usual.'

'I think we've just been insulted,' Freddy said to Larry. They both grinned, earlier enmity forgotten in the face of a common 'enemy'.

'And I suppose you want *me* to talk to the postal workers?' asked Dorothy Finnegan from the corner. 'I wondered what I was doing here.'

'Well . . . you *do* work there part-time,' Nell Norton said. 'But if you don't want to . . .'

'I'd be happy to, as long as you tell me what you want to know.' Dorothy, recently widowed, had taken a part-time job as counter worker at the Post Office, glad of the distraction and the small additional income. 'There are all kinds of cliques and factions down there – you wouldn't believe it.'

'Oh, yes I would,' Margaret Toby said. 'I used to be a secretary in a big firm and I know all about politics in the work place, believe me. You be careful.'

Dorothy smiled. 'I will. And all they can do is make me quit, anyway. I've already had an offer from Mr Naseem to manage his supermarket part-time to give him some freedom, so I'm not bothered what they think of me over there at the "Aren't We Great" Postal Centre.' She accepted their congratulations with pleasure.

'Are we all agreed, then?' Mrs Toby asked, looking around. There were shrugs and raised eyebrows, but nobody actually refused to help out. 'Right. Then the first thing we have to do is discuss the case –' She glanced at Emily. 'Discuss *both* cases and decide what it would be helpful to find out.'

The following evening Matt was released from the hospital and was now sitting in his apartment talking to Max, the cat. He had been allowed out but warned to take things easy for a while. He'd also been given a stern talking-to about the handling of diabetes and provided with a little machine for testing his own blood regularly. It was a lot to take in, but he felt a lot better about having been diagnosed. And the fact that he didn't have to inject insulin, as his father had, was a great relief. New medicines were being developed all the time, he told Max. It wasn't going to be a big problem.

Talking to Max was his main form of relaxation, after reading, and while the cat never offered a comment or response, he did have the habit of appearing to listen with interest and enjoyment to all that Matt had to say on any given topic.

Dominic Pritchard had just left, having consumed two cups of coffee and some of Mrs Norton's cookies, which Matt bought regularly from Just Desserts. He and Matt had had quite a discussion, to which Max had been privy throughout.

'He's right, you know,' Matt said. 'There *are* similarities between the two crimes. And I have every right to go on investigating Frog's case, I'm not barred from *that* one.'

Max, who was seated on a footstool in front of the fireplace in which a gas log flickered, blinked his eyes and seemed to nod agreement.

'Surely George will see that,' Matt continued. 'I mean, I am still Sheriff, legally. I think I'll go down and pull the case notes and go over the whole thing again. I've been wanting to do that anyway. And now that Dominic is so convinced . . . well, it's my duty.'

Max yawned.

'I know it's late,' Matt agreed. 'But We Never Close, remember? And I'm damned if I'm just going to spend my time sitting around and talking to you. No offence.'

None taken, apparently, for Max didn't move.

'It's driving me crazy, you know. I thought I would practically hug Dominic when he arrived, I was so glad to see someone intelligent to talk to. No offence again.'

Max licked a paw reflectively, then tucked it back under his chest alongside the other one. He resembled a marmalade meatloaf, sitting there.

Matt stood up, rather startling the cat, who had become

143

accustomed to the drone of his voice. He blinked up at the tall figure that towered above him.

'I'll be right back,' Matt said and headed for the staircase.

When he got downstairs there was only Duff Bradley on duty. 'Matt?' he said, implying, what are you doing here?

'Look,' Matt said. 'I'm only off the Armstrong case – I haven't resigned, you know. And I feel fine, thanks.'

'Oh. Good,' said Duff, who was relatively new on the staff and still didn't quite know how to take Matt's sense of humour. 'Everybody else is out on patrol. I'm on the 911 desk. Not much happening, though. There's a dance at the high school we're keeping an eye on and somebody reported a prowler over by the new mall. Oh, and Mrs Hartsung and her husband had a fight. Susie and Charley are over there now, either holding them apart or bathing their wounds.'

The Hartsungs were regular customers and provided loud entertainment for their neighbours at least twice or three times a month.

'I just want to go over some case notes.' Matt went to a filing cabinet. 'Not the Armstrong case,' he added hurriedly.

'Oh, sure – I never thought it was,' said Duff, who had briefly thought exactly that.

'Frog okay?' asked Matt.

'Yeah, he's asleep. He usually goes off early, once he's taken his night-time pills,' Duff said. 'No trouble.'

Matt looked at him. 'So he takes sleeping pills?'

'Well, I don't know what they are, exactly.' Duff reached for a bottle on the side of his desk. He read off the name, which meant little to either of them. 'But they sure knock him out – we don't get a peep out of him until breakfast. Then he gets up and does all these stretching exercises. Makes a hell of a noise while he does them – I guess they must hurt or something. Poor guy.'

'Ah,' Matt said. 'That's interesting.'

'Is it?' asked Duff. 'Listen, there's something else.' He

lowered his voice to a confidential level. 'He keeps saying he needs a massage. What does he think we're running here, some kind of brothel or something?'

'I think he means a proper physiotherapy massage,' Matt said, amused at Duff's small outrage. 'He has something wrong with his back and joints, Duff. Something with a long name that's pretty painful.'

'Oh. I didn't know.' Duff looked worried. 'Should he see a doctor or something? I mean, being cooped up all the time, maybe he should be getting some kind of other treatment. We don't want to get sued because we didn't treat him right.'

'I don't think Frog will sue us,' Matt said. 'But I will call his doctor and see what we should do, if anything.' He copied the doctor's name from the medicine bottle onto a slip of paper and inserted it into the case file. 'I should have thought of it before. I'll ring him in the morning.'

'Good,' Duff said. 'We don't want to be had up for cruel and unusual punishment or anything.'

'No, we certainly don't,' Matt agreed. 'Anything else I should know?'

'Um –' Duff reached a long arm and snagged a piece of paper from the next desk over. 'Susie wrote a note for you. Something about Mrs Pollock at the bookstore?'

Matt took it. 'Okay. I'll look over there in the morning. Take it easy.'

'I always do,' said Duff resignedly.

Matt went back up to his apartment. Max was still on the footstool in front of the fire, although he had turned round to toast his other side.

'I'm going over this thing right from the beginning,' Matt told him, sitting back down with the case notes on his lap. 'There has to be something I've missed. Something we've all missed.'

Max yawned again, lowered his head and went to sleep, soothed by the sound of rustling paper and Matt's occasional low comment.

The lights in the apartment were still on well after midnight, long after the dance at the high school had broken up, long after the prowler at the mall had slipped away and long after the reconciled Hartsungs had gone to sleep in one another's arms.

The lights were also on late at the pool hall.

Snakehips Turkle was waiting for his turn at the table. He leaned on his pool cue and took a drag on the cigarette that hung from the corner of his mouth, skilfully evading the stream of smoke that rose to join the murk that floated beneath the nicotine-stained ceiling of the hall.

Flaky Bingham was about to sink the seven and maybe the eight. Snakehips looked around the room. Nobody much was paying attention to them.

'Hey, Flaky,' Snakehips said.

'Dammit, don't talk when I'm lining up my shot,' Flaky complained, straightening up and reaching for the chalk cube beside him on the scarred mahogany.

'Yeah, sorry.' Snakehips was not in the least sorry. He wanted to beat Flaky this time. 'Didn't you know Moony Packard pretty well?'

'Yeah. So?' Flaky bent down again, sighting along the cue.

'Well—'

'Hey, I said hold it a minute.'

'Okay, okay.'

Flaky shot and sank the seven, but missed the eight. It had never really been on, but he'd seen it done before and thought he might have had a chance.

Snakehips moved forward and began to circle the table, although he saw right away what his shot would be. 'What did you think of him?' he asked Flaky.

The other man shrugged. 'Not much. Real blowhard, all very high and mighty about what other people did right and wrong. Sure didn't like this place much. Said it ought to be shut down.'

'People just don't understand,' Snakehips said sympathetically, took his shot, sank the eight, moved around checking out the nine. 'Men need to relax.'

'Prezactly,' Flaky said. 'I told him. But he never listened once he got started on something. Only thing ever shut him up was when they called the races over at Grasper Haven's, which is where I knew him from.'

Startled, Snakehips stood up and stared at Flaky, hardly able to make him out on the other side of the low-hanging lamp that was suspended over the table between them. 'He went to Grasper's?'

'Hell, yes – didn't you know that? I thought everybody knew that. Was like a sickness with him. He fought hard, but every once in a while he ended up there. Bet on any damn thing when he was in the throes, Moony would. Sad to see.'

'I had no idea,' Snakehips said, sinking the nine and reaching for the chalk cube that Flaky had replaced on the side of the table. 'Did he lose bad?'

Flaky gave a short bark of laughter. 'Hell no – Moony almost always won. He had a real big win the day before he died. That's what kept him coming back. He loved to win and he loved to strut, did Moony. Gave us all the eye while he was counting up his winnings – look at me, boys, ain't I the smart one? Wonder it took so long for somebody to cave his head in like they did.'

'But at the Golden Perch he was always going on about the evils of gambling,' Snakehips marvelled, shaking his head.

'Was he? Doesn't surprise me,' Flaky said. 'Of course, none of us ever hung out at the Golden Perch, you know. Kind of rich for our blood. Not as comfortable as here or Grasper's.'

Well, that was true enough, Snakehips conceded. The bookie and the manager of the Triangle Pool Hall had much in common when it came to décor – old sofas, busted out chairs, battered tables – nothing that couldn't be easily and cheaply replaced after a fight. And the Triangle was deeply permeated not only with the friendly stench of tobacco, but with the addition of the rich hoppy smell of beer, the fulsomeness of baloney, and the tang of pickles and mustard. A man could let his belt out at the Triangle – even though after a visit to Grasper's he was probably having to take it in a notch or two. It was a layer of Blackwater life that Snakehips dipped into now and then. Other times he could rise up to the Golden Perch or even, on occasion, to Vic Moss's establishment out in the country. Snakehips was a social slider and he followed his money wherever it took him. Mind you, he had acquired his nickname earlier in his life, when he had made his living as a burglar who was known for slipping in and out of places without touching the sides, as it were. But he was reformed now. Mostly because of arthritis, but also because the excitement had gone. The Turkles, a family of contrasts, never stuck to things for ever. Some of them were bad, some good and the rest were usually politicians.

'I guess there was a lot we didn't know about Moony,' Snakehips reflected and missed his next shot deliberately. Letting Flaky win might make him more talkative. Shame, but there it was. 'Big winner, hey?'

'Hell, yes. I thought everybody knew that.'

'Nope – nobody knew it that I know,' Snakehips said. 'He didn't exactly drive around in a Cadillac or anything.'

'Well, he must have put it somewheres,' Flaky said. 'Grasper hated him but he never banned him because people kind of took heart at Moony winning and figured they could too.'

'And?'

Flaky shook his head. 'Never did. Which was fine with Grasper. Well, you know how he is.'

'Oh, yeah, I know how he is,' Snakehips said grimly, having lost many a buck to the bookie in the past.

'He figured Moony was like . . . like free advertising,' Flaky said. He straightened up. 'Hey – you don't suppose they had something going there, do you?'

'Like what?'

'Like maybe Grasper let him seem to win and then took part of it back on the sly, like they do with a shill out in Vegas?'

'I don't think Grasper has that many brains,' Snakehips said. 'And anyway it would go against his nature to pay out anything for nothing. If Moony won all that often, he must have done it on his own. He must have been lucky.'

'Not when coming through Cotter's Cut, he wasn't,' Flaky said.

'No, well . . .' Snakehips waited until Flaky completed his next shot. 'You figure it was Frog Bartlett killed him?'

'No, I do not.' Flaky straightened up and looked flushed with both success and annoyance. 'I think Matt Gabriel jumped the gun there. I think it was all politics, which isn't like Matt, but I reckon they pushed him into it. Makes me mad when I think about it.' He shrugged. 'So I don't think about it.'

'Yeah, but if Frog didn't do it, who did?'

'Well, now . . . that's interesting. You don't suppose it was Grasper, do you?'

'I don't know,' Snakehips admitted. 'You mean, maybe Moony won too often?'

Flaky made a face. 'Aw, Grasper ain't that bad.'

'No – he has a few good points – like the one on the top of his head,' Snakehips agreed. They chuckled edgily, glancing around. A lot of people owed Grasper Haven money and you never knew who was listening. Grasper could ban you in the blink of an eye and where would a man get any excitement then?

'So if not Grasper, then who?' Snakehips asked.

'Why should you care?' Flaky wanted to know, frowning.

Snakehips shrugged. 'I like old Frog, the crabby bastard. He's got himself a young lawyer believes in him now. Wants to make a fight of it.'

'And you want to help?'

'Naw – I was just wondering whether Grasper was making odds on it, is all,' Snakehips said easily. 'Wonder what the field would be – late entries, that kind of thing.'

149

'Ah.' Flaky nodded. This he understood. 'Well, there's his brother, crazy Frank. And maybe Mr Potter, the supervisor down at the Post Office – they hated each other's guts. You know Potter?'

'Can't say I do,' Snakehips admitted. 'He related to Carter Potter?'

'Cousin,' Flaky said. 'On his mother's side. Potter is one of those bleeding-heart liberals and he didn't take kindly to Moony's brother Frank making all those protests in front of the Post Office them times.'

'What times?'

'Vietnam, and Cuba and Grenada, and I don't know what all.' Flaky began to laugh. 'That man can do more with paint than most folks think of in a lifetime. Potter blamed Moony for not keeping his brother under control, but he couldn't fire Moony just because of his brother. Moony was a good worker and he'd worked there a hell of a lot longer than Potter.'

'So what you're saying is, one way and another, there were quite a few folks who could have killed Moony,' Snakehips continued.

'Yeah – but not many of them had enough brains to get hold of Frog's monkey wrench to do it with,' Flaky pointed out. 'You got to admit, that's prime evidence.'

'So you'd bet against him getting off?' Snakehips asked.

Flaky shrugged again and leaned down to line up his next shot. 'If I was a betting man I'd have to, wouldn't I?'

'Oh, sure . . . if you were a betting man,' agreed Snakehips and they both laughed. Snakehips's laughter became a little strained, as Flaky proceeded to clear the table. He now owed the 'non-betting man' twenty bucks. It looked like being a very expensive evening.

FIFTEEN

GEORGE EYED FRANK PACKARD WITH some alarm.

For the past twenty minutes Packard had been going on about how America was going to rack and ruin, that the government was run by a bunch of pinkos, that 'preverts' and homos were everywhere you looked, especially on television, that women ought to know their place and other examples of how modern-day life outraged him. Instead of running down, as George had hoped when it first began, Packard seemed to get more and more excited, his face growing practically puce and sweat running down his temples to drip off his jaw.

George had never seen a man in a sociological snit before. If Matt had been there he would have known what to do, but George – aside from getting in an 'um' and a 'but . . .' and an occasional 'Could we talk about . . .' – was completely flummoxed. He decided to try simple volume. 'Look, Mr Packard –' he said more loudly than he had spoken up to then.

Packard glared at him, irritated but stalled by the interruption. 'What?'

'I'd like to talk about Jack Armstrong.'

'Bastard,' Packard stated. 'He had me beat up, you know.'

'Are you sure it was Armstrong behind it?'

'Those two gorillas work for him – who else would it be?' Packard demanded. 'He's just another example of what I mean when I say that the country—'

'He's dead, Mr Packard,' George interrupted.

151

'Well, I know that,' Packard said. 'That's not news.'

'No. You were at the rally, weren't you?'

'Sure, I was there.' Packard leaned back in the leather easy chair. Perhaps, George thought, Frank had tired himself out after all. He could hope, anyway.

'And you were on the stage – at the end?'

'Yeah, I was up there. Bastard Molt nearly got me with that chair. If I hadn't jumped out of the way it would be me in the hospital instead of that pissant Berringer.'

'Mr Berringer was unlucky.'

'Mr Berringer is always unlucky,' Packard said. 'Everyone knows that.' It was true, the Town Clerk was accident-prone, but it was usually when he was trying to do his best that things went wrong for him. Nobody blamed him, but he saw more of the local hospital emergency room than was usual. Some people complained that he was cornering the market in plaster of Paris. None the less, Mr Berringer persevered with his civic duties. It was a matter of pride over crutches, he said.

'Did you notice Sheriff Gabriel's gun?'

'No. Why should I?'

'Somebody took it.'

'Did they, now?' Packard looked sceptical. 'That's what he says, is it?'

'It's true.'

'Oh, *sure* it is. It's a good thing to say, isn't it, since he knew somebody would trip over Armstrong's body sooner or later. Bit of careful planning, if you ask me.' Packard leaned forward. 'And I bet he had that stuff on his hands you test for, didn't he? Proving he'd fired a gun?'

'We *all* saw him fire his gun into the air at the high school auditorium, in order to get people to stop running around and punching each other out,' George said. 'That test would have been useless.'

'Even so,' muttered Packard. 'It wouldn't surprise me none if he did it. They're all in it, you know. Just like they were all in it for Moony – wanted to get him out of the way.'

'Why would they want to do that, Mr Packard? And who's "they", anyway?'

'Oh –' Packard waved his hand vaguely. 'The government's got people all over. People you'd never suspect were in it.'

'In what?'

'The conspiracy to overthrow the country.' Packard leaned forward and lowered his voice to intimacy.

'Why would the government overthrow the country?' George asked in some confusion. 'They already *have* the country.'

'Not the *whole* government,' Packard said impatiently. 'Just certain ones in power, dotted here and there throughout the fabric of the government, the elected and the non-elected, conspiring to bring a new kind of tyranny to this great country, one far worse than the one we endure now.' His slightly singsong delivery revealed a source other than his own fevered brain for this particular theory. George wondered again whether somebody should give Packard a psychiatric going over. Now that his brother was dead, who was going to keep him in line, look after him, keep him out of trouble? He scribbled a little message to himself in his notebook about contacting someone concerning Frank Packard, who was again displaying that earlier gleam in his rheumy eye. 'And they hated Moony, you know. He was the messenger.'

'The messenger?' George's voice cracked a little. He wished he could take off his tie.

'Of course. He took mail everywhere, he knew who got letters and who didn't, who sent them too. He could get news around, he could wake people up, show them the truth, stop the conspiracy in its tracks by not delivering things. He was dangerous, was Moony. That's why they had him killed.'

'Who had him killed?'

'All of them,' Packard said with considerable satisfaction. 'Molt, Armstrong, Berringer, Attwater, Gabriel . . . they all got together and put him out of the picture. I don't know which one actually done it, but they all knew. They all agreed. Poor Moony didn't stand a chance.' Now a tear appeared in each of the squinty blue eyes. 'I miss him. I miss my brother. Nobody understands. We didn't talk much, but we were brothers and that's what mattered. Moony should have been careful. I told him time and again to be careful, but Moony liked to talk. He talked too much down at that damn Golden Perch, if you ask me. Somebody got mad. Somebody got real mad and *biffed* him –' Packard slammed his left fist into his right palm. 'Biffed him to death. Bastards, all of them.'

'Mr Packard, I promise you that none of those men had the least reason to harm your brother,' George said firmly.

'Hah! What do you know about it?' Packard suddenly shouted. 'Maybe you're one of them too. You work for Matt Gabriel, you'd do what he tells you to do. Did you do it? Did you biff my brother?'

George tried to keep his voice level, while at the same time bracing his feet for a quick rise should it become necessary to beat a retreat. He should have listened, he should have brought Hardwicke or one of the others along. Or Susie – except that Susie had been on duty last night and was probably sleeping cosily right now. Briefly the image of a sleeping Susie Brock crossed his mind and he smiled.

'What are you laughing at?' Packard screamed, standing up. 'I'm right, aren't I? You did it, you did them both and you're covering up by pretending to investigate, but you have no intention of doing anything about it!'

George stood up too. 'We have Frog Bartlett in jail, Mr Packard. He did it. He killed your brother. We have proof.'

'Crap! Crap, crap, crap! *You* did it, *you*! Of course – I shoulda seen it right from the beginning – it's all part of it, all part and parcel of it.'

'*Mr Packard*!' George shouted. '*I did not kill your brother and neither did any of those other men. Do you understand*?'

'No, I don't! Get out of my house, dammit. Get out of

my house!' Packard shouted back, little flecks of spittle emerging with the words. Waving his arms like windmills, he started for the shotgun that hung over the fireplace.

George got. 'If you fire that gun I'll have to arrest you!' he yelled over his shoulder. 'Threatening an officer . . .'

Packard didn't fire the gun. He slammed the door after George and from behind it George could hear his laughter filling the room. The man was definitely nuts.

George felt out of breath, as if he had been running. He was not accustomed to dealing with crazy men. He was not used to making his own decisions, drawing his own conclusions, and he felt badly the need for Matt to be back in charge. He had only come to see Packard because of that half-wit Pritchard's insistence that the two murders were linked. If you asked him, it was altogether possible that Frank Packard had 'biffed' his own brother to death.

He sat behind the wheel of the jeep and considered.

An interesting thought, that.

But *why*?

Damn.

'At least I'll have enough money to look after myself,' Mrs Armstrong said in an almost uninterested voice. 'He left everything to me. I know he did. I'll sell the company and live somewhere warm. I hate the winters here. I'm a Southern girl, used to warmth.'

Susie thought she had detected a Southern inflection in the woman's voice. The hospital room was overheated, they always were, and she was already uncomfortable. But she wanted to make this interview count. It was the first one she'd done on her own and, after George's ham-fisted dealings with the widow on announcing her husband's death so abruptly, she felt it was important to take it slowly, to ease herself into the woman's confidence, if that were possible.

'Where were you born, Mrs Armstrong?' she asked.

'In Savannah,' Mrs Armstrong replied. 'I was Miss

155

Savannah the year I met Jack. He was putting up an office building in town and he was one of the judges of the contest. He voted for me, of course.' She looked at Susie, her eyes suddenly sharp. 'Your boss will get to keep his badge now, won't he?'

'I expect so.'

'Did he kill Jack?' She seemed genuinely curious, asking her question as if it were ordinary conversation. Or perhaps it was the sedative repressing her emotions. Susie was beginning to wonder if this strange woman had any emotions other than self-concern, however. The scream and the subsequent hysteria the other day *could* have been a performance of the 'Bereaved Wife' as imagined by a middle-aged self-styled Southern belle.

'No, he did not kill him,' Susie said firmly. She had to believe that and she did.

'Oh. I heard some talk that he might have.' The woman in the bed seemed almost disappointed. 'Do you know who did?'

'No, I don't. I was hoping you might be able to help me.'

'Well, *I* didn't kill him,' the widow said, picking at a loose thread in the blanket that lay over her lower body. She leaned back against the mound of pillows behind her. 'I can't even get out of bed.'

'I never . . .'

'Because I get all his money, you might have thought that I did,' she said. 'But I didn't. And I didn't arrange to have anyone kill him either, in case you were wondering about *that*.'

'It never entered my mind.' Susie's answer was automatic.

'Oh, pooh. Of course it entered your mind. It would enter mine if I were you.' Mrs Armstrong gave her a sly smile. 'Do you think I should run for sheriff in Jack's place?'

'I'm afraid it's too late for that, nominations are closed,' Susie said idiotically. Mrs Armstrong was taking over the interview. What a strangely powerful woman, she thought. Even ill, even lying in a hospital bed, even sedated. It was like being in the room with a live grenade. 'Do you know if your husband had any enemies, Mrs Armstrong?'

The woman in the bed gave a small, fox-like bark, presumably of laughter. 'Of course he did. He was a nasty, nasty man. Didn't you know that? He was ruthless. He made a lot of enemies.'

'Was he nasty to you?'

'Oh, no. Oh, absolutely not. Jack was good to me. Very very good. He had to be.'

'Why was that, Mrs Armstrong?'

'Because I knew all his dirty little secrets,' she said smugly. 'And if you think I'm going to tell them to you you're wrong. A wife can't be forced to testify against her husband, isn't that right?'

'Your husband isn't on trial, Mrs Armstrong.' Susie was surprised she should think so.

'Isn't he? I wonder. Isn't a murder investigation a little like a trial? Aren't you all going to be snooping around, looking for things that tell you about him, asking questions about him, trying to find out why and who and all that? Isn't that like a trial?'

Susie supposed it was, in a backward kind of way. 'It would help us a lot if you were to co-operate with us, Mrs Armstrong. Don't you want us to find your husband's killer?'

Mrs Armstrong sighed. 'Not particularly,' she said, turning her head to look out of the window. 'He's dead, you can't bring him back. Why should I care any more? It's nothing to do with me, who killed him. I'll have his money, I'll be all right.'

'Is that all it means to you?'

Mrs Armstrong didn't look at her, but continued to stare out of the window. 'Of course. When you're as ill as I am, young lady, you live for the day. Today my husband is dead. That's what today is. Dead husband day. Tomorrow will be too.' She closed her eyes. 'I don't want to talk to you any more. I want you to go away.' A slow tear slid out from under her lashes. 'I want everyone just to go away.'

Susie went.

Kay Pink was waiting down the hall. 'Is she asleep?'

'I think so. Or nearly there.'

Kay nodded. 'She wants to sleep, but she always fights it. Afraid she won't wake up.'

'I didn't realize she was that ill.'

'Oh, she isn't,' Kay said in a practical tone as they went back towards the elevator. 'Other than the strep infection she just had, which I admit was very bad, she's right as rain. But she is convinced she has a weak heart – it's a very lady-like affliction – and so she checks in here from time to time for a "rest". From the social round, you know.' Kay put on a la-di-da accent for those last few words, then resumed her normal tone. 'It's just nerves. And a bad case of cocaine dependency, of course.'

'Should you be telling me that?' Susie queried, surprised.

'Tell you what?' Kay asked innocently. 'I didn't tell you anything.'

'Ah,' said Susie. 'I thought you did.'

After getting her coffee from the machine in the Post Office canteen, Dorothy Finnegan sat down with Mary Baker, Marge Cassary and Queenie Turkle. They took up one end of a long table, while at the other end sat several men from the sorting office. There was a gap of three or four places between the two groups, but occasionally an overheard remark was commented on by one or the other. Depended on the weather, mostly. Summer made people loquacious and friendly, winter drew them into themselves.

'Lord, my feet hurt,' groaned Queenie, settling her considerable bulk into her chair and slamming her rather large brown bag onto the table. 'I been looking forward to this all morning.' She reached in and began to produce plastic containers, wrapped sandwiches, pieces of cake and fruit, and a big thermos that contained home-made soup. 'It's tomato with basil today, anybody want some?' she asked.

'Cooked tomatoes give me indigestion,' Mary said. 'But it smells real good.'

They settled to their various meals.

After a few minutes Dorothy cleared her throat. 'I thought I saw Frank Packard out in front, earlier. Carrying some kind of placard? I couldn't read what it said.'

'It said "Down with Government Killers",' Marge told her. 'Whatever that means.'

'He's nuts,' Queenie said around a mouthful of bacon, peanut butter, mayonnaise and lettuce sandwich. 'Always was nuts. I don't know how Moony put up with him all those years.'

'Did they get along?' Dorothy asked.

'Oh, sure. Real close, those two. Moony had to defend him to old Potter all the time.' Osgood Potter was the Post Office manager, a bitter-hearted bully. He did not patronize the staff canteen, which was a blessing to all. 'Frank has a real "thing" about the government and the Post Office to him represents government around here, because we fly the flag. He throws paint, rotten vegetables, whatever, when he forgets to take his pills.' Queenie spoke with vast disgust.

'But if his brother *worked* here . . . I mean, Moony was a mail carrier and all—'

'Didn't seem to make any difference. Moony was the only one who could settle Frank down. And the only one that Potter was afraid of, for some reason. Now that Moony's gone, Potter will get tough with Frank, I bet. He'll call the Sheriff or something. Surprised he hasn't already.'

'It's not the Sheriff now. It's George Putnam,' Marge said. 'Naturally nobody has showed up yet.'

'They're all busy with these murders,' Mary reasoned. 'I'm beginning to think maybe Blackwater Bay is getting to be a dangerous place to live.' She glanced at Dorothy. 'Sorry, Dorothy.'

'Oh, that's all right.' It was almost two years since

Dorothy's husband had been murdered, but people were still worried about her. 'You're right. First Moony Packard and now Jack Armstrong. It's kind of scary. But what I can't figure out is why anybody would want to kill a mail carrier – I mean, nothing was stolen from him, was it?'

'As far as they could tell,' Queenie said darkly.

'What do you mean?' Mary asked.

Queenie finished her soup and started on her coffee along with a third sandwich. 'What I heard, Moony was carrying a lot of money on the day he was killed. What happened to that, I wonder?'

'Money?'

Queenie nodded. 'He'd won a bet. Over a thousand dollars he had from the night before. Probably went straight into Matt Gabriel's election fund.'

'Oh, surely you don't believe that,' Dorothy protested.

'You think Matt Gabriel is honest?' Queenie asked.

'I do,' Dorothy replied firmly. 'I really do.'

'Unh,' Queenie said, chewing. She was a Turkle and that family was never exactly trusting of the law – seeing as so many of its members viewed it from the wrong side, as it were.

'Moony wasn't carrying money,' said a voice from the other end of the table. It was Phil Decker, one of the senior sorters. 'He never carried money like that. He always mailed it to some bank in Grantham rather than lug it around. Did it every time he had a win. Said the US Mail was safer than any wallet.'

'Maybe he was killed because somebody thought he still had that money in his pocket.' Dorothy turned to Queenie. 'How did you know Moony had won that much money?' she asked.

Queenie shrugged. 'One of my boys mentioned it.' She flashed a look at Dorothy that did not bode well for any future offers of soup. 'If you mean—'

'What I meant was, if you knew about it and you didn't know Moony that well, then a *lot* of people might have known it,' Dorothy said quickly. 'It was obviously fairly

160

common knowledge. So it could have been anybody – even some stranger in town who heard about it in a bar somewhere.' She looked around and saw that most of the others had lost interest in the subject, were wrapping up their sandwich papers, finishing their coffee. 'I was just wondering,' she said slowly. 'At least we know Frog couldn't have killed Mr Armstrong.'

'There's a lot of people who might have, though,' said Phil darkly. 'I heard he had some funny friends. And he sure had some enemies.'

'Who?' asked Dorothy.

Phil stood up and crumpled his brown bag and wrappings into a ball, throwing it overhand into the large waste basket that stood against the far wall. 'What does it matter? He's dead, isn't he? Good riddance, if you ask me.'

'Oh, come on, Phil – he brought a lot of business to the town with that mall and everything,' one of the other men said.

'He didn't bring it to my brother.'

Dorothy frowned after him, then turned to the other women. 'What did he mean about his brother?'

'Sam Decker is an electrician. He tendered for the mall job, but Armstrong gave it to some out-of-towner who was a personal buddy – even though Larry's tender was lower. He was plenty pissed off and he wasn't the only one,' Queenie told her. Queenie knew everything, apparently. 'Lots of local companies bid for jobs on the mall, but they got shouldered out by Armstrong's Army.'

'Armstrong's Army?'

Queenie smiled and stood up. 'You never heard of Armstrong's Army? They're contractors from Grantham or wherever. Places you never heard of, even. But they got work from Armstrong all right. I'm talking about *contracts*, honey. That's where the money is – kickbacks and backhanders – Armstrong's Army march on their wallets.' She smiled down at Dorothy. 'Or they did. I wonder what they'll do now that Armstrong's dead. Maybe one of them didn't get what he expected – so Armstrong got what he didn't expect. Who knows?'

They all went back to their work and Dorothy had to be content with that.

Emily opened the door to the store-front that had recently been campaign headquarters for the Elect Jack Armstrong operation. The many desks, where once sat excited and busy supporters, were now empty, littered with crumpled paper and discarded memos. At the back of the large open room was a part-glass partition, through which she could see Irwin Otis seated at a large desk, his head in his hands.

Overhead, red, white and blue streamers sagged and swung in the draught from the open door, and a few rather wrinkled balloons drifted along the floor in front of Emily as she walked towards the back. Otis did not appear to have heard her enter and gave a leap like a startled eavesdropper when she tapped on the glass of the closed door. He stared at her, then gave a sickly smile and nodded. She opened the door. 'Hi,' she said.

'You're too late. The campaign is cancelled.'

'Death in the family.' Emily nodded. She closed the door behind her. 'I heard.'

'No story here.' He sighed. 'Unless you've got employment for a suddenly available campaign manager. I will provide my own candidate buttons and mobile phone.'

'Sorry,' Emily said with a sympathetic smile.

He shrugged. 'I'll live. But it's too late to get on somebody's staff now, and a long time until next fall when they start the next round for Congress and the Senate. I may have to take up alternative endeavours – like garbage collection or ostrich breeding.'

'Any experience?'

'With garbage – plenty. Although mostly hiding it rather than collecting it. Ostriches, no, although I've heard there's money in it if you're successful.'

'Ah,' Emily said. 'In anything, if you're successful.'

'Always some damn catch or other,' Otis grumbled.

'Did you have to hide much garbage on Jack Armstrong?' Emily asked, all innocence.

'No comment.'

'Not speaking ill of the dead?'

'Just not speaking,' Otis said. 'I'm not being coy. The fact is, I knew very little about Jack Armstrong other than that he wanted to be sheriff today and emperor tomorrow. We didn't exactly hit it off on a personal level. He was a whole other kind of person from me.'

'Didn't that make it difficult to work for him?'

'Funnily enough, no,' Otis said, leaning back in his chair. 'You see, I got the feeling there was a lot I didn't *want* to know about him. The way a defence lawyer doesn't want to know whether his client is guilty or not – just enough to get him off. I don't think Jack was a very nice person, although he was never anything but nice to me.'

'Then why . . .'

He stared at her, his hands behind his head, then shrugged again. 'Suppose it doesn't matter now. Old Jack had a lot going on in his life outside this place. And sometimes *in* this place – people coming and going to meetings to which, as they say, I was not privy. "Not now, Win" he'd say. Or "give us a minute, Win" and out I would go, as obedient as any puppy.'

'And who were these people?'

'I don't know. I have ideas, but I don't know. What I do know is that we seemed to have a lot more cash on hand after they'd visited us. I would ask Jack about this, and he would just pat me on the back and say not to worry about it.'

'And did you?'

'Did I what?'

'Worry about it?'

'Sure I worried about it. I mean you can only have so many rich aunts and grandmothers who suddenly pop off and leave you cash in their wills. But it was between him and his accountants.'

'Wouldn't it have rebounded on you if these were illegal contributions? For favours, say?'

'Not if I didn't know about it.'

'They could have claimed you knew about it.'

'Well, maybe. But they can't now, can they?'

'I suppose not. How convenient.'

He eyed her. 'You writing some kind of exposé after the fact?' He didn't appear defensive – just curious. In fact, he seemed to have little or no feelings at all except resignation.

'No – but I am curious to find out who killed him.'

'Ah . . . amateur sleuth. I read those kinds of books too.'

'All this.' Emily gestured towards the outer room and the residue of electioneering that littered it. 'What happens now?'

'I suppose I have to find somebody to clean it up. Or maybe the landlord does,' Otis said. 'I really have never had an experience like this before. All my candidates have at least made it to the election.'

'What about the money?' Emily asked. 'For instance.'

'The election money? God knows. That's for Robarts to figure out.'

'Who is Robarts?'

'The accountant who handled the campaign funds. He's the only other paid employee now. I don't know where the hell he is at the moment. The researchers were casual, paid in cash. I have a contract, so I get paid until Election Day and for the week following. Then nada. Everybody else was volunteer staff. Hence the empty desks. Nothing left to volunteer for. I suppose after all the expenses are paid, any residue of the campaign fund will go to party headquarters and into the general coffers. Robarts would know. Unless he's made off with it. I suppose that's possible – I always thought he looked shifty.'

'Was there much money?'

Otis nodded. 'Oh, yeah. Like I said, a lot of rich aunts and grandmothers.'

'Thousands of dollars?'

'Hundreds of thousands, more like. We were about to make a big push. Mind you, all the stuff that was ordered will have to be paid for, the TV commercials that were made but will never run, the posters and banners and buttons and so on that will never be worn or waved – all that kind of stuff. Rent on this place. You have any suggested use for a couple of thousand leaflets promoting a dead man?'

'Short of finding a candidate with the same name, no,' Emily admitted.

'Into the shredder – it all goes into the shredder. Maybe like my career – doesn't look too good, losing your candidate. Sort of careless.' He looked pale, suddenly.

'You found him,' Emily said.

'Yeah. Only dead man I ever saw before was my grandfather and he died in his bed. Not the same thing at all.' Otis shook himself.

'These "other people" that came to see Armstrong – did they see Robarts as well?'

'Oh, yeah – Mr Robarts was *always* present.' Otis scowled. 'I told Armstrong I couldn't operate like that – I had to know if there was any trouble coming from any direction, but he just laughed it off, said they were "old cronies" and it wasn't anything to do with the election. I told him when you're a candidate for office *everything* has to do with the election. But he . . . slipped out of it. He was a very slippery kind of guy, as a matter of fact, thinking back. Not that I ever would have said any of this if he were still alive, you understand. Now it doesn't matter a damn, I guess.'

'Where could I find this Robarts?' Emily asked. She had carefully not taken notes, most people clam up at the sight of a reporter's notebook. Anyway, the recorder in her handbag was very sensitive.

Otis sighed. 'I'll write it down for you. He's from Grantham, of course, has his practice there, but he was staying up here a few days every week at the hotel. I think he's gone back to the city now. Unless he made a run for Brazil – always possible, I suppose.'

'Did Robarts strike you as the kind of man to kill Armstrong just to run off with his campaign chest?' Emily asked.

'No, not really.' Otis's tone was dismissive. 'I'm just being nuts. He's probably okay.' He handed Emily a page he'd torn from his notebook. 'There you go.'

'Thanks. What about those other men who used to come here to talk to Armstrong? Could one of *them* have killed him?'

'God, I don't know. I never learned who they were or what their connection was with Armstrong. I know they were all from out of town, that their little "get-togethers" were arranged well in advance. But they wouldn't have met here if they had anything to hide, would they? They would have met somewhere quiet, out of the way, right?'

'I suppose so,' Emily conceded. 'Just grasping at straws, really.' She looked at him sympathetically. 'What are you going to do now?'

'I haven't the least damn idea. The Sheriff told me I have to stay until the inquest, but after that I'm free as a bird. All suggestions gratefully received – as long as they're legal.'

'That worries you?'

'Oh, yes – that worries me very much. I have only my reputation to offer, Miss Gibbons. That, plus my considerable skills at manipulating public opinion and researching arcane subjects.'

'Such as?'

He laughed. 'Well, for instance, Armstrong wanted me to find out all I could about transporting old houses to new locations. The costs and so on.'

'Good Lord – what for?'

'Beats me. I turned it over to one of the students. Don't think he ever got around to making a report. More wasted effort, I guess. And once he asked about postal regulations – something weird about importing books or something. Plus the usual on local statistics they all want so as to make their speeches sound like they were really interested – where the farmers stood, what the educational system was like, whether parents were happy with it, what the small businessmen wanted for the town – the normal stuff.' Suddenly he laughed. 'And then there were the brothels.'

'The brothels?'

Otis laughed again. 'Yeah – he wanted to know how many there were in Blackwater County. And how many pool halls.'

'You don't mean the "you've got trouble right here in River City" approach, do you?' Emily asked, as much amused as astonished.

'Beats hell out of me. He was a nosy kind of guy – whatever came into his mind, he wanted to know about it.'

'Really,' Emily murmured. 'That's interesting.'

'Is it?'

'Well . . . maybe he learned more than he should have about something,' Emily ventured. 'Maybe that was why somebody killed him. I understand it was a sort of execution-type killing.'

Otis went pale again. 'Don't remind me,' he said, putting his hand up as if to ward off the image. 'But you could have something there, I suppose. He was always looking for an advantage, for an edge where he could get a grip, you know? Born politician.' Otis seemed to regret Armstrong's passing on a sort of professional level. 'He could have gone far.'

'Apparently as far as he got was too far for somebody.'

'Like your Sheriff? Armstrong was going to beat him at the polls, you know.'

'Oh, I don't think so.'

'Oh, yes . . . we did a survey last week. It was neck and neck, and we had a while to go yet. We were gaining on him every hour of every day. Especially on this other killing. A lot of people think he arrested that ugly guy too fast. Others not fast enough. Funny case all around in that respect. People seem to have strong opinions about that ugly guy – what's his name?'

'Frog Bartlett.'

'Yeah. I never saw him myself. Is he as ugly and mean as they say?'

'Not attractive, but not mean. More short-tempered than mean. I understand he was a good friend to his friends.'

'And a bad enemy to the rest?' Otis asked curiously.

'Frog just seemed to avoid the people he didn't like,' Emily said reflectively. 'The only person who used to get his goat in a big way was Moony Packard.'

'The guy they say he killed.'

'They say.'

'You don't agree?'

'I don't know ... no, I guess I don't agree,' Emily admitted. 'But I don't have any other candidates to offer either.'

'Whereas with Jack Armstrong there is an embarrassment of riches, isn't there? I understand he made a lot of enemies – legally – putting up that mall and planning that real estate development on the edge of town.'

'And the Main Street shopkeepers whose business the mall is ruining. And those "old cronies" you mentioned. And maybe Mr Robarts the accountant. Oh – we have a plethora of possibilities,' Emily said wryly.

'I also hear it was the Sheriff's gun that fired the fatal shot, so he's suspended himself from the investigation,' Otis said. 'Is that wise?'

'In one way, yes – it stops any gossip.' Emily stood up. 'In another way, no – as his deputy has now taken over, God help us all. Be prepared – he will no doubt want to question you.' She started to turn away, then swivelled back. 'By the way – did Armstrong keep any papers here in the office?'

'Now, now . . . don't go all nosy on me,' Otis said, shaking his finger, adult to child. 'But no, he didn't. Just to do with the elections. I know ... I already looked and so did the deputies.'

'And would you tell me if you found anything incriminating or interesting?'

'Legally I still work for the man. Ethically, if I thought

I knew anything of importance I would turn it over to the Sheriff's office. Don't laugh – there are a few honest people left in the world, Miss Gibbons. Some of us are even in politics.'

'It boggles the mind. Thanks, Mr Otis, you've been a big help.'

'Have I? I certainly didn't mean to be,' Otis said. 'Anyway, all Armstrong's business papers are at his office at his home. You'll have to ask his wife about them. Don't blame me if you get your head bitten off.'

'She's in the hospital at the moment.'

He leaned forward. 'Then I suggest you find yourself a nice friendly burglar.'

Nell Norton found Fran Robinson at her desk at the Century 21 realty office, which was a novelty in itself, as Fran was one of their busiest representatives.

'Brought you some of my cookies to have with your coffee break.' Nell poked her head through the door and held out a brown paper bag.

Fran looked up with a grin. 'Why Nell Norton – what are you doing here?'

'I'm looking for information to help Matt, remember?'

'Oh, of course. Say – I'm sorry we couldn't get to the meeting last night. I was showing a house and Don had to go into town—'

'That's okay, I know your time isn't your own,' Nell said. 'Have you got a minute now?'

'Sure.' Fran moved some papers from the chair beside her desk. 'Why the bribe? Are you thinking of moving house?'

Nell snorted. 'Highly unlikely and you know it. No, it was about the meeting. We really need you with us, you and Don, if he's willing.' She went on to explain what Margaret Toby's Big Plan To Help Matt was all about. 'You get around a lot, meet all kinds of folks,' Nell went on. 'And Don knows just about everybody already, one way or another.'

'True enough,' Fran agreed. She was a tall, attractive woman with a ready smile and more energy than six power-stations put together. The Robinsons were neighbours on Paradise Island and had many reasons to be grateful to Matt Gabriel for keeping their lives peaceful after a nasty murder had happened there. 'What do you want us to do, exactly?'

'Well, first of all, I want to know what you know about Jack Armstrong. I mean, you were in the same business.'

Fran shook her head. 'Not really. I sell houses that are already in existence. He sold houses he was planning to build. He was working on spec all the time and the profits were all his own.'

'So none of the houses ever went through you?'

Fran sighed. 'Well, not exactly. Not to the first-time buyers. But we had a few enquiries from folks after they'd been in the houses for a while. They wanted out because the building work was so crappy. They weren't the kind of places we like to handle, frankly.'

'So his houses were that bad?'

'They *looked* all right, he got good designs, but they were cheaply built and costly to maintain.'

'Why did they sell in the first place?'

'Jack Armstrong sold dream houses. That is, houses that you thought were just what you wanted, until you moved in,' Fran said uncompromisingly. 'He used contractors who cut corners and, although I can't prove it, paid off building inspectors to overlook things. He was a flimflammer, a big talker. People were mesmerized. I think when he realized how good he was at it, it seemed natural for him to go into politics. He looked and sounded so trustworthy – unless you really got to know him, looked him straight in the eye. Then you saw the meanness all right.' She sighed. 'He bought up some houses because he wanted the land for his new development. We handled some of those sales and we're sorry we did now, because later we found out he put a lot of pressure on the people who sold to take his offer, even though we often recommended they should hold out

170

for a better one. I think some of them were really scared into selling and that made me angry – made us all angry.' She shrugged. 'But you can only give folks advice, you can't *make* them take it. But, I'm glad to say, there were a few hold-outs who refused to back down, so his plans came to nothing.' She tilted her head to one side. 'One of them was Frog Bartlett, come to think of it. And his neighbour Miss Marsh. Also Mr and Mrs Golightly, opposite them. Those were the three most important ones and they messed up Armstrong's plans completely. I was proud of them, even though it meant losing a commission.'

'Have you ever heard of Armstrong's Army? It was something Dorothy Finnegan picked up on.'

'Oh, yes.' Fran stretched and reached over to open her brown bag of goodies, peering inside with pleasure. 'Those were his cronies – mostly from Grantham. He gave them contracts and they showed their appropriate – or inappropriate – appreciation by contributing to his election funds. Or that's what I hear, anyway. Let's see –' She extracted a cookie and took a bite. 'There was something about unions too. Some stories about workman's comp – it was a nasty little set-up, both on the first property development and on the mall thing. Same contractors on both.' She put her cookie down and drew over a pad. 'I think I can remember them all.' She began to write down names. 'You might have someone look into these guys, because I heard – somewhere – that Armstrong did the dirty on a couple of them. They might have had a good reason to have him killed.'

'Are you serious?' Nell asked, taking the sheet of paper Fran tore off the pad and looking at the names.

'I can't be sure, or specific – but I did hear his so-called army was thinking of rebelling because of all the trouble on the new development getting put back,' Fran said. 'You hear so much gossip in this business you don't know what to believe.' She leaned forward and indicated one name. 'But this guy I *know* was angry at Armstrong – Mel Ottaway. He's a paving contractor from Lemonville and he was the

171

one who was supposed to put in the roads for the new development. He paid out a lot of cash for equipment and materials – and then got stuck with them when the development got red-flagged. I think he may even have gone bankrupt because of it. Somebody ought to talk to him, maybe.'

Nell stood up. 'I'll see what I can do,' she said to Fran, who had finished one cookie and started on another. 'It sounds like he had a motive.'

'And there may be others. I'll ask around.'

SIXTEEN

GOING THROUGH THE CASE FILE for Moony Packard, Matt had seen clearly that there had been a lot of holes in his reasoning and gaps in his investigation. He was ashamed of this and put it down to the distraction of the election. Or maybe the diabetes.

But that was no excuse.

He'd also been finishing up another murder investigation at the same time, but he had worked multiple cases before and managed perfectly well. The fact that the other case had also been one of murder – indeed several murders – might be a reason, but – again – no excuse.

'I am a dunce,' he informed Max as he finished his breakfast. Max, deeply involved with some tuna fish, only flicked his tail. He was not judgemental.

Matt had not slept long, having set his alarm for a much earlier time than usual. It was barely light when he got into his cruiser and started patrolling the streets until he found his man, Homer Brophy, starting on his round.

A stocky person of about fifty-five, Homer had been a mail carrier for almost as long as Moony Packard, although the two men rarely spoke because their routes were in opposite directions. As it happened, both the Packard house and Frog's house were on Homer's round, and he was only a block away from the former when Matt drew up beside him.

'Hey, Homer?'

The postman turned and looked at the police car. 'I'm innocent!' he cried in mock terror, holding up both hands.

In his right was a packet of letters, in his left a couple of magazines in plastic wrappers. 'Hi, Matt. Heard you were sick. Glad to see you back.'

'Homer.' Matt switched off the engine and got out of the car to stand beside the older man. 'How's things?'

'Things are about as usual, Matt,' Homer said consideringly. 'Letters, magazines, the occasional small parcel – you know how it goes.'

'For me it's traffic, drunks and the occasional family feud.' Matt grinned.

'Well, there you are, then.' Brophy waited expectantly to hear Matt's reason for stopping him.

'I'm looking into Moony Packard's death,' Matt said.

'I thought you had that all tied up.' Homer frowned.

'Well, there are still some loose ends,' Matt explained. 'I hate loose ends.'

'And I hate wrongly addressed letters. Same kind of thing.'

'Yes, I guess so. Homer, you said you saw Frog go by on the morning we found Moony's body. Is that right?'

'I told your Deputy Hardwicke all about it,' Homer answered. 'It was about now – say seven o'clock or so – and Frog shot past me going like a bat out of hell. Went around the corner up there and home, I guess. I didn't actually see him pull in, you understand. But it was definitely Frog's van – hard to miss that old thing, sort of distinctive with those dark windows set in the side and all. Most people don't notice them, but I do. Always thought they were kind of sneaky, you know? Can't see what's going on inside. Not that I think Frog would be up to anything dirty in there, he wasn't like that as far as I know. But in the general idea of the thing – dark windows mean secrets. Don't like 'em.'

'Do you like Frog Bartlett?'

Homer shrugged. 'Don't have anything against the man.'

'You took a while to come forward about seeing his van,' Matt said. 'Why was that? Were you trying to protect him?'

174

'No, of course not.' Brophy was a little nettled at the idea. 'I just didn't want to get dragged in on it. Didn't see the point. But my boss said I should . . .'

'At the Post Office?'

'No. I work afternoons at the mall. Security Guard. Not much to it, just walk around looking serious, chase off the kids now and again, sometimes grab a shoplifter or a purse snatcher. Money's good, though. We can all use extra money,' he added self-righteously.

'Absolutely,' Matt agreed. 'And this boss told you to tell us about seeing Frog's van?'

He eyed Matt. 'Yeah. He overheard me talking to one of the guys. He said it was my civic duty to report it. I live next to Glen Hardwicke, see, so I just went over and told Glen. He made me sign an official report. That's how it happened.' Homer's voice was a little defensive. 'What's wrong with that?'

'Nothing at all, just getting background,' Matt said easily. He glanced around him, noting how many houses had lamps on still. 'It isn't really very light yet, is it?'

'Guess not.'

'So when you saw Frog's van go by "like a bat out of hell" did it come towards you or from behind you?'

'From behind me, going towards home.' Homer waved his arm back in a general sweep. 'Scared the hell out of me, if you want to know the truth.'

'So, if it came from behind you, you couldn't really see who was driving, isn't that right? I mean, the back of the van is closed in . . .'

'It had to be Frog,' Homer insisted. 'He'd never let anyone else drive his van. Frog is real fussy about his stuff, everybody knows that. Had to be Frog.'

'But you didn't actually *see* Frog.'

'Not face to face, no. But I saw from the side it was somebody big and hunched-over driving. Just a glimpse, mind, but—'

'But it was Frog's van so you assumed it was Frog?'

Homer began to look uneasy. 'It was Frog.'

175

'You're sure? You'll swear to that at the trial?'

Now Homer was confused. 'What difference does it make? Sure, I'll swear it was Frog going like a bat out of hell come whizzing past me at seven o'clock on the morning Moony Packard died. Isn't that enough?'

'Frog or Frog's van?'

Homer looked away, his brow wrinkling, his eyes focusing elsewhere.

'Well?' Matt asked.

'I guess I could swear it was Frog's van,' Homer muttered. 'Isn't that good enough?'

Matt smiled reassuringly. 'Oh, that's fine, Homer. That will do just fine. Thanks.' He started back towards his car.

'Hey,' Homer called after him. 'Are you trying to make out I'm a liar?'

'No, of course not. Just trying to clarify things so we know exactly where we are. You've been a real help.'

Matt left Brophy staring worriedly after him as he pulled away. He drove on several blocks before pulling over to use the mobile phone to call his deputy direct.

'Charley? Listen, get someone over to Frog Bartlett's house to fingerprint his van, will you?' He listened. 'No, we never had any reason to, but now I want it done. No need to mention it to George – unless he asks. You understand?' Charley apparently understood very well, because Matt grinned and even managed a slight laugh. 'And say, listen, Charley, have you ever seen Frank Packard driving a car? I've seen him on that old Harley of his, but –' He paused as Charley spoke. 'Oh, right, I remember now. Listen, have whoever does the fingerprinting on Frog's van report straight to you or Tilly. I'll call back later. Thanks – I appreciate it.' He replaced the phone and sat there for a while, thinking, then drove over to Main Street and parked in front of Daria's gallery. It was just seven thirty. Dominic Pritchard lived in an apartment above the gallery and he was bound to be up by now.

Dominic made very good coffee.

George Putnam was steeling himself for his next interview. The one with Frank Packard had gone so badly it had undermined his confidence. He wished Matt were doing this. He wished he had left him a list of instructions. He wished he knew what he was doing. More than anything, he wished Susie Brock hadn't insisted on coming along.

It had been arranged that he talk to Mrs Armstrong at the clinic ... but in the presence of her lawyer, who also happened to be George's own father. His father had never witnessed him acting like a deputy or – in this case – a sheriff before. Hard enough to speak with the grieving widow, worse still to do it before a man who had never wanted him to join the police force in the first place.

George was convinced his father thought he was a boob.

That was not, in fact, the case, but George didn't know that. Carl Putnam was a loving father and a fair man, but he rarely showed his feelings to his sons.

As he had been the late Jack Armstrong's lawyer, he now represented the interests of his widow.

He was nervous too.

He hadn't had much to do with Mrs Armstrong. He'd only met her socially, at a few parties, and remembered her as nervy, shrill and rather intimidating. He wanted George to do well, but he also did not want him to get on the wrong side of Mrs Armstrong. She could, if she wanted, switch lawyers in an instant and the Armstrong business brought in some very welcome revenue to the practice.

Sometimes he suspected the sources weren't all that legal, but it paid to know when to ask questions and when not to ask them. He also suspected other lawyers were at work in the background, but he never asked about that either. Carl Putnam was a very careful man.

Mrs Armstrong was sitting up in bed when they arrived more or less together. She was wearing an elaborate and expensive lace bedjacket, and her hair was carefully arranged. Still very pale, despite the expert application of make-up, her icy pale-blue eyes followed them as they made themselves comfortable in the chairs that had been brought in especially for the conference. 'Well, well,' she said. 'I'm certainly popular today. Good-morning, Mr Putnam.'

'Good-morning,' both men said together.

Mrs Armstrong raised an eyebrow. 'Father and son?'

'Actually—' Carl began.

'And I suppose she's the Holy Ghost,' said Mrs Armstrong wryly, indicating Susie Brock. 'I would appreciate it if we could get straight on with this.' Mrs Armstrong was taking command. 'I'm still not very strong and need my rest. I'm not to get excited, the doctor said so.'

'We'll try to be efficient.' Carl Putnam's voice was soothing.

'This meeting is at my instigation,' George said. 'I have some questions that need answers.'

Everyone wondered where he had learned the word 'instigation', including George himself. It had just popped out. Maybe this wasn't going to be so difficult after all. Perhaps he knew more than he thought he did. And then again . . . he wished she didn't have such pale, cold eyes.

'I talked to your little girl there yesterday,' Mrs Armstrong complained. 'What more do you want?'

'We know that you were here in the clinic when your husband was killed—' George began.

'Obviously,' Mrs Armstrong said.

'Do you know of anyone who would want to kill him?'

'One of my many lovers, you mean?' she asked sarcastically. 'One of the dozens of people he cheated in business? Your own boss? Oh, yes – I know lots of people who are glad Jack is dead.'

'Are you one of them?' Susie asked. During lunch she had decided that her earlier softly, softly approach had gained them nothing.

George looked horrified.

'Now wait a minute,' Carl protested.

Mrs Armstrong looked at the girl, apparently unbothered by the direct question. 'In a way, yes. I won't have to answer to anyone now, or accommodate their wishes and tastes. I can live my own life. So in that way I am glad. In all other ways I am sorry. I loved my husband and I will miss him terribly. He made life interesting.' Her voice was calm. Too calm, perhaps. It was a little unnerving.

'Can you be more specific?' George asked. 'About his enemies, I mean?'

The pale eyes fixed on him. 'No,' she said. 'I put such people out of my mind.'

'It would help us a lot,' George persisted.

'I'm sure it would.'

'Please, Irene – surely you want Jack's killer brought to justice?' Carl asked.

'It won't change anything.'

'No, but—'

'Don't you want revenge?' Susie asked.

'No,' Mrs Armstrong said. 'I am not a vengeful person.'

I'll bet you are, Susie thought. I'd bet you're a bitch and a half when you're crossed. You're enjoying this, aren't you? But she said nothing further.

George cleared his throat. The pale eyes turned towards him again. 'Your husband's personal papers are at your home, I believe.'

'I suppose they are. Jack has . . . had an office there.'

'I'd like permission to go through them in order to find out anything we could about possible motives for his murder.'

'No.'

'But—'

'No, not until I can be there too.'

'The doctor tells me you need at least a week longer here, Irene,' Carl said. 'Surely . . .'

'The sooner we cover all the possibilities, the sooner we can nail who did this,' George broke in. 'The longer we wait, the less likely it will be that we can close the case.'

'That is not my problem,' Mrs Armstrong said.

George took a deep breath. 'It is usual for families to

co-operate with the law in these cases, Mrs Armstrong. I can get a Court Order.'

The woman in the bed looked at her lawyer. 'Can he?'

'Probably,' Carl said unhappily. 'Almost certainly.'

'Do you always do this?' she asked George.

'Do what?'

'Harass bereaved widows?'

'I am not harassing you, Mrs Armstrong. I am merely making a polite request. I don't want to go through the courts, but if I have to, part of my reasoning will be that you seem to want to hide something. As you are trapped here and unable to take care of destroying documents yourself, I can understand your reluctance to allow us—'

'Now wait a minute, George,' Carl interrupted.

'What else can it be?' George asked innocently. 'If she refuses to allow us access to her husband's office it must be because something there worries her.'

'Not necessarily,' Mrs Armstrong said with a smile that was quite terrible to see. 'I might just be determined to be difficult. They'll tell you I'm difficult. I am. It pleases me to be difficult. Reactions are so varied. It can be quite amusing.'

George's eyes met his father's across the bed. Carl raised both eyebrows, but said nothing.

'We have already gone through his campaign headquarters,' George said. 'Mr Otis let us in.'

'Then Mr Otis is an ass. But you found nothing, am I right?'

'Nothing,' George agreed. 'All the more reason why we need to assess the contents of your husband's desk, papers, any diaries or relevant documents—'

'No.'

Susie Brock crossed her legs and spoke up again: 'We can make certain you don't make contact with anyone outside, Mrs Armstrong. We can make certain you can't get someone in there to destroy things before we get access. We can instruct the staff here not to carry out any messages, or to allow visitors, to cut off your phone, to isolate you completely starting right now.'

'And why would you do that?'

'To protect you, of course.' Susie's smile was kindly. 'The person who killed your husband might want to kill you too. It's a risk.'

'Nonsense.'

Susie shrugged. 'We just don't know, do we?'

Again Irene Armstrong turned to Carl Putnam. 'Can they do that?'

'Yes.'

'I thought you were supposed to protect me against this kind of thing. They're trying to intimidate me.'

'I can only advise you that it would be sensible to co-operate with the police in their investigation of your husband's murder, Irene. They are within their rights, so far.'

'This is very annoying.'

'We can see that,' Susie said. 'But murder has no respect for privacy, Mrs Armstrong. Once it happens, a life is exposed. Must be exposed, in order to find reasons and clues.'

'Jack's life, not mine,' she snapped.

'If that's what's worrying you, I can be with them throughout their search, Irene,' Carl said. 'I can make sure they only deal with what is relevant. I can look at everything first . . .'

'But anything you find about me is confidential, client privilege and all that? They can't see anything to do with me, just Jack?'

'That's all we want, Mrs Armstrong. As it is, we should have done it already. In view of your attitude, you'll probably be glad to know your maid wouldn't allow us entry without a warrant.' George still burned over the sulky defiance of Tizzy Turkle, standing behind the storm door, glaring at him, saying 'no way, no way' like a parrot. He'd felt like a jerk, standing there.

'Good for her.' Mrs Armstrong was obviously satisfied with Tizzy, even if George wasn't. 'That's her job.'

181

'My job is to find the person who killed your husband. Let me do it.'

Mrs Armstrong closed her eyes and sighed. Perhaps she was tired of being difficult, or maybe she was just bored. She waved a limp hand. 'Do what you like, I don't care any more.' She opened her eyes to look at Carl Putnam. 'But *you* take charge of any bank-books or financial records or anything like that. I want what's due to me and I don't want anything taken away that might interfere with that.'

'I'll make sure that they take only copies of important items,' Carl assured her. 'I'll get receipts for everything.' He looked across at George. 'Aside from a few minor bequests, everything in Jack's will goes to Irene. They're her papers now.'

'Did you know that, Mrs Armstrong?' Susie asked.

'Well, of course I did.' Again, the terrible smile. 'But I was here in the clinic unable to get out of bed. I didn't kill him, if that's what you're driving at.'

'You could have paid someone.'

'With what, my American Express card? I have no money here,' Mrs Armstrong pointed out. 'And the nurses would have noticed any suspicious characters going in and out of my room, now wouldn't they? Especially any wearing an "I am a murderer" badge.'

'You have a phone,' Susie pointed out.

'Yes, I do. And all calls go through a switchboard downstairs, so you could easily find out if I had called Thugs Anonymous, couldn't you?' The smile was condescending now. It was clear she liked sitting up in the high bed, above them. A little edge of power. A haughty view of the local peasants.

'I think we're done here,' George said, with a scowl in Susie's direction. 'Thank you for seeing us, Mrs Armstrong. Does your maid know Mr Putnam, here?'

'Oh, yes. He's been to the house many times to see Jack.'

'Then perhaps you'll just write a note to her, giving us permission to enter the house to search it.'

'To search the office,' she corrected him.

Carl fished a piece of blank stationery out of his briefcase and handed her a pen. She wrote something quickly and passed it back. 'There.' She addressed George. 'You've had your way. Are you pleased?'

'I'm relieved,' George said. 'Thank you.'

'Go away.' Mrs Armstrong closed her eyes. 'Just go away now.'

They left.

'What the hell was that all about?' George demanded as he and Susie got back into the car.

'What?' Susie asked innocently.

'You were antagonizing her.'

'I was, wasn't I?' Susie looked pleased.

'Well, for crying out loud . . .' he began.

'She likes to push people around – she admitted it,' Susie said. 'Like any bully – and she is a bully, George, in her own little way – she collapses if you stand up to her. She would have had you and Mr Putnam in there for hours otherwise, dancing in polite little circles for her amusement.'

'I think we were perfectly capable of handling her.'

'Sure you were – but I kept it short and to the point.'

'Don't do it again. I'm in charge of this investigation, remember.'

'Of course I remember, George. I was only trying to help save you some time. You haven't got any to waste on a silly, selfish woman, when there are more important things to do. She was being awkward for the sake of it and I wasn't amused. Here we are. What's next?' She gave him a big, trusting smile.

'Dad said he'd meet us at the house,' he muttered, starting up the engine. His father's car had already driven out of the parking lot beside the clinic.

'Good,' Susie said. 'We can get that in before we clock off.'

He glanced at her as he pulled out onto the highway and headed back into town. 'Got a date or something?'

'As a matter of fact, I do.' She didn't elaborate.

'Who with?'

'Oh, look – that's a Canadian goose on the river.' Susie pointed out of the window as they crossed the bridge. 'I'm sure it is. Where are the others? They always fly in—'

'Who do you have a date with?'

She gave him a sideways look. 'What's it matter?'

'Well, I'd sure hate to make you late for some important date or other,' he growled. 'Like if we had to spend a long time at the Armstrong house, for instance.'

'There's plenty of time.' Susie leaned her head back against the head-rest. 'Anyway, he'll wait for me. He can fill in the time.'

'Who?'

'Well, if you're going to get huffy about it, never mind,' Susie said in an injured voice. 'Gee, ever since Matt was taken off this case, you've turned into a regular pain in the ass. Delusions of grandeur it sounds like to me.'

'Very funny.'

They didn't speak again until they got to the Armstrong house. When they rang the bell, Carl Putnam opened the door. He smiled. 'I got in, but there's a problem. He always kept his study locked and we can't find the key.'

'I've probably got it,' George said, producing a very full key-ring. 'These were on him when he was killed. Part of his effects. I thought they might be useful.'

'Good thinking,' Carl said approvingly. 'It's this way.'

As they went across the living-room George and Susie looked around. It was beautifully furnished but looked more like a setting for a magazine layout than a home. No family photos, no scatter of magazines or newspapers, nothing out of place. Of course, the maid had had nothing to do but keep everything perfect while Mrs Armstrong was in the clinic and Mr Armstrong was busy campaigning. Even so, there was a coldness about the décor. Pale yellow and willow green keyed into the colours of a beautiful Chinese carpet. Accents were in darker green and gold, with a few raspberry-coloured cushions carefully plumped on the two settees that bracketed the fireplace. Over it was a huge portrait of Mrs Armstrong, very much the Southern belle, gazing out over their heads much as she had done in the clinic. And looking considerably younger and healthier, too.

Tizzy Turkle stood next to a door on the far side of the fireplace. 'I couldn't find one anywhere,' she said to Carl Putnam, pointedly ignoring George and Susie.

'That's all right, we have one.' Carl smiled at her.

Tizzy turned, stared at George and Susie, gave a small snort and stalked out, head high.

Susie looked at George with a raised eyebrow. 'Old enemies?' she asked.

He cleared his throat. 'Not exactly.'

'Ah,' she said knowingly, but he didn't rise to the bait.

Jack Armstrong's office was not tidy. Indeed, it was quite dusty in places – obviously the maid's duties didn't extend to this room at all. There were papers scattered over the desk and one of the drawers of a file cabinet behind the desk was half open. There seemed to be a strong breeze in the room, for the papers on the desk stirred and fluttered.

Looking around, Carl Putnam pointed to a window. 'It's been broken,' he said. He went over to examine it. 'Broken very professionally, in fact.' He turned back to the desk, then looked at George and Susie. 'Someone's been in here already,' he added. 'Somebody got here before us.'

SEVENTEEN

HELEN POLLOCK WAS VERY RELIEVED to see Matt Gabriel come into the bookshop. She hurried over. 'You got my message, then?'

'I did.'

'It's about Jack Armstrong.'

He frowned at her. 'You know I'm not really on that case now, Helen. If there's something you have to say about a crime, or anything else, you should tell George Putnam. He's in charge at the moment.'

'Oh, pooh,' Helen said. 'George is no more the real sheriff of this town than I am and you know it. You just did it for appearance's sake. Everybody is aware of that.'

'There's a little more to it than that. I am a suspect, you know.'

'Rubbish,' Helen said briskly. 'Anyway, I'm glad you're here and feeling better.' She peered at him closely. 'You *are* feeling better, aren't you?'

'I'm fine. Really.'

'Well, all right, if you're sure. I want you to see something. It's nothing to do with the Armstrong murder. At least . . . well, maybe it is, but you'd be a better judge of that than I am. Come back here, there's something I want to show you.'

Matt started down the aisle after her, then glanced around. 'Where's Lisa? There's quite a line at the desk.'

'I had to let her go.'

'You surprise me.'

'I surprised her, too.' Helen's voice was grim. 'In here.'

She went into the storage room at the back of the shop and Matt followed, pausing while she turned on the light and shut the door behind them. She went over to a stack of boxes, removed the top two and stood back. 'In there,' she said, pointing.

Matt went over, hunkered down and opened the box. Unsurprisingly, it was full of books. He glanced up at Helen questioningly and she looked upset.

'Take them out,' she said. 'Have a look at them.'

He did so and was startled to see they were extremely hard-core pornography, both written and photographed. All different – and all demonstrating a deep depravity. Mostly paedophilic, some S&M, other perversions so extreme even he had never encountered them except in a textbook on abnormal psychology.

He glanced up at her worriedly. 'I didn't think you dealt—'

'I don't,' Helen snapped. 'Of course I don't. Those are all special-ordered, through Lisa. By Jack Armstrong. Paid for in cash up front.'

'They're pretty disgusting.'

'Indeed.' Helen's face was flushed. 'I'd be grateful if you would dispose of them for me, Matt. I really don't want to touch them myself.'

He stood up, dropping the last volume he'd examined back into the box with the others. 'I can understand that. What I can't understand is what Armstrong . . . I mean, I don't think I ever heard any indication . . .'

'The All-American Boy,' Helen said with heavy irony. 'No children, you notice.'

'His wife is not very well.'

Helen sighed. 'And that is supposed to excuse it?'

'No, of course not. These things don't start suddenly with a sickly wife,' Matt said. 'This is evidence of deep-seated problems.'

'Problems.' Helen was disgusted. 'I know – harsh upbringing, cruel parents, all that sort of thing. Horse feathers.

187

I saw him grow up, his parents were fine, he had pretty much everything he wanted.'

'Maybe that was the trouble,' Matt said helplessly. 'How can we tell what went on in someone's secret mind?' He paused. 'Or perhaps he was just selling the stuff for profit?'

'He'd have to charge a hefty price, then. Some of those books are incredibly expensive, as you might imagine. She didn't get them for him wholesale either. One of them – one of the worst – cost over three hundred dollars. According to Lisa, that is.'

'Was she taking a cut?'

Helen shook her head. 'I think so. She seemed to think Armstrong was doing some kind of "research" on sexual problems. That's apparently what he told her, anyway. He had a list of publishers, the exact books he wanted and so on. She put the orders through under my business name – so now it's on record somewhere that I deal in this sort of garbage. I expect I'll be gettting some very bizarre sales promotion material in the future on the strength of it.' She looked suddenly as old and ill as she really was. 'I don't understand how Lisa could have been so stupid. She said he told her that only a young person could understand how important it was to have this kind of information when it came to stamping out immorality, that I was too old to understand and wouldn't have helped him, which is damn true. But she bought it, bought it all.'

'Maybe he was telling the truth,' Matt said.

'Oh, really? You believe that?' Helen stared at him. 'You really believe that? Then you're as naïve as she was. Nobody needs to *see* that sludge to know how bad it is, how it might affect someone. All you have to know is that it exists. And as far as I know – and I've lived here all my life and so have you – we've never had much trouble of that kind in Blackwater. If anybody would have known about it you would. Or the local doctors. Small towns – it would have come out somehow. No, he wanted that for himself, or for someone he knew all too well, believe me.'

'We'll never know, now,' Matt said, bending down to close the box, then lifting it up. 'Not for sure.'

'Doesn't it matter? Doesn't it tell us what kind of man he was?'

'It tells us we didn't *know* what kind of man he was,' was all Matt would allow. 'Still don't.' He shifted the box to a more comfortable position. 'I'll pass this along to George, Helen. It will be easier for me than it would have been for you.' He realized that her hesitation to do this herself had been born of embarrassment at displaying that kind of material to a younger man. As if, by even touching it, it had her tacit approval or interest.

'Thank you,' Helen said quietly. Now that she had moved the burden to his shoulders she seemed suddenly tired. 'I just don't know this business any more, Matt. Don't understand half of what I *do* sell – some of the modern novels come pretty close to that kind of thing these days. *American Psycho*, for instance, lots of what they call "airport books". What is it they say – they're "pushing the envelope"? I didn't know we were in an envelope, other than common decency and respect for one another. It just makes me feel sick. Maybe I should sell up like Bob says, get out of it altogether.'

'I'm told the classics still sell steadily,' Matt said gently. 'And textbooks. And children's books. And cookbooks. And gardening books. And biographies. And self-help books. And—'

She managed a laugh. 'All right, all right, you've made the point.'

'Besides, you're the only bookshop in town. Where would we get our information and culture from if you weren't here?'

'Oh, one of the big chains will push in eventually, you can be sure of that,' she said wearily. She watched him shift the heavy box from one hip to the other. 'You take that away, Matt. Do what you have to do. I'll plod on, doing what I do. Maybe we can keep Blackwater respectable for a little while longer.'

He followed her out into the brightness of the busy bookshop. 'It would be a lot easier if people didn't keep killing each other off,' he said in a low voice. 'Lately I'm beginning to think it's something in the water.'

'Or in the air? I blame television and the movies. Books are still ...' She paused, glancing at the box he held. 'No, I can't even say that, can I?' She sighed. 'I think I'll go home early tonight. Read some poetry. It might clear my mind.'

'Try Dorothy Parker,' Matt suggested. 'It might cheer you up.'

She smiled at him. 'You know, I just might at that.'

Mrs Toby stood beside Maggie Phillips waiting to be served at the delicatessen. 'Shame about all these killings,' she said, eyeing the pastrami in the glass case beside her.

'Sure is.' Maggie had her eye on a nice piece of salami.

'Do you think Frog Bartlett killed Moony Packard?'

'Got no opinion one way or t'other,' Maggie replied, watching in alarm as the counterman reached for the salami. Now somebody else would get it. Peeved, she glanced at Mrs Toby. 'What do you care who killed Moony Packard?'

'Oh, just wondering.' Mrs Toby flushed. This questioning business wasn't as easy in real life as it seemed to be in books. 'He was an odd man, wasn't he?'

Maggie snorted. 'You'd have to ask Sally Dukas about that.'

'Sally Dukas?' Mrs Toby asked ingenuously, knowing full well that Sally Dukas was the big blonde girl who worked at McDonald's.

'He kept her on a string,' Maggie said, stepping forward as the line moved ahead. She still had her eye on the salami, which hadn't been diminished much by the previous customer's depredations. 'On, off, on, off. She was a fool to think he'd ever marry her. Married to that crazy brother of his, you ask me.'

'Sally Dukas,' Mrs Toby mused. 'Mercy me. I never knew.'

Maggie eyed her. 'You don't know everything, Margaret Toby, and don't you forget it.'

Margaret drew herself up. 'I don't forget it. I was only saying . . .'

'Some folks think they run the place,' Maggie muttered. 'I . . .'

'I'll have two pounds of that salami there in one piece, thank you,' Maggie said, ignoring Margaret's outrage. 'And I don't have all day to stand around gossiping either,' she added with a look over her shoulder.

Margaret had no response to that.

Emily Gibbons finally found a parking space on Woodward Avenue, locked up the car and walked back to the Fallon Building where Robarts and Pickering had their offices. She'd phoned for an appointment earlier and if she hurried she might be on time.

She still wasn't sure what she was going to ask Robarts and was hoping inspiration would strike her before she got out of the elevator on the tenth floor.

It didn't.

'Hello,' she said to the receptionist. 'I'm Miss Pritchard. I have an appointment with Mr Robarts.'

The receptionist, a recent high-school graduate from the bored look of her, smiled. 'If you'd like to take a seat, Mr Robarts is on the phone right now. I'll tell him you're here as soon as he's free.'

'Thank you.' Emily sat on one of the two tweed-covered sofas opposite the reception desk and waited. She waited quite a while – either Mr Robarts was a phone freak, or he was having his coffee and doughnuts, or in the john, or just having a quiet snooze in his office.

Finally the girl looked up and beckoned to her. 'Mr Robarts is free now. Second door on the right.' She gestured towards a corridor and went back to her crossword. Obviously a girl out to better herself.

Emily knocked gently on the door indicated, waited a moment, then entered.

Robarts, behind a desk full of papers, glanced up and then stood. 'Miss Pritchard?'

'Diane Pritchard. I've just come from Crabtree and Putnam.' Now this was absolutely true. Before leaving Blackwater Bay Emily had carefully gone and stood in the foyer of Crabtree and Putnam and then gone straight to her car. She also knew that Dominic was listed on the Crabtree and Putnam stationary as D. Pritchard. She knew she was a conniving little sneak. She was quite proud of it. She wasn't certain that Dominic would agree, so she didn't intend to tell him.

'Sit down, please,' Robarts said, all graciousness. He was a very, very small man, practically dwarfed by his desk when he sat down again. His big brown leather chair seemed on the verge of swallowing him up and she felt certain his feet dangled below it. But he was not cute, for all that he was diminutive. He had a narrow, foxy face and thin, reddish hair slicked straight back from a high, domed forehead. 'What can I do for you, Miss Pritchard?' His voice was bigger than he was.

'Well, there are just a few questions we need to clear up, on behalf of Mrs Armstrong, you understand.'

'Oh?'

'Questions of form, really. Particularly in relation to the late Mr Armstrong's campaign funds.'

'I see. And the questions are?'

'What happens to the money?' Emily asked bluntly.

He smiled. 'I'm afraid it goes straight into party funds,' he said. 'It's rare to have a surplus, you understand – usually election campaigns are expensive and absorb every penny given to the candidate. In fact, party funds are normally required to supplement what a candidate raises on his own behalf. In this case – well, we shall have to see when all the expenses are paid, of course – but I imagine there will be a reasonable amount to be paid to the party.'

'To the party and not to Mrs Armstrong?'

'That is the usual procedure, yes. The money is given, after all, to support a candidate's election, not to the candidate himself. As you may know, campaign funds are now regulated very carefully and a complete audit is required after an election – whether the candidate is successful or not. In this case – this very unusual case – we shall undoubtedly have some surplus.'

'The money wasn't actually given to Mr Armstrong, then?'

'No, all cheques were deposited to a separate account, as required by law.'

'All cheques.'

'Yes.'

'And what about cash donations?'

'I don't believe we had any cash donations.'

'Oh, surely – ordinary people contributed as well as companies and wealthy individuals. I've seen it myself, collecting tins at rallies and so on.'

'Ah, of course. Those would be counted up, totalled and deposited in the same account.'

'And what about larger cash contributions given anonymously?'

'I'm sure I would have remembered anything like that and I don't. As I say, it is all regulated.'

'But these kinds of donations have been made in the past.'

His eyes narrowed. 'Are you asking me whether anything irregular was done in this case?'

'No, just making an observation,' Emily said with a smile. His eyes were so black they seemed to have no iris, just flat black, like a shark's. Or was that too easy a comparison? Emily wondered. She did not like Mr Robarts and she sensed he didn't like her for some reason. The fact that she was falsely representing herself didn't add to her confidence. 'I suppose you now have to account for every penny.'

'Oh, yes,' Robarts agreed almost genially. 'Every penny.'

'Will Mrs Armstrong be given a copy of the audit when it is done?'

'If she is interested, of course. However, I was never under the impression that Mrs Armstrong took the least interest in Mr Armstrong's election activities.'

'She takes an interest in money, Mr Robarts.'

'Ah.' He nodded. 'Of course.'

'We'd be interested to see a list of contributors, so that Mrs Armstrong can write thanking them for their support.'

He raised his hands in a helpless gesture. 'I'm afraid I don't have such a list to hand just at the moment. Many people supported him. He was a very charismatic man. Has there been any progress in finding his killer?'

'No, unfortuntely.'

'I understand his opponent, the present incumbent, has removed himself from the case.'

'Yes, that's true. An honourable gesture.'

'He is certain to win now, of course.'

'It seems likely.'

'Very convenient.'

'If you're implying that the murder of Mr Armstrong was political in nature—'

'All acts are political in nature, Miss Pritchard. It's within the realms of possibility that removing a candidate who appeared to be winning was viewed as being useful to the present sheriff's campaign by someone.'

'Useful, but not desirable.'

'No?'

'People are suspicious by nature, Mr Robarts. I would guess that Sheriff Gabriel might lose votes because of that rather than gain them. Oh, by the way, Mrs Armstrong would like the audit of Mr Armstrong's campaign funds to be made public.'

He sat up straighter. 'Made public?'

'Yes. And, of course, as soon as possible. Is that a problem?'

'Well . . . I have a busy practice here and quite a bit on at the moment. We didn't think we would be doing anything about it until after the election. And, as I said earlier, there are expenses still to come in. A final reckoning may take some time.'

'But surely you have records you've kept, day to day, week to week. Isn't it simply a matter of having someone collate them and add things up? Not that I'm an accountant, but it seems to me to be fairly straightforward. I don't see why it would take so long. Surely you could assign it to some junior member of your staff?'

He stared at her for a long time, picked up a pencil and began turning it between his fingers. 'What the hell do you really want, Miss Pritchard?'

'Really want?'

'Yes, let's get onto what really interests you. Or . . . interests "Mrs Armstrong"?'

'Well . . .'

'Why the hurry? What do you think an audit will show? Aren't you really looking for information as to who might have had a reason to kill Jack Armstrong? Me, for instance?'

'Why, good heavens, Mr Robarts . . .'

'Oh, bullshit.' He threw down the pencil he'd been toying with. 'You – she – someone – wants to know whether I skimmed anything off the top or bottom, isn't that right?'

'Would we ever know, Mr Robarts?' Emily countered.

He smiled abruptly. 'No,' he said. 'You'd never know. I am a very clever accountant, Miss Pritchard. No one will ever know whether I dipped into the funds or not. I can tell you that, in fact, I did not. But it is up to you whether to believe it or not.'

'A good investigation could—'

But he was shaking his head. 'No. Not even a *very* good investigation. You want to know whether I stole from Jack and killed him to prevent it being discovered? Then what am I doing here, Miss Pritchard? Why did I see you? Why haven't I fled to Bolivia or someplace with my ill-gotten gains?'

'Because you're a very clever man, Mr Robarts. You said so yourself.'

'Well, you can go back to Mr Putnam – or whoever it

was that sent you – and say that. I am a very clever man. But I am not a killer.'

Emily stood up. 'I don't suppose you would allow us to see the accounts at this point?'

'No, I don't suppose I would.'

'We can get a Court Order.'

'Oh, really? Then do so, by all means. I look forward to co-operating with you – whoever you are. Unusual name for a woman, Dominic, isn't it?'

She felt herself flushing. 'I don't know what you mean.'

'Dear me. I *am* a very clever man, but you are not a very clever young woman, are you? Goodbye, Miss "Pritchard". Oh, and give my regards to Carl Putnam when you get back. When I spoke to him about you a little while ago he didn't sound too happy.'

'Oh.'

He regarded her calmly with those black, black eyes, obviously unprepared to continue the charade. She left hurriedly. Damn, she thought as she went down in the elevator. Damn, damn, damn. Dominic was sure to find out now.

'We should have gone over that place two minutes after we found the body!' George said angrily. They were back in the office and he was furious at the discovery of the presumed burglary.

'Mr – your father didn't think anything was actually missing,' Susie said in a soothing voice.

'How do we know that? We don't know what was there before.'

'No, but your father did. Probably did.'

'Probably isn't enough. He admitted he hadn't been to Armstrong's house for over a month.'

'But we have Armstrong's daybook, his calendar, his files.'

'What's left of them. How do we know what was taken out?' George was pacing and Susie was getting a stiff neck watching him go back and forth, back and forth. She was

196

tempted to put a foot out and trip him but, amusing as that might be, it wouldn't help.

'And the safe was still locked,' she pointed out.

'That doesn't mean anything. It locks when you close it.'

'Yes, but it wasn't broken into.'

'Somebody knew the combination, that's all.'

'But who would know that?'

'My father did.'

Susie was shocked. 'Surely you don't think your *father*—'

'Well, of course not. But if *he* knew, other people might have known. If he made a note of it – and you saw he had in Armstrong's file – anybody in his office could have found it. Or Otis, for instance, he might have had it. Or Mrs Armstrong – and she could have told anyone she wanted to.'

'Her jewellery was still in there – it wasn't a thief, George. Whoever it was, they weren't after anything they could sell.'

'Oh, really? What about papers or photographs that could be worth something – maybe a lot more than those few pieces of her jewellery.'

'Oh – I hadn't thought of that.'

'He was up for election – whoever it was could have been after something compromising, something he could use for blackmail.'

'Or she.'

'What?' He stopped long enough to stare at her.

'Or she, I said. It didn't take much force to break that pane in the french window, did it? It could have been a woman. Perhaps a woman after something that belonged to *her*. Letters, maybe. Compromising letters about an affair with Armstrong.'

'Armstrong wasn't known to be a ladies' man,' George objected.

'Not *known*, no. That's the whole point. I mean, with such a sickly wife, maybe he . . . looked elsewhere for solace.'

'Solace? That's a namby-pamby word for it.'

'There's no need to be crude.'

'Police work *is* crude. Didn't they teach you that? Jeez, you'd think they'd have mentioned things like murder, rape, beatings . . .'

'They mentioned them, they mentioned them . . . but I don't have to use the same words, do I?'

'No, of course not. You're a *lady*, with a degree and everything.'

'That really bugs you, doesn't it?' She was only prepared to take so much from this ox. He might be in charge of this case, but he was not God. Not yet, anyway, although he seemed to be practising a lot for the role.

'Listen—' George began.

'You're straying from the point, people,' Tilly interrupted. 'You're supposed to be concentrating on the Armstrong case.'

'Compromising letters,' George sneered.

'Did you find any bank-books?' Tilly asked.

'Yes – two savings accounts and a cheque-book. Mr Putnam has them, he's checking with the bank that the balances are okay,' Susie answered.

'Insurance forms?' Tilly continued.

'Yes. Mrs Armstrong is going to do very well out of her husband's murder,' George said through clenched teeth. 'We could really stick it to her if she wasn't laid up in that damn clinic. As far as we could tell with a quick look, she's about two million bucks better off than she was when he was alive. And there's probably more someplace, other accounts, maybe, business insurance, that kind of thing. Who knows? Could be three or four million. And she wasn't all that broken up about him either, if you ask me. Not at all.'

'Your father will work it all out,' Susie said.

'In time, in time. Meanwhile, I'm supposed to figure out who killed the bastard and now I've got an unexplained break-in, too.'

'Maybe the break-in happened *before* the killing,' Susie said slowly. 'He wasn't found until after ten the next morning and he was killed during the night. Maybe whoever killed him broke in – maybe Armstrong caught him breaking in, but the guy got the better of him and—'

'And drove him out to the development site and executed him? Get serious,' George said. 'Armstrong was a big strong guy, I can't see him being pushed around like that. He was handcuffed but there were no signs of a struggle – and he would have put up a struggle, even handcuffed. Anybody would.'

'*You* would – that's not to say he did. Maybe he was a chicken-heart, or perhaps—'

'Oh, forget it. Whoever killed him probably wasn't the person who broke in at all. The break-in could have happened the next night, or the one after that, as soon as the word got out that he was dead. The maid never went in there because it was locked, remember? She didn't know when it was broken into – she was as surprised as we were.'

'Yes, that's true,' Susie admitted reluctantly.

'But if everything was there—' Tilly began.

'As far as we could tell,' George interrupted.

'. . . then why break in at all?' Tilly finished. 'What could the reason possibly be?'

'Who knows?'

'Maybe it was just somebody looking for what they could find, knowing the house was empty once Armstrong was dead,' George said. 'Never opened the safe at all. Only sort of searched the desk and files. Took a few knick-knacks as souvenirs. Some ghoul looking for kicks. Possibly it's as simple as that.'

Susie and Tilly exchanged a glance. 'You wish,' Susie said.

George sank down in his chair. 'Yeah – I wish.'

Nell Norton had been to the former offices of the Ottaway Patio and Paving Company and found no one there. The yard was filled with idle machinery, and heaps of gravel and other materials, but the office was dark and locked.

Finally, in the little shop opposite the yard, she discovered that Ottaway himself was in the hospital. 'Bloody ulcer,' was the explanation offered by the little Pakistani man behind the counter who was glad to be able to supply her with the information. Or anything else on offer in his shop, from cigarettes to window cleaner.

Mrs Norton was not that familiar with Lemonville and she drove in circles for about ten minutes until she located the hospital. 'Hate to think if I was having a heart attack or something,' she muttered to herself as she wedged her rather elderly car in between a flashy sedan and a four-wheel-drive off-roader. The parking lot attested to the fact that there was either an epidemic in town, or open visiting hours. The latter turned out to be the case.

When she finally located Mr Ottaway he was in a two-bed ward on the third floor. He did not look like a happy man. She didn't know whether that was due to his illness, or represented his normal state of mind.

'Mr Ottaway?' she ventured.

He turned his head on the pillow. 'Yeah?'

'Of Ottaway Patio and Paving?'

'Yeah. But if you want your patio done you're too late. I'm out of business.'

'Oh, that's too bad.' Mrs Norton's tone was sympathetic as she sat down on the chair beside the bed. 'But I don't have a patio.'

'I don't suppose you have a highway needs repairing either,' Ottaway growled.

'Not just at the moment,' Mrs Norton rejoined. 'I sold my last one on Tuesday.'

'Funny,' he said without a smile. 'Who are you, then? Not from the church are you? I told Father—'

'No, no, not the church. I'm from Blackwater Bay,' Mrs Norton explained. 'A group of us are looking into the Armstrong murder.'

Ottaway stared at her. 'Jack Armstrong?'

'Yes. We have only the one Armstrong murder in Black-water.'

'And not a minute too soon,' Ottaway said with every evidence of satisfaction. 'Bastard.'

'Dear me.'

'He cheated me,' Ottaway went on. 'He cheated me and he destroyed my business and he put me in here.'

'Mr Armstrong did all that?'

'Yes, Mr Armstrong did. And then do you know what he had the damned nerve to do?'

'I can't imagine.'

'He sent me a letter asking me to contribute to his god-damned election campaign. That's when the ulcer started to act up. Can you believe it?'

'I know ulcers have a way—'

'I wanted to cut his heart out when my company went down and he asks me for money. Money I haven't got because of him and his stinking project that never came off. Big talker, Armstrong. He was a big, big talker.' Mr Ottaway was getting a little red in the face and Mrs Norton began to be concerned.

'He's dead now, Mr Ottaway, there's no need to upset yourself.'

Ottaway leered at her. 'Dead, right. Damned dead. Got what was coming to him and no mistake. It was a good day when he got it, a real good day. But it didn't do me any good. I got so excited I went on a bender and busted my ulcer – the ulcer he gave me – wide open.'

'You celebrated Mr Armstrong's death?'

'I sure as hell did. Say, listen, lady – what's it to you?'

'Do you ever go to Blackwater, Mr Ottaway? Have you been there recently? Last week, perhaps?'

'Who wants to know? You haven't told me who you are yet. Why should I talk to you?'

'Because I am an interested party,' Mrs Norton said primly. 'We want to find out who killed Mr Armstrong because suspicion is falling on our sheriff and we know he didn't do it.'

'So you think maybe I did?' Ottaway asked, sitting up with a wince and glaring at her. The man in the next bed, who had been dozing, opened his eyes wide at Ottaway's tone and began to reach for the nursing call button. 'You want to pin it on me?' Ottaway bellowed.

'No, not at all. I have no idea.' Mrs Norton was getting nervous. 'We are just getting some background—'

'Get the hell out of here, lady,' Ottaway shouted. 'Whether I was in Blackwater last week or not is no business of yours.'

'Then you *were* there? I thought you looked familiar. You were at the debate at the Town Hall, weren't you?' Mrs Norton said triumphantly. It wasn't until Ottaway began to shout that she had recognized him as one of the men who had been yelling from the audience on that dreadful night and who, she was fairly sure, had been in the crowd on the stage too. It was the reddened face that did it – he had been so pale when she first came in, but now—

'Get out of here! Stupid old bitch – get away from me!' Ottaway yelled, starting to get out of bed and becoming tangled in the tubes to his intravenous drip.

'Please, please, calm yourself,' Mrs Norton said in alarm, rising quickly and starting to back towards the door. 'There's no need to get excited, it's really just a matter of–' She bumped into a nurse who was rushing in – not in answer to the electronic call, which she had not heard, but because of Ottaway's shouts, which were echoing down the hall.

'Mr Ottaway, get back in that bed!' she commanded.

'Get her away from me!' Ottaway yelled, waving his arms towards Mrs Norton, who was really becoming quite shaken.

The nurse turned. 'I don't know who you are, but you must leave,' she said. 'Mr Ottaway must have complete calm.'

'We *both* need complete calm,' added the man in the other bed, glaring at Mrs Norton. He was totally bald and resembled a shaven ferret. 'Put a No Visitors sign on the door, nurse. Keep out the riff-raff.'

'Well, really . . .' stammered Mrs Norton. She went out into the hall. She had not expected to encounter anything like Mr Ottaway's rage when she commenced her questioning. Perhaps she had been too eager? He had gone up like a geyser when she asked him if he'd ever been to Blackwater. Obviously he didn't like being recognized as having attended the debate the night before Armstrong was murdered. She wished she'd had a book to read on interrogation techniques before she started this.

Was he upset because he'd done it? He had motive, he had – as far as she knew – opportunity. Means? Somebody had stolen Matt Gabriel's gun, probably someone at the debate. Ottaway had it all. She felt excitement rising in her breast. On her way past the nursing station she stopped and spoke to the nurse there who was doing some filing.

Mrs Norton cleared her throat. The nurse looked up, obviously oblivious of the fact that Mrs Norton had been the cause of the noise still coming from Mr Ottaway's room. Had she been, she might not have produced her smile so readily. 'Can I help you?' she asked.

'Yes, I think you can. When did Mr Ottaway come into the hospital?' Mrs Norton enquired.

'Mr Ottaway?'

'Room 326.'

Her face clouded. 'Oh, him. I can tell you that for sure, because it was on my birthday and it wasn't the nicest present I ever had. Last Friday. It was last Friday. Seems like a year ago.' She leaned forward. 'He's driving us crazy.' She suddenly straightened. 'Oh, I'm sorry – he's not a relative, is he?'

'No, he's not,' said Mrs Norton. 'Just an acquaintance. And you all have my sympathy.' She left the hospital with a gleam in her eye and hardly minded at all the new scratch on her rear fender, obviously left by the off-roader in an arrogant swing out of the lot. Mr Ottaway had been admitted to hospital *after* Jack Armstrong had been killed.

She had found a new suspect.

EIGHTEEN

'NOW, YOU *KNOW* WHY I'VE called you all together,' said Mrs Toby. 'It's time to share what each of us has learned.'

'What if we haven't learned anything?' Fran Robinson asked. 'I've been tied up selling houses over the past three days. I haven't even had much sleep.'

'Then you're excused,' Mrs Toby told her. 'But you can still listen and analyse and make suggestions.'

'Oh, yeah.' Fran smiled wryly. 'Unless I fall asleep on you.'

'I'm afraid I haven't much to offer, either,' said Milly Hackabush, who taught Phys. Ed. at the local high school. 'The kids at school have all been *talking* about it, but none of them seems to know anything new. It was a long shot, anyway. Kids are mostly interested in themselves, not grown-ups.'

'True,' agreed Mrs Toby.

'Well, I have something.' Snakehips Turkle proceeded to tell them about Moony Packard's gambling and the fact that he'd had a wad of cash on him the night before he'd been killed.

'Now, *that's* interesting,' said Mrs Toby.

Snakehips leaned back with a gratified look on his face. 'I thought so. Word might have got around.'

'But he mailed it.' Dorothy Finnegan explained about Moony's belief in the US Mail. 'I would think the thing to find out, if anybody can, is how much money he has in this Grantham account of his. And why he didn't want to use the local bank for it.'

'Maybe he didn't want his brother Frank to know about it,' Dorothy said. 'Frank's kind of unstable.'

'That's putting it mildly,' somebody muttered.

'Anybody find out whether anyone but Frog had anything against Moony?' Mrs Toby asked, looking around. Heads were shaken. 'Now, we are proceeding on the assumption that Frog is innocent, but if anybody hears anything to the contrary they have to report it. That's only fair.' She waited but there was still silence, although several people looked less than comfortable.

'We could be wrong about Frog,' Fran said slowly. 'I mean . . . we have to face that possibility. I myself don't think he is a murderer, but I could be wrong. We could all be wrong.'

'The only motive Frog is supposed to have had to kill Moony was the argument they had the night before, no worse than arguments they've had in the past, dozens of times,' Don Robinson pointed out.

'Yes, but there's the evidence of the wrench with Moony's blood on it. Frog's wrench and Frog's fingerprints,' Fran said, looking fondly at her husband but not happy about having to point out the physical evidence that was so damning.

'Of course Frog's fingerprints would be on it, it was his wrench,' Don countered. 'Somebody else could have worn gloves and used it.'

'Mm . . . you're right,' Fran agreed.

'It seems to me we ought to be looking around to see who had it in for *Frog*, then,' Nell Norton said. 'That's an angle we haven't covered.'

Everybody nodded slowly, thinking. 'Anybody find out anything else at all?' Mrs Toby enquired. 'Well, I have. Moony had a girlfriend.'

'Moony Packard had a *girlfriend*?' asked Nell Norton.

'Yep.' Mrs Toby was in her element. '*Cherchez la femme.*'

'Are you getting all this, Tilly?' queried Mrs Norton.

Tilly Moss nodded and continued to write in her reporter's notebook. 'Any idea who it was?' she asked Mrs Toby.

'Yep. Sally Dukas, over at the McDonald's,' she answered. 'It appears she's been after him for some time. He sees her for a while, then stops, then starts up again, then stops again.'

'Ah,' Freddy Tollett said. 'A motive – the woman scorned.'

'Somebody better talk to her,' Snakehips went on.

'Okay.' Tilly was still writing.

Dorothy Finnegan cleared her throat. 'I have something about Jack Armstrong.'

'Wait a minute, Dorothy, let's finish with Moony and Frog first.' Mrs Toby raised her hand. 'This business about Moony trusting the US Mail with cash – seems odd when they tell us never to send cash through the mail.'

'He must have known something,' Freddy suggested. 'Some special thing about the mail only an insider would know.'

'I can't think what it would be,' Dorothy mused. 'Bulky mailers addressed to banks must be a pretty obvious target. Unless . . .'

'Unless what?'

'Unless he addressed it to a person who then made the deposit *for* him,' Dorothy said slowly. 'Like an accomplice or partner, or whatever you want to call it, in Grantham. Then it would just look like an ordinary padded envelope going to a person. Could be a book, a pair of gloves, anything.'

'Who might that be?' Nell Norton asked. 'Did he have another girlfriend in Grantham? Was that why he was on-again off-again with Sally Dukas?'

They all pondered this for a while. 'It must have been somebody he trusted a lot – I mean, a thousand bucks is a fair bunch of money,' Snakehips stated.

'Maybe they took a cut,' Larry said. 'Took a cut they'd agreed on, say five or ten per cent, and then deposited the rest and sent back the stamped deposit slip. Maybe something like that.'

'Getting information out of banks is like trying to retrieve your leg from a hungry crocodile,' Freddy pointed out. 'They don't like to let go.'

'There might be some deposit slips among his papers,' Fran suggested. 'Maybe Matt ought to take another look at them.'

Tilly made a further note.

There was a knock at the back door and Nell Norton went to answer it. She came back with Emily Gibbons, who apologized for being late. 'I just got back a little while ago.' She shed her coat and sat down next to Dorothy Finnegan, who moved along the couch to make room for her.

Mrs Toby brought Emily up to date on what had been revealed and discussed so far.

'So you need to know about Sally Dukas and whether she knows about any other woman in Moony's life.' Emily ticked off on her fingers. 'Or any other *person* in his life, really – I suppose she's the best bet for that, unless you want to try to talk to brother Frank.'

'No, thanks,' said Snakehips.

'And you want to know about his winnings – how much, how often and so on,' Emily continued. 'Also which bank in Grantham he uses.'

'Yes,' agreed Mrs Toby. 'And I'd also like to know the insurance position on Moony and who the beneficiary of that might be. Probably his brother, but you never know, do you? Maybe he left something to Sally. Maybe she got impatient for it.'

'Well, Dominic has learned some things that might be relevant.' Emily leaned back and crossed her elegant long legs. 'First of all, Frog Bartlett was a secret photographer. He has files and files of pictures he's taken of townspeople over the years when they weren't looking.'

'You mean he was a Peeping Tom?' Nell Norton said, horrified.

'Oh, no – nothing like that. They were human interest, very artistic. Really excellent, apparently. Dominic has a whole file of pictures Frog took of Moony and other mail carriers that he's going through to see if there's anything in there that might give us a clue. He won't tell me who's paying for Frog's defence, by the way, although I keep asking him. That's a mystery too. Also, Frog has something called ankylosing spondylitis, which means he has a lot of pain in his spine. That goes some way to explaining his short temper and hunched posture. It also makes him extremely stiff in the mornings. So it seems less likely that he would have got up early and gone over and bashed Moony to death because it would have been very painful and difficult for him. He would have picked another time, another place, maybe even another method, if he'd wanted to kill Moony Packard.'

'That doesn't mean he couldn't have done it,' Larry objected.

'No, but it makes it less likely,' Emily told him. 'We all know that Moony was a holier-than-thou loudmouth, so although he had a public argument with Frog the night before he died, he could also have had other more private enemies.'

'Matt has been wondering about that,' Tilly put in. 'People didn't like Moony much, but he couldn't find anybody who hated him enough to kill him.'

'That doesn't mean one doesn't exist,' Emily insisted. 'We've got to keep looking for possibilities.'

'All right, that's what we have about Moony and Frog,' Mrs Toby said, after waiting a moment for anyone else to speak. 'Now what about the Armstrong thing? Dorothy, you had something you wanted to contribute.'

Dorothy Finnegan cleared her throat. 'Yes. I've been bringing the murders up at work – that's how I got to know about Moony mailing things to people and to himself all the time.'

'Oh, that's a point – was Moony on his own mail route?' Freddy interrupted. 'Did he deliver his own mail?'

Dorothy shook her head. 'No. Homer Brophy delivered to Moony's address. Moony's route was on the other side of town.'

'Oh.' Freddy was clearly disappointed. He didn't elucidate whatever theory he'd had in mind. 'Sorry, go on about Armstrong, then.'

'Well, I mentioned the Armstrong killing and somebody said he brought work to the town, and somebody else said no, he didn't. That he *seemed* to bring work here, but what he actually did was award contracts to his buddies in Grantham and then they hired local brawn just for the donkey work. So there were a lot of local contractors who didn't appreciate him one little bit.' She looked down at her hands. 'They mentioned one name – Sam Decker. Apparently he put in the lowest bid for some electrical work, but the contract went to one of Armstrong's Army, as usual.'

'We know about Armstrong's Army.' Nell Norton glanced at Fran.

'We don't,' Larry said curiously.

Nell explained about the friendly contractors and the shady goings-on. 'Armstrong made a lot of promises concerning his new housing project, apparently, and then when work got held up, a lot of people were in trouble because they'd ordered supplies, hired men and so on, and were stuck with being cash-poor. A couple of them went out of business, although there might have been other reasons for that, but he helped. One in particular is a possibility – a Mel Ottaway over in Lemonville. It seems he got something in the mail last week that made him wildly angry. Armstrong – or presumably one of his team – sent him a letter asking him for a campaign contribution. Ottaway was at the debate the night before Armstrong was killed because he wanted to give Armstrong a piece of his mind.' She told them about her visit to the Lemonville hospital and reported Ottaway's reaction to her questioning. She produced this bombshell with some modesty, considering she had been holding it in all through the Moony Packard discussion. 'Maybe he gave him more than that,' she concluded.

Dorothy cleared her throat. 'I heard there was another investor who'd had a large stake in the project and got cash-flow problems as a result of the stoppage.' She looked around the room. 'Vic Moss.'

Tilly looked up. Vic Moss, who was no relation, was a local 'businessman' who was always viewed with suspicion. Never caught, never charged. His local country club's 'activities' were tolerated because he never allowed anything to get out of hand. Many people were convinced, not without reason, that Vic Moss was up to all kinds of naughty things, but nothing had ever been proved.

'Oh, my,' said Larry Lovich. 'The Mafia. They "execute", don't they?'

'Matt has said a lot of times that Vic Moss may be crooked, but he only preys on his own kind and he's not part of any Family business,' Tilly said. She felt she constantly had to defend Moss because of their sharing the same surname. 'What goes on out at that country club stays out there. And even if Matt decided to bust him one day, Vic has plenty of Grantham lawyers who could get him out of any corner we'd like to put him in. Matt keeps an eye on him, you can bet on that. But he's never even mentioned Vic Moss in connection with Armstrong.' This was a long speech for her and the others listened with respect. After all, she was their channel in and out of the sheriff's office.

'Still, it ought to be considered,' Freddy said. 'Don't you think?'

'I think we should seriously consider Mr Ottaway.' Mrs Norton was trying to hold on to her suspect.

'I have discovered that Armstrong had some very strange backers,' Emily put in. 'You know – strong, silent types. They would arrive without notice, send his campaign manager out of the room and later there would be evidence of big contributions, mostly in cash. They could have been from unions, or something like that. Maybe they were Moss's men. However, his accountant, Robarts, says there were no cash contributions, all by cheque, all above board.'

'You've talked to this Robarts?' asked Nell.

'Yes. For all the good it did me.' She explained about her unsuccessful ruse. She did not tell them about the

211

talking-to she had got from Dominic on her return from Grantham. Apparently Carl Putnam had easily guessed it was she who had 'adopted' her fiancé's identity. Who else could it have been? He'd assumed it had been in pursuit of a 'story' for the newspaper and had dismissed it as a suspect journalistic enterprise. He'd even been, Dominic reported, amused by her audacity. But in return, Emily had been forced to tell Dominic about the Group and what they were up to. When they had parted he hadn't decided whether to be glad or angry about it all. She thought, when he had settled down, that he would be pleased. She was counting on it.

'Robarts is a nasty little piece of work,' Emily went on. 'He knows a lot and he's very, very clever. I suggested that he had a reason to kill Armstrong – that he might have been skimming the campaign money. He denied it, of course. But it is a motive.'

'I think I have something to contribute here,' Tilly suddenly put in. 'When George, Susie Brock and Mr Putnam finally got into Armstrong's office at home, they found out somebody had broken into it.'

At once, everybody's head swivelled to Snakehips Turkle.

He looked puzzled, then outraged. 'I don't *do* that any more!' he said loudly.

'Shame we didn't think of it, though.' Mrs Norton wondered if it had been Mr Ottaway. He had looked so unpleasant she wouldn't put burglary beyond him. Burglary or murder.

'Was anything taken?' asked Larry Lovich.

'Not so far as they could tell,' Tilly said. 'Which makes it all the more odd. There were ornaments there that could have been sold easily for quick cash. A stereo, a television, a fax, a computer – all the usual stuff they look for. His papers had been disturbed, but there's no way of telling if any of them were taken. The files seemed intact, but again – who could tell if certain pages had been slipped out of a folder and others left behind? Only Armstrong himself.'

'And he's dead,' Snakehips said, not without satisfaction.

Again, they all looked at him.

'Dammit,' he expostulated. 'I didn't do it. I wish I had've, then we might know more.'

'What's to do, then?' Mrs Toby asked, rescuing him from any further need for self-defence. She had decided to investigate Nell's Mr Ottaway further herself. She thought perhaps a visit to his wife might be an idea. Meanwhile, she had a job to do. 'Dominic should be told about Moony's gambling and his sending money somehow to a Grantham bank account, about his friendship with Sally Dukas over at the McDonald's. And maybe Dominic will find some clue in Frog's photos – although what could be there I can't imagine. It would be a reason for Moony to kill Frog, maybe, but not the other way around.'

Everyone murmured that that seemed to be the case.

Tilly shook her head. 'Trouble is, George doesn't think the Packard case needs any further work. He's just concerned with Armstrong's murder.'

For the first time, Daria Grey spoke up. 'Matt is actively working on Frog's case, now,' she said softly. 'He's not happy about the case – thinks he was forced to arrest too quickly. Since he now has time on his hands . . .'

'Ah.' Mrs Toby was pleased.

Tilly looked pleased, too. She hadn't seen much of Matt in the past few days and hadn't realized he'd been doing any fresh snooping. Good for him, she thought. 'So Matt should be told what we've found out about Moony,' she said to Daria.

Daria nodded. 'I'll tell him.'

Tilly continued, 'And George should be told about Armstrong's Army and the resentment of the local contractors, especially Ottaway, over the collapse of the housing project. Anything else?'

Mrs Norton looked at Tilly gratefully. At least someone had believed her.

There was a silence.

'I think you should all know about something else,' Tilly went on. 'I don't know if it has anything to do with anything, but Matt did come into the office with a box of books yesterday that Armstrong had ordered through the bookshop. They were . . . not very nice.'

'What do you mean, "not very nice"?' Freddy asked.

'Hard-core pornography,' Tilly said. 'There's no other word for it. George wouldn't even let Susie or me see them. He locked them straight in the evidence room, but Susie took a look after he'd gone out. Even she was shocked and she took psychology when she went to college.'

'I didn't know Armstrong was like that.' Nell was astonished.

'Nobody did,' Tilly said. 'He told the girl he got to order them behind Helen Pollock's back that they were for "research".'

'Hah! I'll bet,' said Larry.

'Well, if that don't beat all,' marvelled Snakehips. 'Maybe that's what the person who broke into Armstrong's office was looking for. Porn.' He looked around. 'Question is – how did he know it was there?'

'You mean another . . .'

'Friend?' Tilly looked disgusted. 'There's rings of these kinds of people, you know. Matt said Helen told him that when Armstrong ordered these books he evidently knew exactly what titles to ask for and which publishers too.'

'Maybe *that's* who bumped Armstrong off,' Freddy said. 'Somebody who knew about his private hobby. Or somebody who shared it and didn't want Armstrong to tell anyone.'

'Well, Armstrong would have been telling on himself then, wouldn't he?' Larry countered.

'Unless he *was* just doing research. Unless he had found out something about somebody . . .' Freddy speculated.

'Oh, come on – was Armstrong the blackmailing type?'

'He was a very nasty little boy,' Milly Hackabush put in abruptly. 'And an even nastier teenager, behind the bleachers. He loved having power over people. He used his friends and undermined his enemies whenever he could.'

Mrs Toby sighed. 'You've done well. But there are a lot of threads to follow up on. Masses of work to be done.'

'Wake up Fran, honey,' Don Robinson said to his wife who had nodded off. 'Work to be done.'

Fran sat up with a jerk, wide-eyed. 'I'm ready. Just point me in the right direction.'

Freddy laughed. 'I never knew anybody who could fall asleep so easily and then wake up so fast.' He smiled at Fran.

'It's a great gift,' Mrs Toby agreed. 'Now we have to make fresh plans . . . before Fran falls asleep again!'

NINETEEN

'I DON'T BELIEVE IT,' MATT said to Daria later that evening as they lay side by side on his king-sized bed. Max, Matt's loyal cat, had snuggled between them as soon as things had settled down. Max was a gentleman who recognized that people seemed to need privacy at certain times. He wasn't sure *why*, his own interest in that side of things having long since been removed, but he accepted that there were times a cat had to stay down and others when a cat was welcome to jump up on the bed and get cozy again.

'Well, it's true,' she told Matt. 'We have a whole army of supporters working for you. But we can't actually *do* anything with what we find out. That's up to you. We're only informants.'

'There's nothing illegal about the police using informants,' Matt acknowledged reluctantly.

'That's what Tilly said.' Daria nodded. 'And we've come up with some very interesting things.'

'Like what?'

She told him.

'My God, that puts a whole different slant on Moony's killing,' he said, aghast that his own investigations hadn't turned up the gambling, the odd mail-yourself habits and the girlfriend in Moony's life. Another example of the poor work he had done as a result of being distracted by the election. He could do a much better job if he weren't interrupted every three years by another campaign. But that way lay despotism, he supposed.

'The problem is, how can we get hold of Moony's papers?

I *knew* there had to be more there than we discovered. There must be bank-books and all sorts of things we didn't see. Frank knows more than he's admitted, of course. And that may be a motive right there. George won't co-operate, will he? Can we get him to search the Packard house?'

'I don't know – why don't you ask him?'

'Then he'll know I'm working on Frog's case.'

'Is that so terrible? You're not getting in his way, are you? He's still in charge of the Armstrong investigation.'

'Theoretically I'm suspended.'

'From the Armstrong case, yes. But not from your position as Sheriff, darling. You still have the authority, except for what you've ceded to George in the one case.'

'I suppose so.'

'So tell him you want a search warrant for Moony's house, that you want a search made for Moony's bank accounts, and to know the position of his will and insurance policies. He can't stop you.'

'If I go into the office people will think I'm working on the Armstrong case.'

'Then get Tilly to do all the paperwork. George will just hand it over to her, as usual, anyway. As a matter of fact, why does George have to know about it?'

Matt turned his head on the pillow and looked at her across Max's ears. His eyes regained a bit of twinkle. 'You know, I don't suppose he does at that.'

'Well, then.' She grinned at him. 'Tilly's on your side, Matt. Although she's – we all are – helping George too.'

'Helping *George?*'

Daria flushed. 'Well – Tilly and Susie are sort of . . . feeding information to George so he will get the right ideas. If you see what I mean. Like checking out this Ottaway, for example.'

'Now, why do I suddenly sense matriarchal manipulation, here?' Matt asked, not certain he approved of this after all.

'You don't. We have lots of men like Don Robinson and Snakehips Turkle, and Freddy Tollett and Larry Lovich on the team. We want to get all this settled as fast as possible, so the election will be straightforward and fair.'

'The election will be straightforward anyway,' Matt pointed out. 'It's too late for another candidate to register, so it's between me and Tyrone Molt. And believe me, if they elect Tyrone they deserve Tyrone and I'm better off out of it.'

'Oh, don't worry – but it would be so much better if this Armstrong thing wasn't still hanging over you so people could vote freely without worries. That's why we're helping George. I mean, he *needs* help, Matt.'

'Hm.' He pondered for a while, stroking Max as he did so. Max purred. Daria waited patiently. She knew Matt liked to think things through thoroughly – it was his way and there was no sense trying to rush him. He cleared his throat. 'Do you think it's too late to call Tilly at home?' he asked.

By the end of the next day, Matt was ready to turn the entire Sheriff's Department over to Tilly, who had really been running it since she was fresh out of high school and went to work for his father. He knew both his father and he had been mere figureheads, that Tilly *really* was in charge, but never was it more clear than now.

She got the search warrant because she was best friends with Judge Dailey's secretary, who knew how to get around the Judge and frequently did.

She found the name of the bank in Grantham where Moony Packard kept his gambling winnings because she was good friends with Nancy Kowalski who worked at Blackwater Savings and Loan and who could find out just about anything she wanted to know about banking via her handy dandy computer, and frequently did.

'Thanks, Tilly,' Matt said, as she reported to him in his apartment that evening.

She waved a hand airily. 'All part of the service. But it still leaves you with a lot to do. And, by the way, George was looking at me very oddly before he left tonight. I think he suspects something.'

Matt shrugged. 'Let him. I am still the Sheriff.'

'Well, that's true . . . speaking legally,' Tilly allowed.

'I have promoted myself to plain-clothes detective,' Matt said firmly. 'A new division of the Sheriff's Department.'

'Ah.'

'And I have a lot of informants, I understand.' He looked at her and raised an eyebrow.

She had the grace to blush, as Daria had the previous evening. 'You don't mind, do you?' she asked. 'I mean . . . really mind?'

'I worry that somebody might ask the wrong person the wrong question and get themselves hurt,' he said. 'You really have to leave the investigating to me, Tilly. And to George.'

Tilly snorted. 'George's present activities leave a lot to be desired. He had Armstrong's home office fingerprinted.'

'Fair enough – I would have too.'

'Oh. And he's looking into Armstrong's will and insurance positions.'

'Good.'

'And he's looking into Mrs Irene Armstrong's past.'

Matt frowned. 'Ah . . . possibly a bit of a side road?'

'I think so. Poor woman's too weak to have wrestled her great big ex-athlete husband into handcuffs, forced him to the ground and then shot him point-blank. Assuming she could have sneaked out of the clinic *and* managed to steal your gun.'

'Is that the way George thinks the murder happened?'

'It is.'

Matt nodded. 'Sounds like he's doing just fine, for the most part. What's the problem?'

'Well . . . it's his *attitude*,' Tilly complained. 'He bosses everyone around, shouts a lot, jumps to conclusions based on very little evidence . . . he had Snakehips Turkle in, questioning him about the break-in at Armstrong's, just because Snakehips has a record.' She neglected to mention how everybody at Mrs Toby's had also jumped to the same conclusion.

Matt chuckled. 'And?'

Tilly had to smile. 'Snakehips pointed out that if he had broken in he wouldn't have left empty-handed in the first place. In the second place he wouldn't have left fingerprints because he always wore gloves. And in the third place he didn't *do* that any more – he's retired on account of arthritis and plain being sick of jail. And then he walked out.'

'What did George say?'

'He slammed things around on his desk for a while, then went over to the Golden Perch for lunch. He slammed the door on the way out too. George is getting a little . . . frustrated.'

'I know how he feels,' Matt said. 'And I can't say he's doing much that I wouldn't be doing in his place.'

'Okay,' Tilly conceded. 'But you would be nicer about it.' She turned to leave, then snapped her fingers. 'Oh – you asked to have Frog Bartlett's van fingerprinted, didn't you?'

'Yes. What did they come up with?'

'Zip. Absolute zero. Not a print on it anywhere. Sorry.'

Matt shook his head. 'Oh, don't be sorry – that's just what I was hoping they'd find. You see, why would Frog bother to wipe his own fingerprints off his own van? He wouldn't. Which means somebody else wiped theirs off instead. Which means somebody *else* was driving Frog's van when it passed Homer Brophy the morning that Moony Packard was killed, because Frog hasn't driven that van since Moony died. I had Dominic check that.'

Tilly looked gratified. 'Then Frog is innocent? I mean, really innocent?'

'I think so. Didn't you think so? Why else are all of you going around playing detective on my behalf?'

'Not because of Frog,' Tilly said. 'Because of *you*.'

'Oh.' It was Matt's turn to blush – but he didn't. He just felt rather humbled and embarrassed enough to get a bit cross. 'That's no reason – we're after justice for Frog.'

'You may be after justice for Frog,' Tilly snapped. 'We're

after a good clean election. We're helping George too, remember? If County doesn't ante up enough of a budget for you to hire the people you need, then we'll step in.'

'Blackwater Bay Irregulars?' Matt asked.

'If you like. Now go hassle that stupid idiot Frank Packard before he burns up every bit of his brother's papers.'

'Good God – he could have, couldn't he?'

Tilly shook her head. 'No – we don't think so. Mrs Naseem lives right across from him and she's been keeping an eye out for trash burning or anything like that. All she's reported is Frank standing on the front porch waiting for the mail to arrive every morning. Real eager for it, he seems to be. The rest of the day he stays inside but there's been no smoke from his chimney and none from the trash burner out back.'

'Mrs *Naseem*?'

Tilly nodded. 'We have people everywhere,' she said grandly and swept out.

Susie had been busy that day too. 'George,' she said in a wistful voice. 'Have you ever heard of something called Armstrong's Army?'

He looked at her, puzzled. 'What the hell is that?'

She shrugged. 'Oh, I overheard somebody use the term and I wondered if you'd come across it in the investigation. I think it refers to the people he always gave contracts to . . . even if they weren't the lowest bidder on a job. And usually the same people too. At least, I think that's what I heard.'

'Really?' George frowned. 'Why would he do that?'

Susie rolled a pencil back and forth under the palm of her hand, pointing it in different directions as if it were some kind of toy car. 'Maybe he thought they were the best people to do the work,' she said innocently.

'He wasn't like that,' George told her. 'I've been talking with my dad about him. Armstrong was hard-nosed, out to make money. If he gave a contract to someone he would have wanted something back for it.'

'Oh,' Susie said. 'That's not legal, is it?'

'It's called a kickback.'

'Of course. That's pretty bad in someone with political ambitions, isn't it?'

'Sure is.' George was thinking. It looked like hard work.

'Well, you know that housing development of his – the one at the edge of town? Where Armstrong's body was found, I mean?'

'Yeah. Say . . . what were you and Duff Bradley doing out there that morning, anyway? It wasn't your usual patrol route,' George said accusingly. It still bothered him, and thoughts of Armstrong and his cronies went right out of his head.

'Oh.' Susie was momentarily taken aback. 'Well, Duff and his wife were thinking about buying one of the houses when they went up, and he wondered what I thought about it. That's all.'

'Your opinion on stuff like that matters to him, does it?' George growled.

'He wanted a woman's point of view, yes.' Susie's chin went up.

'That's what he's got a *wife* for.'

Susie got a little pink. 'He wanted to surprise her.'

'With a *house*? Isn't that the kind of thing people buy *together*?'

'Well, sure . . . but he wanted to know what I thought before he talked to his wife. So as not to waste her time.'

'Hah!' George said. 'I bet.'

'What's that supposed to mean?' Susie wanted to know. She sat up straighter and gripped the arms of her swivel chair.

'I mean you want to watch out what people might think about you driving out into the woods with Duff Bradley.'

'We weren't driving into the woods,' Susie protested. 'What kind of thing is that to say? I have no interest in Duff Bradley as a man. I have a professional relationship with him just as I have with you. If you wanted to buy a house out there and wanted my opinion about the site, I would go out there with you too.'

'Would you?' George asked a little less belligerently.

'Yes, I would.' Susie sat back and her eye momentarily caught Tilly's across the office. 'Anyway, that isn't the point.'

'What is the point, then?' George wanted to know, now slightly distracted by the thought of driving out to look at building sites with Susie Brock. Maybe by moonlight.

'The point is, that's where Armstrong was killed and I think . . . I mean . . . isn't it possible that when the plans for the development were set back, people who had expected to get contracts might have lost money by it? Like maybe somebody lost a lot, and got mad about it. Mad enough to shoot Armstrong? I heard there was a man in Lemonville named Ottaway who lost everything and he was really, really angry at Armstrong.'

'Good God, kill a man over some stupid thing like plumbing?' George expostulated.

Susie cleared her throat. 'Paving,' she muttered.

'What?' George leaned forward.

'He also had some funny people backing his campaign, I hear,' Susie said. 'That man Otis could tell you a few things, I bet.'

'Otis? He's a clown.' George was dismissive.

'Oh, no, he isn't,' Susie contradicted. She ticked off on her fingers the names of several prominent politicians. 'He's worked for all those, and got them elected too. I bet he knows a lot more than he's letting on. I know Emily Gibbons has been trying to get information out of him. She was saying only the other day at the beauty parlour that he was like an oyster but she thought there might be a pearl or two inside.'

'At the beauty parlour,' George echoed.

'It's a useful place to hear things. Don't men talk at the barber's?'

'Only about sports.' That was all *he* ever talked about, anyway. He was thinking again, his forehead deeply creased, his mouth tight. 'Maybe I should talk to that Otis again,' he said slowly. 'And that other guy – what did you say he was called? Ottaway?'

'Do you really think so?' Susie sounded eager. 'Can I come along?'

'No.' George stood up. 'They might not talk in front of a girl.' He walked over and took his coat from the rack. 'Otis is at the Ventnor Hotel, isn't he?'

'I *think* so,' Susie said, who knew very well where Otis was. She was damned if she was going much further in pandering to his stupid male ego. Well, he wasn't stupid, exactly, but he was so easy to lead, his highly polished chauvinist self-image deflected reasonable thought and only admitted ideas that flattered him. Her eyelashes were exhausted from flapping and if she had to swallow one more patronizing remark from this big boob she would choke. In fact, she would *rather* choke. Shame he was so good-looking.

'Right. You two keep an eye on things.' George went out into the cold harsh afternoon to do what a man has to do. Even if it was raining.

Susie and Tilly exchanged a smile.

Such an eager beaver.

'When he gets back, I'll mention Vic Moss,' Susie told Tilly, who nodded sagely.

'Don't forget Robarts the accountant,' she reminded Susie.

'Oh, gosh ... thanks.' Susie made a tiny, tiny note at the side of her blotter, where George couldn't see it.

TWENTY

MATT TOOK CHARLEY HART AND Duff Bradley with him late that night to confront Frank Packard. Frank was asleep when they rang the bell, banged on the door and shouted. He opened up, groggy and off-balance, and was firmly but gently pushed aside.

'Hey!' was all he could manage at short notice.

Matt showed him the search warrant.

Frank was coming to consciousness by the second. 'What the hell do you mean, barging in here like this?' he said. He wasn't original, but he was angry. He was also wearing striped flannel pyjamas. And bedsocks.

'I want *all* your brother's papers, Frank. I want everything he's ever written or got. I want to look over this house. I want you to sit over there and be quiet,' Matt said.

'Listen—'

'I am through listening to you, Frank. You bluster and you roar, but you are hiding something and I am going to find it. Now sit down over there and be quiet, or I'll have one of my men sit on you.'

'Harassment! Bullying! Assault!' Frank shouted.

'There, Frank.' Matt pointed. 'Right there at the end of the couch. And shut up.'

Frank stepped forward. Matt stepped forward. There was a still, quiet moment.

Then Frank spoke, 'Oh, shit,' and went over and sat down at the end of the couch.

'Right,' Matt said. 'I'll take the bedrooms, you check out the basement, Duff, and Charley, you do a tour of

225

the other rooms to start with. You know the kind of thing I'm looking for.'

'Moony never went down the basement!' Frank shouted.

Matt turned. 'And why was that, Frank?'

'He . . . there was no reason for him to go down there,' Frank said sullenly. 'I took care of the furnace and everything.'

'Everything?' Matt asked quietly. 'Like, perhaps, guns?'

'I got a permit for my gun.'

'I know. I checked. A shotgun permit, that's all. What else are we going to find down there, Frank?'

'Nothing to do with Moony. Moony stayed out of there. He . . . he . . . he was afraid of spiders.'

'Dear me,' Matt said. 'And you aren't?'

'Well, of course not. Hey – you – Duff. Stay out of my basement, dammit!'

Duff looked at Matt but Matt gestured for him to go on. 'This warrant covers the whole house and the grounds, Frank. I don't want to hear any more out of you, or I will arrest you for interfering with the police in the pursuit of their duty.'

'You got no duty to search my house!'

'I have a duty to investigate anything in the life of a victim that might have contributed to his death.'

'Then why didn't you do it before?' Frank demanded.

'Because I was stupid,' Matt said easily. 'Criminally stupid.'

That startled Frank into temporary silence and Matt left him to go into Moony's bedroom.

The lights were off in the fish tank and Matt thought he sensed lots of little eyes looking out at him. He wondered if Frank had been remembering to feed the damn things. If not, he supposed he should get the ASPCA onto it. Somebody would want them. Maybe Frank hadn't realized how much they were worth and that he could sell them, once the will was settled, which was an excellent reason for keeping them in good health.

Matt looked for and found the switch that controlled

the tank lights and turned them on. Fortunately the pump seemed to be on a permanent circuit, for it was bubbling away and the water seemed clear. But the fish did not look ... happy? How did you tell if a fish was happy? Matt looked around until he found an old cardboard oatmeal drum inscribed 'Food' in what he supposed was Moony's handwriting, opened it and took out a scoopful. He sprinkled it on top of the tank and the fish went berserk.

So Frank hadn't been feeding them, the stupid bastard.

He sprinkled another scoopful into the water, then set the drum aside. He knew that you could overfeed fish too.

Now he looked around the room. There was definitely a change. The bed was covered with Post Office mailers, lined up headboard to footboard. There had been no evidence of these when he and Susie had taken their fairly casual look around on the day they'd found Moony's body. Even then he'd been distracted, thinking more about the killer than the victim. Maybe thinking more about the election than the murder?

A couple of the mailers were opened, but the rest were not – just addressed to 'M. Packard' at this address. He looked at the postmarks. As he surveyed them, his foot struck something under the bed and he kneeled down to discover quite a few more of the mailers. He pulled some out – they were very dusty. The ones under the bed went back several years, but the ones on the top were all postmarked during the current year. Presumably they, too, had been under the bed. Why hadn't he looked under the bed?

The most recent mailer was actually postmarked three days before Moony had died. That was one of the opened ones. As far as he could tell, all the writing on the address labels was the same as the writing on the large drum of fish food.

Was this why Frank Packard watched so eagerly for the

mail every day? Had Moony been mailing all this to himself? Why? What the devil was it?

He picked up the most recent packet and peered inside: a thick sheaf of handwritten pages. He pulled them out and started to read. 'Jesus wept,' he muttered to himself. 'No wonder he sealed them up.'

Duff Bradley appeared in the doorway. 'You were right, Matt. You can't tell at first, it's all hidden behind a false wall. There's a door behind a stack of shelves with pre-serves on them. My wife does a lot of preserving and I was looking at the labels when I realized they were fakes. I found the catch, eventually, and it swung back nice and sweet. There's automatic weapons, hand-guns, knives, even about a half-dozen grenades. Also some kind of uniforms I never saw before . . . real odd stuff. You'd better come and take a look.'

Matt put the papers back into the mailer, but did not replace it on the bed with the rest. These he wanted to keep with him.

Charley met them in the hall. 'Nothing that I can see, Matt. I looked up in the attic, like you said. There's nothing there but old furniture and some boxes of general crap. Plenty of dust – no recent disturbance that I can see. But if you want me to . . .'

'No. I want you to go out and keep an eye on Frank. Make sure he doesn't go into Moony's bedroom or anywhere else for the moment.' He followed Duff down the cellar stairs that led from the surprisingly well-equipped kitchen.

At one end of the basement there was a neat workshop set-up, with even a small metal lathe and other equipment a gunsmith or armourer might use. 'I should have looked down here,' Matt said resignedly. 'I should have looked everywhere. No wonder Frank seemed so relieved when we left. Once he thought we weren't coming back, he thought he was safe enough. If we'd warned him, if he'd thought there was a chance we'd be back, I imagine the cupboard would be bare by now. Let's see these uniforms you mentioned.'

Duff led the way over to the now open door, which he'd propped back to reveal that that end of the basement had a false wall built into it. Behind it lay Frank's secret. The brothers had been a very secretive pair.

The guns were neatly fixed to the wall with clips. The knives and other hand-to-hand weapons were displayed on a board. There was also a standing rack on which hung about ten uniforms, neatly pressed. They were of various sorts, some dress, some regular, some camouflage fatigues, all in one size. Frank Packard's size. But they had one other thing in common – an insignia that said 'United States Patriots' above a flag in front of which was a raised fist. Under this was embroidered: 'Back to Purity, Back to Unity'.

'I never saw him wear anything like this,' Duff said. 'Not that I ever saw him much . . .'

'Neither have I,' Matt agreed. 'Not him or anyone. I know most of the little groups that exist around the county – I've never heard of this one. Either he wore them under something else when he went to meetings – if there are enough of them to hold meetings – or it's his own fetish outfit that he wears when he's alone. There are a lot of these types around, new groups popping up all the time. They scare the hell out of me.'

'Me, too,' Duff concurred. 'What do you want to do?'

'We'll have to take him in, he has no permits for this stuff. Then we'll call ATF and see what they want us to do. Aside from possessing these, he hasn't broken any other laws as far as we know. As I say, this may be his own fantasy outfit, or it could be he's part of something bigger. He can sleep the rest of the night in the jail so he can't contact anyone else and we'll question him tomorrow. He knew we'd find this. Once he saw the warrant he knew it was over – whatever it is.'

'But Frog is in there,' Duff said, thinking of the new cells.

'We'll keep them separated as much as possible,' Matt told him. 'I need time to go over all this.' He indicated the mailer he held under one arm. 'As far as I can tell, Moony Packard was writing a novel. Or maybe it's short stories – I haven't had time to really look yet.'

'A *novel*?' Duff was astonished.

Matt nodded. 'Seems to me I remember that a cheap way to copyright something is to seal it with wax and mail it to yourself and never open it, so the postmark gives a date of origination. I think that's what this is. Moony Packard put a hell of a lot of faith in the US Postal Service. Both he and his brother . . .' Matt shook his head.

'What?' Duff asked.

'Secrets,' Matt said bleakly. 'Two men, each living two lives. One a vociferous nut who publicly demonstrates against the government and secretly longs for military authority, the other an opinionated but dedicated government servant who secretly gambles and mails handwritten manuscripts to himself. Living together, in this house. God knows what they talked about if they talked to each other at all. What they thought, what they . . .' He shrugged. 'People,' was all he could say. 'People just amaze me.'

'Oh, my God!' Emily clutched Dominic's arm.

He winced. 'Ouch! What's the mat—'

Emily dragged him backwards, away from the windows of Just Desserts. 'He's in there,' she said in a stage whisper.

'Who's in where?' It was still early, although they were running late, having overslept, and Dominic hadn't had his second cup of coffee yet.

'Robarts. He's in there talking to Otis.'

'Really? So what?'

'I told you – there's something fishy about Robarts and now there he is talking to Otis. We've got to find out what they're saying. *You*'ve got to find out what they're saying.'

'Why me?'

'Because they both know me. Go on—' She prodded him. He rubbed his arm and looked at her reproachfully. 'Hurry, hurry.'

'What do you want me to do?'

'Sit at the next table. Eavesdrop.'

'Now, listen—'

'Exactly. Listen. And then follow them. I'll watch from the *Chronicle* office.'

'Follow them? I've got to get to the office,' Dominic protested.

'You can go to the office any time,' Emily said urgently. 'Hurry up, before they finish.'

Dominic closed his eyes, counted to ten, took a good look at his fiancée, sighed and went into Just Desserts, seating himself at the table next to the two men who were in such earnest conversation.

Freddy came over. 'Well, good-morning. We don't often see you in here so early,' he said, with what seemed to Dominic excessive volume.

He improvised. 'Em and I had an argument and I didn't get any breakfast. Any chance of a very large cup of coffee and piece of that maple pecan coffee cake? My blood cries out for sugar and caffeine.'

'You got it.' Freddy started away, then returned. 'It's probably PMT,' he said confidentially. 'She'll be fine by lunch-time.'

'Oh . . . sure.' Dominic nodded, straining to hear what Robarts and Otis were saying. He got up and went past them to get one of the city newspapers Larry and Freddy always had ready for morning customers, then returned to his seat.

He caught the words 'sweetener' and 'trouble' quite clearly, but didn't get the context. Maybe one was asking the other for the sugar bowl, he conjectured. It was really too early in the morning for this kind of thing.

Freddy reappeared beside him with his order. 'Feeling fragile this morning?' he asked as he put down the plate and cup.

'Kind of.' Freddy was blocking Dominic's view of the two men. He leaned forward as if to reach for something – but there was nothing on the table he needed. Freddy raised

231

an eyebrow. 'Back trouble?' he enquired kindly. 'I know how it feels, believe me. Being on my feet all day is killing me, but Larry keeps a stool behind the counter. He can sit down when he gets a moment, but not me, I have to—'

'Freddy, sit down,' Dominic said in desperation.

'Oh. Thanks.' Freddy was always ready to fraternize with the customers.

Dominic leaned towards him. 'You're part of this ... team thing with Emily and Mrs Toby and the others, aren't you?'

Freddy's eyes flashed. 'Yes,' he said, suddenly very quiet.

'The two men sitting behind you ...'

'Yes?'

'Emily thinks they're up to something.'

'Like what? Who are they?' Freddy's voice was almost too low to hear.

'One is Robarts, the accountant who handled Armstrong's campaign funds, the other is his campaign manager. Ex-campaign manager. They really shouldn't need to have anything to do with one another now.'

'I recognized the manager, but I didn't know the other one.'

'Emily says there's something about the funds ... she thinks Robarts was skimming cash out of the funds or something. She wants me to follow them when they leave, but—'

'But what?'

'I have to get to the office.'

'Well, *I* have to serve the customers,' Freddy said. 'We start to get busy about now. What shall we do?'

'I don't know. She's watching from the *Chronicle* office.'

'Uh-oh.'

'Excuse me,' said Robarts to Freddy's back. 'Could we have more coffee, please?'

Freddy shot to his feet. 'I'm *so* sorry. Right away.' He went over behind the counter where Larry stood watching and had a whispered conference with him. Larry looked irritated and shook his head. Freddy appeared to argue for a minute, then sighed heavily and came back to serve coffee

232

to Robarts and Otis. He looked over and shook his head at Dominic. Larry had not approved of him leaving the shop. Dominic glared at Larry, and Larry smiled broadly and waved his fingers in a friendly fashion.

At least they were having more coffee, which gave Dominic a little while longer to think. He still couldn't make out what they were saying, except for the odd word or two. Other people were coming into the shop and the general noise level was rising. He finished his coffee cake and contemplated the empty plate. Well, he would just have to be late to the –

Fran and Don Robinson came in and sat down at a table near the window. Freddy went over to take their order, turned and caught Dominic's eye. He came over.

'Can they do it?' he asked Freddy *sotto voce.*

'Do what?' Freddy asked.

Dominic spoke through gritted teeth. It was not easy. 'Follow them when they leave.'

'Shall I ask them?'

'Yes – but don't go straight from here, get their order first,' Dominic directed.

'This is fun,' Freddy said, manfully keeping down a giggle.

'Oh, God,' Dominic moaned softly to himself.

Freddy went to the counter, got the Robinsons' order and took it over to them. Coffee and what looked like more of the maple pecan coffee cake. It was a popular item, apparently. Freddy leaned down and spoke to them, and they both leaned forward to listen. To Dominic's eye it looked very suspicious, especially when they both looked over at Robarts and Otis, but fortunately those two didn't seem to see anyone else in the room.

Don gave a thumbs-up sign to Dominic on the side of Freddy away from the two 'targets' and Dominic sighed with relief. It was even better like this, he thought. Suppose the two men separated? Which one of them was he supposed to follow? With the two Robinsons on the trail they could always split up.

Unless everyone took to their cars. Had the Robinsons driven over from Paradise Island or walked? Oh, Lord – maybe –

Suddenly Robarts and Otis got up, put on their coats and started to leave. Don and Fran hadn't even touched their coffee cake yet. But, sure enough, after the men had gone out of the door they leaped up as one, shrugged on their coats and went out too, leaving their coffee cups still steaming on the table.

Bless them.

Freddy came over.

'Now, that's bad for business,' he said in a more normal voice. 'It makes it look like Don and Fran didn't like what they ordered.'

'Throw it away and give them a fresh order when they come back.' Dominic laid money on the table. 'On me. And let me know what happens – I'll be in my office.'

'Righty-ho,' Freddy said, scooping up the money. 'Aren't we the clever bunch, or what?'

'Or what.' Dominic went over to the *Chronicle* office to explain to Emily what was going on. He walked on to his own office with her comments ringing in his ears. But what else was he supposed to do? He had a meeting with Carl Putnam and some new clients at ten thirty.

At ten fifty-four Mrs Pickering came quietly into the conference room and laid a small folded note in front of Dominic, then stood waiting. At an opportune moment in the conversation he opened it below the level of the table.

'The accountant went to the clinic, the manager to the hotel,' the note said.

Mrs Armstrong was still at the clinic.

He knew Mona Pickering was also one of the 'team'. Quickly he jotted down 'Call Emily and tell her' and handed it back to Mrs Pickering with what he hoped was a vaguely lawyerly smile. (So much work, so much responsibility, my secretary must even interrupt this important meeting.)

She went out. He broadened his smile and went back to listening to the new client's litany of complaints.

The ATF sent Agent Brokaw.

Fortunately, George was out when he arrived, and Matt took him straight into his office and closed the door.

'The guys at ATF say they have no record of an outfit called "The American Patriots" in this state,' Brokaw announced, when he had settled himself. 'They're coming for the guns and they'll want to talk to your man, but this outfit of his is a mystery.'

'I don't think so,' Matt said. 'I think it's his own little outfit consisting of one recruit: himself. I think Frank Packard is probably certifiably nuts. I also think he might have killed his own brother to cover that up.'

'The mail man?' Brokaw asked in surprise.

'Yes. He said Moony never went down to the basement. Well, what if he did? What if he caught Frank in one of his uniforms, playing with his guns? What if he threatened to tell on him? From what I know of the victim, he was a self-righteous man, religious and loyal to the government to a marked degree. He tolerated his brother's public displays – but if he saw how serious the situation was, maybe he threatened to close Frank down. I've been listening to Frank for most of the morning. He's been carefully planning the overthrow of the government for years, apparently. It's his hobby, his obsession. But his *solitary* obsession. When we told him we'd found his stuff he just snapped – wanted to tell us all about it. Proud of it.'

'They usually are.' Brokaw nodded. 'And if he is as you say, the militia types usually don't want people like him in their groups, because they won't take orders. Why didn't he recruit followers?'

'Because he's a man of absolutely no charisma,' Matt said. 'And I expect he was afraid people might laugh at him. He would have found that difficult to tolerate.'

'Maybe his brother laughed at him.'

'That's very possible.'

'What are you going to do?' Brokaw asked. 'I mean, we want him, but if you think he's your guy for the fratricide—'

Only Brokaw would have used the word fratricide.

'I've called a psychiatrist to talk to him. A local man, but he's supposed to be pretty good. He might get an admission out of him. I don't want to start questioning him and say the wrong thing. I'm not used to handling men like him. It's like talking to a primed grenade.'

'I know the type,' Brokaw admitted. 'But I thought you had a man for the mail man's murder all ready for trial. That you had physical evidence too.'

'We have the murder weapon, it's true. But I've been doing some further investigating.' He told Brokaw about somebody else driving Frog's van on the morning of Moony Packard's murder. 'I didn't say Frank Packard was stupid, just that he was nuts,' he concluded. 'If Moony told him about the fight he had with Frog the previous night, he might have seen it as a golden opportunity to get rid of his brother and pin the crime on someone else.'

'We'd like to move fairly quickly on this,' Brokaw said.

'But you could give me a few days?' Matt asked. 'I've got his place locked down and under observation – they can come and clean it out whenever they like, but I'd like to hang on to Frank for a while longer.'

'I had a talk with them. They have the same thought you had – that he's a solitary. They've checked with their field infiltrators. Nobody's ever heard of him.'

'Infiltrators?'

'You don't think we let these militia wackos run around unobserved, do you?'

'I guess not.' Matt frowned. No wonder the groups were so paranoid. Big Brother *was* watching.

'Can you suggest an alternative?' Brokaw asked a little defensively. 'We don't want any more Oklahoma City surprises.'

'Nope,' Matt said. 'Glad to know you're on the job, Agent Brokaw.'

'Not *me*.' Brokaw looked tired. 'They give me the *good* jobs – like coming to see you every time you come up against another loony situation.'

'We do seem to specialize in them,' Matt admitted with a reluctant grin.

'Do you think it's something in the water?' Brokaw enquired.

'I wouldn't be a damn bit surprised.'

TWENTY-ONE

GEORGE WAS PLEASED WITH HIMSELF. He turned away from the fax machine with a fistful of paper and settled himself at his desk, nodding ever more emphatically with every page he perused. 'I knew it,' he kept muttering. 'I damn well knew it.'

'Knew what?' Susie Brock finally asked in exasperation.

'She had it done,' he said. 'It's plain as the nose on your face.'

'I have a very nice nose.' Susie took exception.

'Yes, yes,' murmured George. 'You do, you certainly do.' He turned over another page.

'George!' Susie spoke very, very loudly. Even Tilly jumped.

He looked up, startled. 'What?'

'What are you reading?'

'Reports from the police department in Savannah,' George said smugly. 'Mrs Armstrong was married before. To a *much* older man named Fred Fiddler. Who died in mysterious circumstances. Nothing was ever proved against her, but there was a lot of suspicion as she inherited quite a bit from him, insurance and estate.'

'What were the circumstances?' Susie wanted to know.

'Get this.' George turned back a few pages. 'He was seventy-nine, she was twenty-two. He owned a lumber mill and a dry goods chain. She met him at a barbecue party held by mutual friends, who introduced them. She married him six weeks later, to the astonishment and dismay of all their friends.'

'"Astonishment and dismay"?' Susie echoed.

'It says right here. Newspaper clipping, gossip column. The guys down in Savannah went to a lot of trouble for us.'

'I guess so.' Susie looked at Tilly, who shrugged. What had George said to the police in Savannah to make them co-operate so readily? It hardly bore thinking about.

'Anyway, they were married for about eight months, and then one night outside his house he got mugged and two days later died of his injuries. The widow was heart-broken.'

'Maybe she really loved him,' Tilly offered.

George just looked at her. 'He was seventy-nine,' he said in what he considered a full explanation of his obvious disgust.

'Well—' Tilly began.

'His kids – he had two grown-up sons – contested the will, which he had made just after marrying Irene Duffield – our Mrs Armstrong. This will left the sons the lumber mill, which was going downhill fast. Everything else went to her. In the will he said they could look after themselves but she couldn't. It seems to me she looked after herself pretty damn well. And still does. She had Armstrong killed all right. There's a pattern there.'

'But she and Jack Armstrong had been married for almost twelve years,' Tilly pointed out. 'Why now, all of a sudden?'

'Because he was blowing all his money on this election thing,' George answered firmly. 'She didn't like to see it dribbling away in what she thought was a dumb fantasy. Plus she was probably turned off by this porn habit he had that we just found out about.'

'Oh,' said Tilly. 'Ah. If she knew,' she added to herself.

'So who did she hire?' Susie asked, returning to the point. 'And how did she arrange it, being as she was flat on her back in the clinic with a high fever at the time?'

'Oh, she probably arranged it even before she went into the clinic,' George said. 'The clinic was just her alibi.'

'They told us she had been pretty sick with that viral infection she developed there.'

'Yeah, well – she didn't count on getting that, did she?' George sounded a bit sulky. 'That was just happenstance.'

'"Happenstance"?' Susie echoed once more.

'Yeah. Bad luck. You know.'

'Oh, yes – I know.' Susie looked at him as he leafed through the faxes again, grinning to himself. 'So, what are you going to do about it?' she finally asked.

'What?'

'Yes, what.'

George, still caught up in the magic of having guessed correctly, he thought, about the murderous proclivities of Irene Armstrong, formerly Fiddler, née Duffield, stared at her.

Susie sighed. 'How are we going to prove it, George?'

'Um . . .' George mumbled.

'Kay Pink says Robarts was in there about half an hour and they were arguing,' Emily confided to Dominic over lunch at the Golden Perch. 'She hung around outside the room, but there were too many other things going on at the time and she had to leave. Mrs Armstrong was very upset when the accountant left and they had to give her a sedative. She kept going on about "cheats and liars", and stuff like that. Apparently there was something about a shortfall in the election chest and they wanted her to make up the difference out of her inheritance. She refused.'

'Hm.' Dominic examined a french fry. 'I wish we knew more details.' He sighed and munched. 'One thing's for sure – it wasn't about Frog Bartlett.'

'Well, we can't put *all* our resources behind Frog,' Emily said. 'We have to get both these things settled before the election. And we don't have much time.'

'I know, I know.' Dominic picked up another fry and inspected it. Emily wondered whether he were looking for gold or just philosophical answers to eternal questions. You never knew with Dominic. 'Did you know that Matt arrested Frank Packard last night?'

'No!' Emily was outraged. 'Why wasn't I told?'

'Nobody was told, including George Putnam, who only found out about it when he arrived at work this morning.'

'What did they arrest him for?' Emily rummaged in her bag for a notebook and pen. 'Killing his brother?'

'I wish,' Dominic said. 'No – for illegal possession of firearms and plotting to overthrow the government.'

Emily nearly choked. '*What?*'

'That's what Matt told me. He says Frank Packard is as nutty as a fruitcake and if he did kill his brother they were going to have a hard time proving it.'

'Did he have a motive?'

'Oh, yes. Apparently Frank thinks he's a one-man army, according to Matt. Spent his evenings strutting around the basement issuing orders to non-existent soldiers. And doing things like sawing off shotguns and sharpening knives and other craftsmanlike pursuits. He says if Moony found out and got nasty or righteous about it – as he was wont to do about most things – then Frank could have taken against him. Also, there is a large life insurance policy and quite a bit in a Grantham bank, all of which goes to Frank because he is the beneficiary of the insurance, and Moony died intestate and there's no other living relatives, so he inherits.'

'That's several motives.'

'Yes. But no proof. And Frank is raving and denies it completely, saying he loved his brother dearly. Although he freely admits to plotting the overthrow of the government. He just hadn't quite decided how to go about it yet, but he was working on it. Oh, yes, he was working on it.'

Emily eyed him. 'You're pleased, aren't you?'

'I think it might supply me with reasonable doubt in the case of Frog's guilt,' Dominic admitted. 'Frank's motives are much stronger than my client's.'

'So your task is over?'

'No – but it's beginning to look a bit easier.'

'So you can help us more on the Armstrong case?'

Dominic sighed heavily. 'More? You have to do *more?* Why can't you just leave it to George? When I was over there seeing Frog he was going on about accusing Mrs Armstrong of setting up the murder herself. He seems to have some kind of proof from her past kind of thing.'

'Good heavens,' Emily said. 'Does he know about Robarts going to see her at the clinic?'

'I have no idea. I certainly didn't tell him.'

'This is getting very complicated.'

'What do you mean, *getting* complicated?' Dominic asked. 'It's always been complicated. I thought the two crimes were connected, but I can't see Mrs Armstrong and Frank Packard in anything together, can you?'

'I don't know,' Emily said. 'It's so outrageous it might be true.'

'Oh, come *on.* Give it up, Em. Frank Packard killed his brother and Mrs Armstrong paid someone to kill her husband. End of story. It's just a matter of proof now.'

'But with Frank refusing to admit he killed Moony and Mrs Armstrong refusing to admit she arranged her husband's death – and make no mistake, she *will* refuse to admit it – how are Matt and George going to prove anything before the election?'

'Um . . .' Dominic said. 'Rubber hoses?'

Sarah Marsh's eyes were wide. 'So you think this might get Frog off without even going to trial?' she asked Dominic.

'I don't know, Miss Marsh, but I think I can use it to show that Frog's motives were pale beside Moony's brother Frank's.'

'But what about the physical evidence?' Sarah said, refilling Dominic's cup. It was tea-time, after all. 'That terrible wrench with all the blood and everything?'

'Well, we think that was planted in Frog's garage. Matt has been suspicious about that all along – it just wasn't like Frog to leave it out like that. Furthermore, the steering wheel, gear shift and door handles of Frog's van had been wiped clean of fingerprints – no man would bother to do that to his own property. Matt is pretty sure someone else was driving the van the morning Moony was killed. It could well have been Frank Packard. The two houses aren't that far apart. Working out a complicated thing like that would be like him – he's half crazy, apparently, but crazy like a fox. If Moony came home and told him he'd had a fight with Frog, Frank might have seized on that as a perfect opportunity to kill his brother and blame it on someone else. It wouldn't have been difficult. Frog sleeps heavily, as you know, because of the pills. And he never locks his garage or his van. A simple matter to get the van out early and never wake Frog at all. Drive to Cotter's Cut, do the thing and drive back, leaving the wrench out in plain view.'

'Mercy.' Sarah was appalled at the cunning of the idea, the cold determination behind it. 'I knew Frank was sort of nuts about authority and all that, but I never thought he was the kind to kill his own brother. They were very close as boys, you know.'

'Were they?' Dominic helped himself to another cookie from the plate that sat on the kitchen table between them.

'Oh, yes. Moony used to suffer from terrible migraines and Frank would look after him. He had to lead him home from school because the headache was blinding and Moony couldn't see where he was going. That's where he got his nickname, you know.'

'Because of the migraines?' Dominic looked puzzled.

'Yes – because the other children noticed that they happened during the full moon. It was sheer coincidence, of course. We were studying astronomy at the time, as I recall. You know, just the basics. And so the children were keeping moon calendars – and one of them noticed, or thought they noticed, that the headaches came at the full moon. I think it was a toss-up whether he got the nickname Moony or Dracula. But Dracula was a little beyond the sixth

243

grade at that time. So Moony he became. He didn't mind – I think he half believed it himself. But he grew out of the headaches, I think. That often happens.'

'Really?'

'Oh, yes. Children can grow out of them, adults can grow into them. Children can suffer from something called "abdominal migraine" too. Often dismissed as "I don't want to go to school tummy aches" but they are quite real. Migraine is a mystery even today. I've read a lot about it because I suffer them myself, you see.'

'Ah.' Dominic nodded.

'They now think it has something to do with the circulation in the brain itself,' she went on reflectively. 'And they are developing new drugs all the time because it is quite common, you know. And it can be very, very debilitating.'

'Did Frank ever have headaches?' Dominic asked.

Sarah frowned. 'Let me think.' Her expression cleared. 'Why yes, later on, during puberty. Not migraines, though. For a while they thought he had a brain tumour, but he didn't. He just had terrific mood changes and periods of irrationality. He never really outgrew it, judging from his recent behaviour. Maybe that's why Moony was so protective of him.'

'Protective? He didn't laugh at him?'

Sarah looked astonished. 'Is that what they think? That Moony laughed at Frank?'

'Or maybe preached at him? From what I understand, Moony Packard was a great one for telling other people what to do, where they were going wrong and so on.'

'Yes, he was,' Sarah agreed. 'But not Frank. Frank looked after Moony when they were little and Moony protected Frank when they grew up. They were real close. That's why . . .'

'Why what?'

Sarah looked forlorn. 'Why, although I would like to believe that someone else killed Moony, not Frog, I find it difficult to see Frank as the killer. Those boys were as

244

close as close could be – I always thought it was why they never married, either of them. They were a couple.'

'Couples break up,' Dominic pointed out.

'Yes, that's true,' Sarah conceded. 'And brothers fall out, I know. But those two . . . it's just so hard to believe. I *want* to believe it, for Frog's sake, but . . .' She shrugged. 'Unless it was over a woman. That can come between brothers. Was there a woman involved at all, do you think?'

Matt parked behind McDonald's and wondered just how to approach Sally Dukas. If it was true that she was the on-again off-again girlfriend of Moony Packard, then she was the one who knew him best, aside from his own brother. And if she knew Moony, maybe she knew about Frank too. It was a long shot, but he wanted to cover all the ends he'd left dangling before. That this was an 'end' that had been turned up by his erstwhile amateur helpers did not dismay him at all.

The only thing that worried him about that loony little group was that they might go too far and get themselves in trouble. He had made an appointment to see them at Mrs Toby's after dinner. They'd done enough. He'd take it from here.

He went in, ordered a Big Mac, fries and a chocolate milkshake, and sat down to watch Sally at work for a while. It was a busy time of day – the high school had just let out – and there were plenty of customers. Sally, plump and friendly, was looking decidedly frazzled by the time the rush had passed. Matt went up to the counter and asked if he could have a word with her in private.

'You a secret Big Mac addict and want forty-seven to go?' Sally grinned.

'No.' Matt smiled back. 'Just want a few words about Moony Packard.'

'Oh.' Her entire demeanour changed. 'I have a break in a few minutes – meet me out back so I can have a smoke while we talk.' She didn't look so cheerful then, nor did she when she emerged from the back door of the restaurant and found him leaning against his car, waiting for her.

She lit her cigarette, blew smoke and peered through it at him. Sally Dukas was a big woman in every sense, even her features seemed too big for her face, but she was attractive in a full-blown-rose kind of way. She pulled off her uniform cap and shook her head. Her blonde hair was slipping out from the hold she'd put on it with bobby pins, hair lacquer and hope. It surrounded her face in a haze. Her blue eyes, however, were sharp.

'I thought Moony was dead and buried,' she said.

'He is,' Matt agreed. 'Don't you want to know who made him that way?'

She shook her head. 'What good would it do me?' she wanted to know. 'If he'd married me like he kept promising to do, then it would matter – I'd be his widow, get his insurance, stuff like that. As it is, I'm his nothing, aren't I?'

'He did propose to you, then?'

'No . . . I got him to promise to marry me, which isn't exactly the same thing, is it? You get sick and tired of the smell of hamburgers and pickles, I can tell you. Moony wasn't much, but he stayed around—'

'I understand sometimes he went off too.'

She tried to push her hair back into some kind of order. Matt put her at well over forty, not enormously bright, but possessed of a natural cunning. 'Oh, sure. They do. But he would come back. He always came back.'

'And do you know where he went off to? Or who?'

'You bet I do. And if I ever meet her face to face I'll scratch her eyes out and bite her nose off, believe me.'

'Name?'

'Why do you want to know?'

'Because finding out all we can about a victim often helps us to track down the victim's killer. There have to be reasons for things, Sally.'

'Motive, you mean. You're looking for a motive?'

'Perhaps.'

246

'I would have one, wouldn't I, if we had been married, that is.'

'Yes, you would.'

She considered this. 'But we weren't.'

'No.'

She nodded. 'But you got that Frog guy in jail for it.'

'He's been accused and arraigned, yes. But not tried yet.'

'Don't you think he done it?'

'No, I don't.'

'Then why'd you arrest him?'

'Circumstantial evidence.'

'And you didn't have no one else in the picture.'

'That's about it. Now—'

'Now you're looking for someone else, right?'

'Right.'

'But not me?'

'No, Sally, not you. Unless, of course, you'd like to volunteer a confession.'

She laughed at that. For a moment, just a fleeting moment, Matt speculated about the possibility that she *had* done it. 'I had a reason to kill him all right,' she said. 'He'd just dumped me. Again. Right the night before he got it.'

'Did you believe he really meant it this time?'

She considered him as she tossed the butt of her cigarette into a nearby dumpster. 'Yeah, I did,' she said. 'So it could have been me, couldn't it?'

'Do you know where Frog Bartlett lives, Sally?'

'No. Why? What's that got to do with it?'

'Where were you when Moony dumped you?'

'Jeez, you're nosy,' Sally observed without rancour.

'It's my job to be nosy.'

'Yeah, I guess.' She rummaged in her trouser pockets for the pack of cigarettes and lit up another, dragging the smoke in deeply, exhaling long and slow while she thought about that. 'We was at my place,' she said finally. 'We always went to my place because of that nutty brother of his.'

247

'You knew Frank?'

'Oh, sure. The one time I met him he called me a harlot and a hussy. Sweet guy. So Moony, he kept me right away from Frank. Said Frank "wouldn't understand" about us and crap like that. I reckoned he just didn't want any hassle at home. He and his brother, they had kind of a strange relationship. Too close, you know? Probably that's why they neither one of them ever got married. Something was funny there. Maybe you ought to think about him.'

'We're considering all kinds of possibilities. But that night before he was killed, Moony came to your place?'

'Yeah. Same old, same old. He come by to tell me about his big win at Grasper Haven's. I thought he was going to share some of it with me – he did, sometimes, when he was feeling big – but not this time. He had it all in one of them padded envelopes, addressed to *her*. I saw it folded up in his jacket pocket and while he was in the john I had a look.'

'And she is?'

'Miss Mary Monahan,' Sally said in an arch singsong voice. 'I don't remember the number, but she lives on someplace called Hyacinth Street in Grantham. Hyacinth Street, for crying out loud. I just bet she's the *sweetest* thing. I asked Moony about her and he got all upset, said I shouldn't have looked at his stupid envelope, and we had a fight and that's when he said we was finished and I was so mad I said fine, and that was that. Off he went. Him and his envelope and his money and his Mary Monahan. I always knew there was someone else and there she was, right in front of my face. I was dumb to waste my time on him, dumb right along. But you don't know, do you? You just don't know.'

'Know what?' Matt asked, writing in his notebook.

'Where to place your bets. Some men look like winners, but they're losers. Sometimes you settle for losers and they turn out to be winners. Moony kept me hanging on, but I should have known better. I been divorced twice, I should *really* know better, right? So, dumb me. I can live with it.'

There was a brief glitter of what could have been tears in her eyes, then she gave a short laugh. 'Don't have much choice at my age.'

'And did you get up early the next morning and kill Moony Packard, Sally? Did you beat him to death in Cotter's Cut?'

'I should have,' she said with genuine regret. 'I'd feel a hell of a lot better now, believe me.'

'You don't mean that.'

She poked him in the chest. 'Don't be too sure. There must be somebody who's feeling satisfied at the moment. If it ain't me and it ain't Frog Bartlett, then who is it?'

'Mrs Ottaway?' Mrs Toby was cautious for the woman looked, if anything, more formidable than her husband, but in a different way. She was younger than he was, a brassy blonde in tight jeans and a very low-cut T-shirt, smoking a cigarette and looking, for all the world, like an unrepentant sinner appearing on the Ricki Lake show ready to confess the way she stole her daughter's boyfriend or shot her sister's husband.

Maybe *she* shot Armstrong, Mrs Toby thought fleetingly.

But when Mrs Ottaway spoke, her voice was soft and tentative, not at all the harsh tones her appearance might have intimated. 'Yes, I'm Mrs Ottaway. What can I do for you?'

'I heard your husband was ill and I came to offer my condolences,' Mrs Toby said. 'Such a nice man. He built my patio, you know.'

'Nice man? You sure you're talking about *my* husband?' Mrs Ottaway wanted to know.

'Mr Mel Ottaway of Ottaway Patios and Paving,' Mrs Toby said.

'That's him.' The blonde nodded. 'Come on in.' She moved back and motioned Mrs Toby into the house. It was a big house with an odd atmosphere. When Mrs Toby entered the living-room she saw why – it was full of packing cases.

'Oh – are you moving house?' she asked brightly.

'I am,' Mrs Ottaway said. 'I don't know what *he* intends to do. They took the house, see. Non-payment of mortgage. He really did it to us this time.'

'I beg your pardon?'

'Trusted somebody he shouldn't have trusted, tried to do things the easy way,' Mrs Ottaway explained. 'Can I get you something to drink? Soda? Coffee?'

'Nothing, thank you.'

'Sit down, if you can find a space.' Mrs Ottaway waved, generously indicating a sofa which was half covered with piles of books and magazines. She herself perched her tight little bottom on the edge of a packing case. 'You not happy with your patio or something?' she asked conversationally.

'Oh, not at all. It's lovely.'

Mrs Ottaway nodded. 'He always did good work,' she conceded. 'So, what do you want?'

Mrs Toby regarded the girl for a moment or two, then made a decision. 'I want to know if your husband went to Blackwater last week,' she said. 'On Wednesday. To a debate at the Town Hall.'

Mrs Ottaway gave a hoot of laughter. 'What the hell do you want to know that for?'

'I just do,' said Mrs Toby. 'I'm very nosy.'

'I'll say. Well, as a matter of fact, he did. So what?'

'Did he come straight home afterwards?'

'Lady, the day Mel Ottaway came straight home from anywhere would qualify for *Believe It Or Not*,' the blonde said. 'He got in about – I don't know – the middle of the night some time. Woke me up, drunk as a skunk, wanting . . . you know. His rights. As usual.'

'Oh, dear.'

'Yeah, oh, dear,' Mrs Ottaway agreed. 'We're splitting up, you know.'

'I didn't realize—'

'Oh, yeah. I hung on for a long time, but hey – I'm outta here. Going to Florida, got a job with my brother-in-law,

250

he owns a bar there. I have had it up to here with Mel Ottaway, patios, paving, bills, promises and black eyes.'

'Oh, dear,' Mrs Toby said again, genuinely distressed. She hated to hear about unhappy marriages. Hers had been so splendid, especially in retrospect.

'Why did you want to know this?'

'Because Mr Armstrong was killed that night.'

'And you think Mel did it?' Mrs Ottaway looked amused, then thoughtful. 'Well, you know, I suppose he could have at that. Armstrong is the guy who broke him and he hated his guts. He's not going to get any alibi from me, if that's what you're after. He came home late. When was Armstrong killed?'

'Late.'

'Uh-huh. Me married to a murderer, if that don't beat all. I sure can pick 'em, hey?'

'That doesn't necessarily mean he's a murderer just because he got home late,' Mrs Toby said hastily. She wanted to be fair.

'Doesn't mean he isn't, either. You talked to – hey, are you the little old lady got him so worked up he opened up the ulcer again?'

'Oh, my – he didn't really, did he?' Mrs Toby was horrified.

'Oh, yeah, he did. By the time his medical insurance runs out he'll have pretty much used up everything,' Mrs Ottaway said thoughtfully. 'I suppose I should feel sorry for him.'

'Do you?' asked Mrs Toby curiously.

The blonde stubbed her cigarette out in a fast-food carton and shook her head. 'Nope,' she said. 'He started out nice and turned real nasty over the past few months. I don't have to live with that. He can, but not me. I'm outta here, like I said.'

'You're deserting him?'

'You think that's wrong.' It was not a question.

'A wife . . .' Mrs Toby began and then remembered the reference to black eyes. She sighed. 'No, it's not wrong.'

'Well, then.' The blonde lifted her backside off the packing case and crossed her arms, pushing up her breasts. They looked like they were trying to escape too. 'Anything else?'

Mrs Toby cleared her throat. 'How long do they think Mr Ottaway will be in the hospital?'

'Couple of weeks at least.' Mrs Ottaway showed little evidence of sympathy. 'Why?'

'Oh – just so we'll know where to contact him.'

'If not there, then in the booby hatch, poor slob,' Mrs Ottaway said. 'He ought to be just about ripe for a straitjacket by then.'

TWENTY-TWO

GEORGE HAD GOT A SEARCH warrant. Rather, Tilly had got it for him and now he faced down Tizzy Turkle and waved it in front of her. 'I get to look everywhere,' he said, a little more loudly than was necessary.

She smoothed her uniform. 'Everywhere?' she asked archly.

Susie Brock stepped out from behind George. 'Everywhere,' she told the girl.

Tizzy moved back, scowling. 'So, big deal.' She walked back into the kitchen and slammed the door.

'She and I . . . once . . .' George began.

'You don't have to explain, George,' Susie said kindly. 'I can see she could be a difficult person to know.'

'Uh – yeah,' George muttered. He was a little frazzled with it all. It had begun with a difficult talk with his father after lunch.

'I think she did it,' he'd told him.

'Did what, George?' Carl Putnam asked, leaning back in his black leather executive chair.

'I think she paid someone to bump off her husband,' George said. And he told him what he had found out about Savannah and the previous marital history of Irene Duffield/Fiddler/Armstrong.

'That doesn't prove anything, George.' Carl seemed very calm.

'It gives rise to suspicion,' George insisted. 'I don't think you should be representing her.'

'Now, wait a minute . . .' Carl sat up straighter.

'I think she's dangerous and crazy,' George went on.

'George . . .'

'And I'm going to prove it,' George concluded.

'Really? And how do you propose to do that?' his father wanted to know.

'I've applied for a search warrant. I want to see *her* cheque-books and bank statements and all stuff like that,' George said. 'She got all excited out at the clinic, remember? Kept telling you she didn't want us to see her stuff only her husband's. She was real worried about it.'

'Yes, I remember,' Carl allowed. 'She's a very nervous woman.'

'Of course she is. Nervous that we're going to find out stuff she doesn't want us to know. What other reason could there be?'

'She's a very private person—' Carl began.

'Crap,' George said brusquely. 'She's scared of being caught, that's all. I'm surprised she hasn't got herself out of the clinic by now . . .' He stopped.

'Yes, I am too,' Carl agreed. 'She's not well, but she could manage with a full-time nurse at home . . . destroy all these incriminating things you seem so certain of finding. She can't be *that* scared, George, or as you say, she would have discharged herself.'

'Hm.' George was not convinced. 'She thinks you're protecting her.'

'I can argue the point,' his father concurred. 'I can oppose the application for a warrant in the interests of my client.'

'Are you going to?'

'I don't think so,' Carl said slowly. 'I don't think you'll find what you're looking for, George. I really don't. But appreciate your coming to tell me.'

George was pensive for a moment. 'I shouldn't have done that, right?'

'It was not your wisest move under the circumstances,' Carl agreed solemnly.

'I thought you ought to know.'

'Why?'

'In case . . . well . . . in case you wanted to come along. To protect your client's interests kind of thing.'

'Are you going to tear the place apart?'

'No!' George was quite offended. 'I am just going to look for evidence that might connect Mrs Armstrong with the murder of her husband.'

'Like a note in her diary saying "today I must have Jack killed" . . . something like that?'

'You're laughing at me,' George said in an injured voice.

'No, as a matter of fact I'm not. But I don't think my client is guilty and I don't think you will find anything that will show that she is.'

'Pretty confident, hey?' George attempted a bluster but it fell flat in the face of his father's calm demeanour.

'Yes. Very confident. Search away.' Carl waved a hand.

George stood up. 'Well, I will, then.'

And now here he was.

He turned to Susie. 'Where do you think we should begin?'

Hyacinth Street was in a quiet residential area with large trees shading the cars that lined the kerb. Many of the houses appeared to have been divided into flats and some were slowly fading into disrepair. A neighbourhood on the way down, but slowly.

Matt found a place to park with some difficulty and walked along until he came to number 4584. It was a clapboard house, very small, tucked between two much larger brick homes and set well back from the street. The front garden, long and narrow, was a mass of rose bushes, now neatly trimmed back for winter. In the summer, he thought, it must be quite a sight. He went through the gate in the cyclone fencing that protected the property on three sides and walked down the path to ring the bell by the front door.

When it opened he smiled and said, 'I'm looking for a Mary Monahan.'

255

The little old lady who stood in the open doorway beamed at him. 'Why that's me!' she said in some delight. 'Who are you?'

After he had been seated, served coffee and cake, fussed over and appraised by faded blue eyes, he explained why he had come.

She dimpled. 'And I thought you were going to arrest me. I thought it was going to be a very exciting afternoon for once. But it's about James, is it?'

'James?'

'James Packard. Oh, I suppose you know him by that silly nickname the children gave him: "Moony". Poor lad, the headaches weren't his fault, they were cruel to taunt him like that. He wept, you know. Wept from the pain and the way they teased him. He was such a sensitive boy. They both were, James and Franklin.'

'Excuse me, Miss Monahan, but you knew them when they were children?' Matt was startled. She must be even older than he'd first thought.

'I was a young maid and cook in that house when they were small,' Mary Monahan told him. 'The Packard family were very well off then . . . before the company failed, that is. Afterwards, well, things were much more difficult. Mr Packard was in the automotive business, but his cars didn't sell. It was only a small factory, and . . . well . . . what with the Fords and General Motors and all, he just couldn't compete. Later he had only the garage and a couple of men working for him, doing repairs and such. It broke his spirit, poor man, but he kept on for the sake of his family. For the boys, you see. And Mrs Packard was such a lovely woman, so devoted to her children. Nothing was too good for them. She went without so they could have everything they needed, those boys. No new clothes for her, no hats, no parties, no social life at all, when before . . .' She sighed. 'But they kept me on because Mrs Packard was not a strong woman and they needed me. When the boys were grown, and Mr and Mrs Packard had passed away, I moved on to another family, and then another. There was never a problem about that. I am a very, very good cook, you see, Mr Gabriel.'

'Judging by this cake, I am sure you are, Miss Monahan. You never married?'

'I had a sweetheart, but he was killed at Monte Cassino. There was never anyone else after that. It would have felt wrong, somehow.' She smiled sweetly. 'Not that I didn't have offers, mind you.' She took a sip of her coffee. 'And James and Frank never forgot me, you see. They kept in touch. At least, James always did.' Her eyes filled with tears. 'I never expected ... when I read that he'd been killed ... so sad. So very sad. I wrote to Frank, of course, but he hasn't answered. It was always James, really. Frank was ...' She cleared her throat. 'Frank has always been a little difficult.'

You have no idea, Matt thought to himself. 'Frank is not well himself, Miss Monahan. There has been a little trouble with guns and so on. He—'

'I knew there would be problems.' Miss Monahan nodded. 'That was one of the reasons I left.' She flushed a little. 'It wasn't right, me living there with two grown men. Guns, you say?'

'Yes. He seems to have ... that is to say ...'

'He's nuts?' Mary Monahan asked brightly. 'You can say it, Mr Gabriel. James and I talked about it often. He didn't quite know what to do about Frank. For a long time it was just about the house, you know, that he would go stamping around shouting and behaving oddly. But lately – oh, in the past few years or so – he's been doing things in public. It wasn't bad enough to get him committed and he wouldn't get the help he needed, wouldn't hear of it, so James just did the best he could each time it happened. James was a very opinionated man, I know, and he could be difficult, but he loved his brother very much. He was very distressed about it. That's why he sent me the money, you see.'

'Well, that's what brought me here, Miss Monahan. The money.'

'Yes. He didn't want Frank to know it was there, you

see. But when he had some extra . . .' She leaned forward. 'I think he gambled, Mr Gabriel.'

'He did, Miss Monahan.'

She nodded. 'I thought that might be it. He was a righteous boy, quite religious in his way, but there was that streak . . .' She pressed her lips together, then continued, 'Anyway, when he had some extra . . . winnings . . . he would send them to me to put into a bank account for him. The bank account was in both names, his and Frank's, and the bank had instructions to notify someone if James died before his brother. I suppose they must have done that by now, don't you?'

'I don't know, Miss Monahan. Whom were they supposed to notify?'

'Some lawyer here in town. It was all worked out, James had worked it all out. I was only the go-between. James liked his little games and schemes, you see. Being a mail man isn't very exciting, you know.' She suddenly went quite pink. 'It's not about what I took, is it?'

'What you took?'

'James insisted I take out ten per cent every time he sent me cash to deposit. I said no, of course not, but he insisted and he checked the deposit slips every time I sent them back to be sure I had. I was very grateful for the money, to be honest. A little windfall now and again is most welcome, you know. There's social security and Medicare and all that, of course, but a little extra here and there . . .'

'Buys those little extras that make life worth living.' Matt smiled. 'Like rose bushes.'

'Oh, you saw my little garden as you came in, of course.' Miss Monahan beamed. 'It looks like nothing at all now, of course. In the winter I call it my stick farm.' She giggled, a most entrancing sound. 'But in the spring and summer – oh, Mr Gabriel, you should see it. A rainbow, that's what it is, a fragrant rainbow. And it keeps me active, you see. So we help each other, the roses and I.'

'Miss Monahan, do you have any idea who the lawyer was

258

who was supposed to administer Mr Packard's account . . . and, I suppose, his will and so on?'

'Why, yes. I have it right here, just in case . . .' She got up and rummaged through a small desk that stood on one side of the tiny sitting-room. She produced a card. 'Mr Theodore Niforos,' she said. 'James seemed to think very highly of him.'

Matt Gabriel thought very highly of him too. Within minutes of meeting the tall, good-looking lawyer he could see why James – Moony – Packard had entrusted his business to the man. Niforos, Van Vechten and Ruzumna had a suite in the Garner Building. It was a businesslike outfit, comfortable but not lavish, and seemed quite busy.

Niforos's ('call me Ted') own office was big but neat, and on his desk were pictures of a very beautiful woman and a handsome family. His secretary had been a sensible-looking woman, efficient rather than mere scenery. Niforos himself was probably about fifty, considering his status, but like many of Greek extraction there was no grey in the black hair and his olive complexion was smooth and showed no sign of age. His smile was ready and reassuring. 'You're the Sheriff of Blackwater County?' he said. 'We hear a lot about your area down here.'

'Most of it bad,' Matt said with a wince. 'The newspapers seem to think we're a kind of Disneyland of eccentrics.'

'Well, considering the one person I've met from your bailiwick I'm not surprised.' Niforos chuckled.

'Moony Packard.'

'Moony?' Niforos raised an eyebrow.

'James. Moony was a childhood nickname that stuck locally,' Matt explained.

'I see. The bank notified me of his death and of course I read about it in the paper. Shocking thing. We expect that kind of thing here in the city, unfortunately, but not in . . .' He paused.

'Disneyland?' Matt smiled. 'I know. Violence has been slowly coming towards us for some time. Drugs, vandalism

259

– all the delights of urban life. We stayed safe for a long time, longer perhaps than most. But . . .' He shrugged.

'Well, what can I do for you, Sheriff Gabriel?' Niforos asked.

'I understand that Moony had a bank account here in Grantham with some unusual aspects to it. Have I got that right?'

'Not as to the bank account, but as to its administration, according to instructions left in his will.'

'We wondered about him having a will . . .'

'Oh, I wrote to Mr Frank Packard immediately after his brother's death,' Niforos said. 'Informing him of the terms of the will and so on. I haven't heard back from him, although I've written several times. In fact, I was preparing to go up to Blackwater myself soon, if I didn't hear. I was very concerned because Mr Packard – Moony, as you call him – was also very concerned about his brother. I understand he's a little . . . unstable?'

'At this moment I have him in jail.' Matt explained the situation.

'Good Lord,' Niforos said. 'And you actually think he might have killed his own brother?'

'I have no idea at the present time. There's no evidence to indicate that, but . . .'

'That puts quite a twist on things,' Niforos reflected. 'You see, under the terms of his brother's will, the house is of course to go to Frank – well, they own it jointly anyway – but all his other assets are to be placed in a trust to give Frank an income but not access to the capital.'

'And how much is the capital, just out of interest?' Matt asked.

'Just under a million dollars,' Niforos said earnestly. 'You can perhaps see why Moony didn't want Frank to get hold of it, considering his state of mind.'

It was Matt's turn to say 'Good Lord'.

'Indeed,' Niforos agreed. 'I believe Mr Packard was just a simple mail man?'

'Yes, that's right.'

'Then I'm at a loss to know where . . .'

'He gambled,' Matt explained. 'He was a very lucky gambler, apparently.'

'I should say so,' Niforos said. 'Mind you, the capital has been accumulating for quite a few years – I met Mr Packard when I wasn't long out of law school . . . and he never withdrew any money. In a way I'm relieved, you know.'

'Oh?'

'Well, the deposits were always in cash, you see. Made through an intermediary—'

'Yes, I've met Miss Monahan.'

'And I wondered where he got it, to be honest. He never explained, you see. Just set up the bank account and that was that. Perhaps that clarifies why he didn't use a local bank,' he added, half to himself. 'I should really have asked, but . . . he wasn't an easy man to talk to, you know. I'm usually pretty good with people, but—'

'He had strong opinions.' Matt nodded. 'He liked to tell people how they should live, but wouldn't take any advice about himself. Miss Monahan said he had always been secretive, even as a boy.' He leaned back and sighed. 'When did he set up this trust thing?'

'Oh, that was more recent. About five or six years ago, I think. Apparently his brother was beginning to show signs of erratic behaviour.'

'That's putting it mildly. He was on his way to becoming the resident town nut-case.' Matt smiled. 'Moony limited his opinions to church and bar, but Frank went the placard, one-man parade and public-nuisance route.'

'Interesting,' Niforos said.

'Yes. More and more interesting the more I find out about them,' Matt agreed. 'You say you've written to Frank?'

'Yes. Now that the trust comes into effect, he will be receiving regular cheques each month. I am a trustee, along with one of my partners and an officer of the bank. Should Frank require special disbursements, for medical care, for example—'

'That's looking pretty likely.'

'Then, of course, we're in a position to see that he gets what he needs. He could, of course, challenge the will.'

'I don't think that's likely.' Matt told Niforos about the uniforms and the plan to overthrow the government. 'Unless he wants to start up a real army, that is.'

'I don't think we would see that as a necessary disbursement,' Niforos said with a quirky smile.

'What happens if we find he did kill his brother?' Matt asked bluntly. 'He can't profit by the death, then, can he? Was there any provision made for that?'

'None at all. There was provision for Frank dying before Moony – various charities and so on, so I suppose that would have some bearing. But Moony, as you call him, was never afraid of his brother, Sheriff Gabriel. The thought would never have occurred to him that Frank would turn violent.'

'We can't always know, can we? Even our own brothers can turn into strangers when mental illness intervenes.'

'That's true. I certainly hope it isn't true in this case.'

Matt realized that he hoped so too.

When Matt got back to the office, George was out and Duff Bradley was minding the phones. 'Call for you, Matt. I left the number on your desk.'

'To do with the Armstrong case? Because . . .'

'No. The shrink who came in to talk to Frank Packard. Who has been raising holy hell back there, by the way, off and on. Whenever one of those talk shows comes on, mostly. I finally told him if he didn't shut up I would cut off his television and if he tried to break anything else I would bust him one. He said it was harassment.'

'It was.' Matt grinned. 'But you dealt with it just fine.' He paused. 'You didn't hit him, did you?'

Duff looked at him reproachfully. 'The shrink left some pills to calm him down, but he won't take them, says we're trying to poison him. He made me take a bite from his hamburger at lunch-time to make sure it didn't have arsenic in it.'

There was a shout from the rear of the building: 'God-damn son of a bitch, you know that's a god-damn lie!'

Duff sighed, glanced at his watch and at the newspaper which lay on his desk open to the television listings. 'That would be the Jerry Nelson show. I've been dreading it all day.' He got up. 'I'd better get him settled down. He's beginning to get on Frog's nerves.'

'And yours,' Matt said, and went into his office and closed the door before Duff could argue the point. After spending a good part of the night with Frank Packard, he could well imagine Duff or anybody else wanting to clout Frank. He'd certainly wanted to himself.

But the man was sick.

It was Harlan Weaver's number on the note and Matt called him back right away. 'Give me about ten minutes – I have a patient on the couch,' Harlan told him in a low voice. 'I'll ring you back.'

Having had so little sleep, Matt dozed off while waiting for Weaver to return his call and when the phone rang he nearly fell out of his chair. 'Gabriel,' he said into the mouthpiece.

'Harlan Weaver, Matt.'

'Hi, Harlan. Your patient all right?'

'Nobody who sees a psychiatrist is all right, Matt.'

'Or so you keep telling them.'

Weaver chuckled. 'Have to make a living, just like you.'

'Uh-huh.'

'So, I talked to your prisoner, Frank Packard, while you were out making the world safe for democracy.'

'And?'

'I think I would like him to have a neurological exam, Matt. I believe there's a physical basis to his behaviour.'

Matt sat up straighter. 'Are you serious?'

'Very. I did some simple tests myself and I got some very suspicious results. It needs an MRI scan and a going-over by a good neurologist. We have one who comes up to the clinic occasionally from Grantham – Dr Hansen. She's excellent.'

'So all his actions . . . all this military stuff, all the protests and shouting at people . . . it could be a brain tumour?'

'It could be something physical,' Weaver said carefully. 'Who's his lawyer?'

'His brother's lawyer is in Grantham, name of Niforos. Good man, I thought, I just talked to him earlier today. I don't think Frank has anyone.'

'Well, this Niforos would be a good starting point. Get onto him and explain the situation. Frank needs representation, Matt. I'm surprised you—'

'We did offer, repeatedly, but Frank seems to think the lawyers are ganging up on him too. I think George was going to get the court to appoint a public defender, but I've been out of the office most of today,' Matt said. 'Sorry. I'll get right on it. You know the FBI and the ATF are interested in him—'

'According to him, the entire government is arrayed against him.' You could hear Weaver's smile down the phone line. 'Every new set of initials just justifies his paranoia. I swear, for a few minutes there, he even had *me* believing him.'

'Does that happen often?'

'Occasionally – which is too often. You wouldn't credit the elaborate fantasy structures some of these people create. Tiny details, special languages, literal castles in the air. Fascinating, really.'

'But in this case—'

'In this case I state my limitations, Matt. He needs to be seen by a neurologist to eliminate any question of a physical basis for his paranoia before I can do anything to help him. If I can – or anyone can. I really do think he should be seen by Dr Hansen.'

'Was Moony Packard crazy?' Matt asked suddenly.

'Did he act like a nut?' Harlan asked in his turn. 'Speaking technically, that is.'

'He had a secret girlfriend, he was a secret gambler, a secret hoarder, a secret writer of romances . . .'

'*Romances!*'

'Believe it or not. I've read some of them. Awful mushy semi-religious stuff, but he seemed to sell them now and again, to these confession-type magazines. He had an agent – which he also kept secret but whose name I found on some correspondence and who also wrote cheques that were deposited to Moony's secret account in Grantham. Frank hid the stuff from us, but we found it eventually.'

'Protecting his brother. That fits in very well with some of what he told me,' Harlan said. 'Mind you, there was also a lot of filial jealousy there. Frank resented his brother's ability to deal with the world and keep a job.'

'Oh, and Moony kept tropical fish,' Matt added.

There was a silence. '*I* keep tropical fish,' Harlan said, after a moment.

Matt grinned. 'Sorry.' He thought for a minute. 'You wouldn't consider adopting a few hundred more, would you?'

'What do you mean?'

Matt explained about Moony's fish and how they were probably being neglected. Harlan said he would talk to Frank about it right away. 'Anyway, what you describe in Moony is unusually secretive behaviour, maybe a little defensive, but it doesn't sound destructive or aggressive. Nope, he just sounds about as nuts as the rest of us. Unless you come up with something more than that, I'd have to say it didn't run in the family. Frank is on his own in this respect.'

'Okay,' Matt said. 'I'll get onto the lawyer right away.'

'Don't let the FBI take him yet, Matt. It would really flip him badly.' Weaver sounded worried.

'You're a good man, Harlan. I'll do what I can.'

Matt hung up the phone, then searched in his pocket for Ted Niforos's number. Out in the rear of the building he could hear Frank Packard yelling something about 'god-damn bolsheviks'.

Sighing, he began to dial.

TWENTY-THREE

GEORGE WAS BEGINNING TO LOSE his temper.

They had searched Mrs Armstrong's room, looked through her bills and her cheque-books, her bank statements and even her diary. Yes, there had been a diary.

Susie read it and said it was a sad diary.

George just thought it was ridiculous.

Susie said it was the diary of a woman whose marriage was dying.

George said that all marriages begin to die the minute they start. They had quite an argument over that.

Susie said that the diary showed Mrs Armstrong was self-centred, egotistical and terrified of losing her looks. She was money-and status-hungry and, towards the last pages, very self-pitying.

George said what about murder?

Susie said no murder. No thought of murder. Susie said Mrs Armstrong loved her husband. She thought he was silly, running for office, she thought he was selfish and a lot of other things, but she loved him.

George said phooey. George said what about the old man?

Susie said what old man?

George said the old man she married in Savannah and had killed off the first time.

Susie said he was talking through his hat. That personally she thought if anyone had got that old man bumped off it had been his sons who hadn't realized he'd changed his will again.

So they had an argument about that.

Now Susie was looking through the kitchen.

She said a lot of women kept things in the kitchen.

George didn't think Mrs Armstrong was one of those women.

So he'd gone back into Armstrong's office.

It didn't look any different from the way they had left it. If anything, it was dustier, but nothing had been moved, so obviously Tizzy Turkle had stayed out. Knowing her natural inclination to do as little as possible, he assumed she would hardly have wanted to add cleaning another room to her list of duties. With Mrs Armstrong in the hospital, all she had to do was dust occasionally, spend her time watching television in her room and help herself to whatever was in the freezer. They'd asked her if she'd heard anything unusual in the nights after Armstrong had been killed, but she'd said there had been nothing. As her room was on the far side of the house from Armstrong's office and she had a habit of playing her television very loudly, they hadn't questioned her further. Maybe they should have.

As if by some mental summons, Tizzy appeared in the office doorway. 'Your girlfriend is going through the kitchen cupboards,' she announced lazily, leaning against the door jamb. 'She collect recipes or something?'

'She's not my girlfriend, she's a sheriff's deputy doing her duty,' George said stiffly. 'I don't think she's looking for recipes.'

'What, then?'

'Information about Mrs Armstrong.'

'What kind of information?'

'Does it matter?'

Tizzy smiled. 'I could tell you a few things.'

'Such as?'

'She was a pain in the ass.'

'Very helpful.'

'But she paid well and was fair.'

'You surprise me.'

'Oh, you shouldn't go by the way she talks,' Tizzy said dismissively. 'She's a lonely woman. He ignored her once he got into this election stuff. He was a different man when that started up. She didn't like it.'

'That's what Susie said.'

Tizzy's mouth quirked. '"Susie"? Funny name for a deputy.'

'You should talk.'

'Now, now, George . . . you liked my name, you said, once.'

Tizzy was very pretty and, although she was doing her best, she was making little impact on George, who had other memories to bolster his resolve. 'No need to go into that now,' he said hurriedly. 'You say she didn't like the election stuff. Did it turn her against him?'

'It wasn't like that. She just felt – left out. And annoyed with the way the money was disappearing. She liked nice things, you see.'

'So she resented the way he was spending his money?'

'Well, yeah.'

'Enough to want to stop it?'

'What do you mean, "stop it"?'

'Enough to want to kill him?'

Tizzy was startled. 'No! She wouldn't do that. She's not like that. What makes you think she's . . .'

'Why is Mrs Armstrong a pain in the ass? Is she demanding?'

'And how. I think they call someone like her a control freak, you know? That's why she gets sick every once in a while, she keeps running around and around, and it wears her out. Everything always has to be just so. She remembers where everything is, and if you move it to vacuum or something, jeez, you'd better put it right back where it was or she notices and gets cross. And her clothes, same thing. She would check the ironing, even the ruffles for crying out loud, and I was supposed to keep track of stuff going to the dry-cleaners or coming back all the time

268

'– she only ever wore anything once. You see her closets upstairs?'

'I saw a room full of closets,' George said wearily. And all of them had held only clothes.

'Yes, you did. And that's only winter clothes. We just put all her summer stuff into storage. Took me a week to get it folded and boxed, and then she had to—'

'Where is it?'

'In the attic – a special cedar-lined room she's got up there.'

'Why didn't you tell me about this before?' George demanded. He pushed himself away from the pedestal on which he had been leaning – one of the two carrying bronze statues of American eagles that bracketed Armstrong's desk. The pedestal rocked and he grabbed the eagle's outstretched wings to steady it. There was a click and the back side of the pedestal – a tall, narrow affair in dark wood – popped open. 'What the hell?' George said, as the rocking pedestal disgorged an avalanche of magazines onto the floor around his ankles. He knelt down and looked at them.

So this was where Armstrong kept his porn. No wonder they hadn't been able to find it.

Tizzy came over and stood beside him. 'Oh, my.'

'You could say that,' George agreed. The visible covers showed this was strong stuff indeed, mostly foreign, some still in their envelopes bearing European stamps. 'Mr Armstrong had some unusual tastes.'

'I never knew that!' Tizzy kneeled down beside George and picked up one of the magazines. 'And I never knew people did *that* . . .' She giggled.

'You've led a sheltered life.' George took it back from her with a deep blush suffusing his cheeks. Tizzy wasn't a virgin by a long chalk, but what they were looking at was enough to shock a downtown prostitute, and that was saying something. Some of the Turkle girls might have loose morals, but there was no sense allowing them to find out about the further shores of deviation, George thought.

Blackwater was a small town and he was supposed to be a guardian of the people. Suppose they decided to try a few of these things themselves? And without him?

'Let me see that!' Tizzy said, trying to snatch it back.

'No.' George held it out of her reach.

'You two enjoying yourselves?' came Susie's voice from the doorway.

Tizzy did not hurriedly disentangle herself from George, but eventually stood up and looked at Susie. 'Dirty books,' she said. 'I never knew Mr Armstrong was like that. He was just as sweet as pie to me, never tried anything, never even said anything wrong.' She almost smiled at Susie. 'Began to feel downright ugly there for a while. Now I see what I was up against I don't feel so bad. You wouldn't catch me doing those things.'

'Not if you were very careful,' Susie agreed sweetly. 'Anything of interest, George?'

'Sort of,' George said, abruptly dropping the magazine he was holding onto the slipping pile. 'Looks like those books he ordered through that girl at Helen's shop weren't a fluke – some of these are two or three years old.' And Armstrong had been campaigning on family values. Hah!

George stood up and nudged the pile of magazines away from him a little, to show his distaste for the matter within. In truth, he felt a creeping fascination and an almost overwhelming urge to look through them, which was very upsetting. He wasn't like that! He was a decent man. After glancing at some of those photographs, however, George wasn't feeling very decent at all. Easy to see how weak people got sucked into the business, he thought. He enjoyed mags like *Playboy*, sure, but was not going to be mixed up with this kind of stuff. No way. He cleared his throat. 'Tizzy says that Mrs Armstrong has a special storage room in the attic for her clothes,' he told Susie, perhaps speaking a little more loudly than necessary. 'Maybe you might find something up there.'

'You don't want me to help you sort through those?' Susie asked, sensing his discomfort and amused by it.

'No, I don't. Go on – show her, Tizzy.'

'Spoil-sport,' Tizzy said in a mock huff. Tizzy was a good girl at heart and had also been very upset by what she had seen. She'd thought she'd been working for *nice* people. That Mr Armstrong! And to think she would have voted for him. She led Susie out of the office. With one backward glance and a twitch at the corner of her mouth, Susie followed.

George sighed and knelt down to restack the magazines and replace them in the hollow pedestal. On an impulse he went over to the other one and twisted the bronze eagle upon it. Another panel popped open at the back of the pedestal. This time nothing slid out, but looking in, George saw stacks of videos. He began to sweat. 'Bastard,' he muttered to himself. 'Dirty bastard.' And there was a VCR right there in the office.

'Ladies and gentlemen, it's good of you, but it's got to stop.'

Matt glanced around Mrs Toby's living-room before continuing. The assembled group looked deeply disappointed.

'I'm not saying that what you've done so far hasn't been helpful, it has. Very helpful. But the closer we get to the killer, the more dangerous questions can be.'

'Are you getting closer?' Don Robinson enquired.

'I think so,' Matt replied. 'It's a matter of putting it all together and looking for the pattern.'

'Can't we help with that?' Mrs Toby asked. 'Sounds like planning out a quilt to me. You get all the elements and then you lay them out on the floor and move them around until it all looks right. I do it all the time.'

Matt sighed and glanced at Daria, who smiled sympathetically. 'She could be right, Matt. You could already have the answer and just not be able to see it.'

'Why don't we run over what we have so far?' suggested Nell Norton. 'Just kind of review the situation.'

'All right,' Matt said. 'We have Moony Packard bludgeoned

271

to death with Frog Bartlett's monkey wrench. Forensics have said it is Moony's blood.'

'Fingerprints?' asked Larry Lovich.

'No fingerprints.'

'Isn't that odd in itself?' This from Freddy Tollett.

'Yes, it is. Homer Brophy saw Frog's van coming from the direction of Cotter's Cut and going towards Frog's house not long after the murder took place, and assumed Frog was driving it. He didn't want to say this, but his boss talked him into it.'

'They didn't get along very well, Homer and Frog,' Fran Robinson said.

'What makes you say that?'

Fran shrugged. 'Just – I don't know – you hear things. I think Frog accused Homer of not delivering all his mail on time or something petty like that. Said he kept it back and looked at it, steamed it open, maybe. Seems to me it was something about photographs.'

'Frog was a keen amateur photographer,' Matt conceded. 'Thanks, Fran – I'll look into that.'

'It might not mean anything,' Fran pointed out. 'I mean, it was just something I heard – I don't even know where or when.'

'The thing about the van was there were no fingerprints in it either,' Matt went on.

'Not even Frog's fingerprints?' Lem Turkle asked. 'He drove that thing all the time.'

'Not even Frog's fingerprints.'

'Well, that's crazy,' Lem stated. 'Nobody keeps their car *that* clean, not even Frog.'

'I agree,' Matt said. 'It begins to look more and more like someone took Frog's van and the monkey wrench with the express intention of murdering Moony Packard and laying the blame on Frog.'

'Conjecture isn't much of a defence,' Dominic said from the corner where he sat with Emily Gibbons. 'I can conjure up this mysterious figure but without something definite –' He shrugged.

'Exactly,' Matt agreed. 'Now Frog sleeps very deeply – my deputies can attest to that. He takes sleeping pills to ease his pain, and it takes him a long time to get up in the morning because he is so stiff and sore.'

'What pain?' Nell Norton asked.

'Frog has something called ankylosing spondylitis.'

'Wow, what the hell's that?' Lem asked. 'Is it catching?'

'No, it's not catching. It's a progressive disease of the spine and joints, very painful. It's what makes him walk hunched over like he does, among other things. But the likelihood of him being awake or supple enough at five in the morning to have bludgeoned Moony Packard to death is small.'

'He could have stayed up all night,' Lem suggested.

'Yes, that's true,' Matt agreed.

'Sort of kept moving around, that kind of thing,' Lem continued, thinking about it and moving himself in a kind of seated shadow-boxing manner.

'He would be exhausted by the end of a day,' Dominic said. 'He insisted on tending his garden, which was a bad thing to do, and on the day in question he had been painting his dining-room, which would have meant he was hurting pretty badly by supper-time. He needed those sleeping pills.'

'How do you know all this?' Larry asked, curious.

'Information received,' Dominic said briefly. From the look on his face they saw he wasn't going to say any more.

'So, with all these things against Frog being the killer, what or whom do we have as an alternative?' Matt asked.

'Nothing,' Freddy said.

'We have Frank Packard,' Matt pointed out.

'You think he might have killed his own brother?' Mrs Toby asked, shocked.

'It's possible. According to a doctor who examined him, he may have some neurological problem that would render him unable to control his actions. He's very paranoid, he suspects everyone of trying to get him. If he thought his

273

brother was turning against him . . .' Matt shrugged. 'We're going to get him examined as soon as possible.'

'Have you asked him?' Fran enquired. 'I mean – just asked him right out if he did it?'

'Yes, I have and he denies it,' Matt answered. 'He says he loved his brother and wouldn't harm a hair of his head.'

'Not that Moony had many,' someone muttered.

'But, if we suppose that Frog didn't do it and Frank didn't do it – who else had a reason to kill Moony?'

'Moony was a big gambler,' Matt told them. 'He had a lot of money on him the night before he was killed.'

'But he mailed that,' Dorothy Finnegan objected.

'Maybe the killer didn't know that,' Matt said. 'Not everybody knew Moony's habit of making deposits by mail.'

'Where did he win the money?'

'Grasper Haven's place.'

'Ah – so anybody in there at the time would have seen him collect it,' Freddy said. 'Including Grasper himself, who hates like hell to let go of a buck, I hear.'

Snakehips Turkle spoke up. 'Flaky Bingham was there – I could ask him who else saw Moony's big win.'

'And Sally Dukas knew.' Matt told them about her seeing the envelope with the name of the 'other woman' on it. He also told them about the 'other woman'.

'Yes, but Sally didn't know she was a sweet little old lady, did she?' Nell Norton pointed out. 'She could have got herself into a jealous rage and . . .'

'Gone over to Frog's place, stole his van and monkey wrench, and then clobbered her erstwhile lover?' Matt asked. 'Why involve Frog?'

'So nobody would suspect her.'

'Yes, but why *Frog*?' Matt persisted. 'What did she have against him?'

'Oh,' Nell said. 'I see what you mean.'

'What did anyone have against *you*?' Larry Lovich asked Matt suddenly. 'I mean – it's the same thing, isn't it? Using your gun to make it look like you killed Jack Armstrong. It's a pattern, if you're looking for a pattern.'

'Like magicians,' Daria said.

Everybody turned to look at her. She blushed.

'Well . . . when they're doing something they don't want you to see, they cause a distraction, don't they? Misdirection, I think it's called. You look at their right hand because they don't want you to see what their left hand is doing.'

'So whose left hand are we talking about? You don't mean Tyrone Molt, do you?' Freddy asked. 'He could have killed Armstrong using Matt's gun so they both would be eliminated from the election and he'd be the only one left and get elected.'

'Does it really mean that much to Molt to be sheriff?' Dominic asked. 'I always thought he campaigned for the publicity.'

'That's what everybody thinks, but what if—'

'I don't think it was Tyrone Molt,' Matt interrupted this wild flight of fancy. 'But again, if you go in that direction, you have to think, who had it in for both Jack Armstrong and me?'

'Or who had it in for both Moony Packard and Frog Bartlett?' Fran asked.

'Homer Brophy,' said Dorothy Finnegan suddenly.

It was her turn to be the centre of attention. 'Homer wanted Moony's route and he had a feud with Frog. But he didn't get it.'

'Get what?'

'Moony's route,' Dorothy said.

'What's so special about Moony's route?' Matt asked.

Dorothy shrugged. 'It's to the best part of town except for the lakeside and that's done by van. All the big houses are on the west side. And no hills, either. It's the easiest, pleasantest walking route in town.'

'On the west side?' Matt asked.

'That's right.'

'So Moony Packard delivered mail to Jack Armstrong's house?'

'Why, I guess he must have,' Dorothy said slowly. 'Sure –

he would have. The Armstrong house is on Parkview Drive, isn't it?'

Matt glanced over at Dominic. 'You might be right after all – there could be a connection. Did you bring those photographs Frog took of mail men I asked you about?'

'Sure, right here in my briefcase.' Dominic produced them. 'But I don't remember anything special about them.'

'You didn't know what to look for,' Matt said. 'Not then.' He started to go through them when the telephone rang and Mrs Toby went to answer it. He was just saying good-night to everyone when she returned.

'It's Tilly, Matt. She says you'd better come quick – there's trouble in town. Real bad trouble.'

TWENTY-FOUR

'WHAT THE HELL HAPPENED?' MATT burst into the office and glared around. Tilly was there, along with Ted Niforos and Harlan Weaver. Neither George nor Duff nor Susie was anywhere to be seen. Harlan was holding a folded handkerchief to his forehead and Niforos seemed groggy too. There was the beginning of a bruise forming on the point of his chin.

'It was awful, Matt,' Tilly explained. 'He went berserk when Dr Weaver tried to sedate him with an injection.'

'My mistake,' Harlan said from beneath the folds of handkerchief. 'I should have knocked him senseless first. Just not used to doing things that way any more.'

'No, it was my fault,' Ted Niforos growled stiffly. 'I was standing in the open door of the cell and he clouted me before I knew what was happening. He shot past me like a greased goat.'

'Maybe it was my fault,' Tilly said. 'He probably wouldn't have taken a rifle if I hadn't thrown myself in front of them to stop him. The cabinet was unlocked because Duff had been cleaning them one at a time. Frank just pushed me over like a feather.' Considering Tilly's size, that was a considerable achievement. 'He took two rifles and some ammunition before I could even pick myself up. I grabbed his legs but he kicked me away.'

A very chaotic picture was emerging.

'Where were the others? Why were you two in with Packard in the first place?'

Harlan sighed. 'Dr Hansen has a block of time tomorrow

morning, so I came over to see if I could take Packard to the hospital tonight and settle him in. Mr Niforos was already here talking to him—'

Matt turned to the lawyer. 'You came up from Grantham?'

'He seemed to need representation pretty quickly from what you said and, since I've been more or less empowered to guard his welfare, it seemed the simplest course of action,' Niforos said. 'It was my wife's bridge night, anyway. I wanted to explain to him just what his options were, that there would be enough money to make sure he was comfortable and he wasn't to worry about the gun thing. With what you said about the doctor's evaluation, it seemed to me we could enter a plea of temporary insanity or *non compos mentis* – something along those lines. But I had to see for myself what he was like.'

'You saw,' Harlan Weaver commented.

'Yes,' Niforos said sadly.

Matt turned to Tilly. 'Did Packard hurt you, Tilly?'

'Just a bruise or two,' Tilly said negligently. 'Mostly in my pride. If George had been here—'

'Where was George? Where *is* George?'

'They – he and Susie – were searching the Armstrong house for evidence that Mrs Armstrong had paid someone to kill her husband.' Tilly was apologetic.

'Bullshit!' Matt said.

'Well, you know George when he gets a bee in his boxers.' Tilly turned to the switchboard. 'I'll get him on his mobile. They must have finished at the house long ago.'

'Where's Duff? And where's Charley Hart – he should have come on duty by now.'

'He did – just a few minutes after Frank took off,' Tilly said. 'Duff was over at the Golden Perch getting dinner for Frog and Frank. Charley and Duff are out trying to find Frank now. Wait a minute.' She spoke on the phone, briefly. 'It's all right. George is out there too, with Susie. They're all looking.'

'Tilly, don't leave,' Matt directed.

'Well, of *course* not,' Tilly said.

'Hey – hey somebody!' came a croaking shout from the cells. It was Frog, trying to get someone's attention.

Matt went through. 'Are you all right, Frog?'

'Hell, yes, I'm fine. Listen, if you want to know where that psycho went, look high.'

'High?'

'Yeah. He kept going on about being on top of the world – just like that old Jimmy Cagney movie that was on this afternoon. Sorry I couldn't stop him for you – are those other guys okay? That Packard, he went apeshit on them the minute he saw that needle the doctor had. Me, I'm used to them.' Frog sighed. 'I need my pills,' he said plaintively. 'And my dinner.'

'Sorry – I'll take care of that.' Matt went out and told Tilly to take in Frog's pills and his dinner, which was going cold on a tray on Duff's desk. He turned to the other two. 'Gentlemen, are you going to stay here, or do you want to join in the hunt?'

'I'm game.' Ted Niforos stood up a bit unsteadily. Harlan Weaver nodded agreement.

'What's left in the garage?' Matt called to Tilly. He'd driven over to Paradise Island with Daria. She had dropped him and then gone back to the meeting. He didn't even want to *think* about what that little group were dreaming up now.

'Nothing,' she called back from the cells.

'We can take my car,' Niforos offered. 'It's parked right outside.'

It was, unfortunately for Matt and Harlan Weaver, a red convertible sports car and all three of them were big men. Harlan got into the front seat with Niforos, who put the top down so Matt could sit up on the back and give directions. It was freezing and Matt jammed his hat down over his ears to keep it on as Niforos took them through the back streets surrounding the station at a breakneck pace.

'Jesus, slow down, will you?' Matt shouted.

'He could be anywhere,' Niforos shouted back. 'He was moving fast.'

'Well, at this pace I wouldn't be able to see him anyway,' Matt said, getting a mouthful of icy wind that made his teeth ache. As they sped down Main Street the election banners snapped and waved overhead. All three were still up – Vote for Molt, Vote for Gabriel, Vote for Armstrong.

'Oh, boy,' Matt said, as Ted turned another corner and slowed down. Up ahead he could see a line-up of police vehicles across the intersection of Trumbull and Heckman Drive. Lights were flashing and a crowd was gathering. 'Frog was right. It's the Heckman Tower. I should have thought of that right away.'

The Cecil G. Heckman Carillon was a feature of Blackwater. Endowed by the Heckman family, it rose nearly a hundred feet above the surrounding streets, embarrassingly phallic and noisy as well. Every day, at noon, the carillon rang out a different tune, never repeating itself over the entire year. The tunes were played by Mabel Terwilliger Heckman and Roger Heckman the Third, who alternated. Mabel favoured Rodgers and Hart, while Roger was more of a Gilbert and Sullivan man. At the base of the tower was a theatre and a small museum, devoted to the admirable life and works of Cecil G. Heckman, former mayor and patron of the arts. He had also been an Eagle Scout and throughout a busy life had maintained a keen interest in knots. In his later years, as an invalid, it became an obsession. Some of the finest macramé in the county could be seen on the walls of the museum, much of it done by Cecil himself. The little theatre was used for many local activities, particularly those with a musical aspect. Twice a year the Blackwater Bay Players put on a light opera, which drew people from all over the county. Nancy Heckman Tupp's School of the Dance gave an annual recital, which delighted many parents. Today there had been some kind of choral competition, Matt recalled.

Ted pulled over beside one of the police cruisers. George

was there. He turned. 'What the hell, Matt? How did he get loose?'

'It's a long story.' Matt climbed awkwardly out of the sports car and stretched his legs. 'Has he shot anyone yet?'

'No, but he's shot *at* a few.' George turned to scan the intersection. 'Charley, get those people the hell out of here, put up a tape, would you? Tell them they're in range. Honest to God, Matt – they're coming out of the woodwork.'

'It's Rent-a-Crowd, always ready for the call,' Matt said.

'Yeah, well, it's their fault.' George pointed towards a van marked clearly with the logo of the local television station. 'They were here to do a story on some choral competition being held in the auditorium and the next thing Packard goes in shooting, scattering everyone and then climbing up the damn tower. They put out a bulletin right away – damn, they're quick.'

'Oh, yes,' Matt said. 'Where there's trouble, there you will find them, causing most of it. Who's left in the museum?'

'Nobody, thank God. They all came flying out. He's up there alone.'

'Have you tried to talk to him?'

Mutely, George held out a bullhorn, which had been pierced by several bullets. 'Oh, yes, I tried.'

'I'm really sorry about this,' Harlan Weaver said from behind them. Both Matt and George turned round. The psychiatrist and the lawyer were stamping their feet and blowing into their hands. It really had turned very cold.

'What does he mean?' George asked Matt.

'I scared him,' Harlan admitted.

'What did you do?'

'He tried to sedate him with a hypodermic,' Ted Niforos explained.

'Oh, swell,' George said. 'Why wasn't I told about this?' he demanded of Matt. 'I'm the sheriff.'

'I'm afraid not.' Matt took out his badge. 'I'm back.'

281

'But I'm handling the Armstrong case—'

'Yes, but I'm handling the Packard case,' Matt said. 'I have priority.'

'That's not fair!' George was so outraged he almost forgot that there was a man with a rifle in the bell tower. He was immediately reminded by a shot. The red and blue revolving light on his cruiser shattered and they flinched from the flying glass.

'Symbol of authority,' Harlan Weaver observed out of the corner of his mouth to Ted Niforos. He raised his voice. 'I wouldn't put that badge back on, Matt, if I were you. If it picks up any light it would make a really good target.'

George immediately moved his badge to his shirt and zipped up his jacket. Matt did the same. 'I forgot,' he said to George. 'Frank is a real good shot. He has a practice range in his basement. And he's using our rifles.'

'Oh, shit,' George said. The Town Council had been generous – they had bought them very good rifles with excellent sights.

'Are you sure everybody is out of the museum and auditorium?' Matt asked again.

'I think so,' George replied.

'You haven't been in to look?'

'I just *got* here.'

'Where the hell were you?' Matt demanded.

George looked embarrassed. 'Susie and I had some stuff to look at over at the Armstrong house.'

'And did you find anything?' Matt asked.

'Yeah – I did. By accident.' And he told Matt about the hidden stacks of porn magazines and the videos. 'I knew you already knew he was a weirdo, so we decided it wasn't urgent and were going up to Begonac for dinner. We went off-duty at six, you know.'

'I know, I know.' They all ducked as another shot rang out. A police cruiser seemed to give a sigh and settled down on one side. Apparently Packard was going for the tyres now.

'Didn't you check with the teachers?' Matt asked.

'I didn't have a chance,' George answered. 'By the time I got here they'd all scattered, taken their cars or their coaches or whatever and got the hell out.'

'So nobody took a head count,' Matt said.

Duff Bradley came over. 'Some of the parents took their kids with them, other kids went with the teachers. It was all pretty messy, Matt. I was mostly concerned with getting everyone out of range.'

'Well, that's understandable.' Matt stood thinking for a moment. 'Okay, I'm going in there,' he announced. 'Give me that horn.'

George handed him the punctured bullhorn and Matt switched it on. Aside from a background squeal, it seemed to be in working order.

'Frank – this is Matt Gabriel.'

Another shot, another tyre on another cruiser went down. That was two – only one was left, along with the jeep.

'Frank, I'm coming in to make sure everyone is out of there and I don't want any nonsense.'

'He'll shoot you, Matt,' Harlan Weaver protested.

'No, he won't.' Matt switched on the bullhorn again. 'If you shoot me the FBI will have a real case, Frank. They'll never let you rest, they'll be after you the rest of your life.'

'Is that true?' Harlan asked the lawyer beside him.

'Hell, no,' Ted Niforos replied. 'But I'm not sure about that deputy – he looks like a man who would keep on the hunt.'

'George?' asked Harlan in surprise.

Niforos nodded. 'Not too dumb, just dumb enough. Look at the way he looks at Sheriff Gabriel.'

Harlan looked. He could see George was miffed at having his temporary authority usurped, but he could also see hero-worship in his eyes when he glanced at Matt. 'Ah. Do you think Frank knows that George would go after him?'

Niforos shrugged. 'You're the psychiatrist. Does Frank know anything at all or is he completely nuts?'

Matt turned to them. 'I guess we're about to find out.'

He took a deep breath, emerged from behind the cruiser and started across the intersection. There was another shot, and the cement about ten feet in front of Matt chipped and smoked.

'Come back, Matt!' George urged.

'He's just showing off,' Matt said over his shoulder and sure enough, there were no more shots. Matt disappeared into the door of the museum. Everybody waited.

TWENTY-FIVE

MATT PAID SCANT ATTENTION TO the displays in the cabinets or the intricate knotted exhibits on the walls. He went through to the open doors of the auditorium and looked in. 'Is there anybody in here?' he called.

He listened. There was no reply. He was about to turn away when he heard a noise. He stopped and listened again. It was a whimper and it was coming from the stage.

'It's all right, I'm Sheriff Gabriel. You can come out, the man with the guns is gone.' In saying this he glanced at the open door at the far side of the little museum, the one that led to the tower. It was open. Frank Packard could come down at any moment and start firing.

There was a movement to one side of the stage and a small face peered around the curtain. Matt was pretty certain it was one of the Turkle children, but he wasn't sure which one, or even to which branch of the family it belonged. There were so many and they kept coming along, more every year.

He strode down the centre aisle and stood before the stage looking up. 'Are you okay?' he asked gently.

The face nodded. There were freckles and there were tear tracks.

'Are you alone?'

The head went from side to side.

'Who else is with you?'

'Mm . . . m . . . my sister.' Another small face looked out, an exact duplicate of the first. Aha. The Turkle twins,

Mamie and Jamie, famed for doing exactly the opposite of what they were told to do. Teachers, friends and family had learned to adjust to this phenomenon, telling them to close their books when they wanted them to read, to stay downstairs when they wanted them to go to bed, to go one way when they wanted them to go the other. In the panic of Frank Packard's appearance the teachers and adults had shouted to the children to get out. So naturally the Turkle twins had stayed behind.

Matt climbed up onto the stage and looked down at them. Nine or ten, they were dressed in some kind of choral garb, the length of their hair the only indication of which was Jamie and which Mamie. Mamie had braids. Jamie had a buzz cut. They were Lem Turkle's grandchildren and, aside from their tendency to do the opposite of what they were told to do, they were therefore probably intelligent and decent kids. Good Turkles rather than bad.

Matt looked around the stage. He walked to the rear and saw there was a door marked 'Exit' that would open onto Trumbull, away from the intersection that was taking Frank's attention at the moment. He went over and tested it. It opened. He left it slightly off the latch and came back to the children.

'Okay. The man with the gun has gone up the tower,' he told them. They nodded. 'I am going up to talk to him. Whatever happens, don't go out that door. Just stay right here until I come down. Okay?'

They nodded solemnly, Jamie's eyes wandering ever so slightly towards the door.

'I'm going up the stairs now,' Matt said, getting down off the stage. 'You stay right there. Don't go out, don't talk to George Putnam . . . you know George?' They nodded again. 'Well, don't go out and don't tell him that I'm going up the tower. And whatever you do, don't go out and tell him there's nobody left in here. All right?'

They nodded again. This time Mamie's eyes went to the door at the rear of the stage.

Matt turned away from them and went up the centre

aisle, not looking back. What if, for the first time, they did exactly what they were told? If Frank knew they were there, he might come down and use them as hostages. Well, Frank would have to deal with him first.

As Matt reached the door to the tower, he heard a noise from the stage. A very quiet noise, as of a door closing. He smiled and started up the stairs.

'Going up the tower,' said Jamie to George Putnam.

'To talk to the man,' added Mamie.

'Damn,' said George. He had thought Matt was just going in to make sure there was nobody left in there. He should have known Matt would try to confront Frank. He had a sudden image of two bodies tumbling from the tower, locked in combat. He shook his head. Matt wasn't *that* brave. But he was stubborn.

'All right, I want everybody right back.' George picked up the bullhorn. 'And down,' he added, before pressing the button.

'Hey, Frank,' he called through the horn. His voice echoed around the intersection. 'Why don't you just come down like a good guy and stop all this shooting? Nobody wants to hurt you, nobody—'

A shot rang out and the red and blue lights on a second cruiser went out.

'Interesting,' Harlan said to Niforos as they crouched beside a leafless rose bush.

'What is?' Ted asked.

'He keeps shooting at the same two cruisers. He's leaving one alone.'

'Maybe he can't get a good shot at that angle,' Ted suggested practically.

'No, it's not that,' Harlan mused, eyeing the tower. 'I think he wants one left intact so he can use it to get away. He's nuts but he's not stupid.'

'They could also use it to chase him or take him in,' Ted pointed out. Crouching so close to the pavement they were both feeling the cold coming up through the seats of their pants. It was not comfortable and Ted thought longingly of his nice warm house and his lovely wife coming home from bridge to find it empty. She would be worried. It would take her about five minutes to think of the answering machine, during which time she would be very upset. He hated her to be upset. And if he hadn't been in such an awkward position he would have wanted to kick himself for acting on impulse and coming up to Blackwater to see this insane man.

'Did you mean what you said to the Sheriff – that it might be a brain tumour or something like that?' Ted asked Weaver.

'It's possible. And that's the problem,' Harlan answered. They were both whispering, which was ridiculous under the circumstances, but they couldn't seem to stop. 'Psychologically, his actions might be predictable, directable. But if it's physical . . . there's no knowing what will set him off.'

The stairs up the tower were narrow and went around the sides in a rising spiral. The carillon bells were controlled by a keyboard, which was in a room at the base of the tower. It had stood, mute, in the corner when Matt passed by. It occurred to him, thinking back over his reading of classic mysteries, that he might turn it on and render Frank unconscious by playing the carillon. The bells going off beside his head would at the very least disorientate the man. But then he thought better of it. Playing the carillon at this time of night would bring people from all over town, either in curiosity or protest, and give a maddened Frank Packard even more to aim at. So far he hadn't gone for people, at least not before Matt had come into the building, but there was no guarantee that would continue.

Slowly and quietly Matt climbed the stairs. From outside he could hear George talking on the bullhorn. From above, he could hear Frank shouting in response and an occasional shot. He knew the twins had told George what he'd wanted them to say. He also knew George was trying to keep Frank's attention away from the stairs below him so Matt could approach safely.

The stairs were wood. They creaked and groaned. As he got closer, there was a scuffling from above and, when he looked up, Matt stared straight into the barrel of one of his own rifles.

'Sneaky,' said Frank Packard. 'I always said you were sneaky. That's why I didn't vote for you.'

'We haven't had the election yet, Frank,' Matt said, as evenly and calmly as he could manage.

'What do you want?' Frank demanded.

'What do *you* want?' Matt countered.

'I want to be left alone!' Frank shouted.

'I can hear you, Frank, I'm right here,' Matt said.

'You want me to talk, don't you?' You got a wire on you or something?'

'Now why would I want a wire?' Matt asked.

'To get evidence for the FBI,' Frank said self-righteously. 'They want to know all about me. They're building up a case. They think they can stop me, but they're wrong. I think you're wearing a wire. I think you want to make me look foolish.'

Matt sighed. 'No, I am not wearing a wire, Frank. And I don't want to make you look foolish, I just want you to come down from here and stop shooting at people.'

'I never shot at anyone,' Frank said. 'You think I'm nuts?'

'You threatened the teachers and the children downstairs.'

'That was only to get them out. I hate kids, little stinky, squealing kids, like a bunch of little pigs. But I wouldn't shoot them. At least, I don't think I would.' He seemed to ponder this for a moment, then shook his head. 'No point.' Then his eyes widened with sudden inner enlightenment. 'Unless the FBI is recruiting kids. Say, they might at that. The IRA uses kids all the time. So did the Vietcong. It's smart, those little bastards don't know any better, offer them a chocolate bar and they'll do anything, why—'

'Frank,' Matt interrupted the manic flow. 'Listen to me. It's cold up here and eventually you are going to have to come down.'

'Am not,' Frank said stoutly. The rifle never moved, it stayed pointed straight at Matt's forehead.

'You don't have a coat. You don't have food or water. There's no toilet. You will fall asleep.'

'Not me.'

'You will, Frank. You will. And when you do we will get you down. But if you come voluntarily it will go much easier, Frank.'

'Take off your coat,' Frank ordered abruptly.

'What?'

'I said, take off your damn coat and give it to me.'

'Sure. Sure.' Matt unzipped the jacket and passed it up to Frank, who leaned down to take it, bracing his feet on either side of the hatch as he did so.

'Don't try and pull me down,' Frank warned.

'I have no intention of doing that.' Matt's voice was reasonable. 'You'd fall right down the tower. I don't want you hurt, Frank. I don't want you killed. But if you insist on this, George will bring in the State Police by morning. They have sharpshooters who will bring you down, Frank. We can't have you up here in daylight, shooting at people. You *know* that. If you were in George's position, you'd do the same thing.'

'Yes, I would,' Frank agreed. 'Take off your shirt.'

'What?'

'I said take off your shirt, I want to see if you're wearing a wire.'

'I'm not wearing—'

'Take off your god-damn shirt!' Frank shouted.

Matt unbuttoned his shirt and let it hang open. 'See? Nothing.'

'Hand it up.'

Matt shrugged off the shirt and handed it up.

'Now your pants.'

'Frank, this isn't—'

290

'Pants!' Frank yelled. 'You could have a wire anywhere. I read about it, I know all about it.'

Awkwardly, Matt took off his uniform pants. He stood, shivering, on the stairway. There was no heat in the tower, it was built of stone and the carillon bay was open on four sides to allow the music to roll out over the town. Cold air poured in from above and down the stairwell.

Frank Packard inspected Matt's shirt and trousers, then peered down at him.

'I'm not taking off my underpants, Frank,' Matt warned in a menacing voice.

'You can come up now,' Frank said and moved back from the hatchway, keeping his rifle aimed at Matt. When Matt emerged into the icy air of the carillon bay, Frank was wedged into the far corner, the rifle resting on his knees. He had put on Matt's jacket.

Shivering, Matt stared at him. 'Now what, Frank?' he asked.

Mrs Toby came back from the phone. 'Tilly says that Frank Packard has escaped and is holed up in the Heckman Tower, shooting at anything that moves.'

'Good Lord,' Daria said, standing up. 'We'd better get over there.'

'To do what, exactly?' Lem Turkle wanted to know and then his face fell. 'My God, the choral competition is going on there – my grandkids are in it!' He stood up too. 'Let's go. If that bastard has hurt my grandkids, I'll kill him myself.'

'Wait a minute, wait a minute,' pleaded Dominic.

'No way.' Emily gathered up her coat and handbag. 'This is a story and a half. I need to get right down there.'

'Me, too,' said Snakehips Turkle.

'Why do you need to get there?' Mrs Toby wanted to know. Her troops were disappearing before her eyes. 'What about our New Plan?' They hadn't actually completed their plan at that point and she knew there was

still a lot of work to do before they brought in the killer
There was much ground to be covered before they could
make a case.

'Hell with the plan,' Snakehips said.

Emily turned on him. 'No pocket picking.'

'Who, me?' Snakehips was all innocent astonishment.

'Yes, you. I know you had to give up burglary because
of your arthritis, but I also know you haven't given up on
everything.'

Snakehips had the grace to look abashed. 'I only take a
little money, never the credit cards, and I always send the
purses or wallets back in the mail.'

'I know,' Emily said. 'And everybody is getting sick
and tired of being part of you not getting bored in your
retirement. This is a bad situation, don't you make it
worse.'

'Oh, hell.' Snakehips was obviously disappointed.

'Are you saying that everybody knows it's him who does
the pickpocketing?' asked Dominic, amazed.

'Of course.' Emily searched in her huge purse for her
car keys.

'Does Matt know?'

'Of course.' She glanced at Snakehips in exasperation.
'Trouble is, nobody has ever lodged an official complaint.
He never takes more than a few dollars and he usually gives
that to charity. Matt knows all about it. He had bills marked
and the whole thing. He was going to talk to him about it,
though – it's gone on long enough.'

'I thought Matt was honest,' Dominic said.

'Of *course* he's honest,' Mrs Toby said. 'But he also
knows there's no point in going to the time and expense
of arresting and trying Snakehips for something so
petty.'

'It's a skill,' Snakehips protested. 'You got to practise a
skill to keep it up.' He drew himself up. 'He should have
arrested me. I deserve respect.'

'You deserve a kick in the pants,' said Don Robinson.
'Did you break into Jack Armstrong's house?'

'No, I did *not*.' Snakehips was firm. 'But I bet I know who did.'

Although most of them were on their way out of the door, they all stopped and turned to stare at him.

'Well?' Dominic finally asked.

Snakehips smirked. 'Take me with you and maybe I'll tell.'

'Frank, I hope to have kids some day,' Matt said, shivering in his socks and shoes. 'I can feel my sperm count dropping by the minute.'

'Very funny,' Frank growled. 'Put 'em on, then. But I keep the coat.'

Matt struggled into his pants and shirt, nearly falling through the hatch at one point.

'Matt, are you all right?' George's voice boomed on the bullhorn. Matt went over to the edge of the bay and looked down. The cruisers were still there, in a half-circle around the intersection. Duff, Susie and Charley were patrolling the perimeter, keeping people back as far as they could, but it was a losing situation. He heard sirens in the distance and realized that George had called in reinforcements from Hatchville and Lemonville. Oh, great – a circus. As he stood there he saw other cars pulling up and recognized them, cursing. He saw Daria, he saw Emily and Dominic, he saw Mrs Toby and Mrs Norton, he saw the Robinsons, Lem Turkle, Larry and Freddy – the whole crew had arrived. He hoped to God they didn't have A Plan.

'I'm fine. Just keep everyone back,' Matt yelled down to George. 'And I mean everyone.' He pointed to the little pack of Blackwater Bay Irregulars who were marching towards the intersection in a determined manner. George turned and looked, then glanced back up at the tower. He waved, but he didn't look very happy.

Matt turned back to Frank. 'Well?' he said. 'What now?'

'Sit down,' Frank directed. He had the rifle pointed at Matt again and it was very steady.

Matt sat in the opposite corner from Frank, his back

pressed against the icy stones of the tower. 'Did you kill your brother, Frank?' he asked quietly.

'I took care of that!' Frank shouted. 'I dealt with that. That's all over now.'

'He was very concerned about your welfare, you know, Frank.'

'I know, I know. That lawyer wrote me all about it.'

'He was a good man, Frank.'

'Of course he was,' Frank shouted, his face red. 'Don't you think I know that?'

'Then why?'

'Why what?'

'Why did you kill him?'

'I didn't kill him, dammit! But I took care of it, like I said. You don't have to worry about that any more. Tit for tat, that's what it was. Tit for tat.' Frank glared at him. 'I don't like you. I never liked you. You aren't tough enough you don't hold the line, you let people get away with stuff. So I'm taking over.'

'I try to keep the peace and protect the people,' Matt said. 'I try to reason with people, talk to them. It isn't always in the best interests of the community to go around officially arresting people for every little thing.'

'Well, you should,' Frank said stubbornly. 'Armstrong would have been tough, except—'

'Except what, Frank?'

'Except he was dirty,' Frank said. 'Moony knew, Moony was going to take care of it. Moony took care of a lot of things. People didn't know. Moony cared about how things should be right and decent. And I was going to back him right up. I know how, I got the equipment, I got the know-how. The FBI knows that, that's why they were after me and Moony. I had to take care of that before Moony got hurt. Then it would have been all right.'

'I don't understand,' Matt said.

'You work for them,' Frank shouted. 'Why should I sit here talking to you?'

'Because you haven't got anything better to do,' Matt

said reasonably. 'Here we are, we might as well talk. Unless you're ready to come down.'

'Into all that?' Frank stood up, looked down quickly, gestured with the rifle and then brought it back to bear on Matt as he sat down again. 'There's a lot of them now. I bet that the FBI is down there and maybe the CIA – they're in it too, they want to get rid of me. I'm dangerous, did you know that? Very, very dangerous.'

'I know that, Frank.'

'Well, don't forget it. Why did you come up here, anyway?'

'Because I don't want anyone to get hurt, including you, Frank.'

'Bullshit.'

'It's true. All I want is to find out who killed your brother, Frank. Don't you want that too?'

'You don't have to worry about that any more, I told you. I took care of that. Tit for tat, I took care of that.' The rhyme seemed to please him.

'Took care of what?'

'Took care of things for my little brother, that's what.'

Matt sat and looked at him for a while, thinking about the things his little group had discovered, that he had discovered, that Dominic had discovered, that George had discovered. 'Oh,' he finally said. 'I see.' And he did.

'I don't know how much longer we should wait,' George was saying to Brokaw. 'It's not kidnapping, it's not a hostage thing. Matt went up there voluntarily.' He turned to Duff, who had a strong pair of binoculars on the tower. 'What are they doing?'

'I can't see anything,' Duff complained. 'A minute ago Frank stood up, but he got down again before anybody could get off a shot.'

'I don't want any shooting,' George said. 'Dammit, no shooting! Matt's up there!'

'But how long is this going to take?' asked Captain Gottschalk from Lemonville. 'I've got a town to police.'

'How much ammunition has he got?' demanded Captain Leavis Butter from Hatchville. 'How many shots has he fired?'

'Jeez, I don't know,' George moaned.

'I got a man can take him out fast,' said Gottschalk. 'Took special training and everything. Got a laser sight. The minute the bastard stands up—'

'And how can he tell at this distance who is standing up?' Susie Brock asked. 'Does he know either man by sight?'

'Well, he's kind of new—' admitted Gottschalk. 'But we haven't got all night, you know.'

'Oh, yes, we do,' George said. 'We got all night and all day and whatever else it takes to get those two down alive. I have priority here, I'm county, you're local. No shooting!'

'You may be county, but I'm a lot older than you, you little pipsqueak,' blustered Gottschalk, deprived of utilizing his newest toy. 'If I want him to fire, he'll god-damn well fire.'

'Over my dead body!' George moved towards him.

'What did the guy do?' Butter wanted to know, suddenly and insistently. There was a brief moment when George and Gottschalk glared at one another, then Butter repeated his question.

'We think he killed his brother.' George turned away from Gottschalk, who stomped off with a determined look on his reddened face. 'But we don't know. He hasn't been arraigned, we're waiting on psychiatric reports—'

'I don't think he did.' Harlan Weaver joined the group. His legs had given out, and he and Ted were no longer prepared to crouch down like a couple of idiots in the greenery. Besides, there hadn't been any shots fired for twenty minutes or more. 'I think he is very, very unstable, however, and should be treated with caution and care.'

'You have no legal cause to use maximum force,' said Ted Niforos firmly. 'There is no proof the man has done anything but escape from custody and steal two rifles.'

'There was all them guns in his cellar,' Charley Hart reminded everyone.

296

'But he never fired them outside his own premises,' Ted said. 'He owned them illegally, but he didn't *use* them illegally.'

'He probably was planning to all right,' Charley argued.

'You can't convict on that,' Ted stated. 'You can't even charge on it – you have no way of knowing what he intended to do. He may simply have been a collector. Subject to laws covering possession, obviously, but nothing more.'

'Dammit, what's going on up there?' George muttered, glaring up at the tower. They had searchlights on it now, brought from Hatchville. They had plenty of men maintaining a wide perimeter, although with difficulty. People didn't seem to realize that they could be picked off, even at that distance, by a good rifle and a good shot. The group around George all turned to look up at the tower.

Where nothing seemed to be happening at all.

'Frank, you're exhausted. You're not well. You're going to catch pneumonia up here.' Matt shivered in his thin shirt, while Packard, wearing his jacket, seemed just as cold.

'Weakening me, aren't they?' Frank's teeth were chattering a little. 'Just standing down there waiting for me to weaken so they can drag me off to the Pentagon and torture me. I know what they're like. I read the books, I know how they operate all right. They hate people like me and Moony. Hate us.'

'But I don't hate you, Frank. And I have jurisdiction here,' Matt reminded him. 'I have first call on what happens to you.'

Frank narrowed his eyes. 'What do you mean?'

'Just what I said. I am the County Sheriff and I am arresting you for murder. You stay in Blackwater County on a capital charge. All the other charges are lesser. You'll be tried here. By your neighbours, not the FBI or anyone else.'

'Wasn't murder.' Frank's voice was weary but stubborn.

'I'm afraid it was,' Matt said patiently. He was feeling

light-headed – it had been a long time since his last cookie at Mrs Toby's house. And he'd forgotten to eat dinner again.

Frank rubbed his forehead with one hand. Slowly at first, then more frantically. 'Hurts.'

'One of your headaches?'

Frank looked up suddenly. 'What do you know about it?'

'I know the doctor thinks there may be something wrong in your brain, Frank. Something that's giving you that pain. Something that's making you very afraid. You are afraid aren't you?'

'Nothing makes sense any more.' Frank rubbed harder.

From below came a voice on the bullhorn. 'Matt – what's going on? Are you all right?' George was calling.

Suddenly Packard's eyes narrowed. 'Don't you move!' he said rather loudly. 'Don't you make a jump for me.'

'I have no inten—'

'I can see it in your eyes, you're going to jump me and drag me down. I knew it, I knew it all along, you're one of them!' Frank began to struggle to his feet, getting his knees tangled up with the rifle. Staggering wildly, he gained his feet. A shot rang out from below and a stone chip clipped his cheek-bone. He cried out and dropped the rifle as he clapped his hand to his face.

Although he was stiff from cold, Matt moved relatively quickly and dived for Frank's knees, bringing him down with a crash that shook both of them to the bone.

'See? See?' Frank babbled. 'They're trying to kill me. They've been trying to kill me all along.' He grasped Matt's shirt, practically strangling him, still strong although blood was flowing freely from his wound. 'You got to protect me. You're the Sheriff, you're still the Sheriff, you got to make them go away. Make them go away.'

'Let go, Frank. Let go and I'll make them go away,' Matt promised in a thin voice.

Gradually, slowly, Frank let go of Matt's collar. Matt

298

rocked back on his heels. 'I'm an old man,' Frank whimpered. 'They got no right to pick on me. Tell them. Tell them that.'

'All right,' Matt said and stood up.

Another shot rang out.

TWENTY-SIX

'HE THOUGHT YOU WERE PACKARD because you were in your shirt-sleeves,' explained George frantically. 'How was he to know you'd given Packard your uniform jacket?'

'He wasn't,' Matt said wearily.

'I told him not to shoot,' George went on. 'But he wouldn't listen. You notice he's buggered off – didn't wait around to see what happened. He knew it was wrong.'

'We'll get it all into the report, George,' Matt said.

They were waiting for the ambulance to get through the crowd. It was making a lot of noise but little progress. Now that the rifleman was down, people had surged forward to see him and to see Matt bringing him down.

'Just sit there.' George looked wildly around for the ambulance. 'Don't try to move.'

'It's only a flesh wound, George,' Matt pointed out. 'It's Frank who needs the ambulance. By the way, he's pretty subdued, but there's no knowing whether he might break out again. I've cuffed him, but you'd better go with him to the hospital. I've given him his rights and I've arrested him for murder.'

'So he confessed to killing his brother Moony?' asked George with some pleasure. 'That should make things easier.'

'No, he didn't confess to killing Moony. He killed Jack Armstrong because Jack Armstrong killed Moony,' Matt said.

'You're joking!' Mrs Toby had come up in time to hear his last statement.

'Margaret, the man is bleeding,' Nell Norton pointed out.

'Yes, I know, but he's not bleeding very badly,' snapped Mrs Toby, shrugging off Nell's admonishing grasp. 'What about Mel Ottaway, Matt? He killed Jack Armstrong, didn't he?'

Matt smiled at her. She so wanted it to be *their* suspect who was guilty. 'No. Moony was Jack Armstrong's mail man. Armstrong regularly got pornography through the mail and perhaps one day one of the envelopes had been torn, because Moony realized what he had been delivering and was furious. When Armstrong upped and ran for election on the basis of family values, Moony was even more furious and probably – in his usual way – confronted Armstrong with what he knew. Threatened to expose him.'

'Oh,' said Mrs Toby, chagrined.

'What?' George stared at all of them.

'Dominic brought some photographs that Frog had taken of mail men. A couple of them showed Moony Packard delivering things to Jack Armstrong's house and Armstrong taking them in personally. Presumably they were the ones you found – you said some were still in their envelopes.'

'Oh, yeah.' George nodded. 'Tizzy told me that he was a real bear about getting the mail himself.'

'I think when Moony Packard threatened to expose Armstrong, Armstrong got the bright idea that he could kill two annoying birds with one stone. Or, as it happened, wrench,' Matt said, as the ambulance finally pulled up. 'He wanted to kill Moony, but he also wanted to get rid of Frog Bartlett – or more precisely, wanted Frog put in a position of vulnerability. He heard somehow about the argument Frog and Moony had at the Golden Perch, and the whole thing probably seemed as if it were designed to help him. His ego allowed for that. He used Frog's van and Frog's wrench. He did it early in the morning when Moony would be on his own and few people would be about. With Frog in jail, he would be able to get hold of

Frog's house and land, and continue building his preciou
housing development.'

'Did Frank know this?' asked Emily, writing furiously.

'Moony had told him that night when he got home tha
he was going to get into Armstrong's house somehow, anc
get some of the stuff that was addressed to Armstrong anc
bring it to you at the *Chronicle*. But Armstrong got to hin
the next morning, before he could carry out his plan.'

'Some sheriff he would have made,' George muttered.

'Frank broke into Armstrong's office after the towr
meeting, trying to do what Moony had intended doing
and Armstrong caught him there. Frank overpowerec
Armstrong. He'd stolen my gun thinking he was going
to use it to threaten Armstrong, but I think by that time
he was fully intending to kill him. Which he did. But he
made Armstrong drive out to the housing developmen
first, so no one would hear the shot. Then he just drove
Armstrong's car home and parked it in the driveway. I
hasn't been touched since – I imagine we might pick up
some fingerprints there.'

'But Armstrong was bigger than Frank,' protested Daria

'Armstrong was a bully and a blusterer, but he usuall)
had someone else do his dirty work for him. When it came
to actual murder he had to do it himself and that made hin
very, very vulnerable,' Matt said. 'He was a coward at hear
and Packard sensed this. That, and fury over his brother'
death, gave him the strength he needed.'

'So they *were* connected, the two crimes,' Dominic saic
with some satisfaction.

'What about Mr Ottaway?' asked Mrs Toby in a smal
voice.

'Mr Ottaway is angry, but innocent,' Matt said. 'Sorry
Margaret.'

She looked at him anxiously. 'But we did help, didn'
we?'

'Yes, you helped a lot. All of you. And I never want you
to do it again.'

Margaret Toby drew herself up. 'I won't promise that.

302

'Oh, Margaret,' said Nell Norton in exasperation.

'Well, I won't. He doesn't know whether he might not need help again, does he?'

Ignoring her, Dominic said, 'Frog is innocent.'

Matt was allowing himself to be ministered to by the paramedics. 'Frog is innocent,' he agreed.

'I know someone who's going to be pleased.' Dominic smiled.

'Who?' Emily pounced, pencil ready.

'A friend,' Dominic said. 'Just a friend.'

'Well?' Frog Bartlett stood in his open door, glaring at Sarah Marsh. 'What do you want?'

'I brought you a cake,' Sarah said steadily. 'You've been through an ordeal. You need to build up your strength.'

'I need to be left alone,' growled Frog. 'I don't like cake.'

'Oh, yes, you do,' Sarah said. 'This is apple-sauce cake made from your own mother's recipe, which she gave me before she died. She said it was always your favourite.'

Frog looked startled. 'She gave you the recipe?'

'She did.' Sarah stood firm, holding the plate out before her. A cold wind made her shiver, but she held her ground.

'But she never gave her recipes to anyone, not even me,' Frog's voice was puzzled. 'She never wrote them down either.'

'Well, she gave them to me,' Sarah said. 'She said you'd only ruin them, but that I should make them for you if you wanted.'

'I never said I wanted any,' Frog protested a little less resentfully. He eyed the cake, high and light and thickly frosted. 'Is that cream cheese frosting?'

'It is. She told me you never wanted any other kind on this particular cake. And she told me plenty of raisins, too.'

'Really?' He looked up from the cake to her face. 'She liked you, I guess.'

'She liked me, she loved you,' Sarah said uncompromisingly. 'So here I am.'

Frog scowled. He looked at the cake, then again at the woman he'd known from a girl. She didn't know about the photographs he'd taken of her, of course, so that was all right. And she didn't know how lonely he'd felt in that jail, how lonely he'd felt for years and years. How hard it had been not to give in to the pain, to keep going without letting people see his weakness. She didn't know any of that. But here she was, plain, sensible, loyal, on his front porch, waiting to see what he'd say. 'You'd better come in. People might talk.'

Mrs Irene Armstrong signed the release that would free her from Mountview Clinic and took back her gold credit card. 'There,' she said. 'You're off the hook.'

'I was never on a hook, Mrs Armstrong,' responded Dr Forrester. 'This time you were genuinely ill and needed looking after.'

'And all the other times I was here?' Irene glared at him.

'You just needed looking after.' He smiled.

Slowly, she smiled back. 'Am I strong enough to sue somebody?' she asked him.

'Is it important?' He looked concerned.

'Oh, yes, it's very important,' she said. 'I want to get a man called Robarts by the balls and I want to get him good. He took Jack's money when Jack wasn't looking and I want it back.' She went to the window and looked out. 'You see that man down there?'

Forrester went over and stood beside her. Down below, in the car-park, a man stood waiting beside a limousine. Not a very big man, not a very impressive man. 'Yes.'

'His name is Otis. He was Jack's campaign manager. I've decided to retain him. We're going to get Robarts together. Then, we'll see.'

'See what?'

'Whether I can run for office myself,' Irene said.

'For office? You? I thought you hated politics.' The doctor was amazed not only by the proposition, but by

the change in his patient. She seemed stronger, purpose-
ful, alive.

'I did. I do. But I have to do something with my life.
We never had kids, Jack and I. We had . . . problems in
that area. So maybe I'll run for office back in Savannah.
There's some paying back I want to do down there too.
Oh, I have a *lot* to do.' She looked up at him. 'I'm not as
old as I look, you know.'

'You don't look old, Irene.' His voice was soothing.

'I did, but I don't any more. I'm going to give them hell.'
She grinned at him and he nodded.

'I just bet you are, Irene. I just bet you are.'

Election Day arrived at last, cold, windy, miserable. At Matt
Gabriel's 'Campaign Headquarters', also known as the
back room of Just Desserts, all was bustle and business.

'We have to get them out to vote,' Daria said firmly.
'They don't have to vote for Matt, necessarily, but they
have to vote.'

'We've got the transport organized,' Larry Lovich said.
'I can pick up about six at a time in our van and Freddy
can take three or four at a time in the car.'

'And we can pick up a few too,' added Margaret Toby.

It was seven thirty in the morning and they were all
huddled around a table.

'We've decided to offer free coffee and a doughnut to
everyone who votes,' Freddy said expansively. 'After all,
the library is only a few steps away.' The polling station
had been set up in the library and would open at nine.
Several of the electoral workers were also in Just Desserts,
stoking up on sweet things for the energy needed in the
hours ahead.

'Have you got a list of the disabled and elderly who want
collecting?' Larry asked.

'Right here.' Daria produced a list. 'Most of them don't
want to come until the afternoon – it takes them a while
to get going in the morning. I'll pick up Aunt Clary,
by the way, don't worry about her. Matt is allowing the

deputies to use the department cars to collect up folks from the country where the roads are difficult – there's a lot of ice this morning.'

'Isn't Matt going out?'

'No – that would look too much like electioneering,' Daria said. 'He'll be here or in his office. I mean, somebody has to look after the community in case we get another murder.'

'God forbid,' said Margaret Toby.

Daria ran her hands through her short, curly hair. 'We've got more important things to deal with. Now, who's driving the speaker car this morning?'

The day wore on. The *Chronicle* had printed the entire story of the siege and the arrest of Frank Packard for the murder of Jack Armstrong, who – it was alleged – had killed Moony Packard. It was all very complicated and all very exciting. Now, they were just hopeful that the voters would see that Matt had done a good job at last.

Matt himself was not so sure.

He and Daria had lunch at the Golden Perch. He told her that the doctors had, indeed, found a tumour in Frank Packard's brain. They would operate, but there was no knowing what the result would be. The existence of the tumour would figure in his defence, of course.

'Poor man,' Daria said again.

Matt looked at her in exasperation. 'You'd feel sorry for Jack the Ripper, wouldn't you?'

'I don't know,' Daria admitted. 'I never met him. I know Frank Packard and, for all his craziness and paranoid ravings, he was always nice to me.'

'You are an artist,' Matt said cynically. 'According to him, artists don't work for the FBI or the CIA.'

'Oh.' After a moment, Daria smiled. 'They actually do, you know. They draw up maps and plans, and illustrate—'

'All right, all right,' conceded Matt.

'Speaking of artists.'

'Yes?'

'I've been talking to Dominic. We're going to try to get

Frog Bartlett to let me mount an exhibit of his photographs at the gallery. I gather they are pretty fantastic.'

'Good idea.' Matt looked pleased, but not cheered.

'You're just coming down with a cold,' Daria said affectionately. 'You aren't used to being out in the open catching killers. You watch too much television, you and Max. It's time you had something else to occupy your evenings. *All* your evenings.'

He looked at her, eyebrows raised. 'Are you giving in at last to my constant proposals?' he asked hopefully.

She smiled at him. 'Maybe.'

Evening fell. The tension was mounting. The polls were closed and the counting had begun. All of Matt's very active supporters were gathered in Just Desserts, waiting to hear the results.

Matt was pacing back and forth. There was no reason to worry. He knew – he was reasonably sure – that Tyrone Molt wouldn't be elected, even if he voted for himself a dozen times.

Suddenly he stopped pacing and stared at Tilly Moss. 'My God,' he said.

She looked at him, worried. 'What is it? What's wrong?'

He blinked and began to laugh. 'I've been so busy all day – I forgot to vote. If I lose by one vote, it will be my own damn fault!'

EXCERPTS FROM THE
BLACKWATER BAY CHRONICLE

November 6.

Mayor:
M. Attwater (incumbent)	8,717
V. Clackhammer	1

City Clerk:
E. Berringer (incumbent)	6,455
B. Tweed	1,937

Sheriff:
M. Gabriel (incumbent)	5,022
T. Molt	56
J. Armstrong (deceased)	640

District Attorney:
S. Mason	5,003
M. Seeton	3,715

Town Treasurer:
D. Overton	8,005
M. Proudfoot	712

Also by Paula Gosling

DEATH AND SHADOWS

A murdered nurse, disappearing drug supplies, a diminishing trust fund and the sudden death of two apparently healthy patients are just some of the problems confronting Blackwater Bay's leading private clinic.

Laura Brandon, recently arrived physiotherapist, niece of the owner of Mountview Clinic and self-appointed sleuth, realises that a lot of people have something to hide. Confronted by tight-lipped colleagues, inter-staff feuds, and strange tales about a shadowy evil that lurks in the woods, Laura begins to believe the theory of a psychotic killer on the loose. Then another, eerily similar, murder occurs and she knows the solution cannot be impersonal.

Fast-paced, entertaining and full of misdirections, Paula Gosling's latest tale from the Great Lakes brilliantly confirms her mastery in the art of the murder mystery.

'Super, swift-sure characterisation, pace, high local colour: Paul Gosling has all the gifts' SUNDAY TIMES

Other best selling Warner titles available by mail: